THE BEST AMERICAN

NONREQUIRED

READING

2017

D0191210

Jan 18

THE BEST AMERICAN

NONREQUIRED

READING™

2017

■

EDITED BY

SARAH VOWELL

AND THE STUDENTS OF

826 NATIONAL

MANAGING EDITOR

DANIEL GUMBINER

A MARINER ORIGINAL
HOUGHTON MIFFLIN HARCOURT
BOSTON ▪ NEW YORK
2017

hmhco.com

ISSN 1539-316x (print)   ISSN 2573-3923 (e-book)
ISBN 978-1-328-66380-1 (print)   ISBN 978-1-328-66407-5 (e-book)
Printed in the United States of America
DOC 10 9 8 7 6 5 4 3 2 1

CONTENTS

Editors' Note

AS AMERICANS ALIVE IN 2017, we have more access to information than any people in the history of humankind and yet, it seems more difficult than ever for us to arrive at a consensus about what is true. It is even more difficult to determine what is right and ethical. This year has been one of confusion, disorder, and disagreement. Our good ship appears to be drifting somewhere, but we are not looking at the same maps, cannot agree on the direction of the prevailing winds, and several of us claim to have scurvy while others dispute the existence of scurvy and believe it is a hoax invented by the Chinese. How did we get here? And how do we chart our course forward?

This book is, and always has been, edited by a committee of high school students. They come from all over the Bay Area and range in age and they meet every Monday in the basement of McSweeney's Publishing, where they read and discuss contemporary literature. They are aided by a guest editor—this year, the inimitable Sarah Vowell—who visits the class several times a year and, in the interim, recommends many of the pieces that the students read in class. As managing editor of the collection, I help guide our conversations on a week-to-week basis, but my guidance is light and our conversations are largely unstructured and unplanned. The point is to have the students converse and debate, to create a space where they are allowed to explore a piece of writing on their own terms.

At the end of the year, after reading through hundreds of pieces, we must select the two dozen or so works that end up in this collection. This is not easy. The students, myself, and Sarah all have differing opinions about what deserves to be included. But we must find common ground, or the book will never get finished. So we huddle around our oblong editorial table and we hash it out. Imagine the Iowa caucuses but with even more shouting. Like all democratic processes, it is messy and imperfect, but in the end, we find a satisfactory common ground. I can think of no better training for the work of citizenship, and at a time when the adults of the world seem incapable of compromising, it is refreshing to watch these brilliant teenagers negotiate, confer, advocate, and ultimately arrive at a consensus.

The resulting product is, I think, much richer and more diverse for having passed through this process of deliberation. In the ensuing pages, you will read a dissent from a Supreme Court justice, a story about a Japanese mermaid, and an exploration of carp theft. There will be modern fables and oral histories and an excerpt from the diary of a man who worked in a gulag in Siberia. We have also included, for reasons that are too lengthy and complex to discuss in this Editors' Note, a poem about a woman frying and eating her husband's pet goldfish. All of the work here inspired our committee in some way, and we hope you find it equally rewarding.

In closing, I'd like to thank Sarah Vowell for her help putting together this anthology. She is just as brilliant and funny as one would expect, and it was our distinct honor to work with her. I'd also like to thank the fearless Stephanie Steinbrecher, who helped with myriad, far-flung tasks, and without whom this volume would not exist. And now, without further ado, I will send you on to Sarah's introduction.

DANIEL GUMBINER and the *BANR* Committee,
June 2017

INTRODUCTION

READS LIKE FICTION. When I was starting out as a journalist in the twentieth century, that was the sort of bigoted, back-handed compliment bestowed upon well-written true stories by people who never chucked *Finnegans Wake* at the floor in an exasperated huff.

For reasons having nothing to do with prose style, "reads like fiction" currently applies to pretty much every flabbergasted article mentioning the president of the United States. Which lately is every article.

Throughout the 2016–17 school year, Daniel Gumbiner and I edited this roundup of writing alongside twelve formidable Bay Area high school students who I call, behind their backs, "the Teen Politburo." Let's just say you don't want to run into any of them in a dark alley and try to talk them out of including two pieces from *The Southern Review.*

During our third month of bickering in a basement in San Francisco, Donald J. Trump, the nontraditional Republican candidate for president of the United States, beat the front-runner, the former senator and secretary of state, Hillary Clinton. By nontraditional I mean unacceptable. His batty antics included being caught on tape bragging that when a man as famous as he is happens upon women, it's acceptable to "grab them by the" slang word for female genitalia inappropriate to use in conjunction with a literary after-school program. Or accusing the father of one of his Republican primary rivals of meeting with Lee Harvey Oswald before he assassinated President Kennedy based on a photo published in the *National Enquirer,* "a magazine that frankly, in many respects, should be very respected." Or badmouthing the Gold Star parents of a fallen Muslim U.S. Army captain who died saving the lives of his subordinates in Iraq. Or doing a heartless impression of a disabled reporter suffering from a disease of the joints. Or saying of Senator John McCain, a former POW in North Vietnam who remained imprisoned with his fellow soldiers even after his captors offered him—the son of Pacific Command's Commander-in-Chief—early release, "He was a war hero because he was captured. I like people who weren't captured." Or referring to Mexicans as "rapists." Or, during a campaign stop in South Carolina, denouncing the Obama administration's landmark nuclear agreement with Iran this way:

> Look, having nuclear—my uncle was a great professor and scientist and engineer, Dr. John Trump at MIT; good genes, very good genes, OK, very smart, the Wharton School of Finance, very good, very smart—you know, if you're a conservative Republican, if I were a liberal, if, like, OK, if I ran as a liberal Democrat, they would say I'm one of the smartest people anywhere in the world—it's true!—but when you're a conservative Republican they try—oh, do they do a number—that's why I always start off: Went to Wharton, was a good student, went there, went there, did this, built a fortune—you know I have to give my, like, credentials all the time, because we're a little disadvantaged—but you look at the nuclear deal, the thing that really bothers me—it would have been so easy, and it's not as important as these lives are (nuclear is powerful; my uncle explained that to me many, many years ago, the power and that was 35 years ago; he would explain the power of what's going to happen and he was right—who would have thought?) . . .

During the Teen Politburo's fifth month in the basement, our new president moved to Washington. As former President George W. Bush reportedly said as he left the Capitol dais after Trump's unnerving inaugural rant about "American carnage" and whatnot, "That was some weird shit."

From the Oval Office, Mr. Trump repeatedly talked up the unparalleled turnout for his inauguration (despite all empirical evidence to the contrary) and dismissed any bulletin or broadcast that questioned him, his appointees, or his policies as "fake news," calling the press "enemies of the people." Meanwhile, a White House official with a straight face coined the phrase "alternative facts." Such developments make me nervous about the Republic our student editors will inherit. On the other hand, hooray for publishing, because George Orwell's book sales are through the roof.

Sidebar. To the people and/or cyborgs of the future (assuming there is one): if, decades from now, you've picked up this volume off the shelf of some library or used book store (assuming those still exist), and you're wondering what living in 2016 was like for a sighing sub-culture of Americans that, no joke, came to refer to themselves as "re-ality-based," touch your pinky to your earlobe or however one accesses archival footage and take a look at one of the year's most interesting television series, *The People v. O. J. Simpson: American Crime Story.*

While depicting an infamous court case from 1995, the look on ac-tor Sarah Paulson's face was pure 2016. Portraying Marcia Clark, the capable and experienced prosecutor in O. J. Simpson's double mur-der trial, Paulson reacts to a colleague's disclosure that even though she and the city's investigators were lining up a "bulletproof" case against the accused, the Los Angeles black community, hardened by decades of police brutality and institutional racism, believed this de-fendant, a beloved black football hero turned movie star, to be inno-cent. So even though Clark and the rest of *The People* were working long hours to accumulate enough damning evidence to get a convic-tion, a big chunk of the actual people rooted for Simpson's acquittal.

"A lot of black people think O. J. didn't do it," says Sterling K. Brown as Clark's fellow prosecutor Christopher Darden.

Paulson blinks, flinches ever so slightly, and murmurs, "What?" Pause. "Really?"

"Yeah," he replies. "I guess they just don't want it to be true. Good looking, charming, talented black kid from the street makes it all the way to the top, then gets pushed off his pedestal and thrown in jail like black men do."

"Oh, come on," she counters, shaking her head, suddenly staring across the fault line separating the ground of verified evidence from the tectonic plate of obstinate belief.

Back in 2011, when President Trump was busy hosting a reality TV show pitting the policy wonk Gary Busey against the national se-curity expert Meat Loaf, the Associated Press published a poll pur-porting nearly eight out of ten Americans believe angels to be real. So we can't blame the all-American tendency toward magical think-ing entirely on Trump. And yet his insistence on dismissing news he doesn't like as fake news is still, I think, news.

When I was about the same age as our student editors, I remember being appalled when then-President Ronald Reagan offered the following statement to explain one of his administration's most disturbing screw-ups, the Iran-Contra scandal: "A few months ago, I told the American people I did not trade arms for hostages. My heart and my best intentions still tell me that's true, but the facts and evidence tell me it is not."

At the time, as an eleventh-grader who was not allowed to turn in algebra assignments without showing her work or term papers without footnotes, the president of the United States saying a falsehood felt true in his "heart" seemed less intellectually rigorous than the average Wham! song. But now that we have a president who can look at aerial photos of a smattering of people on the National Mall and still see hordes, I'm retroactively grateful that even an overly optimistic Hollywood happy face a few years away from full-on dementia like Reagan nevertheless sucked it up and faced an actual fact.

The Sunday after Election Day, Fareed Zakaria moderated a round-table discussion on CNN featuring ex-felon and Anglo-Canadian curmudgeon Conrad Black. Baron Black of Crossharbour—his actual and not at all villainous-sounding title—disregarded the preceding months in which the president-elect repeatedly picked on Muslims, Mexicans, and women *on the record*. Black stated, "The facts are that Donald Trump is not a sexist and he's not a racist. He won the Republican nomination over the established figures in that party."

Playing the Sarah Paulson role, *New Yorker* editor David Remnick responded, "When I hear [Trump] described as not a sexist, not a racist, not playing on white fears, not arousing hate, when he's described in a kind of normalized way as someone in absolute possession of policy knowledge, as someone who somehow is in the acceptable range of rhetoric, I think I'm hallucinating."

Remnick is at the tippy-top of Americans besmirched by folksier folks throughout the campaign as "the elites." Or what his magazine's copy editors hilariously insist on spelling "élites," with an *accent aigu*. As George Saunders wrote of the way Trump's supporters feel "left behind" in the *New Yorker* article included in this anthology, "To them, this is attributable to a country that has moved away from them, has been taken away from them—by Obama, the Clintons, the 'lamestream' media, the 'élites' . . . They are stricken by a sense that things are not as they should be and that, finally, someone sees it their way."

If I can identify an *accent aigu* and find applying it to the word "elite" to be weirdly amusing, does that make me an elite/élite? On the one hand, I have a master's degree and every now and then I write for what the president calls "the failing *New York Times*." As an author, I've even shared a paperback publicist with the aforementioned Mr. Orwell. (Hi, Craig.) On the other hand, I learned what an *accent aigu* is when I took French at my Montana public junior high. Then, after public high school, I attended one of the state land grant universities President Lincoln signed into law in 1862 to educate "the sons of toil." I put myself through said college working at a sandwich joint called the Pickle Barrel, which was about as glamorous as it sounds. On my mother's side of the family, my sister and I, along with our first cousins, are literally the first generation since Reconstruction to not pick cotton. Walker Evans might have photographed the shack where our Okie grandmother lived. When Ma— we called her Ma—was wallpapering her bedroom with newspapers to keep out the cold, did she ever imagine her youngest granddaughter would one day work up the nerve to walk into the office of the school paper and kick start an inky little life among the swells?

I wonder how many of the country's so-called elites come from families that have only been that way for a generation or two. A not terribly elite member of the elite like me got this far almost entirely thanks to public schools, and specifically public school arts programs. It's worth noting that eight out of twelve of the student editors who argued and labored and questioned and cared assembling this anthology attend public schools.

If my fellow editors and I learned anything reading all the essays, stories, and poems that went into this book, along with the heartbreaking legion of wonderful pieces we simply did not have room to shoehorn into it because that Ta-Nehesi Coates made so very many good points, it's that the cheapest, most pleasurable way for a country of strangers to get to know each other and the rest of the world is through reading.

As novelist Elena Ferrante points out in an interview we have included, "The duty of literature is to dig to the bottom." While there are a few dashed off Internet items in this collection because immediacy can have its charms, the bulk of this book contains verses and yarns loner misfits (as well as one Supreme Court justice) in quiet rooms put down on paper after much thought, research, pacing, and procrastination, cranking out draft after draft in order to say what they had to say in precisely the way they wanted to say it to their people, the readers.

In one evocative selection, "I am reminded via email to resubmit my preferences for the schedule," poet Chen Chen of West Texas writes of being stuck performing a humdrum work task while longing to get home to reread Turgenev. Chen pictures himself walking down a story's misty Russian hill to chat with old locals. "I'm sitting with the villagers," he says. And for the length of the poem, he is. Poems, like the words coming out of a president's mouth, are better when they're true.

Sarah Vowell

Sarah Vowell *is the author of seven nonfiction books, including* Assassination Vacation *and* Lafayette in the Somewhat United States. *An original contributor to McSweeney's, she has volunteered with the various writing centers overseen by 826 National since 2004.*

THE BEST AMERICAN

NONREQUIRED

READING

2017

TEJU COLE

■

Fable

FROM *The New Inquiry*

IT WAS TRUE THAT the Adversary had brought other monsters into being. Each had been wicked in its own way, each had been an embodiment of one or other of the seven vices, and each had been strong and difficult to vanquish. Some of those monsters still roamed the land. But what made this new monster remarkable, indeed uniquely devious, was that it wasn't strong at all. In fact, it was weak. The weaknesses through which the other monsters had been vanquished, this monster had tenfold. The new monster was not moral, but it is not in the nature of monsters to be moral. But the monster was also not beautiful, or intelligent, or brave, or well-dressed, or charming, or gifted in oratory, though usually monsters had at least some of those qualities. The Adversary had sent this new monster out, designing it to derive its strength from one source and one source alone, as in olden days was said of Samson and his locks, so that if that source were cut off, the monster would wilt like a severed flower stalk in the noonday heat. The source of the new monster's strength was noise. If it heard a bit of noise pertaining to it, it grew stronger. If it heard a lot of noise, whether the noise was adulation or imprecation, it was full of joy, and grew even stronger. Only collective quietness could vanquish it, quietness and the actions that came from contemplation.

Having thus designed it, the Adversary sent the monster out to Noiseville. "A new monster!" the cry went up, and the monster grew a little stronger. "It grows stronger!" went the chorus, and the monster grew stronger still. And thus it was in Noiseville that the new monster, weaker than all the other monsters ever sent by the Adversary, was the only thing the people of Noiseville spoke about. The sound had reached a deafening roar. In every newspaper across Noiseville, the most read articles were about the monster. On television, the reporters spent most of their time making noise about the monster. On little devices the people carried around with them, it was all monster all the time. If the monster smiled, there was noise in reaction. If the monster scowled, there was noise. If it coughed, there was an uproar of coughing and commentary on the manner of the monster's coughing. The Adversary was astonished by how well his little stratagem had worked. The monster smiled and scowled and coughed, and learned to say the things that generated more noise. And on and on it grew.

"But it is so weak!" the people shouted. "It is not beautiful, or intelligent, or brave, or well-dressed, or charming, or gifted in oratory. How can it grow in strength and influence so?" And if the noise went down even one decibel, the monster did something again, anything at all, and the noise went up. And the people talked of nothing but the monster when they were awake, and dreamed of nothing but the monster when they were asleep. And from time to time, they turned on each other, and were distraught if they saw their fellows failing to join in the noise, for any quiet form of contemplation was thought of as acquiescence to the monster. Other monsters in the past had been drowned out by sufficient loudness. Besides, this was Noiseville, and there was no question of not making noise, there in the home of the loudest and best noise in the world, the most beautiful noise, it was often said, the greatest noise in the history of the world. And so the noise swelled to the very limits of Noiseville, and the new monster grew to gargantuan size as had Gulliver in the land of the Lilliputians, and their ropes were powerless against it, and there seemed no limit to its growth, though it was but the eighth month of that year.

ELIZABETH LINDSEY ROGERS

■

One Person Means Alone

FROM *The Missouri Review*

BEFORE TAIGU, people warned me: China was a fiercely social country. After I arrived, I rarely went anywhere unaccompanied. I was ushered into crowded noodle stalls and into corner stores stuffed with plum juice, chicken feet, and hot-water thermoses. I often needed help at the post office, with its hundreds of strict regulations and wisp-thin envelopes you sealed with a depressor and paste. Students took me to the White Pagoda and the courtyard of H. H. Kung, the only historical sites in town that hadn't been destroyed during the Cultural Revolution. Eventually, I'd be invited into my Chinese colleagues' small apartments, where several generations of the family often lived together. I'd be generously served five kinds of dumplings, the bowl full again before I had the chance to set down my chopsticks.

In the unheated, Soviet-feeling building where I taught university English, I waited in line with other women to use toilets without doors or stalls. At first, I tried to turn my face away from the others, demurring. But there was no use trying to hide anything about our bodies here: whose stomach was upset, or who was crying, or who was on her period that day. We saw it all. We offered stacks of tissues when someone had run out of their own supply.

I lived in a tiny brick house, the tiles on my roof painted with evil eyes to ward off badness. I'd often wake to the arguing of an unknown college couple, shouting their insults right in front of my window, just a few feet away from where I had been sleeping. I'd stumble into the kitchen, startled to find a stranger outside the back door, shaking my (was it mine?) jujube tree and picking up the fruits from the ground.

Like most teachers at the agricultural university, I lived on campus, and I wasn't hard to find. My thoughtful students showed up on my front stoop, bearing jars of weird, floating grains and fermented vegetables sent by their grandmothers. "If you eat this for six days," they'd say, "you will be well."

The word was out: I was sick a lot. It was my first time living abroad, and the new microbes were hard on my body. In Taigu, there was delicious street food as well as contaminated cooking oil, air, and groundwater. Shanxi province, even by Chinese standards, was an environmental disaster. The coal plants were next to the grain fields, pink and green smoke rising out of the stacks. On a good day, you could see the mountains that surrounded campus. Most of the time, they were hidden by pollution. Particulate matter caked the windowsills in my house.

People were curious about me. I was asked daily by strangers in the market square what country I was from and why I had come to Shanxi province—sort of the West Virginia of China, except that it was on the edge of the desert—as opposed to the more glamorous Shanghai or Beijing. They also asked how old I was, how much money I made teaching at the university, if I'd eaten that day yet, and, if so, what had I eaten? And why was I "a little bit fat," they said, but not as fat as some Americans? How often did I need to color and perm my hair? (It was reddish and was curly on its own, I said.) Was that American living in the other half of my duplex my boyfriend? (He was not.) Well, did I at least have a boyfriend in the States? (Sarah, my girlfriend from college, was teaching down in Indonesia, but I didn't explain her, for obvious reasons.) And, occasionally, from students and younger friends: What did I think of the movie *American Pie Presents: Beta House*? Was it an accurate portrayal of American university life?

Eventually, I borrowed my friend Zhao Xin's laptop so I could watch the pirated version with Chinese subtitles. I was horrified. One of the thankfully forgotten sequels of the original *American Pie*, it made me squeamish during scenes of a fraternity's hazing ritual, something about attaching a bucket of beer to some guy's genitalia.

There was also one exaggerated fire-hose moment, a sorority sister experiencing female ejaculation for the first time. As for the question of whether this resembled university life in the United States, I told them, in all honesty, I wasn't sure. I had just graduated from a small, studious college in the Midwest. Despite its sex-positive atmosphere, things were, all in all, pretty quiet there, with some nerdily themed parties but no Greek life at all.

In truth, I'd had plenty of sex in college, but that had to be my own business. More specifically, I didn't reveal my lesbian identity to anyone in China, at least at first. I responded to boyfriend questions with a simple "No." I didn't know what the consequences of coming out might be, and I couldn't take the risk. Keeping this a secret, I'd come to realize later, was part of what made me feel so isolated that first year in China, even though other people surrounded me.

As a student in America, my life had been pretty communal. Still, like a number of Generation Y, middle-class, considerably selfish Americans, I thought I was fiercely independent and staged myself as the protagonist in my own life story. Very little prepared me for the level of social responsibility and interconnectedness that came with moving to Taigu. One of the first words I learned was *guanxi*, which can be roughly translated as "social connections," or maybe "relationships." If you had *guanxi* with others, you could count on them for most everything, and they could count on you; if you failed to foster a sense of *guanxi*, people would resent you or think of you as selfish, even though they might not say it out loud. *Guanxi* emphasized—or mandated— the whole you were a part of rather than the part you played alone.

I embraced this idea the best I knew how. My American co-fellow, Ben, and I mounted a disco ball in our living room and started hosting weekly dance parties for our Chinese friends: social activity for the greater good, something students reported as scarce on our small-town, farm-school campus. At these parties, at first, we'd awkwardly stand in a circle. But then the sorghum-alcohol punch we provided began to take effect, and our loopy, arrhythmic movements took over the room. Over time, we perfected our playlist: a mix of American '80s and '90s hits and cheesy Chinese pop songs. By our second year in China, our living room floor was beginning to split from people's dancing enthusiasm.

The Americans got a wild reputation on campus. Our parties were on Thursday nights, but then we got a noise complaint from the university's vice president, who happened to live in a house just thirty feet from our front door. When we showed up on his porch the morning after, with a giant fruit bowl and profuse apologies, he smiled and invited us in, as if nothing bad had happened. Our *guanxi*, the neighborhood harmony, seemed to be restored.

Overall, however, I was not the best at fostering *guanxi*. I often found myself hungry for space between others and myself: a necessary measure to quiet the buzz in my dislocated brain. I'd draw the curtains and hole up in my side of my foreign-teacher duplex, the door to my side half closed. This action was usually perceived as hostile or a symptom of possible depression.

"Why is she not coming out here?" I heard someone ask Ben on the other side of my door. "Is she sad about something? Why is she alone?"

The word *alone* in Mandarin can be translated in various ways. The expression I heard on the other side of my door, traveling by myself on a train, or walking down the street solo was *yi ge ren*. *Yi* is "one"; *ge* is a kind of counting word, placed between a number and an object. And *ren* means "person" or "people." The expression "Are you *yi ge ren*?" when translated literally is "Are you one person?" In context, though, I began to understand this as a way of asking, "Are you on your own? Are you alone?"

Of course, I was rarely 100 percent alone, unless you counted when I was asleep or in the single-person bathroom in my apartment. I had come to Taigu paired with Ben, another recent college graduate, and there were two more Americans living in the house next door to us, doing their second year of the same teaching fellowship we'd all received. Most of our life outside of class involved a mixed group of American fellows and Chinese graduate students, with a few older Chinese undergraduates mixed in. We ate dinner together most nights at the hot pot place, just outside the campus gate, or at one of the noodle stalls at school.

Every once in a while, though, I'd find myself walking alone in public. I was not afraid: not near my house, not on the other side of campus, not even in the bleak brick-and-mud Taigu village alleys scattered with trash and piles of used coal pellets. There were terrible stories, real or imagined, of people getting snatched up around here and having their organs harvested. There was a line of massage parlors, a sort of red-light district, the neon signs flickering on and off.

When I passed another person, I'd see what I came to know as the Look: not threatening but a look more of curiosity or even shock, mostly due to my obvious non-Han appearance. Sometimes they'd ask me where I was from. Some would say nothing. Some would even ask me if I was okay, if I had eaten, and where I was going.

I don't know whether it was the fact that we lived in the ultramilitarized People's Republic or just that Taigu men are not the type to cat-call, but I always maintain that China felt like the safest place I'd ever lived. Perhaps my outsider status as a Westerner protected me. Years later, when I returned to the United States, finding myself living in a host of smaller towns, as well as cities like Chicago, Washington, DC, and New Orleans, I was shocked at how often some stranger on the street would whoop at me or stare for too long or start to walk too close. In my own homeland, strangely, I felt the most unsafe being by myself.

In a country of a billion people, personal space isn't just something that's frowned upon; it's often impossible to find. Even a small town like Taigu—just forty thousand people—was no exception. If you wanted to be alone in the daytime, you could ride your bicycle past the grain fields and the coal- and bauxite-processing plants to the even smaller village at the edge of the mountains, where there were several temples in the outcroppings.

In China, university dorms are not named after famous educators or benefactors but are instead referred to by serial numbers: "26 building," "27 building," and so on. I soon discovered that the undergraduates were living eight to a room: four sets of bunk beds pressed against the walls, one shared table in the barely existent center of the room. The graduate students, thought to be deserving of a bit more space, were also in dorms but housed in groups of four. The first time I entered a dorm room at the agricultural university, it was as if I was entering a unit in a warehouse. I saw schoolbooks, clothes, shoes, packages of dry noodles, and clothes-washing bowls crammed beneath the lowest bunks and around the perimeter. The room's one narrow window was strung with several drying lines for shirts and underwear. It was the middle of the day, so the students were elsewhere.

My friend Wang Yue, a twenty-year-old English major, pointed disapprovingly to one of the lower bunks and told me that a pair of her roommates—two nineteen-year-olds who preferred to be called by their self-selected English names, Sky King and Toni—always slept side by side in this single bed. They were obviously in the early stages of a romance. "It's like they wish the rest of us weren't here," Wang Yue told me, rolling her eyes.

It was unclear to me where her disdain came from. Was it just homophobia? Was she annoyed because these women had upset the *guanxi* and balance of the group, prioritizing their personal interests over the harmony of the whole? Or was it because they were two women, finding a loophole in the single-gender dorm, the thing that was supposed to keep students focused on school, not on sex?

Everyone on campus was struggling for intimate space. The foreign teachers' houses were adjacent to a small, circular garden where the willow and birch trees created a shadowy canopy over a few park benches. This was hardly a hidden place, but it was more secluded than the rest of campus. If I passed by at nightfall, I'd see the flash of someone's limbs wrapped around another body, and then another couple on the next bench, just a few feet away. This was the official campus hook-up area, a kind of twenty-first-century drive-in theater. The students called it the *qingren shulin*, or "Lovers' Forest."

Even the privacy in my half-a-duplex was not a thing I could always count on. My girlfriend, Sarah—who also had a teaching fellowship, but down in Indonesia—managed to visit China the first fall I was there, during her Ramadan break from school. We'd spent a large part of our senior year in college in bed together, but coming to teach in Asia, as well as our physical separation, had resulted in an almost celibate life for both of us. Desperate, we tried to cram as many sessions as possible into those two weeks of her visit.

One late Friday afternoon, we got interrupted by Ben's frantic knocking on the door to my bedroom. He warned us that Xiao Zhang, a staff member for the Foreign Affairs Office, had just come over, and she was about to walk in any minute. She needed to see something on my side of the house, and right now, apparently.

A wave of indignation passed through me, which was instantaneously replaced by panic. I didn't have any closets to hide inside. There were no locks in our house, except on the front door. And it was no use to pretend to be out: Xiao Zhang and the office staff members, for all sorts of reasons, regularly came into our apartments when we weren't home and would have no trouble coming into the bedroom. The units belonged to the university, after all; we were just living in them.

Flushed, I pulled on my tossed-off clothes and rushed out into the foyer area, apologizing for my delay. I tried to close the bedroom door behind me, but, like most doors in the house, it didn't fully latch. Xiao Zhang advised me, in the slowest Mandarin she could manage, about getting some sticky paper to try and trap the mice that had invited themselves in just after the weather had turned. "Right," I kept saying, nodding, hoping to make the conversation as short as possible. I stopped understanding her instructions after a while. My language skills were not up to snuff, especially when I was panicked.

But it was clear from her hand motions that she was describing what happens when the mouse actually dies its horrible death inside the adhesive. She even went so far as to mimic a rodent scream, just so I would be prepared. I stood fidgeting. On the other side of the partially cracked door, Sarah was hidden under the duvet, still undressed and trying not to move.

Besides teaching, eating, and the lessons with my Chinese tutor, I spent a few late afternoons a week at the campus's indoor swimming pool. The idea of swimming, especially in a poor, dry province like Shanxi, sounded luxurious in theory. In practice, the pool felt like an environmental apocalypse, so gritty and chemicalized that you could barely make out the T's on the tiled bottom. The water smelled like a mix of spoiled vegetables and bleach. The chlorine powder was dispensed in satchels that looked like giant artificial jellyfish floating just above the underwater jets.

One week, I ran into my student and his friends on their way back from the pool building. He told me they had closed the pool down for a couple of days. "They must change the water this week," he told me assuredly, in English. "It is the first time in seven years they will change the water." I hoped something had been lost in translation.

The pool scene was, despite this, pleasant enough. Of course, if you headed there with the sole intention of swimming a bunch of laps, you'd be frustrated. Like everywhere else, the pool was full of bodies, especially in the shallow end. For every fifteen meters I swam, I'd usually stop to talk to someone: a student, or a friend, or sometimes a complete stranger. If I didn't stop, I'd likely collide with them in the water anyway.

Right away, I noticed that most of the women stayed in the shallow end, trying to develop the basic skills to pass the university's swimming test. The lifeguards/pool keepers, all middle-aged men with beer guts and sagging swim trunks, were impressed with my sessions in the deep end and with my swimming skills. "You have a good *sui jue*," one of them told me, which literally translates to "feeling of the water."

But my sense of the water wasn't intuitive so much as it was another marker of my Western, middle-class upbringing. I thought of the series of photos in my mother's albums back in North Carolina: me at six months, fat and smiling, at baby swim class at the YWCA; me at four, splashing in the waves at the beach; my first swim-team picture at the age of six, posed next to the diving board. In China, however, swimming pools were scarce, and most natural bodies of water seemed apocalyptically contaminated. For most of the Chinese students, the university was the first place they'd had access to anyplace where they could swim.

The women at the pool intimidated me. It was not because of their swimming. It was the locker-room shower scene that I found daunting: an enormous, packed-to-the-gills mob of bodies and steam.

Unless you are very wealthy in Shanxi, most homes do not have their own shower. Chinese towns have public bathhouses. At university, similarly, there were no showers in the dorms themselves; showering was something most people did a couple of times a week in one of the university's provided facilities. Or, if you bought a swim pass, you could take your showers at the pool.

At any given time, the showers at the pool had four or five people gathered around each showerhead, taking turns to rinse. To pass through this shower room, even just on your way to or from the pool, was to push through a crowd of women and soap and hair. Much to

my Puritan dismay, it was almost impossible to find unscented anything in rural China, including laundry detergent or maxipads, and
the shower room was no exception. The air was overwhelming with
its shampoo and soap perfumes, freesia and juniper and lavender. In
the fog, it was a humid, scented forest, with limbs reaching in every
direction.

I had never seen so many naked bodies together, been close to
so many people at once. Most of the women, being students, were
in their twenties: their skins completely smooth, their breasts small,
their bodies angular and narrow by my own Western standards.
Many of them had tied a red string around their hips, with a jade pen-
dant for luck. There were some older women, too, who were teachers
or lived in the community. Their bodies were considerably rounder,
more weathered by time. Some had caesarean scars that had never
faded, their bellies divided by the pink line.

The level of intimacy here terrified me. In this shower space, my
own shame came from what I couldn't hide: the obvious strangeness of
my Caucasian body and its larger proportions of fat, muscle, and hair.
It was one thing to walk through Taigu, wearing jeans and a jacket I'd
bought in town, and be stared at immediately because of my red curls
and pale skin. It was another to enter the shower room, for it to be obvious that the hair in my crotch was as red as that on top of my head.

"Wow," my friend Wang Hui Fang said the first time she got a look
at me, not long after we had met. We weren't even showering then; she
and I and our other friend were just changing into our bathing suits,
stuffing our clothes into a shoebox-sized locker with no lock. "*Name
hong!*" she exclaimed, an expression meaning "really, really red."

When she saw my embarrassment, she switched to English and
tried to reassure me.

"It is very interesting," she said with enthusiasm. She grabbed,
then, at the nonexistent flesh on her own waistline. "I am really getting fat," she said, as if she meant to comfort me.

So I usually rushed through the shower room at the pool, being there only long enough to rinse off, my frantic quality probably causing me to get even more attention than I would have otherwise. Sometimes I avoided the shower room altogether, opting to
walk home shivering, with the chlorine eating away at my hair. I was

choosing, then, to use my own showerhead in my apartment, which was simply attached to the wall and got everything else in the tiny bathroom wet: sink, toilet, trashcan, floor. Even in the privacy of my own bathroom, showering could be a messy, unbounded experience.

Once I went with Wang Yue to visit her hometown of Datong in the north of Shanxi province, another cold, dusty, coal-mining city that borders Inner Mongolia. On Saturday afternoon, we went to a public bathhouse near her family's apartment.

The showers were strangely empty that day, much less crowded than the pool building's at school. Several middle-aged women turned to look at me incredulously and then went on with their scrubbing. With all that empty space in the tiled room, I actually felt cold, despite the hot water beating down on me.

I admitted to Wang Yue then that I felt embarrassed showering at the pool at school. To make things even weirder, I pointed out, I was a teacher. The shower room called to mind one of those teaching-anxiety dreams, I explained, when you suddenly find yourself naked in front of one of your classes. Wang Yue looked me at, confused. It hadn't occurred to me that the "teaching naked" dream might be specific to my cultural background.

"Like, what if I see one of my students in the showers?" I asked her, reframing my point. "That would be embarrassing."

"Why?" she asked. "I mean, like . . ." she said, her English colloquialisms flawless, "they are also there taking a shower, right? They don't care. They are doing the same thing as you." She offered me her bottle of soap. She had a point.

In this new phase of my life, where I felt exposed all the time, there was still so much in the culture that seemed guarded, so much information I'd never be privy to. At the start of the day's classes, I frequently got notes from missing students who gave vague excuses for their absences. "Dear Teacher," the notes usually read, in English. "I am sorry I will not attend class today. I have something to do."

In Mandarin, the expression *you shi* means you have some kind of business to deal with, the specifics of which might be private and need not be explained in detail. There is no good translation for this phrase, at least in my experience, though my students tried. What these *somethings* were, I never found out.

Despite the communal culture, there was a limit to how much of myself could be seen. I had my own secret. My first year in Shanxi, I felt I couldn't explain to any Chinese person—mostly because of the conservative social mores of where I was living—how much I longed for Sarah and how impossible communication had become, given unreliable Internet access and my crackling phone as well as the unpredictable restrictions from the government in Beijing. We found our Skype calls going silent.

As exhilarating as it was to be living abroad, there was also, for me, the day-to-day panic I didn't know how to explain to others, which came from an accumulation of small things: not being able to read all the characters on the bus schedules or figure out how to send a package. Or what to do when you eat something that gives you violent diarrhea all night and when the water source to your toilet is cut off, in a province with severe shortages, between 10 p.m. and 7 a.m. When I think back on China, even my good days had an undercurrent of deeper, untranslatable anxiety. It was that dislocation that only comes when you find yourself living, all of a sudden, on the other side of the world and not understanding how anything works. On bad days, I felt that I shouldn't have come to China. As an outsider, maybe I had no business being in Shanxi at all.

At night, I lay awake in my cold little bedroom, listening to the rat inside the radiator vent toenailing his way out onto the dark floor. China is a pretty loud place, but at night in Taigu, there was only this, plus one other noise: a train, about a mile away, from Xi'an on its way to Beijing, sounding its horn into the crisp, landlocked night. I could hear its pitch shift as it grew closer, then farther away. A sort of reverse alarm clock: I heard this every night at the same hour. Years later, when I think of the word *alone*, I still hear this sound.

That first spring, when I'd been in China nine months, Sarah finally broke up with me over the phone, the result of a multicall argument we couldn't seem to resolve while in two separate countries. Neither of us would back down. "This is impossible," she admitted and then hung up, as if some unknown force in the universe was responsible for what was happening to us. Despite the fact that we were already physically separated, and knowing the unlikely odds for relationship survival—several countries between us, two new cultures to adapt to, no plans to see each other until later in the summer, and being immature, in our early twenties—the breakup blindsided me.

I wasn't out to any of my Chinese friends yet. So the night after the phone call I spent wallowing in the company of the Americans next door, eating, in alternation, seaweed-flavored potato chips and beef-flavored potato chips. (We would eventually start calling them "breakup chips," since hardly any American's long-distance relationship survived while one member of the couple was living in China.) We drank large bottles of Xue Hua, a mediocre Chinese beer. The next morning, I woke at dawn, hungover and disoriented, to the loudspeaker narration of a campuswide exercise routine. I couldn't decipher any of the voice's directions except for the counting parts. "Three . . . four . . . five . . . SIX!" the voice kept saying, the reason for this emphasis unclear to me.

My grief that spring was enormous, maybe even out of proportion. Before China, I had never been particularly weepy, especially not after a breakup. Now I cried anytime I was not in front of a group of students: during dinner, during my Chinese lessons, after I bought vegetables in the square, while sweeping my floor or wiping the black coal dust from the windowsill. In Shanxi, all my usual emotions became augmented in ways I didn't understand, and the boundaries for who should and shouldn't know my feelings became more and more unclear.

Everything I ate made me sick. I started to resent hosting the usual dance parties, giving a thin-lipped smile as twentysomethings flooded my house. It wasn't long before my new Chinese friends put two and two together, even though I had never directly explained to them that Sarah, who had visited in the fall, was my girlfriend. I did not have to spell it out. "Oh! You have *xin shi*," they would tell me, letting my lesbianism be implied rather than stated outright.

When it comes to emotional matters in China, there is a variation of the vague expression *you shi*, the usual "I have business" or "I have something to do." If you say you *xin shi*, it means, more specifically, you have a matter of the heart to deal with, or something is weighing on you, or that you're worried in an all-consuming way. The word *xin*, written in Chinese, is an actual pictograph meaning "heart." *Xin shi* was how my friends referred to struggles with their boyfriends or girl-friends, or, occasionally, even more sensitive matters. (One close Chinese friend, I eventually discovered, had had three abortions in the past four years, all of which she'd kept a secret from her family and most of her friends at school.) The phrase is useful and can serve as a euphemism if you want it to, allowing you to both guard the details of your situation while also offering the gesture of an explanation.

The first time I uttered the phrase, it was because it was a bad day for me, my eyes still red and swollen when I entered the grain-seller's store to buy a half kilogram of flour. After I asked for the flour, the woman nodded, looked hard at me like an all-knowing mother. "*You xin shi*," I said, and she seemed to accept that.

"This poor foreigner," I heard her say to her husband, shaking her head, as I was heading out of the door. But that was the last time she'd refer to me as *foreigner*. I'd always be one, but the next time I came in to buy something, she called me Luo Yi Lin, the name I'd been given by a Mandarin tutor just after I'd arrived to China.

Not surprisingly, being with other people could sometimes distract me from my breakup. But I preferred to hang out with my friends one-on-one rather than be in the crowd. My favorite thing to do that spring was to sit on my stoop late into the evening with my Chinese tutor at the time, Zhao Xin (or "Maggie," as she sometimes called herself), drinking cheap beer and talking. Maggie had slowly become my closest friend in Shanxi. She was less demure than most of the Chinese women I knew—she cursed and played badminton and got angry at her boyfriend a lot. With the formal hour of the Chinese lesson long past, our conversations tended to get crasser and crasser as the night went on. These sessions, I maintain, are how I finally got conversational in Mandarin.

Maggie showed up at my house one spring night, appearing like a ghost on the dirt path leading up to my porch. She was coming from her graduate program's class party. "I had dry white wine," she kept saying, over and over, in English. Something was off about the translation: there was no dry white wine, at least the kind made from grapes, anywhere in town. Maggie only spoke English to me when she was drunk; it was her secret code to let you know what she'd been up to.

She had missed the dorm curfew, so she stayed with me. We shared my double bed, talking loudly and rudely for a while, scaring off the mice. She kept asking me, in English, with a strange British accent I'd never heard, if I had any beer in the kitchen. I didn't.

Far away, we heard the train pass, its timbre now more muddled than what I remembered in the colder months. Why was that so? We lay on our backs next to one another, our shoulders just barely touching. The ends of her black hair crossed onto my pillow. I could smell her shampoo. The room felt still, big around us. What was this? It was a closeness I hadn't felt in a long time.

I was thinking about what could happen, what would not happen between us. We got quiet. I wanted to know what she was thinking. Finally, she rolled toward me and reached across my arm. I held my breath and froze.

In a teasing, nonsexual way, she grabbed the hem of my shirt and tried to tickle me on my stomach, the way my sisters would do when we were kids. She stopped suddenly, with the heel of her hand just below my ribs.

"It's strong here!" she said, jubilant and surprised, pointing to my upper abdomen. "I like it."

When I exhaled, it came out as a laugh. She rolled back onto her back. A thin sliver of moonlight was wedging its way through the bedroom curtains. Our chattering thinned out, and the room went still again. I heard her breathing shift toward sleep. Our shoulders were still touching.

Language-wise, I finally gained the confidence to spend a good chunk of that first summer traveling alone. On a warm night in June, I stood beside the railroad tracks outside Taigu Railway Station, balancing my backpack across my feet. Alongside me was a small group of students with tiny suitcases, farmers with burlap bundles across their backs, and a handful of men and women who carried nothing except poker cards and the sunflower seeds and pears they would snack on. When the train to Beijing approached, a red light and a low honking in the dark, it slowed only long enough for the twenty or so of us to climb on: not from a platform but directly from the dusty ground. A train attendant reached her hand out to grab mine.

From Taigu to Beijing, a trip I'd made many times, took nearly eleven hours, meaning we'd wake up just before the train pulled into Beijing Station. And then it was another twenty-four hours to Inner Mongolia, the first new place on my journey, where I'd end up, for several nights, sleeping in a yurt, under quilts and on the floor. A hole at the top of the tent showed the pollution-free, star-spangled sky.

On that train to Inner Mongolia, we passed through a dry mountain range that eventually leveled out against the grasslands: a kind of lush prairie filled with long shadows, the sky enormous and flat and blue. The herds wandered in the distance, a scatter of white co-ordinates. I sat on a foldout seat by window, talking to strangers for hours. "Are you *yi ge ren?*" they would ask me, surprised, wanting to know if I was really traveling by myself.

I was, I said. And I wasn't, in another sense. At night, in my train compartment, I slept on the high bunk with my backpack nestled under my head. There were two strangers on the bunks below me, and three more against the opposite wall. We were together, if only for tonight. A man across the way snored rhythmically, precise. I could still feel my grief from the past year close to the surface, but it felt good not to be alone as I drifted into an on-and-off sleep. The six of us jostled across the terrain, passing towns and villages in the dark. Occasionally, I woke to the train's deceleration and the *thunk* of a new rider being hoisted aboard.

Back in Taigu, I had finally gotten over the showers at the swimming pool. Because my American co-fellows were men, they couldn't help me with this. I faced my fear by always entering the shower surrounded by my women friends. This is what all the women did; I don't know why it took so long for me to figure out that it was my aloneness, not just my foreign body, that made people stare.

After a long afternoon in the pool, with our hands turned as wrinkly as Shanxi's jujubes, we climbed out of the water and slipped into our plastic slippers, careful not to fall as we headed into the tile corridor. We passed the open toilet stalls, the stench pricking my nose, just before the perfumed smell of the shower room took over. We peeled ourselves out of our suits and wrung them out with our hands. I could feel my breasts swaying a little as I stepped over the tile ledge, the cold air grabbing my bare skin. As I crossed into the foggy threshold, I heard, in English: "Teacher!"

I had finally run into a group of my students. They were undergraduate freshmen, English majors. I had only seen most of them when they were wearing their glasses, so I hardly recognized them at first. Luo An, who introduced herself as "Annie" in my class, looked at me in a dreamy, blurry sort of way. She was one of her class's leaders and the most forthright in English, talkative and clear.

"Do you come here often to have a shower?" she wanted to know immediately. "And are you by yourself?"

"I usually shower at my house," I told her. I motioned to my friends in front of me. "We are together today."

The smallest student, who called herself Stella, nodded at me demurely, her wet bangs and bob still hanging in a perfect square around her face. She was less than five feet tall. Undressed, her body seemed to be solely composed of bones and skin, barely pubescent. Her chest was almost completely flat. At this point, I remembered my own shame, that I was also naked. They must all be looking at the weirdness that is my body, I thought to myself: my red bush, sturdy thighs, and sizeable butt. I could feel my face growing hot, despite the cold air.

But I resisted the urge to turn away. There is nothing weird here, I told myself. I was twenty-three years old. The students were nineteen: barely even women yet, but still women, nonetheless. Toward the end of my conversation with my students, it hit me that they were treating me in much the same way they had at the times we'd run into each other in the marketplace, fully clothed. Seeing their teacher out in public was seeing their teacher out in public, regardless of the circumstances.

I slipped further into the steam, the showers' whooshing noise, the clamoring of female voices, their exact words getting lost in the larger din. I placed my plastic caddy at the edge of the room, with the dozens of others, what seemed like hundred of bottles of shampoo and body wash crammed inside, washcloths draped over the handles. By now I had run out of all of my preferred Western toiletries—my last holdout from my former day-to-day life in the United States—

so it was next to impossible to tell my basket from the others.

On the one wall where there were no showerheads, I saw a dozen undressed women lean against the tile, as if poised for a series of painful tattoos. Instead, their friends vigorously scrubbed their backs. The scrubbers wore hand-shaped loofahs, what looked like textured oven mitts, and rubbed so hard—more like scoured—that the top layers of skin began visibly pilling in some places. Of course, I had no loofah mitt of my own, but Wang Hui Fang insisted that she use hers on me. "You first," she said. "Then me."

Eventually I turned, putting my hands on the tile wall. I glanced over my shoulder. There had been a handful of women staring at me since I entered the shower room, but once they realized that I was with friends, they went back to their showering, seemingly losing interest.

The scrub hurt almost as much as I imagined it would. Wang Hui Fang worked in long, shoulder-to-butt strokes, the friction so fierce that it felt like my skin was lit. At first I thought this force was unnecessary, but then I remembered the swimming pool's chemicals and what the bottoms of my feet looked like: almost black in the dry, dead parts at the edges of my heel, and the ball of my foot its own dingy plateau. I had made the mistake of trying to go barefoot in my apartment a few times, earlier in the year, and I had paid the price. I couldn't seem to get all the Shanxi dust off my body, no matter how hard I tried under my tiny home showerhead, no matter how many times I mopped my apartment.

Pronouncing me done, Wang Hui Fang handed me the fluorescent pink mitt, and I looked for an open showerhead to wash it out and rinse myself. There were none. "Just push your way through," she suggested. I edged slowly into the crowd, waiting and waiting, my backside getting cold, until finally a woman stepped out from under the spray, and I got my clearance. I rinsed the mitt off first and then myself. The water was hot, and the pressure was good, much better than the lukewarm trickle of the sad shower in my apartment. I was not alone. I was so close to the stranger next to me that when I bent forward, my shoulder brushed hers. The woman and I turned to look at one another at the same time, both of us sort of smiling in acknowledgment. The collision was inevitable; the room was very full. Neither one of us felt the need to apologize.

■

How to Stop a Black Snake

FROM *The New York Times*

NEAR CANNON BALL, ND—Last Sunday, the Oceti Sakowin camp at Standing Rock in North Dakota was slick with icy, packed-down snow. The mud was glass. Veterans poured in, having traveled all night to support the people protecting their water from the Dakota Access Pipeline.

I linked arms with Loretta Bad Heart Bull, and we teetered up to the central prayer circle with Art Zimiga, an Oglala Hunkpapa Vietnam veteran who had just been gifted a pair of crampons. The sun was still warm, the air scented with burning cedar.

The sudden announcement that an easement to cross the Missouri River had been denied by the United States Army Corps of Engineers, dealing the pipeline an apparent setback, sent roars of joy, waves of song, disbelief, joy again, all through the camp.

Dancers swirled, women gave high-pitched Lakota trills, people roared "Mni Wiconi," water is life. Some wept, sank to their knees, waved wands of smoking sage. Loretta grabbed my arm and tugged me closer to the circle, into the crowd. She is a no-nonsense, funny, sharply dressed woman. Everybody let her through.

I crushed up next to Vermae Taylor, from Fort Peck, Montana, who had been back and forth to the camp since August. She told me that this moment was the happiest she'd been in all of her 75 years. Mary Lyons, an Ojibwe elder from Leech Lake, beamed and held my arm. She was there for her great-grandchildren.

This was supposed to be *it*, the end of months of desperation. In spite of the tribe's strenuous objections, Energy Transfer Partners, the company building the pipeline, had chosen a route that could threaten water that the tribe, as well as farmers and ranchers, depend on. As the pipeline neared, water protectors committed to peaceful action chained themselves to drilling equipment and tried to pray on a butte where Sitting Bull walked.

While the victory strengthens the tribe's position, most people around me were aware that the struggle was not over. Energy Transfer Partners had called the denial of the easement a "political action" and said it was committed to finishing the pipeline. People were not breaking camp, but digging in.

My family has been taking turns at Standing Rock, and last weekend was mine, so I drove from Minneapolis. I have poor cold-weather-camping skills, and the Prairie Knights Casino and Resort was bursting, with people slumped asleep in lobby chairs. I felt lucky to be able to stay in Loretta's home, snug on a windy hill, overlooking Barren Butte. Her house is a tidy haven, often filled with visitors. We got home late, collapsed. I drank glass after glass of water.

It was delicious water. *That's what this is all about*, said Loretta. She was drying traditional chokecherry cakes in an electric food dryer. The day, with its huge range of emotions over the surprise decision, seemed endless. I had actually come to talk to the veterans, who were still arriving as we left. More than 2,000 had signed on and more were expected along with snow.

Like many Standing Rock Lakota, Loretta is from several generations of veterans. Her father, Joseph Grey Day, was awarded a medal as a code talker. The night before, I had been at the first veterans' gathering at Sitting Bull tribal college. There, I met Duane Vermillion, a local Marine and Vietnam veteran who was unsurprised that so many veterans were arriving. "If a call is put out to ask for help, our friends will answer," he said. Duane's grandfather George Sleeps From Home was also a code talker, and Duane's father served in Korea.

Native Americans have always maintained an outsize presence in the military, serving on a per-capita basis in higher numbers than any other ethnic group. American Indians fought in the Civil War and World War I before we even had citizenship. Many Native Americans volunteered to serve in World War II and Korea before they were included in the Voting Rights Act, and in Vietnam before the American Indian Religious Freedom Act of 1978.

That's right. In a country founded on religious freedom, Native Americans were not granted the right to legally practice our own religions until 1978.

Since then, indigenous spirituality has become a powerful uniting force. Each tribal nation has its own rituals and observances, but we hold in common the conviction that our earth is a living mystery upon whose tolerance we depend.

In the Missouri Breaks, you feel that presence acutely. But the flat aqua expanse of Lake Oahe in view of the Oceti Sakowin camp is another story. The lake isn't natural, and was forced on tribal people when the Army Corps flooded the fertile bottomlands of the Missouri River. Up north, the project displaced the Hidatsa, Mandan, and Arikara people. Down here, the Lakota. After so many other acts of dispossession, it was said that many elders died of broken hearts.

The Black Snake is what Lakota people call the Dakota Access Pipeline. It will extinguish the world. For a people who have endured the end of their way of life so many times, who can doubt the truth of their vision, which coincides with scientific truth about the relationship of fossil fuels to catastrophic climate change?

On Monday, I said goodbye to Loretta, who packed me an egg sandwich. I drove home chased by snow. Along I-94 there were the familiar signs, simple black-and-white admonitions, Be Nice, and Be Polite. It could have been the camp motto. So many young non-Native people have been drawn to this cause. I thought about the spindly girl with wild ringlets, smiling as she served me a plate of wontons and strawberries in the food tent. I worried. Did she have wool socks? A subzero sleeping bag? After a blizzard, there is usually deep cold.

Which was how things felt — a storm of emotion and then the glaring truth of our political reality, in which fossil fuel interests expect a presidential blessing.

Still, someday, I hope we look back to Standing Rock as the place where we came to our senses. Where new coalitions formed. Where we became powerful together as we realized that we have to preserve land, water, the precious democracy that is our pride, the freedoms that make up our joy.

I hope we look back at the images — the blurred features behind the riot-gear-clad men looming over a praying woman, the costumes of intimidation, the armored Humvees confronting young people on horseback, and see how close we came to losing the republic. But we didn't. We woke up. We understood that the people who had persevered through everything, including Wounded Knee, knew how easily the world could end. So they were fighting for the water of life, for everyone.

SMITH HENDERSON

■

The Trouble

FROM *American Short Fiction*

THE BOY DAWDLED DOWN the road into Tenmile with the practiced nonchalance of a troublemaker, shifting along like a raccoon, miming terrific fascination at the foil wrappers and sun-scalded aluminum cans blown flat into the weeds at the side of the two-lane highway, stopping for items worthy or simply shiny, peering, sometimes picking one up, and then moving on. The sun had eased into the trees of the mountain, and Henry was at the put-in by the river watching the kid cross the bridge into town. Songbirds darted to their final assignations in the bleeding light. The bats pitched themselves at right angles into the mayflies milling above the water. Henry tossed the crust of his sandwich out his pickup window high over the river and watched as bats honed and dove for the morsel. The boy arrived at the town square. Henry started his truck and rolled alongside the boy, who did not look up.

"Son," he said. The kid stopped. Thumbed his pockets. Henry dropped the truck into park and left the engine running. "You from around here?"

A tall, handsome kid. Vivid blue eyes, hair black and shiny as a beetle shell.

"Nope. My aunt has a place somewheres."

"You don't know where?"

"Nope."

"You mind I ask her name?"

"Nope," the boy said.

Then the boy didn't say who his aunt was.

"You wanna give me that name?"

"My aunt?"

In the shaded dusk, Henry could not tell if the boy was a smart-ass or just profoundly stupid.

"Yes."

A streetlamp winked twice and came full on.

"It's Brenda Parks," he said, straightening up into the light. "I don't figure you know where her place is," he said.

"There's only six thousand people live in Tenmile, son. Get in."

The kid smirked and looked away. Like a plan had come off or was set in motion. He dashed around the truck and got in. Said his name was Keith. He'd been praying for a ride since Forsyth, where he'd been looking for his uncle. He said he was eighteen, but Henry didn't believe it. The scar on his arm was from a fight in Seattle. So was the tattoo. Seattle had marked him up good. But then he found Jesus, the Lord's forgiveness. He wasn't gonna lie about nothing no more. He had stuck needles in his arm and had been on the wrong path. He wasn't gonna lie about it. He was saved and had decided to find his aunt, see if he could get a clean start. His uncle—the one in Forsyth—said she was in Tenmile, so that's how Keith come to be here. All of this was the truth.

"I see," Henry said at the conclusion of this biography. They went past the bars, the barbershop, and Dairy Queen, then out on the county road.

"This some kind of fire truck?" the kid asked.

Henry said it was. The first water tender he owned, in fact. A twelve-hundred-gallon tank bolted and welded to a Ford F-150. Did the boy have a driver's license? Would he be looking for work? Could he study up for the kind of test you need to take to drive an even bigger truck and operate a pump and enter into the profession of wildfire fighting and dust suppression? Henry smiled at the boy over the last part as if to say it really wasn't a profession at all, that the boy'd almost be doing him a favor to take the job.

"Holy shit." The kid fairly vibrated at his good fortune. "Pardon me."

Henry plucked a business card off the dash.

"Keith, you come out to this address tomorrow morning at eight. Ask for my mother, Kelly, to get you started on the paperwork."

"Holy cow."

Henry pulled into the drive. A grave unsmiling old woman hefted herself out of a wicker chair on the porch and tilted her head back to look at them stopping.

"One favor. You tell your aunt who gave you a job."

"I sure will." He scanned the card for Henry's name. "Thanks, Mr. McGinnis."

"Folks call me Daddy. Tell your aunt that Daddy brought you home. Daddy got you a job already."

Henry went to the Sunrise Café. The old boys down there, the farmers, loggers, and the cripples and layabouts drawing social security. He used to bring his daughter Jill when she was little, pigtailed or tutued, and she'd carry on *daddydaddydaddydaddy Daddayyy* until he stopped whatever he was doing and gave her a quarter for the gumball machine or sent her around the corner to the tobacco shop to get him a cigarillo and a candy cane, don't tell your mother, wink. Spoiled her mostly. So the old boys got to calling him Daddy. And over the years it spread to his crew, his clients, his suppliers, the parts guys, and the rest of the town. Now everybody called him that.

The old boys all said *Hey Daddy* when he came in. They were fingering their change, braiding rope, and watching out the window for something to occur. All cowboy hats and cigarettes and coughing and taking medications. Pearl-snap buttons like a line of aspirin clinging to the rondure of their guts.

Old Burt waved Henry over with a big red arm tufted white with hair that gave him the pink aspect of a prize pig. Burt had suggested the previous autumn that maybe Henry should run for mayor, said that a picture of Henry—thick-necked and flannelled and smiling—would look just about boss with two words right under him: *Vote Daddy.* Everybody knowing Henry McGinnis. Everybody liking Henry McGinnis.

Henry had said he'd think on it.

He sat at the counter and ordered a cup of coffee. Burt read aloud the rodeo results from the paper. He turned and folded the paper and glanced at Henry and spoke to the room in general.

"Says here a kid was attacked by an owl," Burt said. "Cross-country skiing up in the high country with his family it says."

"A goddamned *owl*?" old Rosignol asked. "Let me see that."

Burt handed to paper to Rosignol and went over to where Henry sat. They shook and greeted one another.

"Take a walk?"

"Make that a to-go Marcie."

Henry expected another entreaty but not the whole gang filing out after them. Burt took his arm, the rest of the old boys trailing behind. They talked about the owl and Rosignol and Rosignol's new F-150 pickup and arrived at the end of the square, where beyond was a squat row of bars and after that nothing but an empty field and then the timber. Henry stopped. At a gesture from Burt, the others crossed the street and went to the courthouse in the middle of the square. Burt cleared his throat, the effort showing in the quilting of his throat.

"Have you all decided?" he asked.

Henry said he was thinking about it.

"You'd make a helluva mayor Henry. You pay well. You bring business. Hell, *you are* the Tenmile Chamber of Commerce. Running for office? Shit. Ain't no thing but a chicken wing. Imagine what you could do, all the business connections you got in Polson. And Kalispell?"

Burt had Henry's shoulder pinched ever so lightly in his fingers and thumb. Henry waited until it was uncomfortable for Burt to leave it there, then he spoke.

"Let me get this straight. You'd have me employ the town. You'd have me bring business here. And now you'd have me run for mayor and govern." Burt grinned at his boots. "Is there anything else can I do for you, Burt?"

He looked up at Henry under his flaring white brows, palmed his nape, and said, "Well, I got this crick in my neck."

Henry just sucked his teeth at the joke. The old boys milled around the courthouse lawn, looking for some sign of what was decided.

"All kidding aside," Henry said. "You know what seventy percent of my business is? Dust. I piss on dirt for a living."

Burt narrowed his expression, rubbed his jaw. Said, "And you feel like what you got already is just about your fair portion."

"Something like that."

Burt nodded, thought better of what he was about to say, and punched Henry soft in the arm.

"We'll line up behind you. All I can say is, you'd make a fine mayor, Daddy."

What Henry believed in was family and that all the blessings in his life proceeded from this belief. He was the richest man in Tenmile—even if that wasn't saying much—and he put close to seventy grand in wages in the town's pockets the year prior. Martha Baumgartner even thanked him for hiring her boy in a rambling four-page letter, the upshot of which was that her son Ben had been about to join the Marines or go to college, and Henry had saved the boy from both of those evils. He wrote her back saying the kid was a natural grease monkey and born water tender driver, even though neither was true. Henry hired young and he hired dumb. It was that simple.

The kid who'd walked into town, Keith, was no different. Worse, if possible. Poor in the uptake of new information and skills. Little inherent work ethic or simple sticktoitiveness. It took the better part of April to get him certified. On a practice run up to Tub Gulch, Henry followed in another truck as the boy pissed 3,000 gallons of potable on the road. Henry tried the CB. The logging road was too narrow to pass, so he honked and flashed his lights. Nothing.

When they got to the site, Henry asked was his damn radio broke.

The kid flipped it on. Said that it didn't look like it was.

Henry took off his cap and worked his temples. The kid watched him closely, like Henry was at charades. Henry beckoned him to the back of the truck and showed him where the valve dripped the last drops of the water. The kid asked him what happened.

"You didn't close the cam lock is what happened."

"Shit."

"Imagine there's a dirty, hungry, thirsty fire crew up here. Needing to cook and shower. I want you to imagine them looking at you right now."

The boy peopled the meadow with sincere concentration.

"Man," he said with considerable awe. "I bet they'd be fuckin' pissed."

Henry's daughter Jill was something Henry liked to show off when she was younger, somewhere between the MEC 650 shotgun-shell reloader in his den and the pressure washers and concrete drains he had installed out in the truck bay. At parties and barbecues, he used tell her to come on over and do that dance she learned in that dance class down in Polson. She'd ask which one suspiciously, and he'd say the one that was costing him an arm and a leg, to his guests' laughter, her embarrassment. He'd soothe her on his knee. Times he could coax a warbled tune out of her. But as she grew taller and plumper and her talents more vague, he quit asking her to do anything for company. She would just stand there looking at her phone or pluck some invisible sweater pill or dandelion seed from her new bosom, and ignore whoever her father wanted her to meet, men who now seemed content to just look at her and did not laugh. Not at all.

The case with Keith was likewise. She came around the house as Henry was explaining to the nigh-idiot why you don't simply pour the old engine oil into the ditch. Henry called her over to meet the kid, but she didn't hear or didn't care and went out on the dirt road. She crossed it kicking white dust up to the hem of her dress with her cowboy boots, and dipped into the ditch opposite looking for something, pointing it out to herself, ducking down to get it. She mounted the road grunting and came back. Along her thigh she swung a dead chicken by the neck. Henry called her again, and she came over with the bird.

With her other hand she typed something on her phone, who knew what. "Another'n got out and got hit," she said. A pickup full of boys barreled up the road as if to prove her point. She raised a chin at them and grinned vaguely in the direction they were headed.

Henry pecked her on the cheek, put an arm around her, which she seemed mainly to tolerate.

"This is Jill," he said.

Keith's mouth slowly opened but he didn't say anything with it.

Henry told Keith she was homeschooled and raised animals in 4-H and had already taken practice tests of the SAT and wanted to be a veterinarian or maybe even a pilot, and though it would kill him, she would probably go to college in Washington or at least the University of Montana. He pushed the hair out of her eyes.

"Daddy," she said. "*Don't.*"

Keith watched him kiss her cheek. She had a toothpick in her mouth and moving it around in there made a powerful impression. The chicken bled. Spots of blood on her dress, her boot.

"Keith wants to go into the ministry," Henry announced.

Jill squinted up at the late morning sun, yawned, and fluffed the dead bird's white feathers.

"You got a little blood on you," Keith said, pointing at her foot.

"I better clean up," she said, ducking out from under her father's arm.

"I'll see you at church then?" Keith said to her.

She backed away, dead chicken, sundress, toothpick, smile.

"If you sit by the window you will."

As the weeks went on, Henry's mother Kelly came to adore Keith. Mornings Henry'd come into the dispatch office where she kept the books and find the boy leaning over the desk showing her a thing he'd drawn and wanted to tattoo on his shoulder. Things he said were straight out of Revelations, dragons and horsemen. Visions more commonly airbrushed on vans.

"You don't got nothing to do?" Henry would say to him.

"Sure thing, Daddy."

His mother smiled and shook her head as the boy departed.

"I thought you hated tattoos," he said to his mother. He dropped into the office chair on clicking casters and groaned with the springs.

"I do. He's just something else to listen to."

"Listen to?"

"To look at then." She fluttered her eyelashes, making fun of herself.

"Mother."

She shrugged.

Now in his fifties, Henry had come to look like her in the mouth and jowl, and it bothered him, though he never thought so in actual words. Just a feeling he had, passing a mirror. His resemblance to her had nearly startled him when Burt brought over that *Vote Daddy* poster he'd done up. Now he saw her mouth in the mirror every time he shaved. How we are each a late version of someone preceding us.

"He's got Jill in a lather," she said.

Maybe he'd grow a mustache or beard. He wondered how that would look on a *Vote Daddy* poster.

"Asking if she can bring me my lunch and every other thing just to get a look at him," she said.

"What?"

"Jill."

"Jill what?"

"And Keith."

Henry scoffed.

"He's an idiot."

"Why'd you hire him then?"

Henry leaned forward and scanned the large calendar on the desk for upcoming jobs. She watched him a minute and then got up and went to the file cabinet, stopped, turned around, and sat again. He glanced up.

"What?" he said.

"Because of Brenda Parks."

"How's that now?"

"Brenda's popular with them in the church, and he's her nephew. So if you were to run for mayor—"

"Mama, I ain't running for mayor. We need a lot more jobs or a big fire season to cover our nut." He tapped the blank week on the calendar. "You don't know how dry it's gonna be this summer."

"Maybe the mayor's allowed to start forest fires," she said wryly.

She looked at him with a face that was his face, and it embarrassed him. The thought of all those posters going up all over.

The fires up past Deerwater, deep in the Purcell Range, issued from a spectacle of heat lightning that lit the night sky an awful purple like some kind of novel ordnance. The dawn met grim pennants of smoke, and by then the fires had scorched several thousand acres. Tenmile smelled of smoke and then a nicotine halo shrouded the sun and to go outside was to come back in smelling like a campfire.

The wildfire was big and close. By noon Henry and his crew had already been up to the fire camp at Fourth of July Creek three times, filling the huge bladders of potable and the remote dip tanks for the helicopters, and pumping straight from the Kootenai River and racing up the mountain to douse the fire line directly. Sweltering smokejumpers manifested at the roadside in small bands, coated in soot. Henry stopped and sprayed the men down. A crew of trench diggers and chainsaw men marching up the road stopped when Henry honked and they too stood in the spray and trudged Indian-file dripping back into the lodgepoles to help set backfires.

Henry was heading back to camp in the late afternoon when his mother radioed. Keith. The kid had attached a potable bladder to the water truck, opened the valve, and wandered off for a cigarette. When he came back the mess chief was screaming murder about the pond under his kitchen. A number of the firefighters' individual tents were flooded, their clothes and belongings sopping wet. Keith had banjaxed half the camp.

"Fire him."

"Henry—"

He cut her off but knew she couldn't hear him until she quit speaking into the CB, so he repeated himself: "Fire him. Fire him. Fire him."

"He's just a kid—"

Henry flipped off the CB.

Reputation was everything, mayoral candidate or not. Henry went straight to the campsite and helped the mess crew tote the propane tanks and kitchen burners to dry ground, strung up lines by himself, hung clothes and sleeping bags, and met the truckloads of sooted firefighters coming off the mountain in the dark, explaining and apologizing. Most of them were too bushed to do any worse than brush by him, drop their pulaskis, and curl up on the ground like dogs.

It rained, first in timid drops that impinged Henry's dusty lot in polka dots and then in great waving drapes across the meadow in back of his property. A full day of small drizzle under gray shapeless scud and witchy cold. Henry cooked a can of chili on his dash heater as he sat on standby at the fire camp. At least everything was wet now. Maybe they'd forget. He realized, with relief, that none of these firefighters were from Tenmile, that none would vote here. Then this relief embarrassed him.

He finally got the all-clear to go home in the dark downpour, ate mutely with his wife, and fell asleep to the purl of gutter water by the window. He woke before dawn, before the rooster cockadoodle, with it still raining or raining again. He fixed his coffee and eggs. The day lit. The rain eased.

Going out to drop a bag of garbage in the dumpster, he discovered Brenda Parks's Buick behind the outbuilding. For a moment he wondered what her car was doing there. Where it could not be seen from the house. He pitched his coffee into the wet grass and jogged back the inside.

He flung open Jill's bedroom door. Her head thrown back, clutching her robe closed over her chest, her own hand over her mouth. The boy's legs such that it only slowly dawned on Henry she was astraddle him backwards. He watched the boy's toes curl. Jill didn't even notice him.

When Keith slunk out to the car, Henry stepped from behind the dumpster and crowned him with shovel handle. Henry slipped and nearly fell in the mud.

"I ever see you again, I won't stop. You hear me?"

Keith goggled at the inchoate blur talking to him.

"You hear me?"

"I can't hear anything this ringing in my ear."

Henry hit him again, hard in the knee. Keith scrambled into his car, turned it over, and went away forever.

Henry had, in fact, witnessed his grandson's conception. Had occasioned it, one could say, hiring that boy loping into town. All of the trouble fell squarely in his lap.

What Henry did not see but imagined and could not stop imagining: Keith sniffing around the house, sidling up, ogling and charming and seducing his daughter. It was Henry's whole setup that was to blame, then. Putting this kind of business on the same property as his house. His family. It seemed so inevitable now. Did he not know the sheer natural fact that since she was thirteen, his crew had thought and spoke crudities about her, sexual and violent animal things, snatches of which had wafted into her ears as she passed the outbuildings to fetch her grandmother or these very men for dinner, things they said involving parts of her body, and which pooled in her thoughts and made her picture herself as a mere constituency of thigh and neck and breast?

He did know. He could not unhear these things any more than she.

In fact, his silence was permission.

A man with a placard waited across the street, already at this hour of the morning. WHAT PART OF "THOU SHALT NOT KILL" DO YOU NOT UNDERSTAND? read his sign. Leaning on the placard and sipping his coffee, the man watched them pull in and back out of a STAFF ONLY space right up front. His face untroubled, a little optimistic even. He stood on the street corner in front of a hotel. The hotel sign said *Welcome Soroptimists.*

Henry's family hadn't been down to Missoula in years and they would not be back for years more. He drove around and around the clinic in wider and wider circles. So early in the morning and with no one on the sidewalks, it was astonishing how many cars there were, the dearth of spaces. They entered an unpromising lot. Even the handicapped spaces were taken. Henry parked on the grass under a tree. They could just ticket him then.

He told Jill and Reba to wait in the pickup. The maple trees were grand and cool. Showing off. In Tenmile, no one had planted trees. Trees were for the mountains. But here. It was an initiative to have planted trees. Henry would plant trees in Tenmile when he was mayor. In the town, around the bald square. Take care of this business and plant trees.

Yes. He wanted to be mayor. If he was mayor, perhaps he would deserve his life.

The clinic was a brick house on a rise above street level. Henry mounted the steps that ran through a cinderblock wall. A guard picking up trash in the grass told Henry that the clinic wouldn't open until the doctor arrived, but Henry was welcome to wait out front. Henry looked across the street at the man leaning on his sign and sipping his coffee. The man tugged up his sleeve to look at his watch, as if waiting for his shift to start.

"He don't get holy rolling until he finishes his coffee," the guard said. "But don't worry. He can't come within a hundred feet of here."

A car pulled up in the staff spot. A nurse, from the look of her pink scrubs, parked her sedan in front of the cinderblock wall and asked did the guard want her to run for donuts.

"Oh come on now, you witch," he said to her. "She's undermining my willpower," he said to Henry, tapping his gut. "Now lookit that. She went and got them already anyhow."

The nurse set the donuts on the hood of her car, shrugged innocently.

Henry said he'd wait with his family in the yonder lot. He pointed in that direction, but the guard was telling the nurse to get them donuts up to him pronto. He went and sat on the bench by the front door and rubbed his hands together.

When Henry got to down to street level, the man with the placard nodded at him like a coach on the opposite sideline. Henry had a mind to go over there, but that was it. Just a mind to go over, no idea what he'd say to the fellow. And the wind was odd. From the windrows it gusted up last year's old gray leaves. They spread like an opening palm and fell into a sudden stillness.

When the explosion happened, it rattled and blurred the visible world, it hurt his teeth, and he expected something collapsing, something falling from the sky. He pivoted around into a crouch between two cars, and when the guard's body dropped into the street before him, he did not immediately recognize it as such and looked up wondering generally now what the fuck are they doing now the goddamn sonofabitches, hot debris pelting him and smoking the sonofabitches. Jesus. A white cloud of smoke in front of the clinic. Burning green leaves.

The taillights on the car were flashing, the noise—car alarm. He warily rose, scanning the street. The flashing lights of other vehicles in automatic hysterics. The smoke caught in one of those odd gusts shunted sideways down the street and halted just like a person might stop to take in this scene. He turned and could just make out Reba and Jill inside the pickup in the distant lot, what confused expressions they wore. He touched his chest to show them he was fine and gestured at them to stay put.

He warily approached the guard in the middle of the empty street. He'd been blown out of his shoes, his clothes, naked save his service belt. The exposed bones of his glistening face were flensed and obscene. He did not move or even bleed, just smoked and in places bubbled.

Screaming. From somewhere, screaming.

Henry made for the nurse next to her car. Burned donuts sweet in the air. A trace of aqua fortis. When Henry knelt, he cut his hand on the car. He sucked his hand and looked where an array of hot nails and screws spiked out of the fender, and told of a homemade bomb he would realize later. He bent over the nurse, her scrubs ripped open and bloody as the day she was born. From black holes the length of her seeped ribbons of blood. But she drew breaths and screamed again. Again and again like an infant. Henry felt for her jugular, femoral, auxiliary arteries. He tilted her to check underneath and her clothes and backside were pristine. He took her quivering hand.

She passed out or simply quit shrieking. He checked her breath and her pulse again, both faint and steady. People arrived, blanched, and departed. Someone touched his shoulder, uttered things, and left. There was a vibration in his pocket. He would realize later it was his phone, his wife calling and calling him from the pickup.

The police and paramedics arrived and pulled him from the woman's side, and he heard his daughter yelling, "Daddy! DADDY!" He swagged heavily to the truck. Jill and Reba shouted at him for leaving them there and not answering his phone and slapped and clutched at him as he negotiated the key into the ignition, started the truck, and got them the hell gone. Saying, "Okay okay okay."

Henry and his mother, wife, and daughter sat around the kitchen table, silent. Jill rubbed her belly as if her pregnancy were evident. The coffee had ceased steaming and the sun had gone up so far during their muted impasse that there was just a little quadrangle of light on the corner of the table. Like the last slice of cake. A housefly planed figure eights.

Jill had changed her mind.

Henry said that nothing had changed. They had decided before and what was settled was still settled. He set his palms on the table to indicate finality.

Kelly got up and rinsed her cup in the sink. Reba fingernailed a spot of cream on the table, ran rays from it. Jill jiggled in the chair like it was hot or vibrating under her, waiting for her mother or her grandmother to say something. She looked hard at her mother.

"You said we never should have gone, Mama. You said that."

Henry passed his bandaged hand across his forehead as if to smooth the thoughts in there. What Jill said was true. On the way back Reba prayed. Begged forgiveness, thanked the Lord for sparing Henry. Said to God that they never should have gone to the clinic. Now she only nodded.

"He doesn't even know," Jill said. "Keith will come back when he knows he's a daddy."

"He's a fuckwit," Henry said.

Jill leaned forward and spilled her hair onto the table. Sobbed there. "We could keep it," she said, her voice hard and wet on the wood under her hair.

"No, it's not—"

"If you just loved it, Daddy."

His words were like flintsparks, hot, quick, and seeking fuel: "I won't ever love it, Jill."

Her face rose white and ominous, and she stood, and a good majority of her love for him evaporated right then forever.

She went to her room, slammed her door, of course. The fly landed on her cup. Disappeared over the lip of it.

Reba leaned on an elbow toward him. "I'm gonna pretend," she said, "that what happened, what awful things you saw, is why you just said that."

"Wonderful," Henry said. "You changed your mind, too."

But she was already away from the table.

His mother was leaning against the sink, looking at him sadly. He'd never seen her cry. She didn't now, but this was close to it.

"Christ, you too?" he asked.

"No. Not that."

"Then what?"

"Henry. You're my son. You could've been killed."

He tasted his cold coffee, got up, and went out the side door.

That he could have been killed did not change how he felt. People die and people almost die all the time. Only the fortune in his life would ever astonish him. His ten water trucks, the nurse tankers, the 5,000-gallon water tenders. Four buildings. Mountains all around, and the acreage on three sides his too. That was a miracle. Death you could count on. His life he wasn't so sure he deserved.

He walked out to the truck bay. A pair of his crew were grab-assing when he came up in the cavernous outbuilding, and they snapped to at the sight of him.

"Hey Mr. McGinnis. We about got this one lubed."

"Good. Where's the rest of you all?"

"Jeff and Church went for them parts you ordered. Ken and Ben are getting our lunch. Nick's around."

The two young men stood there greased to the elbows and waiting for him to say something. Warm oil in the air.

"You all can knock off early. Say, three?"

"Sure thing, Daddy."

The heating sun made a corrugated panel boom into shape and sounded like someone had dropped a rubber hammer on it, and he flinched. The young men witnessed this without comment, glanced a couple times at his bandaged hand. Henry asked if they heard what had happened. They had.

"Was it gnarly?"

"Yes."

"Man."

"So it's got around then?" Henry asked. "That we were down there? What we were down there for?"

They nodded. Henry put his hands on hips and affected an authority he didn't feel.

"I want to be really clear," Henry said. "I don't want any of you talking to my family about what happened. Any of you breathe a goddamn word about it to Mrs. McGinnis or my daughter and you're fucking fucked."

"We wasn't—"

"You hear?"

"Yessir."

"In fact, don't talk to her at all. Don't so much as talk about her or look at her or nothing. I so much as get a whiff of you thinking about her, you'll lose more than your goddamned job."

Despite his efforts, Henry could not bury the incident and get them on with their lives. Two detectives from Missoula—nice enough, mustached and earnest and not even taking notes—had a hard time believing Henry or his family didn't see anybody except the man with the placard. And the FBI agents in their black sedans and black sunglasses had a harder time. All those cars at the scene, and not one single person before the blast? The bomb had a remote detonator, not a timer. Someone had seen *them*—Henry and his family—and had decided to spare *them*. They should think about that, the FBI said.

Reba wouldn't even listen to Henry about another clinic, the one in Spokane. At supper, Jill and Reba closed ranks—sitting close and stubborn and binary in some new and powerfully thwarting way—and left him puncturing the air with his fork when he tried to change their minds. And the sun went down, him at the dining room table, through the picture window there. An explosion of light from under the clouds and above the trees as the sun gloried in the last of the day. The murmuring behind Jill's closed door was unbearable.

He went to his mother's. She sat on the porch swing that his father had made and that to this day didn't so much as creak. A filigree of roses on the armrests. The sheer skill and love in it. He sat next to her on it.

"She's fifteen," he said.

"Pshaw. In my day, you got pregnant, you got married. I's fourteen, you recall."

"I know."

"Like I used to say, if you don't like me, blame your father. He raised me."

"I hate when you say that."

Her cackling had startled a starling from the eaves.

"There ain't a lick of him in my face, you know that? It's all your side of the family," he said.

"That's too bad. He was a handsome devil." She pushed the swing with her feet. "How's your hand?"

"It's fine." He touched it. "I'm okay. I was really lucky."

She nodded. "You want something to drink?"

He turned to her.

"Why you all like him so much?" he asked. "That kid, I mean."

"Keith? I don't know that we like him *so much*. Some people just have charisma, and you believe in them." She touched a rose on the armrest. "I got some sun tea in there."

"I'm all right. I just feel so helpless."

"You're far from helpless, Henry. You're wonderful. You're more successful than I ever imagined. But you're just Jill's daddy. And my boy."

He felt hot shame like he hadn't felt since he'd been a child, and she brought him sun tea but the glass sweated in his bandaged hand and he wanted something stronger, so he left.

He drank often. Afternoons alone in his office with a bottle or in his pickup by the river. An evening he spent a few hours at pinball in the Ten High with glasses of cold beer. The air conditioner cooled and then goosebumped his arms and neck. He felt considerably better. Burt and some of the old boys came in with wadded currency for dollar poker and bags of fried chicken that bloomed dark with grease. The belled pinball music gave him away in the corner, and Burt waved him over. His beer was empty so he went up to the bar and ordered another. The old men smoothing out their dollars looked up under hooded crow-footed eyes with something like sorrow in them, and Henry knew.

"A little walk, Burt?"

They took their beers outside with them. They squinted against the sunset until their pupils pinned, and then walked away from the sun boring into the mountains.

"How you all doing?" Burt asked.

"Fine."

"Anything we can do. Just let me know."

"Sure."

"They find out who—"

"They don't know shit."

"Some kind of world we got going on."

They didn't stop at the end of the square but instead walked along the road out of town and to the bridge where they leaned over the rail. Henry spat into a pool just below them and fish the color of the stones, brown and green, flicked and dashed away.

"All because of our business down in Missoula. Our *private* business," he said.

"Come again?"

"Why you're gonna drop me," Henry said.

He looked at Burt, and Burt watched the water dishing the two of them faintly in the pool

"Well now, there was that flood up at the fire camp. That's a black eye right there. Now, *I* know that isn't your fault. But there it is anyhow."

Henry drank. Burt set his large pink hand on Henry's shoulder.

"The boys asked if I'd throw my hat in. We'd like to have you aboard, Daddy."

Henry removed the hand. Told Burt what he could do with his hat.

On the Fourth of July, a roman candle caught the brush behind the old auto shop. Henry got a single truck out there at the same time the rural fire department arrived. The kids who were responsible for the fire scattered like tomcats when Henry spotted them peeking out from a pile of tires. The department fighters headed for the timber that was starting to catch, while Henry and a couple of his boys drove right into the thigh-high flames in the field with the back sprinklers blasting. The fire uncovered old Fords and Studebakers that stood out stark and abstract, their smoking frames hissing where the water hit them.

Henry and his crew fetched shovels from behind the cab and

went to putting out hot spots by turning sod. The wet and black earth steamed where they worked. The fire department guys looked like they had a handle on the flames on the mountainside, but it was hard to tell what was going on in the smoke and the thick of the timber. For a while they watched a red city fire truck spray the wilderness. Large hawks sat nearly motionless and cruciate in thermal updrafts, looking for rabbits and mice flushed out by the flames.

"Let's go look for spot fires," Henry said to his boys, "before they have a chance to make more trouble."

They spread out and went to work. Just beyond the smoldering area in front of him, a large hawk swooped down, snatched something from the wet unburned grasses, gliding low near the smoking earth, before it pumped itself skyward. Henry went to where this hawk had found prey. He moved his boot in the bearded darnel and wild columbine there, turning up clutch of wet eggshelled pheasants on folded wings not yet for flying. Moving like bats on their elbows and just as blind. Henry gripped the shovel and stood guard over the hatchlings, certain that they all had another thing coming.

MEAGAN DAY

■

Excerpt from *Maximum Sunlight*

FROM *Wolfman Books*

The following is an excerpt from Meagan Day's debut book, Maximum Sunlight, *which delves into life in a former mining town in Nevada's Great Basin. It was published by Wolfman Books, a small press in Oakland, California, dedicated to experimental nonfiction, poetry, and artist books.*

Sky, Sand, Sky, Sand, Sky, Sand

Most of unincorporated America is relatively civilized. Beyond the borders of small towns we encounter rural houses, roads, crop fields, livestock, scattered machinery, an array of anthropogenic junk. In the East there is scarcely an unobstructed acre, but even in the West we eventually spot power lines, drilling equipment, ranch fences.

But the edges of Tonopah, Nevada, are sharp. There are houses and trailers with yards full of trampolines and car parts, and then suddenly there is only earth and sky. Tonopah, Nevada, is an island of civilization in a vast humanless sea.

In the desert, up is sometimes difficult to distinguish from down. After heavy rains, water pools between the blackbrush and mirrors the stratosphere. Just after sunset the crisp horizon dissolves into a hazy bluish band. An inverted Fata Morgana will sometimes appear, actual hills collapsing into an imaginary limit. Tough bald hills slope at impossible angles, as if molded under the heel of a giant. It's easy to envision dinosaurs pounding this dry terrain with legs the size of refrigerators.

In Tonopah, I meet a man who warns me of the dangers of driving off-road in the desert at dawn and dusk. He crashed doing this once, going 120 mph on his three-wheeler. "I broke my neck out in the dunes and ripped my face off," he says. "I told them there was no way I was going to the hospital, to just give me a beer and wipe the sand out of my lips and my eyes."

This man has just spent a night in jail for a DUI and is sipping plain Coke through a straw. "I know where it sits now, the three-wheeler," he says, "and every time I see it I just get flashbacks to when I was flying off it—sky, sand, sky, sand, sky, sand. And that's why you don't ride at twilight. At twilight, you can't tell what a shadow entails."

The Cascadian Race

In the centuries since the arrival of Europeans, Nevada's Great Basin has inspired scores of esoteric origin theories. In 1924, "Was the Garden of Eden Located in Nevada?" made the front page of the *San Francisco Examiner*. The article was about the research of archaeologist Alain Le Baron, who claimed to have found petroglyphs not far from Tonopah that resembled Egyptian and Chinese characters, but predated both. He called the petroglyph site the Hill of a Thousand Tombs and believed it was evidence of an alternative anthropological timeline. His theory held that a prehistoric society called the Cascadian Race originated in Nevada and proceeded from there to populate the rest of the world.

Earlier yet, in 1917, an amateur geologist named Albert E. Knapp claimed to have found a fossilized human footprint from the Triassic period—the imprint of a shoe made of stitched dinosaur hide. This led him to believe that humans and dinosaurs had coexisted in Nevada's Great Basin 200 million years ago.

The *New York Times* took Knapp's finding somewhat seriously, as did Nobel Prize–winning Oxford scientist Frederick Soddy, who used it to support his pet theory of a superior race of prehistoric humans that destroyed itself after achieving scientific mastery over atomic energy. In Soddy's account, the sophisticated civilization made a technical mistake that wiped them out, leaving us—their more primitive counterparts—behind to literally reinvent the wheel.

These theories share a design: desertion by superior progenitors, the Great Basin as the point of origin for a flourishing society that eventually evacuates the region. This motif of abandonment can be located, too, in less fringe mythologies of the Nevada desert. Nevada, like California, experienced a Gold Rush that produced enormous wealth in the late nineteenth and early twentieth centuries. Tonopah was known as a place where millionaires were minted. But the money made in Nevada boomtowns was soon taken elsewhere, mainly to California or back East in the pockets of savvy capitalists. Briefly, many of these towns were opulent. Now they are the residue of imperial advancement. Decade by decade their elegance fades.

"What do you think people in big American cities think about Tonopah?" I ask a woman in her fifties named Linda who's smoking a Winston 100 inside a casino called the Tonopah Station. "Like on the East and West Coast," I explain, "places like LA and New York."

She's playing electronic keno, a game that has a reputation as a working-class diversion—it was once considered too blue-collar, even, for gambling houses on the Las Vegas Strip. All around us colorful lights flash on gaming screens. The décor in the Tonopah Station is Western-fantasy, all wagon wheels and old saloon signage. The soundtrack is contemporary country, punctuated by bleeps from the gaming machines. The bar adjacent to the gaming room is doing decent business though it's only one in the afternoon.

"Well, aside from Vegas, I don't think they think about us at all," she says matter-of-factly, ashing into a tray provided by the house. "They probably don't know what Tonopah is, though it used to be a big important town. But we're out here."

Counter-Eaters

The first time I passed through Tonopah, I lost an hour wandering its complicated streets, wide-eyed and straining with curiosity. I took one photograph on that first encounter. It shows the window of a white brick house. On the windowsill is a gold trophy. I remember that it was snowing. The trophy pricked me, a small sharp surprise, like what Roland Barthes means when he writes about the *punctum,* that subtle aspect that demands acute attention and inspires a groundswell of emotional attachment for reasons that elude reason. Tonopah itself is unsentimental. Its relics are not enshrined so much as worked around, even ignored. But I grew nostalgic all the same. I lost the photograph, but I see it clearly in my mind.

That first visit, I was especially transfixed by the Clown Motel, a pair of shabby two-story blue buildings at the edge of town. A plywood cutout in the shape of a clown points to a hand-painted sign announcing that truckers are welcome. Directly adjacent to the motel is a Gold Rush–era graveyard, a few paces from the parking lot. I stared at the motel in amazement thinking *Why does this exist? Who the hell lives here, works here?* I had no frame of reference.

The route between Reno and Vegas is five hundred miles of America with essentially zero cultural profile. That's roughly the distance between Boston and Washington, DC, a stretch that encompasses hundreds of hyper-distinct cultural enclaves. Even rural Nevadans themselves, like Linda at the casino, will admit that they are neither contradictions to nor embodiments of any particular social archetype. The nation draws a blank on rural Nevada.

In 1940, the Works Progress Administration published a guidebook to the state that betrays a kind of sour-grapes attitude toward Nevada's abandonment in the broader American imagination:

> Relatively few Americans are familiar with this land. If the citizen of other states is asked what he knows about Nevada, he is apt to laugh and mention gambling and divorce . . . Pressed for the state's physical characteristics, he will usually mention the Great Basin, envisioned as a huge hollow bowl . . . There are various reasons for this vast ignorance about the sixth largest state in the Union, but the chief one has always been the reticence of Nevadans themselves. They have always known their State's great beauty and are unusually sensitive to it, but humbled by long neglect on the part of the vast traveling public, it is only recently that they have begun to tell the world about Nevada.

And yet, when it comes time to enumerate the specificities of Nevadan culture, all the writers can muster is that Nevadans like to *eat at counters,* a characteristic so trivial and generic as to be absurd.

It is doubtful whether there is a restaurant in the state without one; even the smartest places feature counters. Usually the board is high and the stools are mounted on a small platform. No Nevadan is quite sure why he likes "counter-eating."

Rural Texans have the stalwart cowboy, Iowans have the forthright yeoman, and Mainers have the hard-bitten seafarer with rubber boots up to his knees. Nevadans have the counter-eater. Evidently I am not the first to grasp at straws.

In recent years, perhaps Cliven Bundy's high-profile standoff with the federal government has replaced the counter-eater of yore with the modern right-wing libertarian weapons stockpiler. But that still doesn't explain what a clown-themed motel is doing next to a graveyard in the middle of the treeless wilderness, or what that trophy was doing in that window.

For years, I'd think of Tonopah and be socked with the realization no matter what dramas and excitements visited my own life, some kind of existence continued out there in the desert, inscrutable to me. My enigmatic compatriots—I was and remain both curious about and troubled by this blind spot. I came to Tonopah to write, eventually, not because I wanted to answer a specific question, but because I had no idea what kinds of questions even applied.

We Are After Freedom

From the balcony of a dive bar amid a cluster of short-term residences called Humbug Flats, you can see every building in Tonopah. Small ranch-style houses with tidy facades alternate with puzzling complexes of shacks, sheds, and mobile homes. The town sits in a saddle slung between steep hills, and the houses are crowded together, gradually terraced on the gentler slopes.

Tonopah is a striking anomaly, a small town in the middle of a great desert characterized by relative density rather than by sprawl.

The cause of this peculiar urban geography is that Tonopah is completely surrounded by public land. You can't build on it, but you can do just about anything else—hunt and trap, rummage for rocks and artifacts, drive your four-wheeler or pre-runner as fast as your heart desires. At the town's border, roads turn to dirt and extend faintly across the desert toward distant purplish mountains.

I'm told that there are two forms of entertainment in Tonopah: drinking and off-roading. People drink because of the isolation— "there's nothing else to do"—while the off-roading is a consequence of proximity to hundreds of miles of unobstructed public land. So these recreational proclivities spring from the same source: the desert, which functions as both the town's playground and its quarantine.

Tonopah sits roughly halfway between Vegas and Reno on route US 95, about three and a half hours away from each. Its population is less than 3,000, and even at that it's the biggest town for more than a hundred miles in any direction. To the west is the imposing Sierra Nevada mountain range, with its snowy crests and flamboyant vistas. On the coastal side of the Sierras is California's productive Central Valley and its lush coastline. On the inland side of the divide spans the Great Basin, an arid region characterized by spindly mountain ranges stretching north to south and the flat desert valleys between them. From an airplane, the ranges look like slithering snakes.

Wallace Stegner wrote that one has to get over the color green in order to appreciate the American West. Natural green is a rare sight in the region around Tonopah, but hypnotic combinations of bruised purple and burnished gold at sunrise and sunset make a decent substitute.

In the bar of the Mizpah Hotel—built in 1907, carefully restored in 2011 after long abandonment, and now the most upscale business in town—I overhear two men introducing themselves to the bartender as federal employees. "The dreaded BLM," they say, and laugh. The Bureau of Land Management controls nearly 48 million acres in Nevada, about 67 percent of the state. Its mission is sprawling and contradictory—it monitors the health of plants and wildlife, maintains trails and recreational areas, and issues permits for drilling, mining, and cattle grazing.

With so many interests competing for its use, Nevada's BLM land is a battleground for opposing visions of the role of the federal government and the meaning of the term *public*. Consider the Cliven Bundy standoff: Bundy was up against the agency over unpaid cattle-grazing fees, a private disagreement that quickly turned ideologically epic. "We are after freedom," he told the press of his ad-hoc encampment of far-right armed militiamen. "We are after liberty. That's what we want." The BLM was the enemy in the Bundy party's fight for nothing less than independence.

In theory, the people of Tonopah are not thrilled about the BLM. They wrinkle their noses at its mention—to many it's both a symptom and agent of federal authoritarianism, bureaucratic tyranny, and government overreach. At the same time, somewhat confoundingly, people tell me that Tonopah is a stronghold of individual liberty (one calls it "the last bastion of free America") precisely because they can largely do whatever they want out in the desert. The very same people who despise the BLM call the neighboring desert "the people's land" and refer to it proudly as "my backyard." There would be no bobcat trapping or informal desert drag racing if the land were private.

Managed though it is, BLM land is the freest and most open land in America. Perhaps the people of Tonopah have grown accustomed to a degree of autonomy with which the rest of us are unfamiliar, for their primary complaint about BLM land is that it's not free enough.

Horse Management

I stop in at the University of Nevada in Reno and speak to Leonard Weinberg, an expert on grassroots right-wing politics, about the political landscape of Nevada. Nevada owes its blue-state badge largely to the Reno and Las Vegas metro areas, he tells me. The rural parts, by contrast, are characterized by staunch libertarianism.

"Nevada has the lowest rate of church attendance of any state in the union," Leonard says. "So it's not like the South. What we call the Cow Counties, including Nye County where Tonopah is, are overwhelmingly right-wing Republican, but the issues that excite people there aren't questions of morality and traditional values like you have with Southern religious right-wingers. Additionally, racial prejudice is not the driving force of right-wing politics here the way it is in the South."

Instead of the Ku Klux Klan or Christian family values groups, far-right organizations and movements here primarily include the Tea Party, the Sovereign Citizens, the Oath Keepers, and various armed militias united in their deification of the founding fathers, fear of socialism, hatred of the federal government, contempt for taxation, mistrust of all politicians, and abiding commitment to the Second Amendment. "The main issue that gets people going is the government telling them what to do with their property," Leonard tells me.

"What's the situation with the wild horses?" I ask. I've read that they're a major source of tension between the federal government and rural Nevadans.

"Wild horses are accused of eating too much rangeland, harming cattle operations," he says. "There's a tussle that goes on between ranchers' associations and the environmental types who are defenders of wild horses. The ranchers want fewer wild horses roaming this territory."

They got their wish in 2007, when seventy-one wild horses wandered onto the Tonopah Test Range, a highly classified military base, and died of nitrate poisoning after drinking the water there. This was not the first year horse poisoning had been recorded there—Tonopah Test Range employees were even known to have operated a betting pool to guess how many would die. The poisoning may not have been intentional, but neither was it unwelcome.

At the Mizpah Hotel bar, one of the BLM employees—an abandoned mine specialist—explains, "They're not really wild. They're feral, and they need to be managed somehow. So there's a federal program to manage them, and there are areas called horse management areas, or HMAs." The bureau, for its part, is "just trying to deal with the situation and listen to all sides the best we can."

I ask Leonard if rural right-wingers in Nevada are patriotic. "They would probably tell you that they are," he says, "but that's debatable. I remember there was one Iraq War general who retired to Douglas County," a bit west of Tonopah, "and said that it reminds him of Iraq—everyone hates the American government and they all have weapons. There are people here for whom the Second Amendment is the only part of the Constitution with which they're familiar, and they consider defending it to be the ultimate act of patriotism."

"Is immigration a big right-wing issue in Nevada?" I ask.

"Sure, there's anti-immigrant sentiment in Nevada. But even that manifests more as loathing for the federal government than for individual Hispanic people. There's racism here, no doubt," he concedes, but there's also an individualist live-and-let-live streak that precludes certain forms or manifestations of prejudice that one finds in other conservative regions, namely the South.

"Keep in mind that the Nevada state nickname is Battleborn," he says, "because it was created during the Civil War as a non-slave-owning state. There's a fair amount of pride associated with that here. In a sense, the anti-slavery cause relates to the local theme of 'Leave me alone, do whatever you want to do but just stay out of my way.'" He laughs and says, "In fact, now that I think about it, that seems like it should be the state motto," in place of the ill-fitting All for Our Country.

Time Machine

Tonopah is, in many ways, the apotheosis of rural right-wing Nevada. It's an isolated town in an isolated and isolationist state, a self-reliant town in a state where rural residents not only prize but insist on self-reliance, a town fully surrounded by federal land in a state that feels besieged by the federal government.

Unsurprisingly, many people I speak to in Tonopah are vocal about their right-wing political views. I hear that the government is planning to confiscate private citizens' firearms, that Barack Obama is not an American citizen, and that Obamacare is the biggest current threat to American liberty besides Islamic terrorism.

Most people I speak to, however, tell me they don't care for politics at all. I ask one woman whether she's more liberal or conservative. "I don't follow that stuff," she answers, annoyed. "All I know is I wish I had a time machine so I could go back to the 1700s with George Washington, back in the time when people didn't rob their neighbors so much."

Another person tells me, "I don't talk about politics. I can't do anything about it anyway, and that pisses me off. And I don't vote because they already know who's gonna win."

At one point I ask a room full of people, who've all been open and obliging so far, if I can talk to them about their political views. They bellow "No!" in unison, followed by rowdy laughter and clinking of beer bottles. One quietly mumbles that he likes Hillary Clinton, and his friend quickly interjects, "He doesn't speak for us," but declines to clarify her own political leanings.

Perhaps the people I'm speaking to consider political inquiry an invasion of privacy. Or maybe they really don't care—maybe Tonopah is simply too far removed, geographically and in its unique local concerns, from the nation at large for people to feel invested in national politics. It's possible that, just as America has neglected rural Nevada in elaborating its pantheon of cultural archetypes, so too have the people of rural Nevada turned a blind eye to the goings-on of the nation.

Maximum Sunlight

Like an island, Tonopah is strictly circumscribed. There are limitations on its latitude—because of the BLM, the town its prohibited from sprawling. The population remains steady and financial resources scarce, so Tonopah residents don't build up, either. They just don't build much at all.

Many live in timeworn houses or inventive structures made from repurposed parts of other edifices. Architecturally, the town speaks a junkyard vernacular. Every sliver of space is a profusion of materials and textures—corrugated tin, rusted steel, weathered wood, chipped paint, mortar, rebar, drywall, old cars and furniture put out to pasture. Whatever your vantage point, you can see a whole lot without turning your head.

Beyond the town limits, the nearest trees can be found in neighboring Goldfield. The natural landscape is characterized by stony crags and desolate flats meagerly populated with nondescript grasses and shrubs. Ninety percent of the earth's surface is pale dirt so dry that it whips into dust at the slightest disturbance.

If you say the word *plant* to people in Tonopah, their minds first turn to the Crescent Dunes Solar Energy Project just west of town.

The solar plant is a mystical arrangement—10,000 mirrors surround a 600-foot tower filled with molten salt. From the highway, in the afternoon when the sunset illuminates the tip of the tower, Crescent Dunes looks like a candle flickering in the desert. From overhead, with its mirrors arranged in a circle nearly two miles in diameter, it looks like a throng of pilgrims encircling the Grand Mosque of Mecca. All day long the mirrors swivel to capture maximum sunlight.

The rollout of Crescent Dunes has been mostly quiet and efficient. Only one occurrence betrayed the formidable, almost occult power of the machinery. For unspecified reasons, employees staging a test adjusted the mirrors so that they directed light at a focal point 1,200 feet above ground, twice as high as the tower. The suspended field of light attracted birds, which flew into the solar flux and were immediately incinerated. Scientists noted over a hundred "streamers"—trails of smoke and vapor—left behind by individual cremated birds.

The plant's owners apologized for the "avian incidents" and redirected the mirrors back down at the tower. Since then, the plant has continued preparatory testing without drama, but locals regard it with more trepidation than they did before. Some say it's badly built. They say if you look at it closely, you can see that it leans.

Between 2011 and 2013, over 4,000 people worked on the construction of Crescent Dunes. Many were Tonopah residents—particularly those hired to assemble the mirror panels—but the majority were specialists from elsewhere who left once construction was completed. A company called Cobra brought out a lot of Spaniards. There were hundreds of them during the preliminary stages, living in the Mizpah Hotel or Humbug Flats or even the Clown Motel. There are still a handful of Spaniards in town. They speak poor English, but drink and play pool with the locals.

Now only a few dozen people are employed to oversee daily operations on the site. Crescent Dunes mines sunlight, and like every mine in the history of the region, its peak employment window was astonishingly brief. This is the nature of industry here: residents wait for news of a new mine or plant or infrastructure project, strike while the iron's hot, and know not to expect anything permanent.

Thunderhead

I'm standing on Main Street looking for people to interview, feeling graceless and unprepared. Finally I get up the nerve to approach an older man in Carhartt overalls, a bucket hat, and dark sunglasses. He's sitting on a bench with an ancient laptop balanced on his knees. "Hi," I say too eagerly, surprising him. I scale it back. "I'm writing about the town. Can I talk to you about living here?"

He takes off his sunglasses and sizes me up. "Well, I'm not from here originally," he answers, then pauses, searching for the most concise way to let me down.

"Ma'am," he finally decides, "I'm a Baptist minister, and my opinion of Tonopah is not high. There are behaviors in this town to which I'm not accustomed." He smiles, pleased with his pithy assessment. "So I'd better pass."

The first person to accept my invitation is the town bookseller. He leads me through his store, its shelves abundant with volumes crammed in at strange angles, to a dim kitchen lined with dark green floral wallpaper. We sit in folding chairs with our elbows propped on a red-and-white checkered plastic tablecloth. "So," he begins, but says nothing else, evidently waiting for me to speak first.

I ask his name. Joe. I ask his age. Seventy-three. I ask if he's from here. He shakes his head. "So what brought you to Tonopah?"

"Well first," he says, "what brings you here? You writing a travel piece?"

"Sort of," I say, "but I'm less interested in tourism and more interested in daily life. I used to drive through here sometimes and it always gave me a strange feeling. It's like its own planet, so far away from everything else. And I did some research and learned about the mines, and the wild horses, and the nuclear testing, and the military planes and everything." My face flushes. "So I'm just curious, I guess."

This is good enough for Joe. He leans back and folds his arms across his chest. "I was living out in California before this," he begins. "I moved here in 2008, after I retired. I'm a sober alcoholic, been sober for over twenty-four years. My sponsor in AA was dying, and I hadn't quite figured out what I wanted to do yet in my retirement. He said he wanted me to take Alcoholics Anonymous to the wilderness."

Having already decided on Nevada, Joe conducted an Internet search for the town that had the most drug and alcohol arrests and the paltriest recovery resources. "Winnemucca and Tonopah tied as far as the most arrests, but Winnemucca already had meetings," he says.

Joe lives off his pension and savings, and opened the store for essentially the sole purpose of establishing a space for Alcoholics and Narcotics Anonymous meetings. In the back of the store is a meeting room with inspirational posters on the wall, pamphlets for the taking, and folding chairs assembled around a white folding table. The shop barely makes any money, he admits. And he's not particularly bookish himself—he tells me he's read only two books since he opened the place seven years ago. The first was a mystery novel, and the second was "more scientific," though he can't remember the subject matter.

I ask him what the impact of the meetings has been so far. "It's given some people their life back," he says. "It's given some people life who never even had a life. I started drinking at ten years old," he confides easily. Like many sober alcoholics, he has his story down pat, each phase measured in years and each turning point attached to a precise age, a highlight reel from a life of internal struggle. "There's a lady in town who started drinking at nine years old. She comes to the meetings. Until you learn to live a different way, you don't know any better."

"We just had a man named Chuck die at the end of June," he continues. "He was six years sober. He used to be a fall-down drunk and he used drugs intravenously. He had just lost his job shortly before he came to AA, and was several months behind on his rent. He was ready to commit suicide." Chuck heard about the meetings at Joe's bookstore through a friend, and Joe helped him get back on his feet, putting him to work shelving books.

"Chuck died right here in this store of a heart attack," Joe tells me, nodding toward the entrance where a sagging couch greets visitors, be they customers or addicts. On the coffee table in front of the couch is a jigsaw puzzle, only the perimeter completed. Joe's balding Chihuahua shivers in its tiny dog bed. The carpet is brown and flecked with lint. The shelves in the back are draped in clear tarps for a repair job that's been put on indefinite hold.

Despite Chuck's early death, his body battered by decades of substance abuse, Joe considers his story a success. He shows me a framed picture of a man grinning through a biker beard that's as gray and dense as a thunderhead. "Chuck was a good friend," he says with soft eyes.

I ask him why people drink so much here. "That's what there is to do," he replies.

"How many bars are there in town?"

"There's the Mizpah, the Tonopah Liquor Company," he counts on his fingers, "the Station House, the Bug Bar, the Bank Club, the Tonopah Brewery. And there used to be the Club House. That was a hard-drinking dive bar. A miserable place. Bar fights every night. Closed earlier this year, but the drunks still sit right out front on the sidewalk there."

Then he says, with sudden urgency, "I got out before I killed anyone. I had blackouts all the time. I could've killed someone in a bar fight or car accident and not even known why I was in jail when I came to. I said I couldn't do that."

He shakes his head vigorously. "And people in this town, they're suffering. So you see? That's why I'm here."

Sensitives

"The people are still living on the history," says Wilma, who works in the office of the Clown Motel. "Many of them are descendents of the original miners. And many are miners themselves. Out in Round Mountain or Silver Peak, mostly. There are generations of them who've lived here since the 1900s, and their attitude is pretty much still the same. Wild West."

"What do you mean by that?" I ask her. She's probably in her early fifties but has a girlish face and round, earnest eyes. Her waist-length red hair is bound by a scrunchy at the nape of her neck. When she speaks, each r sound shades slightly into a w.

"The miners used to drink a lot," Wilma replies. "That was their only other thing besides mining. They would sleep in the mines for like seven days, and they would come out and they didn't have family to go to because they were single guys or their family was way back somewhere else, so the only thing they had was the alcohol. That's staying, that kind of attitude."

I tell her that she's not the first person to bring up booze when explaining the town to me, and her laugh betrays a bit of concern. "Alcohol use in this town is tremendous," she says. "I mean, wow. It's a huge situation." Her affect is now serious, a bit stunned. "I don't know much about the drugs. Meth is pretty prevalent here, I know that. But the alcohol, yikes, it's way out there. You can see it at night in the town. It keeps 'em low, keeps 'em icky."

Wilma pauses to take a phone call, and my eyes scan the room. To my left are several shelves of clown figurines, over five hundred of them. A sign hanging in the middle reads:

SPECIAL CLOWNS FROM
AROUND THE WORLD NOT FOR SALE

Behind me are two life-size clown dummies. One is an early iteration of Ronald McDonald, while the other is more of a Barnum & Bailey type.

"Don't look into that one's eyes," says Wilma, placing the phone back on the receiver. She gestures toward the old-timey one clad in a rainbow jumpsuit. Several fingers are missing from its life-size hands. Wilma was afraid of clowns when she first came to work here, she tells me. She's mostly gotten over it, but that one still strikes her as "a little off."

The Clown Motel sits at the western edge of town. For the phobic, there's no skirting the issue—there's a clown on every door and clown paintings above every bed. Adding to the potential fear factor is the cemetery right next to the motel, visible from nearly every vantage point.

"Are people freaked out by this place?" I ask. The smaller clown figurines are cheerful portrayals with oversized shoes, accordions, and juggling pins—vestiges of a time when clowns enjoyed more favor in the hearts of the masses. The whole history of clowns is on display: There are porcelain harlequins with cherubic faces and rosy cheeks, hobo clowns with patches on their pants and sympathetic frowns, and polka-dotted buffoons with frizzy orange hair poking out above their ears. One, however, is obviously a later creation, fabricated after John Wayne Gacy Jr. and the movie *It* transformed the clown into a popular object of dread. Teeth bared and eyes crazed, it's perched in a metal cage like a lethal zoo animal. This figurine is prominently displayed near the front desk, demonstrating a wry self-awareness on the part of the Clown Motel's management.

"Oh sure, people are scared," she answers. "But we still get a lot of business. Some people actually come here to face their fear. I've seen 'em faint and I've seen 'em scream. It's not uncommon to see somebody walk in and their face turn pure white." She tells me she's even met people who were sent here on the advice of their therapists.

"If you ask me, the Clown is not nearly as scary as the cemetery next door," she says. "There's a lot of paranormal activity there. We get tons of researchers. Psychic people, sensitives, ghost hunters. They always find something."

"What's a sensitive?" I ask.

"People that are so sensitive they can feel the entities around them," she explains. "Ghost hunters bring sensitives with them, and if the sensitives feel like something's going on, that's when they start their cameras. And sure enough, bam. There's a lot of activity in this town, because there was a lot of death here. The mines were so dangerous. A lot of death."

I ask her why she came to work in the Clown Motel if she was afraid of clowns. "My husband and I were really down on our luck when we first arrived here," she answers. "We had a car that was acting like a real idiot." She explains that she was on her way from Texas to California when her car started to falter, just past Las Vegas. By the time they got to Tonopah, "the car decided that it didn't want to go any further," she laughs. "Piece of work is what it was."

She and her husband slept in their busted car in the parking lot of the Bank Club, a local small-time casino with an adjoining Chinese restaurant, for about three days. "Then one of the nice people at the grocery store told us, 'Hey, go talk to Hank P., he can help you out.' So we did and he offered us a job."

Hank P. owns the Clown Motel, along with a large share of the retail space on Main Street. I tell her I've already heard stories about Hank P., that he employs people who have no money, people who have substance abuse problems, homeless people, out-of-town drifters. I've heard that he gives them work at the Clown, or the pawnshop, or the Economy Inn, and that he often hooks these people up with places to stay. She nods her head in agreement with everything I'm saying. "He just cares," she says finally. "He cares about the people and the town. He's descended from one of the original families. He wants to rise the place up."

I don't tell her that in the few interviews I've conducted thus far I've also heard him called a loan shark and a slumlord, that I've heard him accused of exploiting the desperation of the local down-and-out. People seem either bitterly resentful of Hank P. or eternally grateful to him.

"He helps you get on your feet," Wilma continues. "Like Jeff. He's one of the hard-ups. He has a real problem with alcohol, major. And he comes off of it and he's a sane person, and then he leaves for a while. He does it in waves. It's a cycle. And Hank always hires him back."

I ask her if Hank ever has problems with the people he helps out. "Yeah, I mean sometimes he has to forcibly get the money from them because folks like to use and abuse. And he's a *strong* person." She emphasizes this by leaning forward across the counter. "You don't mess with Hank P."

"Is this a violent place?" I ask. Night is falling and my car is parked closer to the center of town, so I'll need to walk.

"Well there are bar fights," she says laughing, "so try not to get into one of those. We used to have a place called the Club House. That was a hang spot, but it just got closed down. It was a fighting, brawling kind of place. It was a really cool place though, with a beautiful old bar and a lot of history. People would go just to hang and let loose. It was *the* spot."

I tell her I'll avoid bar fights and thank her for her time. "Hey if you go to the cemetery," she adds, "just watch your phone battery. The cemetery always drains phone batteries."

Tiny

Outside the pawnshop is a sign that reads, "Free Lifetime Parking reserved for Hank P." He owns this building, and I've heard that Jeff works here. But even though it's the middle of the day, The Hock Shop is locked up and there's no one in sight. On the door is a hand-scrawled sign announcing three open beds in a mobile home, available immediately for solar or construction workers. The sign says to call Hank P. if interested, and that rooms at the Clown Motel are also available weekly or daily.

I keep walking down the block, past the Tonopah Liquor Company and the shuttered Club House. A middle-aged man sits on the sidewalk with an open beer in hand. I pass within two feet of him, but he doesn't lift his head.

On the other side of the Club House is a small storefront whose handwritten sign says The Hock Shop 2. A guy out front is holding a pair of dancing Native American dolls. He looks to be in his early forties, with unkempt blonde facial hair, sunburnt skin, and a jumble of improvised tattoos. I tell him I'm a writer working on a story about the town and ask him if he'd be up for an interview.

"Just as soon as I put price tags on these drunk Indians," he says with a chuckle. "They're for storing whiskey, see?" He shows me the openings where the liquor flows in and out.

I wince and say, "Oh. Look at that."

The shop is more like a storage unit, barely any attempt at organization or attractive display. The guy, named Zachary, invites me to sit in a metal folding chair, pushing aside an ashtray on a cluttered table so I can rest my arm. I take stock of his appearance: blue eyes, baseball cap, missing teeth.

Suddenly he remembers something and gets up. "Sorry," he says, turning the sign on the door from closed to open. "We're having a little sale. A lady in town, Barbie, her husband committed suicide two weeks ago, so I'm donating twenty percent of all my profits for the weekend to help her cover the funeral costs."

"Is Barbie a friend of yours?" I ask.

"Kind of. She works at Giggle Springs," he says, referring to the gas station and convenience store across the street. I later learn that the name is a mistranslation of the town's Paiute name, which does not mean "laughing water" as the original owner had believed. "She's a real nice lady that helps anybody out in town. When I came to this town I didn't have nothing. And the gentleman that owns this building gave me this store to run, gave me the house I live in, and everything else. So somebody helped me, and now it's my chance to help someone else." The gentleman, of course, is Hank P.

I ask him where he came from, and he says Arkansas, though he's originally from Aberdeen, Washington. "The hometown of Kurt Cobain," he adds.

"How does Tonopah stack up?" I ask.

"It's a quiet little town," he says, "but there's too many alcoholics here. There are about twenty of them that sit out front of my store every day. It's irritating. A few of them live in apartments up above the Hock Shop. If you went into the Hock Shop and talk to that guy, his name is Jeff, he's drunk from the time he wakes up to the time he passes out."

"Jeff seems to have a real reputation," I say.

"Oh yeah," he confirms. "He comes into my store all the time and helps himself to my stuff. All my jewelry from Africa ended up in his store for sale."

"Do you live in these apartments back here?" I ask. He scoffs and says you couldn't pay him to live there. The apartments are on the backside of the building. I can see them from my motel room, and have observed the comings and goings of various men clad in dirty jeans, often accompanied by muscular off-leash dogs.

"Are the guys who live back there Hank P.'s guys?" Zachary nods his head yes. I ask if he's friends with any of them.

"No. I'm not friends with any of Hank P.'s guys," he says with a sneer. Zachary is himself one of Hank P.'s guys, but evidently envisions himself a cut above the rest. "Actually I can't say that. There is one guy that works for him as a mechanic that I'm friends with personally. But he and I have a similar background, so we get along pretty well. The other guys are all just a bunch of worthless drunks."

"Do you think it's good that Hank helps them out?" I ask.

"Yes and no," he responds. "It's good that Hank gives them something productive to do for the day, otherwise they just sit here and bother people. But it's bad that he gives them the money that he does, because he knows they're just gonna go out and drink. That's the only time they come in and work for him is when they need money for booze. And I have a problem with that."

Bells jingle and a Latino man walks in, wobbly on his feet.

"Hey Lee," says Zachary coolly.

"Has anybody come in here and tried to sell you a DeWalt drill?" Lee asks, leaning on a cane to steady himself.

"Nobody's tried to sell me anything stolen," answers Zachary. "They know better. Everything that comes into my shop goes to the sheriff's department for thirty days and then comes back."

"That DeWalt cost me $170," Lee says in protest. "That sucks. That was expensive."

"Well, I'll keep my eyes out. If someone brings it in I'll snatch it up and call the sheriff's office."

"I think he left town," Lee says, shaking his head.

"Who was it?" Zachary asks. "Nate?" Lee nods yes, anger glowing in his eyes. "Nate left," Zachary confirms. "He owed Hank a lot of money. He split, man."

Lee is quiet, disappointed. Abruptly he lifts his cane and brings it down hard. "I hate thieves," he declares.

"Trust me, so do I," says Zachary. "I've had many thieves in here try and steal stuff from me. They were willing to go to jail for fifteen dollars—hey, fine by me. They don't realize that I can put handcuffs on 'em myself and take 'em to jail." He turns to me and straightens his back as he boasts, "I work for the sheriff's department here and in Mineral County. I can arrest people." Somehow I doubt this is entirely true.

Lee is silent, stewing. After a long pause he says resignedly, "Well you have my number," and turns to leave. Before he exits he looks over his shoulder and says, "Hey, you want these?" He's waving a stack of envelopes.

Zachary asks what they are.

"My bills!" says Lee, and laughs from his belly, his spirits temporarily lifted. The bells jingle again, and he's gone.

Zachary turns to me. "He's one of the drunks I was telling you about. He had a dog called Tiny. It was a really big dog. He had that dog for twenty years. And somebody from California come and hit it with a car, and it had to be put down. Lee's been drunk ever since."

Stuff Out There That Isn't There

Throughout the Cold War, the United States Air Force ran a classified program to test the capabilities of its aircraft against foreign fighter planes. The USSR-based Mikoyan-Gurevich Design Bureau was building exceedingly agile aircraft and supplying them to the United States' Cold War enemies. By the late 1960s, as the Vietnam War came into full swing, American air-to-air combat losses due to these planes—known as MiGs—were growing worrisome.

In 1967, under a program called Have Doughnut, the United States acquired a Soviet MiG from Israel. The plane had been handed over by an Iraqi fighter pilot who chose to defect rather than drop napalm on Iraqi Kurdish civilians. It was flown to top-secret Area 51, between Tonopah and Las Vegas, to be poked and prodded by the United States Air Force.

Over the next decade more captured MiGs were flown in, and secret dogfights began to take place over the Nevada desert. To keep the program under wraps, airspace was fully restricted and the area was blotted out in red ink on aerial maps—furtive measures that contributed to Area 51's prominent place in conspiracy theories about UFOs and insidious government plots.

In 1979, these foreign technology evaluation tests were relocated to nearby the Tonopah Test Range, known as Area 52. The fighter pilots there, known as the Red Eagles, lived in a dormitory called Mancamp, which consisted of "a chow hall, an Olympic-size stainless steel pool, bowling alleys and a sports field that was lit up at night," according to an interview given by pilot John Manclark after the official declassification of the secret program.

Some pilots played the role of aggressors—they were tasked with flying Soviet planes and replicating enemy tactics so that trainees could troubleshoot effective responses. Several pilots died flying the unfamiliar aircraft, for which the United States had no manuals. "We didn't know what 90 percent of the switches did," said Manclark. "We had one switch that we just labeled BOMB EXPLODE."

At the same time, Lockheed was busy building the F-117 Nighthawk at the Tonopah range. It was America's first stealth aircraft, designed to avoid radar detection in enemy airspace. The engineering of the F-117 was a highly classified black project and the Tonopah Test Range a black site. Thousands of personnel worked on the project, and were flown to Tonopah on Mondays and back out to the Las Vegas area on Fridays. They were prohibited from telling their families where precisely they went all week.

The United States government came up with a cover story involving a surrogate aircraft, justifying the program's existence to the civilian world and deflecting suspicion. Early biometric technology was used to screen everyone who entered the base, and vehicles that came too close to the range were searched and their occupants warned away.

The F-117 flew only in the dark, and its manuals were kept inside a hyper-secure vault. The pilots were called Bandits and wore patches featuring scorpions, sphinxes, atomic symbols, grim reapers, and eagles with lightning emanating from their talons. One patch featured an image of the plane and the embroidered words, "To those who hide at night, beware of those in the shadows."

Eventually, the Nighthawk was ready for war. In 1991, leaflets rained down on Iraqi villages showing the plane wreaking havoc and warning civilians to "Escape now and save yourselves." The aircraft dropped thousands of bombs during the Gulf War, and continued to operate through the '90s.

Only one Nighthawk was ever lost to U.S. enemies—the aircraft, named Something Wicked, was shot down by Serbs in Yugoslavia in 1999. There is speculation that the missing equipment was acquired by China or Russia for study, bringing full circle Tonopah's relationship to the top-secret world of foreign aircraft exploitation.

While Tonopah's Area 52 is not as ubiquitous in conspiracy theories as neighboring Area 51, the site's combination of strict confidentiality and global impact lends itself to paranoid interpretations. Most residents know bits and pieces of what takes place in the desert outside their town, but nobody knows everything. Parts of the history are still classified, and secret projects are still underway.

Proximity to the genuinely clandestine inspires eccentric worldviews in locals, or at least an increased openness to what might elsewhere be considered crackpot conspiracy theory. But few people dwell near government black sites—information about the land we live on is readily obtainable, largely predictable, and often mundane. If secret plots are actually unfolding in your backyard, orchestrated by absentee elites intent on consolidating global power, it becomes difficult to dismiss other theories that follow the same pattern. For some residents of Tonopah, the mystery of nearby government activity is understandably destabilizing.

"Do a lot of people believe in UFOs around here?" I ask Wilma at the Clown Motel.

"Oh yeah," she says unreservedly, her eyes growing wide. "A lot of people have *seen* UFOs here. I'm one of them. I've seen multiple UFOs throughout my life. I know it sounds crazy. But I had people with me who witnessed it."

I ask her to describe what she's seen in Tonopah. "I've only seen one here," she says. "It was a couple years ago and I was walking home from work at the Clown. I saw this thing come flying in, no sound at all, right in the middle of town. There was no denying it was freaky. It did a little back and forth thing, a very intelligent type of movement, and then it went straight up into the universe. I mean, c'mon!"

"Why do you think people see so many UFOs here in this part of the country?" I ask.

"It could be the Indian reservations," she explains soberly. "That's a huge possibility. The governments are not allowed to touch the UFOs or even try to go after them in the reservation areas. I know that for sure. And the Native Americans are firm believers in UFOs. It's part of their whole thing."

Mounted on the wall to her left is a placard that boasts a silhouette of the F-117 against a map of the Middle East, pockmarked with little cartoon explosions. It reads TONOPAH STEALTH—1ST TO STRIKE IN THE GULF.

I suspect that Wilma would believe in UFOs whether or not she lived near a secret government site. Throughout our conversation, she eagerly divulges theories about additional forms of paranormal activity (while she has not seen a ghost at the Clown, she has smelled one—it wafted in on a cold wind and "smelled like a very ancient perfume"). Other residents surprise me a bit more, like Clifford who works at Joe's bookshop.

A self-described computer nerd who moved here six years ago from Southern California, Clifford speaks matter-of-factly. "I help Joe out in the bookstore," he says, "but my skill set is more technical. Computer networks, information systems, business systems."

He gets excited when I mention the Tonopah Test Range and the stealth bomber built there. "Oh man, it's an awesome piece of war machinery," he says. "It's a killing machine. The designers were all told to design different parts—the wings, the cockpit. There was no collaboration whatsoever. That's how they keep the secrecy of the design." He relishes both the technical sophistication and the cloak-and-dagger gravity of the project.

"Somebody told me they're building another secret plane out there," I offer.

"That's what I heard," he affirms. "Man, the security measures that they have in place are serious. If you wander off the beaten path and end up on the test site, within minutes security will come out of nowhere and be all over you. It's very tightly controlled." I had read accounts of wayward explorers who suddenly found themselves surrounded by a swarm of military vehicles, unaware that they had trespassed from public into top-secret land.

I ask him if the secrecy has any effect on people living in town, if it fosters theories about covert activity. Clifford strikes me as a rationalist, and I'm expecting to chuckle together about local kooks. Instead he says, "I mean, I don't know. I've seen some pretty weird stuff myself that I have no explanation for here in Tonopah. I've seen flying objects that I couldn't identify. The flight path and the flight pattern, the maneuverability, there's nothing that we have that I'm aware of that can maneuver like that."

He continues, "I've seen glowing orbs in the sky. They go one direction and then another and then they just disappear. Then they reappear somewhere else, and it makes no sense."

I ask him if the flying objects could be military technology and not intelligent extraterrestrials. "Absolutely," he says, relieved by my suggestion. "Here in Nevada, there's so much open ground that it's a lot easier to test aircraft without having to worry about communities getting an eyeball on it. They mostly fly out in the middle of nowhere. Sometimes a camper or a hiker will see something, but they largely go undetected." He lights a cigarette and leans back in his chair, taking a long first drag. "The stuff we see is just one fraction of what goes on out there."

Later, I'm at the Tonopah Liquor Company conducting an interview when a man comes up to me and says quietly, "So you're a reporter."

I nod my head and he says, "I work for the government. Listen. If you go up into the hills, find the golf balls. And when you've found the golf balls, look southeast. There's stuff out there that isn't there, if you know what I mean. It isn't there, but it is."

I never learn his name, and I never find the golf balls.

SIMON PARKIN

■

So Subtle a Catch

FROM *Harper's Magazine*

IN APRIL OF LAST YEAR, under the crisp light of an embryonic English spring, Darren Wakenell pulled his Citroën hatchback onto the gravel driveway of Timberland, a private fishery nestled improbably among stratospheric smokestacks on an industrial estate about an hour's drive from London. Wakenell is a postman turned fishery-enforcement officer with the UK's Environment Agency, and Timberland is one of some 300 fisheries that he and his partner, Stephen Robinson, patrol.

Along the ramshackle banks of Timberland's Mystery Lake, one of five waters the fishery comprises, Wakenell parked his car within sight of a few wispy-haired men lounging on deck chairs. Each seat was surrounded by a jumble of angling equipment and grubby Tupperware, and was separated from the others by enough distance to spare the men, and their dogs, the necessity of interaction. Robinson, a former military-police officer in khaki pants and a knife-proof vest, led the approach. "If it all kicks off with one of these guys," Wakenell warned me in a whisper, "just walk back to the car. We'll handle it." He fingered an extendable truncheon that hung from his belt and strode toward a middle-aged man who was patiently ignoring our presence.

After a few minutes, the man looked up from a margarine tub full of writhing maggots and offered a conciliatory smile. "Nice to see the Environment Agency showing a presence round these parts," he said, drawing his rod license from his wallet without being asked. "They've had a lot of problems, haven't they? People keep taking the carp."

* * *

The carp grows in estimation the farther east he travels. In the United States, he is often branded a rough fish or, more damningly, a trash fish, a catch that is good for neither cuisine nor sport, food nor glory. The so-called Asian carp, an unscientific amalgam of four species, is loathed up and down the Mississippi River, where he outcompetes local fish and is known to leap from the water at the sound of a propeller, bruising the eyes and breaking the bones of passing sailors.

When he comes to England, the carp's fortunes elevate considerably. Here, as Izaak Walton wrote three and a half centuries ago in *The Compleat Angler,* the carp is regarded as "the Queen of Rivers, a stately, a good, and a very subtil fish." Indeed, in 2015, a drawing of the fish was printed on the rod license, which most anglers carry in their wallet as though it were a cherished family photograph. As the fish enters Poland he discovers that he is no longer merely good: now he is considered a delicacy, eaten in place of turkey or ham as the nation's favourite Christmas dish.

By the time he reaches Japan, the carp has grown in both confidence and chic. Gone is the glum pallor and gormless mouth. Here the koi—a variety of the common carp—is prized not for subtlety but for its opposite: his papery fins and drooping mustache are judged to be the height of aquatic elegance. In Japan the fish may be considered a family heirloom, even a life companion. Hanako, the longest-living specimen on record, was born in 1751 and handed down through generations until she died, two centuries later, at the unlikely age of 226. Her final owner, Komei Koshihara, described Hanako in a 1966 radio broadcast as his dearest friend.

If the Japanese prize the carp's longevity, the Polish his taste, and the Americans his absence, for English anglers the one attribute that counts above all others is his weight. In Britain you're not considered an accomplished fisher of carp until you've landed a twenty-pounder. Fishermen peer into the watery murk at sunrise, hoping to catch a glimpse of a thirty-pound colossus—something you could, as one angler likes to quip, "put a saddle on." A forty-pounder will make the lake in which he lives famous, drawing anglers from across the country to camp out for days on end. A fifty-pounder tempted from his lake will have his picture published in angling magazines. The landing of a sixty-pound carp regularly makes national headlines.

According to Environment Agency estimates, each year more than 4 million people in the UK engage in "coarse fishing," the British term for nongame freshwater angling, and that figure continues to rise. To meet the surging demand, many British landowners have dug holes on their estates, filled them with carp, and established new fisheries. It's a lucrative business: bids for a permit to fish the best week of the season at a reputable British still water can exceed $2,000.

Fisheries need big, braggable fish to justify such prices, but the moneymakers, the forty-, fifty-, and sixty-pounders that can turn their captors into heroes, take years to grow and are rarely offered for sale. As a result, the growth of the British angling industry has been shadowed by a booming market in stolen carp. Nearly 2,000 people were prosecuted for illegal fishing last year, with license cheats paying more than $600,000 in fines. Bruno Broughton, a fisheries-management consultant, estimated that organized carp thefts in recent years have yielded hauls worth "in excess of £100,000" each—more than $120,000.

"This form of crime is a lot more widespread than is believed," says Alun Bradshaw, a wildlife-crimes officer for the police who regularly works with the Environment Agency to catch carp thieves. "Some fishery owners do not care how they get their fishery stocked, so long as they get some large carp that will attract anglers looking to catch large fish." A rangy man with close-cropped dark hair, Bradshaw is responsible for investigating fish crime in the county of Cambridgeshire. The recent spike in carp theft, he suggested, was a matter of simple economics. Anglers risk a $6,000 fine if they are caught stealing fish, but with forty-pounders selling for more than twice that, poachers stand to make sizable profits if they escape the law.

In the summer of 2014, Bradshaw received an email from a local angler that noted a series of suspicious photographs on the Facebook page of a recently founded commercial fishery near the city of Peterborough. The anonymous fisherman said that the carp in the photographs had been taken from a local river and nearby lakes; he knew because he'd caught them before and recognized their features. Within a few weeks Bradshaw had collected enough information to act on the tip. He and ten other police officers and Environment Agency staff met around the corner from the Peterborough fish farm to execute what they called Operation Vulcan. "Officers approached the house and a static caravan on the fishery, and the two suspects were arrested on suspicion of handling stolen goods," Bradshaw told me. For the next six hours the team netted the lake, removing the carp one by one and photographing each specimen, looking for deformed fins, missing scales, and other distinguishing marks that would positively identify a translocated fish.

Bruno Broughton told me that the first recorded cases of organized carp theft in the UK date to the mid-1960s. A man caught two large fish in Knotford Lagoon, a former gravel quarry, and decided to transfer them to a lake close to what is now the Leeds Bradford Airport. He came unprepared, however, and had to order a taxi for himself and the fish, which he'd wrapped in wet sacks. The driver, who had never had a pair of live carp in the back of his taxi before, recounted the story to his friends, and news of the crime soon reached the police.

Fifty years later, carp crime remains, in the majority of cases, equally unsophisticated. In England, it usually involves cars and the cover of darkness. While some thieves use a conventional rod and line, police have seen other methods as well, ranging from the blunt (sending an electric current through the water and netting the unconscious fish as they float to the surface) to the innovative (attaching baited lines to bungee cords that keep self-hooked fish from breaking free). Carp are able to survive almost indefinitely in a small amount of aerated water, Broughton explained to me, which makes it easy to transport a fish in a tank or tub until a buyer can be found.

The roots of England's obsession with gigantic carp can be found at Redmire Pool, a tiny lake near the Welsh border. It was here, eighty years ago, that Donald Leney, a nonangling fish farmer, seeded the nation's interest in the fish. Redmire sits at the base of a green hill less than a kilometer from Bernithan Court, a small, stately home that fell into disrepair during the 1890s. (Turkeys took over the drawing room.) In 1926, Lieutenant Colonel Ernald Barnardiston bought the estate, and as part of his renovation work he decided to stock a nearby lake with carp. (To compensate, perhaps, for evicting the turkeys.) Eight years later, Leney delivered fifty yearling carp, all between five and a half and eight inches long, that he'd obtained from a Dutch farm north of Vaassen. The Barnardistons rechristened the lake Redmire after discovering that the fish churned up red sand while they fed.

Redmire became famous in 1951, when a local angler caught a mirror carp that weighed 31.4 pounds, a new British record. His feat attracted attention, and the following year that attention turned to adulation when, at the end of an overnight session, a former World War II pilot named Richard Walker caught a common carp weighing an unprecedented forty-four pounds. Walker, who had been eating cans of ravioli during his night's fishing, named the catch after his pasta. Instead of returning him to the water, he called the Bristol Zoo to inquire whether they wanted to rehome the massive carp. Reportedly, the zookeeper who answered the phone misheard the weight as fourteen pounds and declined Walker's offer. London Zoo's line was clearer, apparently, since Ravioli was soon carried to the city by two zoo employees in the back of a van.

Walker's Redmire record stood for three decades, until, in June 1980, a young angler named Chris Yates stuck three pieces of sweet corn to the end with a bit of Plasticine. Using a rod that Walker had fashioned in 1955, Yates hauled a 51.5-pound mirror carp from the same waters that had hosted Ravioli. "Casting at that fish was like casting at the sun," he later wrote of the experience. "I suddenly lost my focus in a fever of anticipation." Yates described the fish, which he named the Bishop, as a "perfect monster."

Redmire's trio of consecutive records gave the lake a peculiar mystique, but by twenty-first-century standards, even its monsters become somewhat less impressive. Using heated tanks and high-protein diets, British fish breeders today are regularly able to push carp as high as thirty pounds and beyond.

There currently remain, however, only a handful of known sixty-pounders in England. The largest of these lives in Cranwells, a twenty-acre lake on the Wasing Estate, about an hour from London's

Piccadilly Circus. To taxonomists, he's known as a mirror carp, after the broad and lavish scales slung across his back, but to the legions of anglers who hope for an opportunity to hunt this white whale among freshwater leviathans, he's known as the Parrot.

The Parrot is a descendent of the carriageload of fish that Donald Leney delivered to Redmire in 1934, and at 68.1 pounds he now holds the official British record. (In September, a thirty-three-year-old investment banker named Tom Doherty caught a 70.4-pound carp in Shropshire; the fish, however, named Big Rig, is believed to be an immigrant, reared in France, leading to the contesting of the title. Doherty says he has received death threats related to the disputed claim.) Brian Humphries, who runs a windshield-replacement business in Gloucestershire, stalked the Parrot for four years before catching him. He's lifted the fish out of the water three times now, and has compared landing the carp to wrestling Mike Tyson. If the Parrot decides that he's not ready to be reeled in, Humphries told me, there's not a lot that you can do. "At the end of the day he's essentially a giant reproductive muscle," he said. "If he doesn't want to be caught, you just have to let him go."

At Wasing, the lawns are manicured to uniformity, the hedges are sculpted into firm, pleasing shapes, and the hillsides are arranged in a tectonic cascade that leads the eye across Berkshire with an elegance that would make Capability Brown shrink with envy. Cranwells—home to several fifty-pounders in addition to the Parrot—is the most exclusive and prestigious of Wasing's eight fishing lakes. Only sixty permits are made available each year, and they cost $1,000 each. A person who secures a permit is allowed to renew the membership annually for life, which means that aspiring members must wait for existing permit holders to depart, decease, or fall into disgrace.

Applications for the two or three permits that become available each year for Cranwells are heavily vetted. Since their assets are freely swimming in the water, the fishery's owners want to ensure that members are trustworthy and competent enough to deal with a fish like the Parrot. Mike Bampton, the head bailiff at Wasing, told me that landing a carp that large requires a donkey-load of mats, nets, slings, and antiseptic. "Very few carp anglers have the necessary equipment to deal with a fish of this size once it's on the bank," he said.

To protect their fish from thievish attention, some fisheries have begun in recent years to ask members not to publicize photographs of their fish on the Internet. But the Parrot is too famous for such measures. "Everyone knows where he lives," Bampton said. "You'd never keep a fish like that quiet." A soft-spoken, rakish middle-aged man with the stride of someone used to covering vast stretches of countryside on foot, Bampton first began fishing at Wasing in the early 2000s, several years after the three-year-old Parrot arrived from a local fish farm. For the past two years he has managed a team of fifteen other bailiffs; they are, essentially, the Parrot's security detail. Every day and night the bailiffs patrol the lake, checking the anglers' permits and ensuring that the three gates that guard the lake from the main road remain padlocked at all times. "It's not to say you couldn't do it," Bampton said, as we shuddered over a pocked pathway in his mud-wrecked four-wheel drive. "But the thief would have to get in here first. We are fussy about the gates."

Broughton, the fisheries consultant, believes that the Parrot is protected precisely because of his fame. "This fish is so well known among anglers that it would be like stealing the *Mona Lisa*. It may be priceless, but it would be almost impossible to sell on." What's more, there remains the difficulty of catching the elusive monster in the first place. Though some consider him a mug fish, the term given to a carp that is landed too often and considered reckless or slow to learn, the Parrot was caught only six times in the past two years. And even if a crooked angler got lucky (or resorted to brute force), the Parrot's protectors are ever vigilant. "There are a lot of us down here a lot of the time," said Bampton. "Even if nobody's fishing, there are bailiffs always around to keep an eye on anything that's going on."

Bampton told me that while anglers often attempt to bribe him for a permit at Cranwells, nobody's ever been "stupid enough" to offer him money for the Parrot. But the inside carp job has precedent. In 1999, Brian Barbrook, a bailiff employed by Thames Water, was asked to empty a reservoir of fish before it was drained. He was supposed to distribute the haul of fish, which included several large carp, to other reservoirs around the borough. Instead, he used ten of the fish to pay off a debt, and allegedly offered some of the others to a fish dealer, Anthony Silvester. "He showed up looking official in a Thames

Water uniform, driving a Thames Water van," Silvester told me. Silvester bought the fish, each of which carried forged papers, and sold them on to lake owners around the country. But since he hadn't received the appropriate receipts, he alerted the Environment Agency. Barbrook was arrested that November. He denied involvement in the thefts. He was fired, and the next year he was charged with stealing fish worth a total of $30,000. (To this day Barbrook maintains his innocence. "I only ever wanted to run the best fishery," he told me. "I was simply redistributing surplus fish. It was a big hoo-ha about nothing.")

Steve Broad, the editor of *Carpworld* magazine, said that the case against Barbrook became especially well known because it was the first to establish that carp can be individually identified by their scale patterns. Today, whenever there is a raid on a fish farm that is suspected of selling stolen carp, wildlife officers release mug shots of the fish in hopes that local anglers will recognize a carp they'd previously caught and provide photographic evidence of the catch. In the wake of Operation Vulcan, Alun Bradshaw sent out a press release under the headline DO YOU RECOGNISE THESE FISH?

For Bradshaw, it was the criminal, rather than the fish, who got away. The Peterborough case collapsed because police couldn't confirm that the anglers knew the carp were stolen. Bradshaw remains convinced that some of the carp he recovered from the farm were contraband, but he admits that there's nothing to be done. The fish will remain in the fishery's lake, and on Facebook.

At Timberland, Wakenell took the rod license from the angler with the tub of maggots and jotted down the number in his black notebook. "It's the Polish, isn't it?" the angler said. "They take the carp out and eat 'em. Why aren't you lot doing something about that?"

The Environment Agency is, in fact, working on the problem—or, at least, the perceived problem. As we walked back to the car, Wakenell pointed out a sign fastened to a lamppost. It displayed a series of large, crossed-out red circles. One showed a stick figure running with a large fish under his arm. Another showed a fish sizzling on a saucepan. "Everybody can see what this means," Wakenell said.

Right-wing tabloids in Britain have seized on the idea that the

rise in carp theft in England is the fault of foreigners. ANGRY AN-
GLERS BLAME EASTERN EUROPEAN MIGRANTS FOR DRAMATIC
DECLINE IN CITY RIVER'S FISH STOCKS, exclaimed a *Daily Mail*
headline in 2010. The indignation was further fueled by the news
that *Angliya,* Britain's Russian-language newspaper, had urged its
immigrant readers to "catch their own" fish instead of shopping
in markets. In 2010, the paper printed a cutout guide to four well-
stocked lakes. At one of the recommended lakes, in Northampton-
shire, seven Eastern European anglers were caught with the guide
about a month after its publication. "Incidents of thefts for personal
consumption have risen in prominence in the last decade," said
Broughton. "And it's true: most of those caught for this crime have
been people of Eastern European origin from countries where there
is a culture of fishing for food."

Whether or not Broughton's opinion is correct (neither the police
nor the Environment Agency tracks the ethnicities of those caught
stealing carp), in 2011 the Angling Trust hired Radoslaw Papiewski,
a Polish fisherman, to run a project that aims to educate migrant anglers about UK fishing culture. Nevertheless, Papiewski believes that
the threat immigrants pose to England's prize carp has been exaggerated. "Carp is a good food source in Europe, but it's usually farmed
for specific food purposes, and I doubt that many people would like to
eat anything from the commercial fishery," he says. "There is also a
misunderstanding of the size of the fish we eat. Big fish are fatty and
have old meat, which tastes unpleasant. In Europe we generally don't
eat a carp that weighs more than eight pounds. Some of these stories
are simply made up and escalate from angler to angler."

When I visited Mike Bampton at Wasing, he told me that he had recently noticed a curious trend. "When the Parrot isn't caught for a
month or so, people begin to panic," he said. "They worry that he's
died or been stolen. I've even had people saying to me they're thinking of joining a new ticket because they think the Parrot is gone.
Then, sure enough, a week later he's caught and they're all happy
again.

"I'm not like that," he told me. "I fish for the love of carp. I don't
fish because I just want to catch the largest one."

Bampton's uncorrupted love of carp was rewarded in late 2014, when, after fishing through the night, he felt something take his bait. He stood up and looked into the water. "It's only then I realized it was the Parrot," he recalled. "You always think in the back of your mind that it might be, but when it finally is . . . well, the bulk and the tail. It's huge."

The Parrot's weight—equivalent to that of a ten-year-old boy— affords him considerable strength. After the fish took the bait, he dragged Bampton's rowboat around the lake for close to an hour. Once the fish tired, Bampton and two friends were able to lug him from the water, slop him into a sling, and lay him on a mat to keep him safe from harm. "Everyone told me about the snout," Bampton said. "But it wasn't till I first saw him on the bank . . . well, it's a character fish, isn't it? And the rest is so pretty. The scales. The shape. He's not dumpy. He doesn't have a belly. The weight is evenly distributed. And he's so long. You can't imagine a fish getting that large." Bampton treated the Parrot's fresh wound with antiseptic, took a photograph, and then rushed him back to the water. "It took me a week to recover from the encounter," he said, "to realize just what I'd achieved."

It's that sense of achievement, so closely tied to the size of the catch, that keeps both the angling industry and its criminal shadow alive. Carp theft may be on the rise, but it's not the only reason that a fish goes missing. Sometimes, after a three-day stretch quivering under a bivouac, when no fish has bitten for hours, it's tempting to blame a spectral thief who empties the lake in the middle of the night. In those moments, the frustrated mind turns not to the one that got away but to the one that perhaps is no longer there.

As the sky, a unanimous shade of English gray, began to darken over the ancient Wasing Estate, Bampton surveyed his lake, which he so dutifully and so earnestly protects. The few anglers within his view sat on the shore higgledy-piggledy, staring at the motionless water. Twenty yards away, a barge carved soundlessly along the adjacent river, which is open to the public.

"That canal gets busy in the summer," Bampton announced forebodingly. "Makes me nervous."

ANNA WIENER

■

Uncanny Valley

FROM *n + 1*

MORALE IS DOWN. We are making plenty of money, but the office is teeming with salespeople: well-groomed social animals with good posture and dress shoes, men who chuckle and smooth their hair back when they can't connect to our VPN. Their corner of the office is loud; their desks are scattered with freebies from other start-ups, stickers and koozies and flash drives. We escape for drinks and fret about our company culture. "Our culture is dying," we say gravely, apocalyptic prophets all. "What should we do about the culture?"

It's not just the salespeople, of course. It's never just the sales-people. Our culture has been splintering for months. Members of our core team have been shepherded into conference rooms by top-level executives who proceed to question our loyalty. They've noticed the sea change. They've noticed we don't seem as invested. We don't stick around for in-office happy hour anymore; we don't take new hires out for lunch on the company card. We're not hitting our KPIs, we're not serious about the OKRs. People keep using the word *paranoid*. Our primary investor has funded a direct competitor. This is what investors do, but it feels personal: Daddy still loves us, but he loves us less.

We get ourselves out of the office and into a bar. We have more in common than our grievances, but we kick off by speculating about our job security, complaining about the bureaucratic double-downs, casting blame for blocks and poor product decisions. We talk about our IPO like it's the deus ex machina coming down from on high to save us—like it's an inevitability, like our stock options will lift us out of our existential dread, away from the collective anxiety that ebbs and flows. Realistically, we know it could be years before an IPO, if there's an IPO at all; we know in our hearts that money is a salve, not a solution. Still, we are hopeful. We reassure ourselves and one another that this is just a phase; every start-up has its growing pains. Eventually we are drunk enough to change the subject, to remember our more private selves. The people we are on weekends, the people we were for years.

This is a group of secret smokers, and we go in on a communal pack of cigarettes. The problem, we admit between drags, is that we do care. We care about one another. We even care about the executives who can make us feel like shit. We want good lives for them, just like we want good lives for ourselves. We care, for fuck's sake, about the company culture. We are among the first twenty employees, and we are making something people want. It feels like ours. Work has wedged its way into our identities, and the only way to maintain sanity is to maintain that we are the company, the company is us. Whenever we see a stranger at the gym wearing a T-shirt with our logo on it, whenever we are mentioned on social media or on a client's blog, whenever we get a positive support ticket, we share it in the company chat room and we're proud, genuinely proud.

But we see now that we've been swimming in the Kool-Aid, and we're coming up for air. We were lucky and in thrall and now we are bureaucrats, punching at our computers, making other people—some *kids*—unfathomably rich. We throw our dead cigarettes on the sidewalk and grind them out under our toes. Phones are opened and taxis summoned; we gulp the dregs of our beers as cartoon cars approach on-screen. We disperse, off to terrorize sleeping roommates and lovers, to answer just one, two more emails before bed. Eight hours later we'll be back in the office, slurping down coffee, running out for congealed breakfast sandwiches, tweaking mediocre scripts and writing halfhearted emails, throwing weary and knowing glances across the table.

I skim recruiter emails and job listings like horoscopes, skidding down to the perks: competitive salary, dental and vision, 401k, free gym membership, catered lunch, bike storage, ski trips to Tahoe, off-sites to Napa, summits in Vegas, beer on tap, craft beer on tap, kom-bucha on tap, wine tastings, Whiskey Wednesdays, Open Bar Fridays, massage on-site, yoga on-site, pool table, Ping-Pong table, Ping-Pong robot, ball pit, game night, movie night, go-karts, zip line. Job list-ings are an excellent place to get sprayed with HR's idea of fun and a twenty-three-year-old's idea of work-life balance. Sometimes I forget I'm not applying to summer camp. *Customized setup: design your ul-timate work station with the latest hardware. Change the world around you. Help humanity thrive by enabling*—next! *We work hard, we laugh hard, we give great high-fives. We have engineers in TopCoder's Top 20. We're not just another social web app. We're not just another project-man-agement tool. We're not just another payment processor.* I get a haircut and start exploring.

Most start-up offices look the same—faux midcentury furniture, brick walls, snack bar, bar cart. Interior designers in Silicon Valley are either brand-conscious or very literal. When tech products are pro-jected into the physical world they become aesthetics unto themselves, as if to insist on their own reality: the office belonging to a home-shar-ing website is decorated like rooms in its customers' pool houses and pieds-à-terre; the foyer of a hotel-booking start-up has a concierge desk replete with bell (no concierge); the headquarters of a ride-sharing app gleams in the same colors as the app itself, down to the sleek elevator bank. A book-related start-up holds a small and sad library, the shelves half-empty, paperbacks and object-oriented-programming manuals sloping against one another. It reminds me of the people who dressed like Michael Jackson to attend Michael Jackson's funeral.

But this office, of a media app with millions in VC funding but no revenue model, is particularly sexy. This is something that an of-fice shouldn't be, and it jerks my heart rate way, way up. There are views of the city in every direction, fat leather loveseats, electric gui-tars plugged into amps, teak credenzas with white hardware. It looks like the loft apartment of the famous musician boyfriend I thought I'd have at twenty-two but somehow never met. I want to take off my dress and my shoes and lie on the voluminous sheepskin rug and eat fistfuls of MDMA, curl my naked body into the Eero Aarnio Ball Chair, never leave.

It's not clear whether I'm here for lunch or an interview, which is normal. I am prepared for both and dressed for neither. My guide leads me through the communal kitchen, which has the trappings of every other start-up pantry: plastic bins of trail mix and Goldfish, bowls of Popchips and miniature candy bars. There's the requisite wholesale box of assorted Clif Bars, and in the fridge are flavored water, string cheese, and single-serving cartons of chocolate milk. It can be hard to tell whether a company is training for a marathon or eating an after-school snack. Once I walked into our kitchen and found two Account Managers pounding Shot Bloks, chewy cubes of glucose marketed to endurance athletes.

Over catered Afghan food, I meet the team, including a billionaire who made his fortune from a website that helps people feel close to celebrities and other strangers they'd hate in real life. He asks where I work, and I tell him. "Oh," he says, not unkindly, snapping a piece of lavash in two, "I know that company. I think I tried to buy you."

I take another personal day without giving a reason, an act of defiance that I fear is transparent. I spend the morning drinking coffee and skimming breathless tech press, then creep downtown to spend the afternoon in back-to-back interviews at a peanut-size start-up. All of the interviews are with men, which is fine. I like men. I had a boyfriend; I have a brother. The men ask me questions like, "How would you calculate the number of people who work for the United States Postal Service?" and "How would you describe the Internet to a medieval farmer?" and "What is the hardest thing you've ever done?" They tell me to stand in front of the whiteboard and diagram my responses. These questions are self-conscious and infuriating, but it only serves to fuel me. I want to impress; I refuse to be discouraged by their self-importance. Here is a character flaw, my industry origin story: I have always responded positively to negging.

My third interview is with the technical cofounder. He enters the conference room in a crisp blue button-down, looking confidently unprepared. He tells me—apologetically—that he hasn't done many interviews before, and as such he doesn't have a ton of questions to ask me. Nonetheless, the office manager slated an hour for our conversation. This seems okay: I figure we will talk about the company, I will ask routine follow-up questions, and at four they will let me out for the day, like a middle-school student, and the city will absorb me and my private errors. Then he tells me that his girlfriend is applying to law school and he's been helping her prep. So instead of a conventional interview, he's just going to have me take a section of the LSAT. I search his face to see if he's kidding. "If it's cool with you, I'm just going to hang out here and check my email," he says, sliding the test across the table and opening a laptop. He sets a timer.

I finish early, ever the overachiever. I check it twice. The cofounder grades it on the spot. "My mother would be so proud," I joke, feeling brilliant and misplaced and low, lower than low.

Home is my refuge, except when it's not. My roommate is turning thirty, and to celebrate we are hosting a wine and cheese party at our apartment. Well, she is hosting—I have been invited. Her friends arrive promptly, in business casual. Hundreds of dollars of cheese are represented. "Bi-Rite, obviously," she says, looking elegant in black silk as she smears Humboldt Fog onto a cracker. My roommate works down on the Peninsula, for a website that everyone loathes but no one can stop using. We occupy different spaces: I am in the start-up world, land of perpetual youth, and she is an adult like any other, navigating a corporation, acting the part, negotiating for her place. I admire and do not understand her; it is possible she finds me amusing. Mostly we talk about exercise.

Classical music streams through the house and someone opens a bottle of proper Champagne, which he reassures us is really from France; people clap when the cork pops. My roommate and I are the same age but I feel like a child at my parents' party, and I am immediately envious, homesick. I send myself to my room, lock the door, and change into a very tight dress. I've gained fifteen pounds in trail mix: it never feels like a meal, but there's an aggregate effect. When I reenter the living room, I suck in my stomach and slide between people's backs, looking for a conversation. On the couch, a man in a suit jacket expounds on the cannabis opportunity. Everyone seems very comfortable and nobody talks to me. They tilt their wineglasses at the correct angle; they dust crumbs off their palms with grace. The word I hear the most is *revenue*. No—*strategy*. There's nothing to do but drink and ingratiate myself. I wind up on the roof with a cluster of strangers and find myself missing my mother with a ferocity that carves into my gut. In the distance I can see the tip of the famous Rainbow Flag on Castro Street, whipping.

"Oakland," one of them says. "That's where we want to invest."

"Too dangerous," says another. "My wife would never go for it."

"Of course not," says the first, "but you don't buy to *live* there."

By the time the last guest has filtered out, I am in leggings and a sweatshirt, cleaning ineffectively: scooping up cheese rinds, rinsing plastic glasses, sneaking slices of chocolate cake with my damp hands. My roommate comes to say goodnight, and she is beautiful: tipsy but not toasted, radiant with absorbed goodwill. She repairs to her room with her boyfriend, and I listen from down the hall as they quietly undress, ease into bed, turn over into sleep.

Ours is a "pickax-during-the-gold-rush" product, the kind venture capitalists love to get behind. The product provides a shortcut to database infrastructure, giving people information about their apps and websites that they wouldn't necessarily have on their own. All our customers are other software companies. This is a privileged vantage point from which to observe the tech industry. I would say more, but I signed an NDA.

I am the inaugural customer support rep, or Support Engineer. My job involves looking at strangers' codebases and telling them what they've done wrong in integrating our product with theirs, and how to fix it. There are no unsolvable problems. Perhaps there are not even problems, only mistakes. After nearly three years in book publishing, where I mostly moved on instinct, taste, and feeling, the clarity of this soothes me.

I learn the bare minimum, code-wise, to be able to do my job well—to ask questions only when I'm truly in over my head. Still, I escalate problems all the time. I learn how to talk to our customers about the technology without ever touching the technology itself. I find myself confidently discussing cookies, data mapping, the difference between server-side and client-side integrations. "Just add logic!" I advise cheerfully. This means nothing to me but generally resonates with engineers. It shocks me every time someone nods along.

This is not to confuse confidence with pride. I doubt myself daily. I feel lucky to have this job; I feel desperately out of place. My previous boss—breezy and helpful, earnest in the manner of a man in his early twenties bequeathed $4 million to disrupt libraries—had encouraged me to apply for the role; I had joined his publishing start-up too early and needed something new. "This is the next big company," he had said. "It's a rocket ship." He was right. I had been banking on him being right. Still, there are days when all I want is to disembark, eject myself into space, admit defeat. I pander and apologize and self-deprecate until my manager criticizes me for being a pleaser, at which point it seems most strategic to stop talking.

I convince myself and everyone else that I want to learn how to code, and I'm incentivized to do it: I'm told I will be promoted to Solutions Architect if I can build a networked, two-player game of checkers in the next few months. One lazy Saturday I give it three hours, then call it a day. I resent the challenge; I resent myself. I tell everyone I can't do it, which is a lesser evil than not wanting to. In this environment, my lack of interest in learning JavaScript feels like a moral failure.

Around here, we nonengineers are pressed to prove our value. The hierarchy is pervasive, ingrained in the industry's dismissal of marketing and its insistence that a good product sells itself; evident in the few "office hours" established for engineers (our scheduled opportunity to approach with questions and bugs); reflected in our salaries and equity allotment, even though it's harder to find a good copy-writer than a liberal-arts graduate with a degree in history and twelve weeks' training from an uncredentialed coding dojo. This is a cozy home for believers in bootstrapping and meritocracy, proponents of shallow libertarianism. I am susceptible to it, too. "He just taught himself to code over the summer," I hear myself say one afternoon, with the awe of someone relaying a miracle.

Our soft skills are a necessary inconvenience. We bloat payroll; we dilute conversation; we create process and bureaucracy; we put in requests for yoga classes and Human Resources. We're a dragnet—though we tend to contribute positively to diversity metrics. There is quiet pity for the MBAs.

It's easy for me to dissociate from the inferiority of my job because

I've never been particularly proud of my customer-service skills. I'm good at subservience, but it isn't what I would lead with on a first date. I enjoy translating between the software and the customers. I like breaking down information, demystifying technical processes, being one of few with this specific expertise. I like being bossy. People are interesting—unpredictable, emotional—when their expensive software product doesn't behave as expected. Plus, I am almost always permissioned for God Mode.

After a year, my job evolves from support into something the industry calls Customer Success. The new role is more interesting, but the title is so corny and oddly stilted in its pseudosincerity that I cannot bring myself to say it out loud. This turns out to work to my advantage: when I change my email signature to read "Technical Account Manager" instead, it actually elicits a response from previously uncommunicative clients who are—I regret having to buttress stereotypes—always engineers, always founders, and always men.

I visit a friend at his midsize software company and see a woman typing at a treadmill desk. *That's a little on the nose,* I whisper, and he whispers back, *You have no idea—she does Customer Success.*

My coworkers are all skilled at maneuvering something called a RipStik, a two-wheeled, skateboard-like invention with separated pivoting plates, one for each foot. They glide across the office, twisting and dipping with laptops in hand, taking customer calls on their personal cell phones, shuttling from desk to kitchen to conference room. Mastering the RipStik is a rite of passage, and I cannot do it. After a few weeks of trying, I order a tiny plastic skateboard off eBay, a neon-green Penny board with four wheels that looks coolest when it's not being ridden. I come into the office over the weekend and practice on the Penny, perfecting my balance. It's fast, dangerously so. Mostly I put it under my standing desk and then get onboard, rocking back and forth as I work.

The billboards along the stretch of the 101 that sweeps Silicon Valley have been punchy and declarative lately, advertising apps and other software products that transcend all context and grammatical structure. "We fixed dinner" (meal delivery). "Ask your developer" (cloud-based communications). "How tomorrow works" (file storage). The ads get less dystopian the farther you get from the city: by the airport, they grow international-businessman corporate, and as the land turns over into suburbs you can almost hear the gears shift. A financial-services company—one that's been around for more than a century, a provider of life insurance, investment management, and, in the 1980s, bald-faced fraud—holds a mirror to an audience that perhaps won't want to recognize itself. The ad reads, "Donate to a worthy cause: your retirement."

I attend a networking event at an office whose walls are hung with inspirational posters that quote tech luminaries I've never heard of. The posters say things like "Life is short: build stuff that matters" and "Innovate or die." I am dead. Our interior designer tried hanging posters like these in our office; the front-end engineers relocated them to the bathroom, placed them face to the wall. The event is packed; people roam in clusters, like college freshmen during orientation week. There are a few women, but most of the attendees are young men in start-up twinsets: I pass someone wearing a branded hoodie, unzipped to reveal a shirt with the same logo. I Google the company on my cellphone to see what it is, to see if they're hiring. "We have loved mobile since we saw Steve Jobs announce the first iPhone," their website declares, and I close the browser, thinking, *how basic.*

The tenor of these events is usually the same: guilelessly optimistic. People are excited to talk about their start-ups, and all small-talk is a prelude to a pitch. I'm guilty of this, too; I'm proud of my work, and our recruiting bonus is 15 percent of my salary (alignment of company–employee goals and incentives). I talk to two European men who are building a food-delivery app geared toward healthy eaters, like people on the Paleo diet. They're extremely polite and oddly buff. They say they'll invite me to their beta, and I am excited. I like to be on the inside track. I want to help. I tell them that I know a lot of people on the Paleo diet, like the guy in marketing who stores plastic baggies of wet, sauteed meat in the communal refrigerator. I chatter on about Paleo adherents and people who do CrossFit and practice polyamory, and how I admire that they manage to do these things without detrimental physical or emotional consequences. I've learned so much about polyamory and S&M since moving to San Francisco. Ask me anything about *The Ethical Slut*; ask me anything about *Sex at Dawn*. That night, I download the healthy-food app and can't ever imagine using it.

My opinion doesn't matter, of course: a few months later I'll find out that the Europeans raised $30-odd million after pivoting to a new business model and undergoing a radical rebranding, and I'll find this out when our company starts paying them thousands to organize the catering for our in-office meals. The food is served in sturdy tinfoil troughs, and people race to be first in line for self-serve. It is low-carb and delicious, healthier than anything I've ever cooked, well worth someone else's money, and every afternoon I shovel it into my body.

Our own 101 billboard is unveiled on a chilly morning in November, just a few months after I've started. Everyone gets to work early; our office manager orders fresh-squeezed orange juice and pastries, cups of yogurt parfait with granola strata. We've arranged for a company field trip around the corner. We walk in a pack, hands in our pockets, and take a group photograph in front of our ad. I forward it to my parents in New York. In the photograph we've got our arms around one another, smiling and proud. The start-up is still small, just thirty of us or so, but within a year we'll be almost a hundred employees, and shortly thereafter, I'll be gone.

I have lunch with one of the salespeople, and I like him a lot. He's easy to talk to; he's easy to talk to for a living. We eat large, sloppy sandwiches in the park and gaze out at the tourists.

"So how'd you end up choosing our company?" I ask. Roast turkey drops from my sandwich onto the grass.

"Come on," he says. "I heard there were a bunch of twentysome-things crushing it in the Valley. How often does that happen?"

I lean in and go to a panel on big data. There are two venture capitalists onstage, dressed identically. They are exceptionally sweaty. Even from the back row, the place feels moist. I've never been in a room with so few women and so much money, and so many people champing at the bit to get a taste. It's like watching two ATMs in conversation. "I want big data on men watching other men talk about data," I whisper to my new friend in sales, who ignores me.

Back at the office, I walk into the bathroom to find a coworker folded over the sink, wiping her face with a paper towel. There aren't many women at this company, and I have encountered almost all of them, at one point or another, crying in the bathroom. "I just hope this is all worth it," she spits in my direction. I know what she means—she's talking about money—but I also know how much equity she has, and I'm confident that even in the best possible scenario, whatever she's experiencing is definitely not. She's out the door and back at her desk before I can conjure up something consoling.

Half of the conversations I overhear these days are about money, but nobody likes to get specific. It behooves everyone to stay theoretical.

A friend's roommate wins a hackathon with corporate sponsorship, and on a rainy Sunday afternoon he is awarded $500,000. (It is actually a million, but who would believe me?) That evening they throw a party at their duplex, which feels like a normal event in the Burning Man off-season—whippits, face paint, high-design vaporizers—except for the oversize foamcore check propped laterally against the bathroom doorframe.

Out by the porch cooler, I run into a friend who works at a company—cloud something—that was recently acquired. I make a joke about this being a billionaire boys' club and he laughs horsily, disproportionate to the humor. I've never seen him like this, but then I've never met anyone who's won the lottery, seen anyone so jazzed on his own good luck. He opens a beer using the edge of his lighter and invites me to drive up to Mendocino in his new convertible. What else do you do after a windfall? "You know who the real winner was, though?" he asks, then immediately names a mutual acquaintance, a brilliant and introverted programmer who was the company's first engineering hire, very likely the linchpin. "Instant multimillionaire," my friend says incredulously, as if hearing his own information for the first time. "At least eight figures."

"Wow," I say, handing my beer to him to open. "What do you think he wants to do?"

My friend deftly pops off the bottle cap, then looks at me and shrugs. "That's a good question," he says, tapping the lighter against the side of his beer. "I don't think he wants to do anything."

An old high school friend emails out of the blue to introduce me to his college buddy: a developer, new to the city, "always a great time!" The developer and I agree to meet for drinks. It's not clear whether we're meeting for a date or networking. Not that there's always a difference: I have one friend who found a job by swiping right and know countless others who go to industry conferences just to fuck— nothing gets them hard like a nonsmoking room charged to the company AmEx. The developer is very handsome and stiltedly sweet. He seems like someone who has opinions about fonts, and he does. It's clear from the start that we're there to talk shop. We go to a tiny cocktail bar in the Tenderloin with textured wallpaper and a scrawny bouncer. Photographs are forbidden, which means the place is designed for social media. This city is changing, and I am disgusted by my own complicity.

"There's no menu, so you can't just order, you know, a martini," the developer says, as if I would ever. "You tell the bartender three adjectives, and he'll customize a drink for you accordingly. It's great. It's creative! I've been thinking about my adjectives all day."

What is it like to be fun? What is it like to feel like you've earned this? I try to game the system by asking for something smoky, salty, and angry, crossing my fingers for mezcal; it works. We lean against a wall and sip. The developer tells me about his loft apartment in the Mission, his specialty bikes, how excited he is to go on weeknight camping trips. We talk about cameras and books. We talk about cities we've never visited. I tell him about the personal-shopper service my coworkers all signed up for, how three guys came into work wearing the same sweater; he laughs but looks a little guilty. He's sweet and a little shy about his intelligence, and I know we'll probably never hang out again. Still, I go home that night with the feeling that something, however small, has been lifted.

Venture capitalists have spearheaded massive innovation in the past few decades, not least of which is their incubation of this generation's very worst prose style. The Internet is choked with blindly ambitious and professionally inexperienced men giving each other anecdote-based instruction and bullet-point advice. *10 Essential Start-up Lessons You Won't Learn in School. 10 Things Every Successful Entrepreneur Knows. 5 Ways to Stay Humble. Why the Market Always Wins. Why the Customer Is Never Right. How to Deal with Failure. How to Fail Better. How to Fail Up. How to Pivot. How to Pivot Back. 18 Platitudes to Tape Above Your Computer. Raise Your Way to Emotional Acuity. How to Love Something That Doesn't Love You Back.*

Sometimes it feels like everyone is speaking a different language—or the same language, with radically different rules. At our all-hands meeting, we are subjected to a pep talk. Our director looks like he hasn't slept in days, but he straightens up and moves his gaze from face to face, making direct and metered eye contact with everyone around the table. "We are making products," he begins, "that can push the fold of mankind."

A networking-addicted coworker scrolls through a website where people voluntarily post their own résumés. I spy. He clicks through to an engineer who works for an aggressively powerful start-up, one whose rapid expansion, relentless pursuit of domination, and absence of ethical boundaries scare the shit out of me. Under his current company, the engineer has written this job description: "This is a rocket ship, baby. Climb aboard."

I am waiting for the train when I notice the ad: it covers the platform below the escalators. The product is an identity-as-a-service app—it stores passwords—but the company isn't advertising to users; they're advertising their job openings. They're advertising to me. The ad features five people standing in V-formation with their arms crossed. They're all wearing identical blue hoodies. They're also wearing identical rubber unicorn masks; I am standing on one of their heads. The copy reads, "Built by humans, used by unicorns."

We hire an engineer fresh out of a top undergraduate program. She walks confidently into the office, springy and enthusiastic. We've all been looking forward to having a woman on our engineering team. It's a big moment for us. Her onboarding buddy brings her around to make introductions, and as they approach our corner, my coworker leans over and cups his hand around my ear: as though we are colluding, as though we are five years old. "I feel sorry," he says, his breath moist against my neck. "Everyone's going to hit on her."

I include this anecdote in an email to my mom. The annual-review cycle is nigh, and I'm on the fence about whether or not to bring up the running list of casual hostilities toward women that add unsolicited spice to the workplace. I tell her about the colleague with the smart-watch app that's just an animated GIF of a woman's breasts bouncing in perpetuity; I tell her about the comments I've fielded about my weight, my lips, my clothing, my sex life; I tell her that the first woman engineer is also the only engineer without SSH access to the servers. I tell her that compared with other women I've met here, I have it good, but the bar is low. It's tricky: I like these coworkers— and I dish it back—but in the parlance of our industry, this behavior is scalable. I don't have any horror stories yet; I'd prefer things stay this way. I expect my mother to respond with words of support and encouragement. I expect her to say, "Yes! You are the change this industry needs." She emails me back almost immediately. "Don't put complaints about sexism in writing," she writes. "Unless, of course, you have a lawyer at the ready."

A meeting is dropped mysteriously onto our calendars, and at the designated time we shuffle warily into a conference room. The last time this happened, we were given forms that asked us to rate various values on a scale of one to five: our desire to lead a team; the importance of work-life balance. I gave both things a four and was told I didn't want it enough.

The conference room has a million-dollar view of downtown San Francisco, but we keep the shades down. Across the street, a bucket drummer bangs out an irregular heartbeat. We sit in a row, backs to the window, laptops open. I look around the room and feel a wave of affection for these men, this small group of misfits who are the only people who understand this new backbone to my life. On the other side of the table, our manager paces back and forth, but he's smiling. He asks us to write down the names of the five smartest people we know, and we dutifully oblige. I look at the list and think about how much I miss my friends back home, how bad I've been at returning phone calls and emails, how bloated I've become with start-up self-importance, how I've stopped making time for what I once held dear. I can feel blood rush to my cheeks.

"Okay," my manager says. "Now tell me: why don't they work here?"

Morale, like anything, is just another problem to be solved. There is a high premium on break/fix. To solve our problem, management arranges for a team-building exercise. They schedule it on a week-night evening, and we pretend not to mind. Our team-building begins with beers in the office, and then we travel en masse to a tiny event space at the mouth of the Stockton Tunnel, where two energetic blondes give us sweatbands and shots. The blondes are attractive and athletic, strong limbs wrapped in spandex leggings and tiny shorts, and we are their smudge-edged foils: an army of soft bellies and stiff necks, hands tight with the threat of carpal tunnel. They smear neon face paint across our foreheads and cheeks and tell us we look awesome. The event space warms up as people get drunk and bounce around the room, taking selfies with the CFO, fist-bumping the cofounders without irony, flirting with the new hires who don't yet know any better. We play Skee-Ball. We cluster by the bar and have another round, two.

Eventually, we're dispatched on a scavenger hunt across the city. We pour out of the building and into the street, spreading across rush-hour San Francisco, seeking landmarks; we barrel past tourists and harass taxicab drivers, piss off doormen and stumble into homeless people. We are our own worst representatives, calling apologies over our shoulders. We are sweaty, competitive—maybe happy, really happy.

The meeting begins without fanfare. They thought I was an amazing worker at first, working late every night, last out of the office, but now they wonder if the work was just too hard for me to begin with. They need to know: Am I down for the cause? Because if I'm not down for the cause, it's time. They will do this amicably. Of course I'm down, I say, trying not to swivel in my ergonomic chair. I care deeply about the company. I am here for it.

When I say I care deeply, what I mean is I am ready to retire.

When I say I'm down, what I mean is I'm scared. I cry twice during the meeting, despite my best efforts. I think about the city I left to come here, the plans I've canceled and the friends I haven't made. I think about how hard I've worked and how demoralizing it is to fail. I think about my values, and I cry even more. It will be months until I call uncle and quit; it will take almost a year to realize I was gaslighting myself, that I was reading from someone else's script.

It's Christmastime; I'm older, I'm elsewhere. On the train to work, I swipe through social media and hit on a post from the start-up's holiday party, which has its own hashtag. The photograph is of two former teammates, both of them smiling broadly, their teeth as white as I remember. "So grateful to be part of such an amazing team," the caption reads, and I tap through. The hashtag unleashes a stream of photographs featuring people I've never met—beautiful people, the kind of people who look good in athleisure. They look well rested. They look relaxed and happy. They look nothing like me. There's a photograph of what can only be the pre-dinner floor show: an acrobat in a leotard kneeling on a pedestal, her legs contorted, her feet grasping a bow and arrow, poised to release. Her target is a stuffed heart, printed with the company logo. I scroll past animated photo-booth GIFs of strangers, kissing and mugging for the camera, and I recognize their pride, I empathize with their sense of accomplishment—this was one hell of a year, and they have won. I feel gently ill, a callback to the childhood nausea of being left out.

The holiday party my year at the company began with an open bar at 4 p.m.—the same coworker had shellacked my hair into curls in the office bathroom, both of us excited and exhausted, ready to celebrate. Hours later, we danced against the glass windows of the Michelin-starred restaurant our company had bought out for the night, our napkins strewn on the tables, our shoes torn off, our plus-ones shifting in formal wear on the sidelines, the waitstaff studiously withholding visible judgment.

I keep scrolling until I hit a video of this year's after-party, which looks like it was filmed in a club or at a flashy bar mitzvah, save for the company logo projected onto the wall: flashing colored lights illuminate men in stripped-down suits and women in cocktail dresses, all of them bouncing up and down, waving glow sticks and light-sabers to a background of electronic dance music. They've gone pro, I say to myself. "Last night was epic!" someone has commented. Three years have passed since I left. I catch myself searching for my own face anyway.

ANDREW SULLIVAN

■

I Used to Be a Human Being

FROM *New York Magazine*

I WAS SITTING in a large meditation hall in a converted novitiate in central Massachusetts when I reached into my pocket for my iPhone. A woman in the front of the room gamely held a basket in front of her, beaming beneficently, like a priest with a collection plate. I duly surrendered my little device, only to feel a sudden pang of panic on my way back to my seat. If it hadn't been for everyone staring at me, I might have turned around immediately and asked for it back. But I didn't. I knew why I'd come here.

A year before, like many addicts, I had sensed a personal crash coming. For a decade and a half, I'd been a web obsessive, publishing blog posts multiple times a day, seven days a week, and ultimately corralling a team that curated the web every twenty minutes during peak hours. Each morning began with a full immersion in the stream of Internet consciousness and news, jumping from site to site, tweet to tweet, breaking news story to hottest take, scanning countless images and videos, catching up with multiple memes. Throughout the day, I'd cough up an insight or an argument or a joke about what had just occurred or what was happening right now. And at times, as events took over, I'd spend weeks manically grabbing every tiny scrap of a developing story in order to fuse them into a narrative in real time. I was in an unending dialogue with readers who were caviling, praising, booing, correcting. My brain had never been so occupied so insistently by so many different subjects and in so public a way for so long.

I was, in other words, a very early adopter of what we might now call living-in-the-web. And as the years went by, I realized I was no longer alone. Facebook soon gave everyone the equivalent of their own blog and their own audience. More and more people got a smart-phone—connecting them instantly to a deluge of febrile content, forcing them to cull and absorb and assimilate the online torrent as relentlessly as I had once. Twitter emerged as a form of instant blog-ging of microthoughts. Users were as addicted to the feedback as I had long been—and even more prolific. Then the apps descended, like the rain, to inundate what was left of our free time. It was ubiq-uitous now, this virtual living, this never-stopping, this always-updat-ing. I remember when I decided to raise the ante on my blog in 2007 and update every half-hour or so, and my editor looked at me as if I were insane. But the insanity was now banality; the once-unimagina-ble pace of the professional blogger was now the default for everyone.

If the Internet killed you, I used to joke, then I would be the first to find out. Years later, the joke was running thin. In the last year of my blogging life, my health began to give out. Four bronchial infec-tions in twelve months had become progressively harder to kick. Va-cations, such as they were, had become mere opportunities for sleep. My dreams were filled with the snippets of code I used each day to update the site. My friendships had atrophied as my time away from the web dwindled. My doctor, dispensing one more course of antibi-otics, finally laid it on the line: "Did you really survive HIV to die of the web?"

But the rewards were many: an audience of up to 100,000 peo-ple a day; a new-media business that was actually profitable; a con-stant stream of things to annoy, enlighten, or infuriate me; a niche in the nerve center of the exploding global conversation; and a way to measure success—in big and beautiful data—that was a constant do-pamine bath for the writerly ego. If you had to reinvent yourself as a writer in the Internet age, I reassured myself, then I was ahead of the curve. The problem was that I hadn't been able to reinvent myself as a human being.

I tried reading books, but that skill now began to elude me. After a couple of pages, my fingers twitched for a keyboard. I tried medi-tation, but my mind bucked and bridled as I tried to still it. I got a

steady workout routine, and it gave me the only relief I could measure for an hour or so a day. But over time in this pervasive virtual
world, the online clamor grew louder and louder. Although I spent
hours each day, alone and silent, attached to a laptop, it felt as if I
were in a constant cacophonous crowd of words and images, sounds
and ideas, emotions and tirades—a wind tunnel of deafening, dead-
ening noise. So much of it was irresistible, as I fully understood. So
much of the technology was irreversible, as I also knew. But I'd begun to fear that this new way of living was actually becoming a way
of not-living.

By the last few months, I realized I had been engaging—like most
addicts—in a form of denial. I'd long treated my online life as a sup-
plement to my real life, an add-on, as it were. Yes, I spent many hours
communicating with others as a disembodied voice, but my real life
and body were still here. But then I began to realize, as my health and
happiness deteriorated, that this was not a both-and kind of situation.
It was either-or. Every hour I spent online was not spent in the physical world. Every minute I was engrossed in a virtual interaction I was
not involved in a human encounter. Every second absorbed in some
trivia was a second less for any form of reflection, or calm, or spirituality. "Multitasking" was a mirage. This was a zero-sum question. I
either lived as a voice online or I lived as a human being in the world
that humans had lived in since the beginning of time.

And so I decided, after fifteen years, to live in reality.

Since the invention of the printing press, every new revolution in
information technology has prompted apocalyptic fears. From the
panic that easy access to the vernacular English Bible would destroy
Christian orthodoxy all the way to the revulsion, in the 1950s, at the
barbaric young medium of television, cultural critics have moaned
and wailed at every turn. Each shift represented a further fracturing
of attention—continuing up to the previously unimaginable kalei-
doscope of cable TV in the late twentieth century and the now infinite, infinitely multiplying spaces of the web. And yet society has
always managed to adapt and adjust, without obvious damage, and
with some more-than-obvious progress. So it's perhaps too easy to
view this new era of mass distraction as something newly dystopian.

But it sure does represent a huge leap from even the very recent past. The data bewilder. Every single minute on the planet, YouTube users upload 400 hours of video and Tinder users swipe profiles over a million times. Each day, there are literally billions of Facebook "likes." Online outlets now publish exponentially more material than they once did, churning out articles at a rapid-fire pace, adding new details to the news every few minutes. Blogs, Facebook feeds, Tumblr accounts, tweets, and propaganda outlets repurpose, borrow, and add topspin to the same output.

We absorb this "content" (as writing or video or photography is now called) no longer primarily by buying a magazine or paper, by bookmarking our favorite website, or by actively choosing to read or watch. We are instead guided to these info-nuggets by myriad little interruptions on social media, all cascading at us with individually tailored relevance and accuracy. Do not flatter yourself in thinking that you have much control over which temptations you click on. Silicon Valley's technologists and their ever-perfecting algorithms have discovered the form of bait that will have you jumping like a witless minnow. No information technology ever had this depth of knowledge of its consumers—or greater capacity to tweak their synapses to keep them engaged.

And the engagement never ends. Not long ago, surfing the web, however addictive, was a stationary activity. At your desk at work, or at home on your laptop, you disappeared down a rabbit hole of links and resurfaced minutes (or hours) later to reencounter the world. But the smartphone then went and made the rabbit hole portable, inviting us to get lost in it anywhere, at any time, whatever else we might be doing. Information soon penetrated every waking moment of our lives.

And it did so with staggering swiftness. We almost forget that ten years ago, there were no smartphones, and as recently as 2011, only a third of Americans owned one. Now nearly two-thirds do. That figure reaches 85 percent when you're only counting young adults. And 46 percent of Americans told Pew surveyors last year a simple but remarkable thing: They could not live without one. The device went from unknown to indispensable in less than a decade. The handful of spaces where it was once impossible to be connected—the airplane, the subway, the wilderness—are dwindling fast. Even hiker backpacks now come fitted with battery power for smartphones. Perhaps the only "safe space" that still exists is the shower.

Am I exaggerating? A small but detailed 2015 study of young adults found that participants were using their phones five hours a day, at eighty-five separate times. Most of these interactions were for less than thirty seconds, but they add up. Just as revealing: The users weren't fully aware of how addicted they were. They thought they picked up their phones half as much as they actually did. But whether they were aware of it or not, a new technology had seized control of around one-third of these young adults' waking hours.

The interruptions often feel pleasant, of course, because they are usually the work of your friends. Distractions arrive in your brain connected to people you know (or think you know), which is the genius of social, peer-to-peer media. Since our earliest evolution, humans have been unusually passionate about gossip, which some attribute to the need to stay abreast of news among friends and family as our social networks expanded. We were hooked on information as eagerly as sugar. And give us access to gossip the way modernity has given us access to sugar and we have an uncontrollable impulse to binge. A regular teen Snapchat user, as the *Atlantic* recently noted, can have exchanged anywhere between 10,000 and even as many as 400,000 snaps with friends. As the snaps accumulate, they generate publicly displayed scores that bestow the allure of popularity and social status. This, evolutionary psychologists will attest, is fatal. When provided a constant source of information and news and gossip about each other—routed through our social networks—we are close to helpless.

Just look around you—at the people crouched over their phones as they walk the streets, or drive their cars, or walk their dogs, or play with their children. Observe yourself in line for coffee, or in a quick work break, or driving, or even just going to the bathroom. Visit an airport and see the sea of craned necks and dead eyes. We have gone from looking up and around to constantly looking down.

If an alien had visited America just five years ago, then returned today, wouldn't this be its immediate observation? That this species has developed an extraordinary new habit—and, everywhere you look, lives constantly in its thrall?

* * *

I arrived at the meditation retreat center a few months after I'd quit
the web, throwing my life and career up in the air. I figured it would
be the ultimate detox. And I wasn't wrong. After a few hours of silence, you tend to expect some kind of disturbance, some flurry to
catch your interest. And then it never comes. The quiet deepens into
an enveloping default. No one spoke; no one even looked another
person in the eye—what some Buddhists call "noble silence." The
day was scheduled down to the minute, so that almost all our time
was spent in silent meditation with our eyes closed, or in slow-walk-
ing meditation on the marked trails of the forest, or in communal,
unspeaking meals. The only words I heard or read for ten days were
in three counseling sessions, two guided meditations, and nightly
talks on mindfulness.

I'd spent the previous nine months honing my meditation practice, but, in this crowd, I was a novice and a tourist. (Everyone around
me was attending six-week or three-month sessions.) The silence, it
became apparent, was an integral part of these people's lives—and
their simple manner of movement, the way they glided rather than
walked, the open expressions on their faces, all fascinated me. What
were they experiencing, if not insane levels of boredom?

And how did their calm somehow magnify itself when I was surrounded by them every day? Usually, when you add people to a room,
the noise grows; here, it was the silence that seemed to compound itself. Attached to my phone, I had been accompanied for so long by
verbal and visual noise, by an endless bombardment of words and
images, and yet I felt curiously isolated. Among these meditators, I
was alone in silence and darkness, yet I felt almost at one with them.
My breathing slowed. My brain settled. My body became much more
available to me. I could feel it digesting and sniffing, itching and pul-
sating. It was if my brain were moving away from the abstract and
the distant toward the tangible and the near.

Things that usually escaped me began to intrigue me. On a meditative walk through the forest on my second day, I began to notice
not just the quality of the autumnal light through the leaves but the
splotchy multicolors of the newly fallen, the texture of the lichen on

the bark, the way in which tree roots had come to entangle and overcome old stone walls. The immediate impulse—to grab my phone
and photograph it—was foiled by an empty pocket. So I simply
looked. At one point, I got lost and had to rely on my sense of direction to find my way back. I heard birdsong for the first time in years.
Well, of course, I had always heard it, but it had been so long since
I listened.

My goal was to keep thought in its place. "Remember," my
friend Sam Harris, an atheist meditator, had told me before I left,
"if you're suffering, you're thinking." The task was not to silence
everything within my addled brain, but to introduce it to quiet, to
perspective, to the fallow spaces I had once known where the mind
and soul replenish.

Soon enough, the world of "the news," and the raging primary
campaign, disappeared from my consciousness. My mind drifted
to a trancelike documentary I had watched years before, Philip
Gröning's *Into Great Silence,* on an ancient Carthusian monastery
and silent monastic order in the Alps. In one scene, a novice monk is
tending his plot of garden. As he moves deliberately from one task to
the next, he seems almost in another dimension. He is walking from
one trench to another, but never appears focused on actually getting
anywhere. He seems to float, or mindfully glide, from one place to
the next.

He had escaped, it seemed to me, what we moderns understand by
time. There was no race against it; no fear of wasting it; no avoidance
of the tedium that most of us would recoil from. And as I watched
my fellow meditators walk around, eyes open yet unavailable to me,
I felt the slowing of the ticking clock, the unwinding of the pace that
has all of us in modernity on a treadmill till death. I felt a trace of a
freedom all humans used to know and that our culture seems intent,
pell-mell, on forgetting.

We all understand the joys of our always-wired world—the connections, the validations, the laughs, the porn, the info. I don't want to
deny any of them here. But we are only beginning to get our minds
around the costs, if we are even prepared to accept that there are
costs. For the subtle snare of this new technology is that it lulls us

into the belief that there are no downsides. It's all just more of every-thing. Online life is simply layered on top of offline life. We can meet in person and text beforehand. We can eat together while checking our feeds. We can transform life into what the writer Sherry Turkle refers to as "life-mix."

But of course, as I had discovered in my blogging years, the family that is eating together while simultaneously on their phones is not actually together. They are, in Turkle's formulation, "alone to-gether." You are where your attention is. If you're watching a football game with your son while also texting a friend, you're not fully with your child—and he knows it. Truly being with another person means being experientially with them, picking up countless tiny signals from the eyes and voice and body language and context, and react-ing, often unconsciously, to every nuance. These are our deepest so-cial skills, which have been honed through the aeons. They are what make us distinctively human.

By rapidly substituting virtual reality for reality, we are diminish-ing the scope of this interaction even as we multiply the number of people with whom we interact. We remove or drastically filter all the information we might get by being with another person. We reduce them to some outlines—a Facebook "friend," an Instagram photo, a text message—in a controlled and sequestered world that exists largely free of the sudden eruptions or encumbrances of actual hu-man interaction. We become each other's "contacts," efficient shad-ows of ourselves.

Think of how rarely you now use the phone to speak to someone. A text is far easier, quicker, less burdensome. A phone call could take longer; it could force you to encounter that person's idiosyncrasies or digressions or unexpected emotional needs. Remember when you left voicemail messages—or actually listened to one? Emojis now suffice. Or take the difference between trying to seduce someone at a bar and flipping through Tinder profiles to find a better match. One is deeply inefficient and requires spending (possibly wasting) con-siderable time; the other turns dozens and dozens of humans into clothes on an endlessly extending rack.

No wonder we prefer the apps. An entire universe of intimate re-sponses is flattened to a single, distant swipe. We hide our vulnerabilities, airbrushing our flaws and quirks; we project our fantasies onto the images before us. Rejection still stings—but less when a new virtual match beckons on the horizon. We have made sex even safer yet, having sapped it of serendipity and risk and often of physical beings altogether. The amount of time we spend cruising vastly outweighs the time we may ever get to spend with the objects of our desire.

Our oldest human skills atrophy. GPS, for example, is a godsend for finding our way around places we don't know. But, as Nicholas Carr has noted, it has led to our not even seeing, let alone remembering, the details of our environment, to our not developing the accumulated memories that give us a sense of place and control over what we once called ordinary life. The writer Matthew Crawford has examined how automation and online living have sharply eroded the number of people physically making things, using their own hands and eyes and bodies to craft, say, a wooden chair or a piece of clothing or, in one of Crawford's more engrossing case studies, a pipe organ. We became who we are as a species by mastering tools, making them a living, evolving extension of our whole bodies and minds. What first seems tedious and repetitive develops into a skill—and a skill is what gives us humans self-esteem and mutual respect.

Yes, online and automated life is more efficient, it makes more economic sense, it ends monotony and "wasted" time in the achievement of practical goals. But it denies us the deep satisfaction and pride of workmanship that comes with accomplishing daily tasks well, a denial perhaps felt most acutely by those for whom such tasks are also a livelihood—and an identity.

Indeed, the modest mastery of our practical lives is what fulfilled us for tens of thousands of years—until technology and capitalism decided it was entirely dispensable. If we are to figure out why despair has spread so rapidly in so many left-behind communities, the atrophying of the practical vocations of the past—and the meaning they gave to people's lives—seems as useful a place to explore as economic indices.

So are the bonds we used to form in our everyday interactions— the nods and pleasantries of neighbors, the daily facial recognition in the mall or the street. Here too the allure of virtual interaction has helped decimate the space for actual community. When we enter a coffee shop in which everyone is engrossed in their private online worlds, we respond by creating one of our own. When someone next to you answers the phone and starts talking loudly as if you didn't exist, you realize that, in her private zone, you don't. And slowly, the whole concept of a public space—where we meet and engage and learn from our fellow citizens—evaporates. Turkle describes one of the many small consequences in an American city: "Kara, in her 50s, feels that life in her hometown of Portland, Maine, has emptied out: 'Sometimes I walk down the street, and I'm the only person not plugged in . . . No one is where they are. They're talking to someone miles away. I miss them.'"

Has our enslavement to dopamine—to the instant hits of validation that come with a well-crafted tweet or Snapchat streak—made us happier? I suspect it has simply made us less unhappy, or rather less aware of our unhappiness, and that our phones are merely new and powerful antidepressants of a non-pharmaceutical variety. In an essay on contemplation, the Christian writer Alan Jacobs recently commended the comedian Louis C.K. for withholding smartphones from his children. On the Conan O'Brien show, C.K. explained why: "You need to build an ability to just be yourself and not be doing something. That's what the phones are taking away," he said. "Underneath in your life there's that thing . . . that forever empty . . . that knowledge that it's all for nothing and you're alone . . . That's why we text and drive . . . because we don't want to be alone for a second."

He recalled a moment driving his car when a Bruce Springsteen song came on the radio. It triggered a sudden, unexpected surge of sadness. He instinctively went to pick up his phone and text as many friends as possible. Then he changed his mind, left his phone where it was, and pulled over to the side of the road to weep. He allowed himself for once to be alone with his feelings, to be overwhelmed by them, to experience them with no instant distraction, no digital assist. And then he was able to discover, in a manner now remote from most of us, the relief of crawling out of the hole of misery by himself. For if there is no dark night of the soul anymore that isn't lit with the flicker of the screen, then there is no morning of hopefulness either. As he said of the distracted modern world we now live in: "You never feel completely sad or completely happy, you just feel . . . kinda satis-

fied with your products. And then you die. So that's why I don't want
to get a phone for my kids."

The early days of the retreat passed by, the novelty slowly ceding to
a reckoning that my meditation skills were now being tested more
aggressively. Thoughts began to bubble up; memories clouded the
present; the silent sessions began to be edged by a little anxiety.

And then, unexpectedly, on the third day, as I was walking through
the forest, I became overwhelmed. I'm still not sure what triggered
it, but my best guess is that the shady, quiet woodlands, with brooks
trickling their way down hillsides and birds flitting through the moist
air, summoned memories of my childhood. I was a lonely boy who
spent many hours outside in the copses and woodlands of my native
Sussex, in England. I had explored this landscape with friends, but
also alone—playing imaginary scenarios in my head, creating little
nooks where I could hang and sometimes read, learning every little pathway through the woods and marking each flower or weed or
fungus that I stumbled on. But I was also escaping a home where
my mother had collapsed with bipolar disorder after the birth of my
younger brother and had never really recovered. She was in and out
of hospitals for much of my youth and adolescence, and her condition made it hard for her to hide her pain and suffering from her sensitive oldest son.

I absorbed a lot of her agony, I came to realize later, hearing her
screams of frustration and misery in constant, terrifying fights with
my father, and never knowing how to stop it or to help. I remember
watching her dissolve in tears in the car picking me up from elementary school at the thought of returning to a home she clearly dreaded,
or holding her as she poured her heart out to me, through sobs and
whispers, about her dead-end life in a small town where she was utterly dependent on a spouse. She was taken away from me several
times in my childhood, starting when I was four, and even now I can
recall the corridors and rooms of the institutions she was treated in
when we went to visit.

I knew the scar tissue from this formative trauma was still in my
soul. I had spent two decades in therapy, untangling and exploring it,
learning how it had made intimacy with others so frightening, how it

had made my own spasms of adolescent depression even more acute, how living with that kind of pain from the most powerful source of love in my life had made me the profoundly broken vessel I am. But I had never felt it so vividly since the very years it had first engulfed and defined me. It was as if, having slowly and progressively removed every distraction from my life, I was suddenly faced with what I had been distracting myself from. Resting for a moment against the trunk of a tree, I stopped, and suddenly found myself bent over, convulsed with the newly present pain, sobbing.

And this time, even as I eventually made it back to the meditation hall, there was no relief. I couldn't call my husband or a friend and talk it over. I couldn't check my email or refresh my Instagram or text someone who might share the pain. I couldn't ask one of my fellows if they had experienced something similar. I waited for the mood to lift, but it deepened. Hours went by in silence as my heart beat anxiously and my mind reeled.

I decided I would get some distance by trying to describe what I was feeling. The two words "extreme suffering" won the naming contest in my head. And when I had my fifteen-minute counseling session with my assigned counselor a day later, the words just kept tumbling out. After my panicked, anguished confession, he looked at me, one eyebrow raised, with a beatific half-smile. "Oh, that's perfectly normal," he deadpanned warmly. "Don't worry. Be patient. It will resolve itself." And in time, it did. Over the next day, the feelings began to ebb, my meditation improved, the sadness shifted into a kind of calm and rest. I felt other things from my childhood—the beauty of the forests, the joy of friends, the support of my sister, the love of my maternal grandmother. Yes, I prayed, and prayed for relief. But this lifting did not feel like divine intervention, let alone a result of effort, but more like a natural process of revisiting and healing and recovering. It felt like an ancient, long-buried gift.

In his survey of how the modern West lost widespread religious practice, *A Secular Age,* the philosopher Charles Taylor used a term to describe the way we think of our societies. He called it a "social imaginary"—a set of interlocking beliefs and practices that can undermine or subtly marginalize other kinds of belief. We didn't go from faith to secularism in one fell swoop, he argues. Certain ideas and practices made others not so much false as less vibrant or relevant. And so modernity slowly weakened spirituality, by design and accident, in favor of commerce; it downplayed silence and mere being in favor of noise and constant action. The reason we live in a culture increasingly without faith is not because science has somehow disproved the unprovable, but because the white noise of secularism has removed the very stillness in which it might endure or be reborn.

The English Reformation began, one recalls, with an assault on the monasteries, and what silence the Protestants didn't banish the philosophers of the Enlightenment mocked. Gibbon and Voltaire defined the Enlightenment's posture toward the monkish: from condescension to outright contempt. The roar and disruption of the Industrial Revolution violated what quiet still remained until modern capitalism made business central to our culture and the ever-more efficient meeting of needs and wants our primary collective goal. We became a civilization of getting things done—with the development of America, in some ways, as its crowning achievement. Silence in modernity became, over the centuries, an anachronism, even a symbol of the useless superstitions we had left behind. The smartphone revolution of the past decade can be seen in some ways simply as the final twist of this ratchet, in which those few remaining redoubts of quiet—the tiny cracks of inactivity in our lives—are being methodically filled with more stimulus and noise.

And yet our need for quiet has never fully gone away, because our practical achievements, however spectacular, never quite fulfill us. They are always giving way to new wants and needs, always requiring updating or repairing, always falling short. The mania of our online lives reveals this: We keep swiping and swiping because we are never fully satisfied. The late British philosopher Michael Oakeshott starkly called this truth "the deadliness of doing." There seems no end to this paradox of practical life, and no way out, just an infinite succession of efforts, all doomed ultimately to fail.

Except, of course, there is the option of a spiritual reconciliation to this futility, an attempt to transcend the unending cycle of impermanent human achievement. There is a recognition that beyond mere doing, there is also being; that at the end of life, there is also the great silence of death with which we must eventually make our peace. From the moment I entered a church in my childhood, I understood that this place was different because it was so quiet. The Mass itself was full of silences—those liturgical pauses that would never do in a theater, those minutes of quiet after communion when we were encouraged to get lost in prayer, those liturgical spaces that seemed to insist that we are in no hurry here. And this silence demarcated what we once understood as the sacred, marking a space beyond the secular world of noise and business and shopping.

The only place like it was the library, and the silence there also pointed to something beyond it—to the learning that required time and patience, to the pursuit of truth that left practical life behind. Like the moment of silence we sometimes honor in the wake of a tragedy, the act of not speaking signals that we are responding to something deeper than the quotidian, something more profound than words can fully express. I vividly recall when the AIDS Memorial Quilt was first laid out on the Mall in Washington in 1987. A huge crowd had gathered, drifts of hundreds of chattering, animated people walking in waves onto the scene. But the closer they got, and the more they absorbed the landscape of unimaginably raw grief, their voices petered out, and a great emptiness filled the air. This is different, the silence seemed to say. This is not our ordinary life.

Most civilizations, including our own, have understood this in the past. Millennia ago, as the historian Diarmaid MacCulloch has argued, the unnameable, often inscrutably silent God of the Jewish Scriptures intersected with Plato's concept of a divinity so beyond human understanding and imperfection that no words could accurately describe it. The hidden God of the Jewish and Christian Scriptures spoke often by not speaking. And Jesus, like the Buddha, revealed as much by his silences as by his words. He was a preacher who yet wandered for forty days in the desert; a prisoner who refused to defend himself at his trial. At the converted novitiate at the retreat, they had left two stained-glass windows depicting Jesus. In one, he is in the Garden of Gethsemane, sweating blood in terror, alone before his execution. In the other, he is seated at the Last Supper, with the disciple John the Beloved resting his head on Jesus's chest. He is speaking in neither.

That Judeo-Christian tradition recognized a critical distinction—and tension—between noise and silence, between getting through the day and getting a grip on one's whole life. The Sabbath—the Jewish institution co-opted by Christianity—was a collective imposition of relative silence, a moment of calm to reflect on our lives under the light of eternity. It helped define much of Western public life once a week for centuries—only to dissipate, with scarcely a passing regret, into the commercial cacophony of the past couple of decades. It reflected a now-battered belief that a sustained spiritual life is simply unfeasible for most mortals without these refuges from noise and work to buffer us and remind us who we really are. But just as modern street lighting has slowly blotted the stars from the visible skies, so too have cars and planes and factories and flickering digital screens combined to rob us of a silence that was previously regarded as integral to the health of the human imagination.

This changes us. It slowly removes—without our even noticing it—the very spaces where we can gain a footing in our minds and souls that is not captive to constant pressures or desires or duties. And the smartphone has all but banished them. Thoreau issued his jeremiad against those pressures more than a century ago: "I went to the woods because I wished to live deliberately, to front only the essential facts of life, and see if I could not learn what it had to teach, and not, when I came to die, discover that I had not lived. I did not wish to live what was not life, living is so dear."

When you enter the temporary Temple at Burning Man, the annual Labor Day retreat for the tech elite in the Nevada desert, there is hardly any speaking. Some hover at the edges; others hold hands and weep; a few pin notes to a wall of remembrances; the rest are kneeling or meditating or simply sitting. The usually ornate and vast wooden structure is rivaled only by the massive tower of a man that will be burned, like the Temple itself, as the festival reaches its climax, and tens of thousands of people watch an inferno.

They come here, these architects of our Internet world, to escape the thing they unleashed on the rest of us. They come to a wilderness where no cellular signals penetrate. You leave your phone in your tent, deemed useless for a few, ecstatically authentic days. There is a spirit of radical self-reliance (you survive for seven days or so only on what you can bring into the vast temporary city) and an ethic of social equality. You are forced to interact only as a physical human being with other physical human beings—without hierarchy. You dance, and you experiment; you build community in various camps. And for many, this is the high point of their year—a separate world for fantasy and friendship, enhanced by drugs that elevate your sense of compassion or wonder or awe.

Like a medieval carnival, this new form of religion upends the conventions that otherwise rule our lives. Like a safety valve, it releases the pent-up pressures of our wired cacophony. Though easily mockable, it is trying to achieve what our culture once routinely provided, and it reveals, perhaps, that we are not completely helpless in this newly distracted era. We can, one senses, begin to balance it out, to relearn what we have so witlessly discarded, to manage our neuroses so they do not completely overwhelm us.

There are burgeoning signs of this more human correction. In 2012, there were, for example, around 20 million yoga practitioners in the United States, according to a survey conducted by Ipsos Public Affairs. By 2016, the number had almost doubled. Mindfulness, at the same time, has become a corporate catchword for many and a new form of sanity for others. It's also hard to explain, it seems to me, the sudden explosion of interest in and tolerance of cannabis in the past fifteen years without factoring in the intensifying digital climate. Weed is a form of self-medication for an era of mass distraction, providing a quick and easy path to mellowed contemplation in a world where the ample space and time necessary for it are under siege.

If the churches came to understand that the greatest threat to faith today is not hedonism but distraction, perhaps they might begin to appeal anew to a frazzled digital generation. Christian leaders seem to think that they need more distraction to counter the distraction. Their services have degenerated into emotional spasms, their spaces drowned with light and noise and locked shut throughout the day, when their darkness and silence might actually draw those whose minds and souls have grown web-weary. But the mysticism of Catholic meditation—of the Rosary, of Benediction, or simple contemplative prayer—is a tradition in search of rediscovery. The monasteries—opened up to more lay visitors—could try to answer to the same needs that the booming yoga movement has increasingly met.

And imagine if more secular places responded in kind: restaurants where smartphones must be surrendered upon entering, or coffee shops that marketed their non-Wi-Fi safe space? Or, more practical: more meals where we agree to put our gadgets in a box while we talk to one another? Or lunch where the first person to use their phone pays the whole bill? We can, if we want, re-create a digital Sabbath each week—just one day in which we live for twenty-four hours without checking our phones. Or we can simply turn off our notifications. Humans are self-preserving in the long run. For every innovation there is a reaction, and even the starkest of analysts of our new culture, like Sherry Turkle, sees a potential for eventually rebalancing our lives.

And yet I wonder. The ubiquitous temptations of virtual living create a mental climate that is still maddeningly hard to manage. In the days, then weeks, then months after my retreat, my daily meditation sessions began to falter a little. There was an election campaign of such brooding menace it demanded attention, headlined by a walking human Snapchat app of incoherence. For a while, I had limited my news exposure to the *New York Times*'s daily briefings; then, slowly, I found myself scanning the click-bait headlines from countless sources that crowded the screen; after a while, I was back in my old rut, absorbing every nugget of campaign news, even as I understood each to be as ephemeral as the last, and even though I no longer needed to absorb them all for work.

Then there were the other snares: the allure of online porn, now blasting through the defenses of every teenager; the ease of replacing every conversation with a texting stream; the escape of living for a while in an online game where all the hazards of real human interaction are banished; the new video features on Instagram, and new friends to follow. It all slowly chipped away at my meditative composure. I cut my daily silences from one hour to twenty-five minutes; and then, almost a year later, to every other day. I knew this was fatal—that the key to gaining sustainable composure from meditation was rigorous discipline and practice, every day, whether you felt like it or not, whether it felt as if it were working or not. Like weekly Mass, it is the routine that gradually creates a space that lets your life breathe. But the world I rejoined seemed to conspire to take that space away from me. "I do what I hate," as the oldest son says in Terrence Malick's haunting *Tree of Life*.

I haven't given up, even as, each day, at various moments, I find myself giving in. There are books to be read; landscapes to be walked; friends to be with; life to be fully lived. And I realize that this is, in some ways, just another tale in the vast book of human frailty. But this new epidemic of distraction is our civilization's specific weakness. And its threat is not so much to our minds, even as they shape-shift under the pressure. The threat is to our souls. At this rate, if the noise does not relent, we might even forget we have any.

VIET DINH

■

Lucky Dragon

FROM *Ploughshares*

I.

THE SECOND DAWN rose in the east, at nine in the morning. Hiroshi had never before seen such radiance. It rivaled the sun. He stood
on deck with Yoshi, and the light crushed them beneath its purity.
Hiroshi closed his eyes, but even so, the brightness pierced his head.
The other crew members clamored to see this strange, unexpected
light. But Hiroshi returned to the tasks of the day. He consulted Sanezumi about their current bearing. He examined the nautical charts,
the curves and byways of the ocean unfolding beneath his forefinger.
Last night, he dreamt of a large school of tuna, a flotilla so dense that
the ocean became the blue-black from their scales. Their eyes flashed
like diamonds in the waves. Each time the crew pulled in the nets,
the smallest of the fish dwarfed him. They entered the hull without
struggling, their flesh tender and firm, bellies thick and marbled
with fat. When he woke, Hiroshi knew that it was an omen. Dreams
were unreliable things, sinuous and slippery as eels, but morning
had not yet come, and he felt the gentle listing of the boat with a single coordinate in mind: *east.*

But soon after the second dawn, Sanezumi pointed at a line of
chop on the water's surface. The water recoiled, and before Hiroshi
had time to react, it was upon them. The wall of air thrust over the
boat, an avalanche of sky. Their clothes trembled as it passed. The

men shouted, necks tense and strained, but nothing penetrated the ringing deep in their ears. Hiroshi's feet vibrated. His men gestured at the distant blaze blossoming from the horizon. Many had lived through the Toyko firebombings—Masaru's left arm was gnarled with scars—but Hiroshi instead remembered the Philippines. His unit had gotten trapped in its position, and he hunkered down in a trench, face pressed against the mud escarpment. Mortars whizzed overhead; shrapnel fell like ice. The Americans were approaching. He felt their progress, a drumbeat in the earth. Only he and Yoshi and a handful of others were still alive. His comrades had sprung from the trench, guns raised in defiance, and were cut down before they had taken ten steps. Hiroshi should have been with them. In the creaking and moaning of the ship, he sometimes heard the voices of the fallen, calling to him from subterranean depths.

After an hour, the fire had cleared from the sky, but now came the rain of ash. It smelled of electricity. The men watched, mouths agape, awed by flakes the size of flower petals, warm to the touch. It clung where it landed, and when Hiroshi wiped it off, it disintegrated into a glittery sheen. It whispered underfoot. Yoshi flapped his arms, sending forth white plumes, as if he were dancing in a snowstorm. Some men held out plastic bags to catch it as it fell. Hiroshi looked to see from where it had come, but if the sky had once been clear and blue, it was now a peach smear. For a few minutes, the rain was a wonder, a miracle. But ash continued falling for the next three hours. It came down so heavily that the boat seemed mired in fog. The men dared not open their eyes. They left footprints where they walked. The ash gathered on the surface of the water, forming gray masses. The crew retreated inside, waiting for it to stop.

"It's inside me," said Yoshi. "It itches."

Hiroshi exhaled. Residue inside his lungs. He sneezed out pebbles. "You're imagining things," he said.

"I feel it in my chest," Yoshi continued. "Underneath my skin."

That night, the men were too nauseated to eat. In Sanezumi's quarters, Hiroshi rested a hand on his navigator's back. Sanezumi couldn't even keep water down; after each swallow, he retched, and the water rushed out of his mouth and dribbled onto the floor. *You'll be fine,* Hiroshi told him. But in the middle of the night, Sanezumi began vomiting blood.

II.

They spent two weeks at sea, slowly chugging back to Yaizu. Hiroshi radioed that they were returning home, that an unspecified illness had overtaken them, but they could not move any faster. The crew scratched without end. No one slept. They rolled on the ground, unable to ease their burning. They ate as little as they needed to to survive. Kaneda, the cook, served them rice watered down to a milky broth. Even so, nine days after the fall of ash, Sanezumi died. The crew debated whether to preserve his body or put him to rest. It wasn't auspicious to keep a corpse onboard, some argued. But others demanded respect: *If you had died, what would you have us do with your body?* Yoshi insisted on a sea burial. It was Yoshi's tatami mat in which Sanezumi had been rolled, and it was Yoshi's blanket that draped Sanezumi's body down in the cold hull. "He lived at sea and died at sea," Yoshi said. "It's only fitting that the sea take him back." The next morning, they gathered on deck, steadying themselves as the boat bucked and shuddered in the waves. They bowed their heads, and Hiroshi heaved Sanezumi's body over the side. For a short time, he trailed in their wake, but Ryujin seized him, embraced him in foam, and took him to Ryūgū-jō.

The men feared that they would follow Sanezumi into death. But when Hiroshi saw the single character—*kori*—glowing on the horizon, he knew that they were saved. He steered toward the *kori* until he could see the wall of the ice house on which it was painted. The other members of the fishing co-op waited on the dock to gather and unload the catch. Miho was waiting to greet him. Sanezumi's widow was there as well, and when they delivered the news, her wails filled the sky, and the other women crowding around her in a rustle of silk and sympathy could not keep the sound from clutching her throat.

The next day, Hiroshi went to the Shizuoka prefecture doctor, who looked at Hiroshi's body and clucked his tongue inside of his mouth, like a wood-boring beetle. The doctor prodded his skin with a metal rod. Across Hiroshi's chest and legs, roseate patches had spread, the centers peeling off in thick flakes, and underneath, skin the shade of twilight. The doctor shook his head and suggested that he try Tokyo University Hospital. Their appointment was scheduled for a week hence. "In the meantime," he said, "try vigorous bathing."

Miho drew Hiroshi's bath and poured water on his body. He winced as it sluiced over him, washing away the ash and salt in his scalp. But when Yoshi went to the sento to bathe, the boisterous chatter near the main tub stopped when he entered. The tub emptied of people when he stepped in.

"At least my skin has stopped itching," said Yoshi. A small comfort, at best.

At their appointment in Tokyo, he and Yoshi were greeted by a reporter from *Yomiuri Shinbun*. He bowed and introduced himself as Nakamura. He held a slender notebook. Pens were clipped to his shirt pocket. "A student informed me of your condition," he said. "You were near the Rongelap Atoll on March 1, correct?"

"That is correct," Hiroshi said.

"Ah." Nakamura lowered his voice. "We believe that your illness may have been caused by an atomic bomb that the Americans detonated on the Bikini Atoll."

Were they still at war? Hadn't they already been thoroughly humiliated?

"A test," Nakamura continued. "A hundred times more powerful than what had been dropped on Hiroshima." It made sense now: fallout, a black rain that sickened those with whom it came in contact. Yoshi's arms drooped at his sides, as if they were boneless. "If I may," Nakamura continued, "I would like to accompany you during your examination. Your struggle is the nation's struggle."

Hiroshi nodded, as if there were any other answer to give.

III.

Hiroshi no longer recognized his own face. This was not the fault of the photographer—he truly could not recognize himself, not even in a pool of water. His skin had dried and cracked and rehardened into an unfamiliar form. His cheeks were broken into grooves and crevices. The flesh had discolored to the color of algae on the side of a boat. The black-and-white picture could not capture this color, but he saw it on his hands, his legs. He rubbed his finger on the newspaper until his stippled image smeared, and he had merged into shadow.

He horrified Miho—he knew it. She washed her hands constantly. She handled his bowls and utensils as if they were made from lightning. She flinched from him, avoiding even accidental contact. He slept on the ground in front of the door, like a dog. The doctors had said that he wasn't contagious, but what did they know? They hadn't been able to arrest the spread of the illness. Even now it crept down his neck, onto his back. Specialists on radiation sickness from America had flown in. They waved Geiger counters over his body, and the wands crackled like sap-rich pine on fire. The poison was so endemic that it was inseparable from his being.

The government had towed the boat to Tokyo, quarantined where nobody could reach it. It still emitted high doses of deadly, invisible glow. Even so, as captain of the *Lucky Dragon,* Hiroshi's responsibilities now bore down on him more heavily than before. Hardly a day passed without a news agency coming to interview him, flashbulbs popping in his eyes, microphones recording every breath. Every picture promised a new deterioration—*Look what the Americans have done!* But not to him alone: his entire crew. They had all been similarly afflicted, but Hiroshi was the only one who had been photographed.

Nakamura showed him letters from around the world: China, Russia, South Africa, and so, so many from America itself. *You are in our prayers,* they said. *Our heart goes out to you.* Many included money, the stray bills here and there growing into a considerable sum. *Yomiuri Shinbun* had established a fund for the crew, but the money addressed to Hiroshi was his alone. He shared what he could, but this did not stem the tide of resentment. *You should have joined Sanezumi,* he imagined his crew saying, their hearts full of mutiny.

Yoshi remained steadfast: their bond was thicker than blood. They had seen things more horrible than an extra flap of skin growing between their fingers and toes; they had witnessed things more disturbing than the red sores appearing along throats like slashes.

During the escape attempt from the No. 12 Prisoner of War Camp in Cowra, Hiroshi watched his commanding officer, Sugiro, remove a fork from his boot. The tines had been compressed, like fingers inside a tight mitten, and scraped along the concrete floor until they had sharpened to a point. Amidst the machine gun fire, the alarms and claxons, the screaming to run left, right, forward, Sugiro unbuttoned his shirt from the bottom, parting it like he was opening a curtain. On his bare stomach, he pressed the point of the fork into his skin until it dimpled and bled. He dragged the fork down, then to the left, using both hands to keep it steady. Hiroshi bore witness to his bravery, his determination, even as Yoshi hissed at him to hurry, to run. The prisoners-of-war had taken a gun tower. Now was their chance.

Sugiro kept his face inexpressive, his mouth twitching only as the fork caught on something tough, gristly. But Sugiro cut through it and passed into someplace else, a place without walls, barbed wire, sandbags. What did he see when his eyes rolled heavenward? He knelt to one knee before collapsing, his pants cuffs and boot laces blackened with blood. Only after he had fallen did his mouth relax into a smile, a blissful release.

Hiroshi tried to smile now, watching his reflection in his bathwater. Miho had added salt—the only thing that soothed his sores—and the undissolved crystals lay at the bottom of the basin like sand. His lips refused to form the shape his mind commanded. His face was no longer his own.

IV.

Hiroshi had not spoken to his father since after the war, and he had not expected Nakamura to contact him, but the past was beyond his power to change. Nakamura had wanted a quotation, and his father said this: "I have no son. He died during the war. My son would have died rather than allow himself be captured."

Forgiveness would not come in this world, nor the next, but after Nakamura ran the quotation, his shame was exposed for all to see: he was a failed escapee, one of the ignoble. He had returned to Japan with his head hung low, chin attached to his chest. He walked, eyes locked upon the ground, as jeers fell upon him, as if from heaven itself: *Coward. Traitor.*

Then, something further unexpected happened: someone wrote to defend him. Countless others had condemned him: FALSE HERO; A CELEBRATION OF COWARDICE; A SHAME UPON OUR NATION. But the letter supporting him—A VICTIM TWICE-OVER—filled Hiroshi with not so much hope as a fleeting, momentary peace.

"Look at this," Hiroshi said to Yoshi, handing him the newspaper.

Yoshi set it aside without reading. His lips were as thick and rubbery as caterpillars, his skin the color of new moss. "We were cursed even before we went to war," he said. "Our skin matches our souls."

"Nonsense," Hiroshi said—though he sometimes thought the same thing.

Yoshi spread his robe to reveal how the skin on his stomach had separated into scales, each as hard as a turtle's shell. "I wake up each night with my mat in shreds." Yoshi tapped his abdomen. "I bet it could deflect bullets," he said.

"It's still skin," said Hiroshi.

"If we were bulletproof," Yoshi continued, "think of what we could do."

This new Yoshi worried Hiroshi. Yoshi had always been solitary, but now, the village people shook their *omamori* when he approached, and none would look him in the eye. None of his former shipmates, none of the workers at the fishing co-op. He remembered the old Yoshi, whose eyes widened each time they reeled in a catch, wondering aloud how much these fish would garner at Tsukiji Market. The old Yoshi stroked the sides of the tuna, thanking them for providing him a roof over his head and a mat on which to sleep, and when the fish stopped struggling, he licked the brine off his fingers.

The new Yoshi's fingers fumbled with his robe, the rough claws and scales fraying the cotton. He ripped the sash loosening it. He bared his chest, where the scales were as thick as a thumb and cupped the area above his heart. From his pocket, he produced his old service revolver.

"Shoot me," he said.

"Don't be foolish."

"It's a test. If the bullet bounces off, then this is a blessing. If I die, then you will have simply hurried me to my next life."

"I will not."

Yoshi dropped the gun to the floor. "I am unworthy of your friendship," he said, contrite. "Your loyalty."

Hiroshi placed a scaly hand on Yoshi's shoulder. He remembered their escape attempt from the POW Camp. Hiroshi covered the barbed wire with his blanket and flung himself over it. They clambered over the wall surrounding the prison, where Hiroshi found a dead Australian guard at his feet. He'd been bludgeoned, his forehead collapsed. The other prisoners spread out, and floodlights scoured the surroundings, picking out shadows fleeing into the nearby farmland. The prisoners had shed their maroon caps, which were scattered on the ground like pools of blood. The guard couldn't have been older than eighteen. Another boy pulled into war. Hiroshi felt at the guard's waist until he found his gun.

Yoshi ran ahead blindly, flailing his arms, deeper into the darkness. Searchlights arced above their heads. Yoshi's movements were panicked, like a small animal caught in a snare. Hiroshi caught a glimpse of Yoshi's arm, his neck. Yoshi stumbled and fell, and Hiroshi aimed the gun at where Yoshi scrabbled in the dirt. A quick and honorable death. He could kill Yoshi and then kill himself, and when their bodies were returned to Japan, his father would wet his lips with water and cover the family shrine with long sails of white paper. His mother would hold the *juzu* in her hands, repeating a sutra for each bead, before offering incense to him, once, twice, three times. Yoshi would never even know that the bullet had come from him.

Hiroshi, Yoshi whispered, *where are you? Don't leave me alone.*

Close behind them, the prison guards called to each other. No matter where they ran, Hiroshi knew that their recapture was imminent. If they were captured with the dead guard's gun, they would be executed on the spot. Why was one death better than another? What was honorable about smashing in the skull of an Australian boy who was still too young, perhaps, to know pleasure? Had he died for his country so that they could honor their own? Hiroshi clasped both hands around the gun and flung it as far into the distance as he could.

I'm here, Hiroshi responded. *Keep going. I'm right behind you.*

V.

Masaru took a job in an American sideshow. THE HORRORS OF ATOMIC WAR. The poster showed him surrounded by oval cameos: midgets, bearded ladies, legless men. He made a good wage, the villagers said, and he sent back money to his wife, who moved up in the village's esteem. Miho overheard this at market, where she was overcharged for even rice, flour, and salt.

Nakamura had invited Hiroshi to appear on television, but he demurred and referred Nakamura to other crew members. They were men untouched by cowardice, and public opinion of them had swayed from disgust to pity, and now, to sympathy. It was possible that people thought differently of him too. Perhaps they were willing to forgive his conduct in the war. Strange: when he was a man, he had been a monster; now that he was a monster, he was once again a man.

Hiroshi's hair had fallen out, and the top of his head was hard and smooth as a helmet. Deep creases scalloped the length of his forehead, a permanent ridge of worry. Scales ringed his body like ruffles of armor.

Yoshi laughed at the news of Masaru. "You know," Yoshi said, "that his wife used to never touch his burned arm? Now she lives high off his deformity."

"We've had offers too," Hiroshi said. "They will fly us to America."

"Haven't the Americans done enough?" Yoshi said. He raised his arms, as if surrendering. "You know what people call us? They say we are *ningyo*. Mermaids! Already some of the villagers think that if they eat our flesh, they will live forever." He rapped his knuckles against the carapace on his chest. "Maybe they will break their teeth on me."

"*Ningyo* are omens," Hiroshi said. "To catch one is to invite misfortune."

"It's too late to throw us back," Yoshi said. He lifted a scale on his arm. The flesh underneath was gray and bumpy, like lizard skin. "What do you think I taste like? There's enough of me to feed the village for a week."

"You? You're as stringy as week-old beef. And if you taste the way you smell, no one would be able to stomach you."

"We could be a boon to this village," Yoshi said. "Remember the story of *Happyaku Bikuni*? One bite of me and everyone would have eternal life. They would hail us as heroes." Yoshi flexed his hands, the webbing as translucent as kelp. "Or maybe our flesh will poison the village folk, and they will know what our pain is like."

"Why do you say these things?" Hiroshi said. "Why can you not be at peace?"

"Look at us," Yoshi said. "Better to have died in Cowra all those years ago than to live like this today." He exhaled—a wheeze, a gasp. "You should have shot me," Yoshi said. "You should have pulled the trigger."

VI.

Yoshi hanged himself. Hiroshi found him—maybe Yoshi had meant for Hiroshi alone to serve as witness to his bravery, but the truth was that no one ever visited him. He had fastened one end of his obi to the pine beam bracing the ceiling and looped the other end beneath the scales on his neck, where the skin was still soft. A green forked tongue lolled out of his mouth, and his eyes were yellow, glassy, streaked with red.

Hiroshi did not cry out when he saw Yoshi's body dangling there, nor did he cry as he tried to cut his friend down. But his webbed hand could not hold a knife; his fingers were too stiff and clumsy. He slashed at the cloth with his talons until it frayed and snapped. Yoshi's body crashed onto the ground, and Hiroshi cradled his friend, scales scratching against scales. Hiroshi's eyelids had atrophied, but his nictitating membrane flicked ceaselessly to keep his eyes moist.

Soon, people gathered outside Yoshi's door, looking in, hiding their words behind their hands. The crowd grew as news spread, and it seemed as if the whole village were looking in. Hiroshi didn't move. Let them look. They had wished us dead—let them look at the result. He no longer had ears, but he heard them whispering, *If it's dead, we should have the body.* He heard Miho gasp. *How could you say that,* she said. *That's his friend. That's Yoshi.*

Monster's whore, they replied.

Enough. Hiroshi lifted Yoshi's body and walked outside. The villagers trailed him, holding aloft torches. Miho was among them. He smelled the detergent she used to purify herself. Here they were: a procession of monsters.

The villagers shouted, *Give us his body. Give him to us.*

If you want him, Hiroshi said, come take him from me. He gouged a nearby tree with his claws, and none of the villagers dared pass the patch of splinters he had made.

Hiroshi did not know if Yoshi's body would burn, as leathery and resilient as it was. And it would be impossible to bury his body in secret. What if it tainted the land where it lay? Hiroshi walked to the beach with Yoshi in his arms. Miho stopped at the sand. She placed his sandals at the start of the path back to the village, as she used to do when he went swimming. *The water is too cold for me,* she used to say. *But you go on.*

Hiroshi stood at the ocean's edge, the water sluicing onto his feet. He thought once again of Sugiro, the commander who had committed hara-kiri. Perhaps it had been the brave thing, the honorable thing. But Hiroshi had seen a new world blossom, a world born of light and fire, and this world no longer had a place for the proud, the defeated, the disgraced. The old world held onto its illusion of bravery, like the cowardly men up on the hill brandishing their torches, as if they had driven him toward the sea themselves. But all Hiroshi had to do was turn and open his mouth—his square teeth had fallen out weeks ago, replaced with triangular shards—and the men ran off like curs.

He no longer felt the cold. Even waist-deep in water, he felt no unease. Indeed, it seemed comforting. The tide pulled at his body, urging him forward. Yoshi's body was buoyant, and the sea lifted him out of Hiroshi's arms. But there could not be even the remote possibility of Yoshi floating back onto land. A *ningyo* washing up on shore was an omen of war, and they had both seen their fill of calamity. Hiroshi ventured further, deeper, until the light from the stars vanished.

He sensed the thrumming of fish around him: the mackerel low on the ocean floor, a squid curling its tentacles around an unlucky clam, and a school of tuna bustling about, mouths open and hungry. He breathed and exhaled through the slits in his neck. He propelled himself, undulating his torso, and as his eyes adjusted to the darkness, vast forests of seaweed unfurled before him. Fish darted out of his path. He released Yoshi's body. He swam forth, examining the endlessness of the new world, and Yoshi followed in the pattern Hiroshi cut through the water, almost as if he were himself swimming. *Yoshi*, Hiroshi wanted to call out, *where are you? Don't leave me alone.* And Yoshi, now given to the ebb and flow of currents, replied, *Keep going. I'm right behind you.*

■

Homegoing, AD

FROM *The Fire This Time*

HERE'S THE DOWN SOUTH story we didn't tell you: sixteen hours in and Jack can't feel her feet but we never stop. Our uncle asleep at the wheel and we that closer to death with each mile. Turned around again and again, before GPS, we learned North Carolina is a long state: tobacco taller than us, the fields and fields of it, no washing it out of our clothes, the air so wet and thick of it, choking us.

Jack won't fly. Full grown with a dead granddaddy and still she won't fly, she tells us I-95 has always been the way back home so we gun it. Straight through, no stopping, sixteen hours and Jack doesn't care how bad we need to pee, she says, *Hold it.* Sixteen hours till we saw the palmetto trees and smelled the paper mill and knew Savage Road was in sight.

Georgie 'n' em got Grandaddy laid out in the front room like a piece of furniture and ushers fanning the top of Grandmama's head. We couldn't find our place in the business of departing: hams out the oven, lemon cake iced, organ tuned, tea made, napkins folded, the children's black patent leather shoes set out for the dirt road come morning.

Here's the down south story we didn't tell you: Leroy barking at us from the grill because when did everybody stop eating pork and why he got separate meat and when all the women become Nefertiti bangles and headwraps and all us named like Muslims. Our cousins who couldn't make it because he died on the wrong Friday, wadn't payday, and our cousins who did and their many children tearing up the front yard. Our decision to sneak into the woods with red cups,

black and milds, Jim Beam, a blue lighter plucked from the card table, and Toya's gold cap kept in her change purse. The pot of greens
we brought out with us and the mosquitoes keeping company like we
wasn't down in the swamps to bury our dead.

Our cousins know the dark and the heat, but we haven't been
home in so long. Our back sweating and this old bra sticky so more
and more from the red cup. Our cousin say, *Lemme top it off for youse,*
so we oblige and when he said pull, we pulled and when he said blow,
we blew smoke over our shoulder and then into his open mouth, gig-
gling. Our cousin say, *You know they found him in the bed, right?* And
we nod cuz sleep don't come easy no how. He say, *Just like that.* And
our cousin clap when he say *that* and we think of Grandaddy setting
his glasses down on the nightstand one last time. Our cousin say, *You
missed me?* And we smile cuz his hand is on our hip and it's hot out
and he smell good and it's the darkest Charleston has ever been. The
dead of night is forgiving when you're kin. Grandaddy gone and we
sitting up in the woods with brown liquor, necking, our cousin hard
on our thigh. Toya say, *Keep watch for them copperheads,* but copperheads ain't never kill nobody—we got our eyes trained for gators.

We think we can still outrun 'em.

Who threw that rock at the gator?

                                    Don't know   *Where Toya?*

Ya'll there?

                                                              We here.

                          Gator comin, boy, run

    Don't see no gator, cuh   *Well, Gator see us, nigga*

*Runnnnnnnnnnnnnnnnnnnnnnnnnnnnnnnnnnnnnnnnnnnnnnnnnnnnnnnnn
nnnnnnnnnnnnnnnnnnnn*

                so we run
                                    fast

cuz gator made for water   but children born for land.

MASHA GESSEN

■

Autocracy: Rules for Survival

FROM *The New York Review of Books*

"THANK YOU, MY FRIENDS. Thank you. Thank you. We have lost.
We have lost, and this is the last day of my political career, so I will
say what must be said. We are standing at the edge of the abyss. Our
political system, our society, our country itself are in greater danger
than at any time in the last century and a half. The president-elect
has made his intentions clear, and it would be immoral to pretend
otherwise. We must band together right now to defend the laws, the
institutions, and the ideals on which our country is based."

That, or something like that, is what Hillary Clinton should have
said on Wednesday. Instead, she said, resignedly,

> We must accept this result and then look to the future. Donald
> Trump is going to be our president. We owe him an open mind
> and the chance to lead. Our constitutional democracy enshrines the
> peaceful transfer of power. We don't just respect that. We cherish it.
> It also enshrines the rule of law; the principle [that] we are all equal
> in rights and dignity; freedom of worship and expression. We respect
> and cherish these values, too, and we must defend them.

Hours later, President Barack Obama was even more conciliatory:

> We are now all rooting for his success in uniting and leading the
> country. The peaceful transition of power is one of the hallmarks of
> our democracy. And over the next few months, we are going to show
> that to the world . . . We have to remember that we're actually all on
> one team.

The president added, "The point, though, is that we all go forward with a presumption of good faith in our fellow citizens, because

that presumption of good faith is essential to a vibrant and functioning democracy." As if Donald Trump had not conned his way into hours of free press coverage, as though he had released (and paid) his taxes, or not brazenly denigrated our system of government, from the courts and Congress, to the election process itself—as if, in other words, he had not won the election precisely *by* acting in bad faith.

Similar refrains were heard from various members of the liberal commentariat, with Tom Friedman vowing, "I am not going to try to make my president fail," to Nick Kristof calling on "the approximately 52 percent majority of voters who supported someone other than Donald Trump" to "give President Trump a chance." Even the politicians who have in the past appealed to the less-establishment part of the Democratic electorate sounded the conciliatory note. Senator Elizabeth Warren promised to "put aside our differences." Senator Bernie Sanders was only slightly more cautious, vowing to try to find the good in Trump: "To the degree that Mr. Trump is serious about pursuing policies that improve the lives of working families in this country, I and other progressives are prepared to work with him."

However well-intentioned, this talk assumes that Trump is prepared to find common ground with his many opponents, respect the institutions of government, and repudiate almost everything he has stood for during the campaign. In short, it is treating him as a "normal" politician. There has until now been little evidence that he can be one.

More dangerously, Clinton's and Obama's very civil passages, which ended in applause lines, seemed to close off alternative responses to his minority victory. (It was hard not to be reminded of Neville Chamberlain's statement, that "We should seek by all means in our power to avoid war, by analyzing possible causes, by trying to remove them, by discussion in a spirit of collaboration and good will.") Both Clinton's and Obama's phrases about the peaceful transfer of power concealed the omission of a call to action. The protesters who took to the streets of New York, Los Angeles, and other American cities on Wednesday night did so not because of Clinton's speech but in spite of it. One of the falsehoods in the Clinton speech was the implied equivalency between civil resistance and insurgency. This is an autocrat's favorite con, the explanation for the violent suppression of peaceful protests the world over.

The second falsehood is the pretense that America is starting from scratch and its president-elect is a tabula rasa. Or we are: "we owe him an open mind." It was as though Donald Trump had not, in the course of his campaign, promised to deport U.S. citizens, promised to create a system of surveillance targeted specifically at Muslim Americans, promised to build a wall on the border with Mexico, advocated war crimes, endorsed torture, and repeatedly threatened to jail Hillary Clinton herself. It was as though those statements and many more could be written off as so much campaign hyperbole and now that the campaign was over, Trump would be eager to become a regular, rule-abiding politician of the pre-Trump era.

But Trump is anything but a regular politician and this has been anything but a regular election. Trump will be only the fourth candidate in history and the second in more than a century to win the presidency after losing the popular vote. He is also probably the first candidate in history to win the presidency despite having been shown repeatedly by the national media to be a chronic liar, sexual predator, serial tax-avoider, and race-baiter who has attracted the likes of the Ku Klux Klan. Most important, Trump is the first candidate in memory who ran not for president but for autocrat—and won.

I have lived in autocracies most of my life, and have spent much of my career writing about Vladimir Putin's Russia. I have learned a few rules for surviving in an autocracy and salvaging your sanity and self-respect. It might be worth considering them now:

Rule #1: *Believe the autocrat.* He means what he says. Whenever you find yourself thinking, or hear others claiming, that he is exaggerating, that is our innate tendency to reach for a rationalization. This will happen often: humans seem to have evolved to practice denial when confronted publicly with the unacceptable. Back in the 1930s, the *New York Times* assured its readers that Hitler's anti-Semitism was all posture. More recently, the same newspaper made a telling choice between two statements made by Putin's press secretary Dmitry Peskov following a police crackdown on protesters in Moscow: "The police acted mildly—I would have liked them to act more harshly" rather than those protesters' "liver should have been spread all over the pavement." Perhaps the journalists could not believe their ears. But they should—both in the Russian case, and in the American one. For all the admiration Trump has expressed for Putin, the two men are very different; if anything, there is even more reason to listen to everything Trump has said. He has no political establishment into which to fold himself following the campaign, and therefore no reason to shed his campaign rhetoric. On the contrary: it is now the establishment that is rushing to accommodate him—from the president, who met with him at the White House on Thursday, to the leaders of the Republican Party, who are discarding their long-held scruples to embrace his radical positions.

He has received the support he needed to win, and the adulation he craves, precisely because of his outrageous threats. Trump rally crowds have chanted "Lock her up!" They, and he, meant every word. If Trump does not go after Hillary Clinton on his first day in office, if he instead focuses, as his acceptance speech indicated he might, on the unifying project of investing in infrastructure (which, not coincidentally, would provide an instant opportunity to reward his cronies and himself), it will be foolish to breathe a sigh of relief. Trump has made his plans clear, and he has made a compact with his voters to carry them out. These plans include not only dismantling legislation such as Obamacare but also doing away with judicial restraint—and, yes, punishing opponents.

To begin jailing his political opponents, or just one opponent, Trump will begin by trying to capture members of the judicial system. Observers and even activists functioning in the normal-election mode are fixated on the Supreme Court as the site of the highest-risk impending Trump appointment. There is little doubt that Trump will appoint someone who will cause the Court to veer to the right; there is also the risk that it might be someone who will wreak havoc with the very culture of the high court. And since Trump plans to use the judicial system to carry out his political vendettas, his pick for attorney general will be no less important. Imagine former New York Mayor Rudy Giuliani or New Jersey Governor Chris Christie going after Hillary Clinton on orders from President Trump; quite aside from their approach to issues such as the Geneva Conventions, the use of police powers, criminal justice reforms, and other urgent concerns.

Rule #2: *Do not be taken in by small signs of normality.* Consider the financial markets this week, which, having tanked overnight, rebounded following the Clinton and Obama speeches. Confronted with political volatility, the markets become suckers for calming rhetoric from authority figures. So do people. Panic can be neutralized by falsely reassuring words about how the world as we know it has not ended. It is a fact that the world did not end on November 8 nor at any previous time in history. Yet history has seen many catastrophes, and most of them unfolded over time. That time included periods of relative calm. One of my favorite thinkers, the Jewish historian Simon Dubnow, breathed a sigh of relief in early October 1939: he had moved from Berlin to Latvia, and he wrote to his friends that he was certain that the tiny country wedged between two tyrannies would retain its sovereignty and Dubnow himself would be safe. Shortly after that, Latvia was occupied by the Soviets, then by the Germans, then by the Soviets again—but by that time Dubnow had been killed. Dubnow was well aware that he was living through a catastrophic period in history—it's just that he thought he had managed to find a pocket of normality within it.

Rule #3: *Institutions will not save you.* It took Putin a year to take over the Russian media and four years to dismantle its electoral system; the judiciary collapsed unnoticed. The capture of institutions in Turkey has been carried out even faster, by a man once celebrated as the democrat to lead Turkey into the EU. Poland has in less than a year undone half of a quarter-century's accomplishments in building a constitutional democracy.

Of course, the United States has much stronger institutions than Germany did in the 1930s, or Russia does today. Both Clinton and Obama in their speeches stressed the importance and strength of these institutions. The problem, however, is that many of these institutions are enshrined in political culture rather than in law, and all of them—including the ones enshrined in law—depend on the good faith of all actors to fulfill their purpose and uphold the Constitution.

The national press is likely to be among the first institutional victims of Trumpism. There is no law that requires the presidential administration to hold daily briefings, none that guarantees media access to the White House. Many journalists may soon face a dilemma long familiar to those of us who have worked under autocracies: fall in line or forfeit access. There is no good solution (even if there is a right answer), for journalism is difficult and sometimes impossible without access to information.

The power of the investigative press—whose adherence to fact has already been severely challenged by the conspiracy-minded, lie-spinning Trump campaign—will grow weaker. The world will grow murkier. Even in the unlikely event that some mainstream media outlets decide to declare themselves in opposition to the current government, or even simply to report its abuses and failings, the president will get to frame many issues. Coverage, and thinking, will drift in a Trumpian direction, just as it did during the campaign—when, for example, the candidates argued, in essence, whether Muslim Americans bear collective responsibility for acts of terrorism or can redeem themselves by becoming the "eyes and ears" of law enforcement. Thus was xenophobia further normalized, paving the way for Trump to make good on his promises to track American Muslims and ban Muslims from entering the United States.

Rule #4: *Be outraged.* If you follow Rule #1 and believe what the autocrat-elect is saying, you will not be surprised. But in the face of the impulse to normalize, it is essential to maintain one's capacity for shock. This will lead people to call you unreasonable and hysterical, and to accuse you of overreacting. It is no fun to be the only hysterical person in the room. Prepare yourself.

Despite losing the popular vote, Trump has secured as much power as any American leader in recent history. The Republican Party controls both houses of Congress. There is a vacancy on the Supreme Court. The country is at war abroad and has been in a state of mobilization for fifteen years. This means not only that Trump will be able to move fast but also that he will become accustomed to an unusually high level of political support. He will want to maintain and increase it—his ideal is the totalitarian-level popularity numbers of Vladimir Putin—and the way to achieve that is through mobilization. There will be more wars, abroad and at home.

Rule #5: *Don't make compromises.* Like Ted Cruz, who made the journey from calling Trump "utterly amoral" and a "pathological liar" to endorsing him in late September to praising his win as an "amazing victory for the American worker," Republican politicians have fallen into line. Conservative pundits who broke ranks during the campaign will return to the fold. Democrats in Congress will begin to make the case for cooperation, for the sake of getting anything done—or at least, they will say, minimizing the damage. Nongovernmental organizations, many of which are reeling at the moment, faced with a transition period in which there is no opening for their input, will grasp at chances to work with the new administration. This will be fruitless—damage cannot be minimized, much less reversed, when mobilization is the goal—but worse, it will be soul-destroying. In an autocracy, politics as the art of the possible is in fact utterly amoral. Those who argue for cooperation will make the case, much as President Obama did in his speech, that cooperation is essential for the future. They will be willfully ignoring the corrupting touch of autocracy, from which the future must be protected.

Rule #6: *Remember the future.* Nothing lasts forever. Donald Trump certainly will not, and Trumpism, to the extent that it is centered on Trump's persona, will not either. Failure to imagine the future may have lost the Democrats this election. They offered no vision of the future to counterbalance Trump's all-too-familiar white-populist vision of an imaginary past. They had also long ignored the strange and outdated institutions of American democracy that call out for reform—like the electoral college, which has now cost the Democratic Party two elections in which Republicans won with the minority of the popular vote. That should not be normal. But resistance—stubborn, uncompromising, outraged—should be.

TA-NEHISI COATES

■

My President Was Black

FROM *The Atlantic*

"They're a rotten crowd," I shouted across the lawn. "You're worth the
whole damn bunch put together."
— F. Scott Fitzgerald, *The Great Gatsby*

I. "Love Will Make You Do Wrong"

In the waning days of President Barack Obama's administration,
he and his wife, Michelle, hosted a farewell party, the full import of
which no one could then grasp. It was late October, Friday the 21, and
the president had spent many of the previous weeks, as he would
spend the two subsequent weeks, campaigning for the Democratic
presidential nominee, Hillary Clinton. Things were looking up. Polls
in the crucial states of Virginia and Pennsylvania showed Clinton
with solid advantages. The formidable GOP strongholds of Georgia and Texas were said to be under threat. The moment seemed to
buoy Obama. He had been light on his feet in these last few weeks,
cracking jokes at the expense of Republican opponents and laughing off hecklers. At a rally in Orlando on October 28, he greeted a
student who would be introducing him by dancing toward her and
then noting that the song playing over the loudspeakers—the Gap
Band's "Outstanding"—was older than she was. "This is classic!" he
said. Then he flashed the smile that had launched America's first
black presidency, and started dancing again. Three months still remained before Inauguration Day, but staffers had already begun to

count down the days. They did this with a mix of pride and longing—like college seniors in early May. They had no sense of the world they were graduating into. None of us did.

The farewell party, presented by BET (Black Entertainment Television), was the last in a series of concerts the first couple had hosted at the White House. Guests were asked to arrive at 5:30 p.m. By 6, two long lines stretched behind the Treasury Building, where the Secret Service was checking names. The people in these lines were, in the main, black, and their humor reflected it. The brisker queue was dubbed the "good-hair line" by one guest, and there was laughter at the prospect of the Secret Service subjecting us all to a "brown-paper-bag test." This did not come to pass, but security was tight. Several guests were told to stand in a makeshift pen and wait to have their backgrounds checked a second time.

Dave Chappelle was there. He coolly explained the peril and promise of comedy in what was then still only a remotely potential Donald Trump presidency: "I mean, we never had a guy have his own pussygate scandal." Everyone laughed. A few weeks later, he would be roundly criticized for telling a crowd at the Cutting Room, in New York, that he had voted for Clinton but did not feel good about it. "She's going to be on a coin someday," Chappelle said. "And her behavior has not been coinworthy." But on this crisp October night, everything felt inevitable and grand. There was a slight wind. It had been in the eighties for much of that week. Now, as the sun set, the season remembered its name. Women shivered in their cocktail dresses. Gentlemen chivalrously handed over their suit coats. But when Naomi Campbell strolled past the security pen in a sleeveless number, she seemed as invulnerable as ever.

Cellphones were confiscated to prevent surreptitious recordings from leaking out. (This effort was unsuccessful. The next day, a partygoer would tweet a video of the leader of the free world dancing to Drake's "Hotline Bling.") After withstanding the barrage of security, guests were welcomed into the East Wing of the White House, and then ushered back out into the night, where they boarded a succession of orange-and-green trolleys. The singer and actress Janelle Monáe, her famous and fantastic pompadour preceding her, stepped onboard and joked with a companion about the historical import of "sitting in the back of the bus." She took a seat three rows from the front and hummed into the night. The trolley dropped the guests on the South Lawn, in front of a giant tent. The South Lawn's fountain was lit up with blue lights. The White House proper loomed like a ghost in the distance. I heard the band, inside, beginning to play Al Green's "Let's Stay Together."

"Well, you can tell what type of night this is," Obama said from the stage, opening the event. "Not the usual ruffles and flourishes!"

The crowd roared.

"This must be a BET event!"

The crowd roared louder still.

Obama placed the concert in the White House's musical tradition, noting that guests of the Kennedys had once done the twist at the residence—"the twerking of their time," he said, before adding, "There will be no twerking tonight. At least not by me."

The Obamas are fervent and eclectic music fans. In the past eight years, they have hosted performances at the White House by everyone from Mavis Staples to Bob Dylan to Tony Bennett to the Blind Boys of Alabama. After the rapper Common was invited to perform in 2011, a small fracas ensued in the right-wing media. He performed anyway—and was invited back again this glorious fall evening and almost stole the show. The crowd sang along to the hook for his hit ballad "The Light." And when he brought on the gospel singer Yolanda Adams to fill in for John Legend on the Oscar-winning song "Glory," glee turned to rapture.

De La Soul was there. The hip-hop trio had come of age as boyish B-boys with Gumby-style high-top fades. Now they moved across the stage with a lovely mix of lethargy and grace, like your favorite uncle making his way down the *Soul Train* line, wary of throwing out a hip. I felt a sense of victory watching them rock the crowd, all while keeping it in the pocket. The victory belonged to hip-hop—an art form birthed in the burning Bronx and now standing full grown, at the White House, unbroken and unedited. Usher led the crowd in a call-and-response: "Say it loud, I'm black and I'm proud." Jill Scott showed off her operatic chops. Bell Biv DeVoe, contemporaries of De

La, made history with their performance by surely becoming the first group to suggest to a presidential audience that one should "never trust a big butt and a smile."

The ties between the Obama White House and the hip-hop community are genuine. The Obamas are social with Beyoncé and Jay-Z. They hosted Chance the Rapper and Frank Ocean at a state dinner, and last year invited Swizz Beatz, Busta Rhymes, and Ludacris, among others, to discuss criminal-justice reform and other initiatives. Obama once stood in the Rose Garden passing large flash cards to the *Hamilton* creator and rapper Lin-Manuel Miranda, who then freestyled using each word on the cards. "Drop the beat," Obama said, inaugurating the session. At fifty-five, Obama is younger than pioneering hip-hop artists like Afrika Bambaataa, DJ Kool Herc, and Kurtis Blow. If Obama's enormous symbolic power draws primarily from being the country's first black president, it also draws from his membership in hip-hop's foundational generation.

That night, the men were sharp in their gray or black suits and optional ties. Those who were not in suits had chosen to make a statement, like the dark-skinned young man who strolled in, sockless, with blue jeans cuffed so as to accentuate his gorgeous black-suede loafers. Everything in his ensemble seemed to say, "My fellow Americans, do not try this at home." There were women in fur jackets and high heels; others with sculpted naturals, the sides shaved close, the tops blooming into curls; others still in gold bamboo earrings and long blond dreads. When the actor Jesse Williams took the stage, seemingly awed before such black excellence, before such black opulence, assembled just feet from where slaves had once toiled, he simply said, "Look where we are. Look where we are right now."

This would not happen again, and everyone knew it. It was not just that there might never be another African American president of the United States. It was the feeling that this particular black family, the Obamas, represented the best of black people, the ultimate credit to the race, incomparable in elegance and bearing. "There are no more," the comedian Sinbad joked back in 2010. "There are no black men raised in Kansas and Hawaii. That's the last one. Y'all better treat this one right. The next one gonna be from Cleveland. He gonna wear a perm. Then you gonna see what it's really like."

Throughout their residency, the Obamas had refrained from show-ing America "what it's really like," and had instead followed the first lady's motto, "When they go low, we go high." This was the ideal—black and graceful under fire—saluted that evening. The president was lionized as "our crown jewel." The first lady was praised as the woman "who put the O in Obama."

Barack Obama's victories in 2008 and 2012 were dismissed by some of his critics as merely symbolic for African Americans. But there is nothing "mere" about symbols. The power embedded in the word *nigger* is also symbolic. Burning crosses do not literally raise the black poverty rate, and the Confederate flag does not directly expand the wealth gap.

Much as the unbroken ranks of forty-three white male presidents communicated that the highest office of government in the country—indeed, the most powerful political offices in the world—was off-lim-its to black individuals, the election of Barack Obama communicated that the prohibition had been lifted. It communicated much more. Before Obama triumphed in 2008, the most-famous depictions of black success tended to be entertainers or athletes. But Obama had shown that it was "possible to be smart and cool at the same damn time," as Jesse Williams put it at the BET party. Moreover, he had not embarrassed his people with a string of scandals. Against the specter of black pathology, against the narrow images of welfare moms and deadbeat dads, his time in the White House had been an eight-year showcase of a healthy and successful black family spanning three generations, with two dogs to boot. In short, he became a symbol of black people's everyday, extraordinary Americanness.

Whiteness in America is a different symbol—a badge of advantage. In a country of professed meritocratic competition, this badge has long ensured an unerring privilege, represented in a 220-year mo-nopoly on the highest office in the land. For some not-insubstantial sector of the country, the elevation of Barack Obama communicated that the power of the badge had diminished. For eight long years, the badge-holders watched him. They saw footage of the president throw-ing bounce passes and shooting jumpers. They saw him enter a locker room, give a businesslike handshake to a white staffer, and then greet Kevin Durant with something more soulful. They saw his wife dancing with Jimmy Fallon and posing, resplendent, on the covers of magazines that had, only a decade earlier, been almost exclusively, if unofficially, reserved for ladies imbued with the great power of the badge.

For the preservation of the badge, insidious rumors were concocted to denigrate the first black White House. Obama gave free cellphones to disheveled welfare recipients. Obama went to Europe and complained that "ordinary men and women are too small-minded to govern their own affairs." Obama had inscribed an Arabic saying on his wedding ring, then stopped wearing the ring, in observance of Ramadan. He canceled the National Day of Prayer; refused to sign certificates for Eagle Scouts; faked his attendance at Columbia University; and used a teleprompter to address a group of elementary-school students. The badge-holders fumed. They wanted their country back. And, though no one at the farewell party knew it, in a couple of weeks they would have it.

On this October night, though, the stage belonged to another America. At the end of the party, Obama looked out into the crowd, searching for Dave Chappelle. "Where's Dave?" he cried. And then, finding him, the president referenced Chappelle's legendary Brooklyn concert. "You got your block party. I got my block party." Then the band struck up Al Green's "Love and Happiness"—the evening's theme. The president danced in a line next to Ronnie DeVoe. Together they mouthed the lyrics: "Make you do right. Love will make you do wrong."

II. He Walked On Ice But Never Fell

Last spring, I went to the White House to meet the president for lunch. I arrived slightly early and sat in the waiting area. I was introduced to a deaf woman who worked as the president's receptionist, a black woman who worked in the press office, a Muslim woman in a head scarf who worked on the National Security Council, and an Iranian American woman who worked as a personal aide to the president. This receiving party represented a healthy cross section of the people Donald Trump had been mocking, and would continue to spend his campaign mocking. At the time, the president seemed un-

troubled by Trump. When I told Obama that I thought Trump's candidacy was an explicit reaction to the fact of a black president, he said
he could see that, but then enumerated other explanations. When assessing Trump's chances, he was direct: He couldn't win.

This assessment was born out of the president's innate optimism and unwavering faith in the ultimate wisdom of the American
people—the same traits that had propelled his unlikely five-year as-
cent from assemblyman in the Illinois state legislature to U.S. senator to leader of the free world. The speech that launched his rise,
the keynote address at the 2004 Democratic National Convention,
emerged right from this logic. He addressed himself to his "fellow
Americans, Democrats, Republicans, independents," all of whom, he
insisted, were more united than they had been led to believe. America was home to devout worshippers and Little League coaches in
blue states, civil libertarians and "gay friends" in red states. The presumably white "counties around Chicago" did not want their taxes
burned on welfare, but they didn't want them wasted on a bloated
Pentagon budget either. Inner-city black families, no matter their
perils, understood "that government alone can't teach our kids to
learn . . . that children can't achieve unless we raise their expectations and turn off the television sets and eradicate the slander that
says a black youth with a book is acting white."

Perceived differences were the work of "spinmasters and negative-
ad peddlers who embrace the politics of 'anything goes.'" Real America had no use for such categorizations. By Obama's lights, there
was no liberal America, no conservative America, no black America,
no white America, no Latino America, no Asian America, only "the
United States of America." All these disparate strands of the American experience were bound together by a common hope:

> It's the hope of slaves sitting around a fire singing freedom songs;
> the hope of immigrants setting out for distant shores; the hope of
> a young naval lieutenant bravely patrolling the Mekong Delta; the
> hope of a mill worker's son who dares to defy the odds; the hope of a
> skinny kid with a funny name who believes that America has a place
> for him, too.

This speech ran counter to the history of the people it sought to address. Some of those same immigrants had firebombed the homes

of the children of those same slaves. That young naval lieutenant was an imperial agent for a failed, immoral war. American division was real. In 2004, John Kerry did not win a single southern state. But Obama appealed to a belief in innocence—in particular a white innocence—that ascribed the country's historical errors more to misunderstanding and the work of a small cabal than to any deliberate malevolence or widespread racism. America was good. America was great.

Over the next twelve years, I came to regard Obama as a skilled politician, a deeply moral human being, and one of the greatest presidents in American history. He was phenomenal—the most agile interpreter and navigator of the color line I had ever seen. He had an ability to emote a deep and sincere connection to the hearts of black people, while never doubting the hearts of white people. This was the core of his 2004 keynote, and it marked his historic race speech during the 2008 campaign at Philadelphia's National Constitution Center—and blinded him to the appeal of Trump. ("As a general proposition, it's hard to run for president by telling people how terrible things are," Obama once said to me.)

But if the president's inability to cement his legacy in the form of Hillary Clinton proved the limits of his optimism, it also revealed the exceptional nature of his presidential victories. For eight years Barack Obama walked on ice and never fell. Nothing in that time suggested that straight talk on the facts of racism in American life would have given him surer footing.

I had met the president a few times before. In his second term, I'd written articles criticizing him for his overriding trust in color-blind policy and his embrace of "personal responsibility" rhetoric when speaking to African Americans. I saw him as playing both sides. He would invoke his identity as a president of all people to decline to advocate for black policy—and then invoke his black identity to lecture black people for continuing to "make bad choices." In response, Obama had invited me, along with other journalists, to the White House for off-the-record conversations. I attempted to press my points in these sessions. My efforts were laughable and ineffective. I was always inappropriately dressed, and inappropriately calibrated in tone: In one instance, I was too deferential; in another, too bellicose. I was discombobulated by fear—not by fear of the power of his office (though that is a fearsome and impressive thing) but by fear of his obvious brilliance. It is said that Obama speaks "professorially," a fact that understates the quickness and agility of his mind. These were not like press conferences—the president would speak in depth and with great familiarity about a range of subjects. Once, I watched him effortlessly reply to queries covering everything from electoral politics to the American economy to environmental policy. And then he turned to me. I thought of George Foreman, who once booked an exhibition with multiple opponents in which he pounded five straight journeymen—and I suddenly had some idea of how it felt to be the last of them.

Last spring, we had a light lunch. We talked casually and candidly. He talked about the brilliance of LeBron James and Stephen Curry—not as basketball talents but as grounded individuals. I asked him whether he was angry at his father, who had abandoned him at a young age to move back to Kenya, and whether that motivated any of his rhetoric. He said it did not, and he credited the attitude of his mother and grandparents for this. Then it was my turn to be autobiographical. I told him that I had heard the kind of "straighten up" talk he had been giving to black youth, for instance in his 2013 Morehouse commencement address, all my life. I told him that I thought it was not sensitive to the inner turmoil that can be obscured by the hardness kids often evince. I told him I thought this because I had once been one of those kids. He seemed to concede this point, but I couldn't tell whether it mattered to him. Nonetheless, he agreed to a series of more formal conversations on this and other topics.

The improbability of a black president had once been so strong that its most vivid representations were comedic. Witness Dave Chappelle's profane Black Bush from the early 2000s ("This nigger very possibly has weapons of mass destruction! I can't sleep on that!") or Richard Pryor's black president in the 1970s promising black astronauts and black quarterbacks ("Ever since the Rams got rid of James Harris, my jaw's been uptight!"). In this model, so potent is the force of blackness that the presidency is forced to conform to it. But once the notion advanced out of comedy and into reality, the opposite proved to be true.

Obama's DNC speech is the key. It does not belong to the literature of "the struggle"; it belongs to the literature of prospective presidents—men (as it turns out) who speak not to gravity and reality, but to aspirations and dreams. When Lincoln invoked the dream of a nation "conceived in liberty" and pledged to the ideal that "all men are created equal," he erased the near-extermination of one people and the enslavement of another. When Roosevelt told the country that "the only thing we have to fear is fear itself," he invoked the dream of American omnipotence and boundless capability. But black people, then living under a campaign of terror for more than half a century, had quite a bit to fear, and Roosevelt could not save them. The dream Ronald Reagan invoked in 1984—that "it's morning again in America"—meant nothing to the inner cities, besieged as they were by decades of redlining policies, not to mention crack and Saturday-night specials. Likewise, Obama's keynote address conflated the slave and the nation of immigrants who profited from him. To reinforce the majoritarian dream, the nightmare endured by the minority is erased. That is the tradition to which the "skinny kid with a funny name" who would be president belonged. It is also the only tradition in existence that could have possibly put a black person in the White House.

Obama's embrace of white innocence was demonstrably necessary as a matter of political survival. Whenever he attempted to buck this directive, he was disciplined. His mild objection to the arrest of Henry Louis Gates Jr. in 2009 contributed to his declining favorability numbers among whites—still a majority of voters. His comments after the killing of Trayvon Martin—"If I had a son, he'd look like Trayvon"—helped make that tragedy a rallying point for people who did not care about Martin's killer as much as they cared about finding ways to oppose the president. Michael Tesler, a political-science professor at UC Irvine, has studied the effect of Obama's race on the American electorate. "No other factor, in fact, came close to dividing the Democratic primary electorate as powerfully as their feelings about African Americans," he and his coauthor, David O. Sears, concluded in their book, *Obama's Race: The 2008 Election and the Dream of a Post-Racial America.* "The impact of racial attitudes on individual vote decisions . . . was so strong that it appears to have even outstripped the substantive impact of racial attitudes on Jesse Jackson's more racially charged campaign for the nomination in 1988." When Tesler looked at the 2012 campaign in his second book, *Post-Racial or Most-Racial? Race and Politics in the Obama Era,* very little had improved. Analyzing the extent to which racial attitudes affected people associated with Obama during the 2012 election, Tesler concluded that "racial attitudes spilled over from Barack Obama into mass assessments of Mitt Romney, Joe Biden, Hillary Clinton, Charlie Crist, and even the Obama family's dog Bo."

Yet despite this entrenched racial resentment, and in the face of complete resistance by congressional Republicans, overtly launched from the moment Obama arrived in the White House, the president accomplished major feats. He remade the nation's health-care system. He revitalized a Justice Department that vigorously investigated police brutality and discrimination, and he began dismantling the private-prison system for federal inmates. Obama nominated the first Latina justice to the Supreme Court, gave presidential support to marriage equality, and ended the U.S. military's Don't Ask, Don't Tell policy, thus honoring the civil-rights tradition that had inspired him. And if his very existence inflamed America's racist conscience, it also expanded the country's anti-racist imagination. Millions of young people now know their only president to have been an African American. Writing for *The New Yorker,* Jelani Cobb once noted that "until there was a black Presidency it was impossible to conceive of the limitations of one." This is just as true of the possibilities. In 2014, the Obama administration committed itself to reversing the War on Drugs through the power of presidential commutation. The administration said that it could commute the sentences of as many as 10,000 prisoners. As of November, the president had commuted only 944 sentences. By any measure, Obama's effort fell woefully short, except for this small one: the measure of almost every other modern president who preceded him. Obama's 944 commutations are the most in nearly a century—and more than the past eleven presidents' combined.

Obama was born into a country where laws barring his very conception—let alone his ascendancy to the presidency—had long stood in force. A black president would always be a contradiction for a government that, throughout most of its history, had oppressed black people. The attempt to resolve this contradiction through Obama—a black man with deep roots in the white world—was remarkable. The price it exacted, incredible. The world it gave way to, unthinkable.

III. "I Decided to Become Part of That World"

When Barack Obama was ten, his father gave him a basketball, a gift that connected the two directly. Obama was born in 1961 in Hawaii and raised by his mother, Ann Dunham, who was white, and her parents, Stanley and Madelyn. They loved him ferociously, supported him emotionally, and encouraged him intellectually. They also told him he was black. Ann gave him books to read about famous black people. When Obama's mother had begun dating his father, the news had not been greeted with the threat of lynching (as it might have been in various parts of the continental United States), and Obama's grandparents always spoke positively of his father. This biography makes Obama nearly unique among black people of his era.

In the president's memoir, *Dreams From My Father,* he says he was not an especially talented basketball player, but he played with a consuming passion. That passion was directed at something more than just the mastering of the pick-and-roll or the perfecting of his jump shot. Obama came of age during the time of the University of Hawaii basketball team's "Fabulous Five"—a name given to its all-black starting five, two decades before it would be resurrected at the University of Michigan by the likes of Chris Webber and Jalen Rose. In his memoir, Obama writes that he would watch the University of Hawaii players laughing at "some inside joke," winking "at the girls on the sidelines," or "casually flipping lay-ups." What Obama saw in the Fabulous Five was not just game, but a culture he found attractive:

> By the time I reached high school, I was playing on Punahou's teams, and could take my game to the university courts, where a handful of black men, mostly gym rats and has-beens, would teach me an at-

titude that didn't just have to do with the sport. That respect came from what you did and not who your daddy was. That you could talk stuff to rattle an opponent, but that you should shut the hell up if you couldn't back it up. That you didn't let anyone sneak up behind you to see emotions—like hurt or fear—you didn't want them to see.

These are lessons, particularly the last one, that for black people apply as much on the street as they do on the court. Basketball was a link for Obama, a medium for downloading black culture from the mainland that birthed the Fabulous Five. Assessing his own thought process at the time, Obama writes, "I decided to become part of that world." This is one of the most incredible sentences ever written in the long, decorated history of black memoir, if only because very few black people have ever enjoyed enough power to write it.

Historically, in black autobiography, to be remanded into the black race has meant exposure to a myriad of traumas, often commencing in childhood. Frederick Douglass is separated from his grandmother. The enslaved Harriet Ann Jacobs must constantly cope with the threat of rape before she escapes. After telling his teacher he wants to be a lawyer, Malcolm X is told that the job isn't for "niggers." Black culture often serves as the balm for such traumas, or even the means to resist them. Douglass finds the courage to face the "slave-breaker" Edward Covey after being given an allegedly enchanted root by "a genuine African" possessing powers from "the eastern nations." Malcolm X's dancing connects him to his "long-suppressed African instincts." If black racial identity speaks to all the things done to people of recent African ancestry, black cultural identity was created in response to them. The division is not neat; the two are linked, and it is incredibly hard to be a full participant in the world of cultural identity without experiencing the trauma of racial identity.

Obama is somewhat different. He writes of bloodying the nose of a white kid who called him a "coon," and of chafing at racist remarks from a tennis coach, and of feeling offended after a white woman in his apartment building told the manager that he was following her. But the kinds of traumas that marked African Americans of his generation—beatings at the hands of racist police, being herded into poor schools, grinding out a life in a tenement building—were mostly abstract for him. Moreover, the kind of spatial restriction that most black people feel at an early age—having rocks thrown at you for being on the wrong side of the tracks, for instance—was largely absent from his life. In its place, Obama was gifted with a well-stamped passport and admittance to elite private schools—all of which spoke of other identities, other lives and other worlds where the color line was neither determinative nor especially relevant. Obama could have grown into a raceless cosmopolitan. Surely he would have lived in a world of problems, but problems not embodied by him.

Instead, he decided to enter this world.

"I always felt as if being black was cool," Obama told me while traveling to a campaign event. He was sitting on *Air Force One,* his tie loosened, his shirtsleeves rolled up. "[Being black] was not something to run away from but something to embrace. Why that is, I think, is complicated. Part of it is I think that my mother thought black folks were cool, and if your mother loves you and is praising you—and says you look good, are smart—as you are, then you don't kind of think in terms of *How can I avoid this?* You feel pretty good about it."

As a child, Obama's embrace of blackness was facilitated, not impeded, by white people. Obama's mother pointed him toward the history and culture of African Americans. Stanley, his grandfather, who came originally from Kansas, took him to basketball games at the University of Hawaii, as well as to black bars. Stanley introduced him to the black writer Frank Marshall Davis. The facilitation was as much indirect as direct. Obama recalls watching his grandfather at those black bars and understanding that "most of the people in the bar weren't there out of choice," and that "our presence there felt forced." From his mother's life of extensive travel, he learned to value the significance of having a home.

That suspicion of rootlessness extends throughout *Dreams From My Father.* He describes integration as a "one-way street" on which black people are asked to abandon themselves to fully experience America's benefits. Confronted with a woman named Joyce, a mixed-race, green-eyed college classmate who insists that she is not "black" but "multiracial," Obama is scornful. "That was the problem with people like Joyce," he writes. "They talked about the richness of their multicultural heritage and it sounded real good, until you noticed that they avoided black people." Later in the memoir, Obama tells the story of falling in love with a white woman. During a visit to her family's country house, he found himself in the library, which was filled with pictures of the woman's illustrious relations. But instead of being in awe, Obama realized that he and the woman lived in different worlds. "And I knew that if we stayed together, I'd eventually live in hers," he writes. "Between the two of us, I was the one who knew how to live as an outsider."

After college, Obama found a home, as well as a sense of himself, working on the South Side of Chicago as a community organizer. "When I started doing that work, my story merges with a larger story. That happens naturally for a John Lewis," he told me, referring to the civil-rights hero and Democratic congressman. "That happens more naturally for you. It was less obvious to me. *How do I pull all these different strains together: Kenya and Hawaii and Kansas, and white and black and Asian—how does that fit?* And through action, through work, I suddenly see myself as part of the bigger process for, yes, delivering justice for the [African American community] and specifically the South Side community, the low-income people—justice on behalf of the African American community. But also thereby promoting my ideas of justice and equality and empathy that my mother taught me were universal. So I'm in a position to understand those essential parts of me not as separate and apart from any particular community but connected to every community. And I can fit the African American struggle for freedom and justice in the context of the universal aspiration for freedom and justice."

Throughout Obama's 2008 campaign and into his presidency, this attitude proved key to his deep support in the black community. African Americans, weary of high achievers who distanced themselves from their black roots, understood that Obama had paid a price for checking "black" on his census form, and for living black, for hosting Common, for brushing dirt off his shoulder during the primaries, for marrying a woman who looked like Michelle Obama. If women, as a gender, must suffer the constant evaluations and denigrations of men, black women must suffer that, plus a broad dismissal from the realm of what American society deems to be beautiful. But Michelle Obama is beautiful in the way that black people know themselves to be. Her prominence as first lady directly attacks a poison that diminishes black girls from the moment they are capable of opening a magazine or turning on a television.

The South Side of Chicago, where Obama began his political career, is home to arguably the most prominent and storied black political establishment in the country. In addition to Oscar Stanton De Priest, the first African American elected to Congress in the twentieth century, the South Side produced the city's first black mayor, Harold Washington; Jesse Jackson, who twice ran for president; and Carol Moseley Braun, the first African American woman to win a Senate race. These victories helped give rise to Obama's own. Harold Washington served as an inspiration to Obama and looms heavily over the Chicago section of *Dreams From My Father*.

Washington forged the kind of broad coalition that Obama would later assemble nationally. But Washington did this in the mid-1980s in segregated Chicago, and he had not had the luxury, as Obama did, of becoming black with minimal trauma. "There was an edge to Harold that frightened some white voters," David Axelrod, who worked for both Washington and Obama, told me recently. Axelrod recalled sitting around a conference table with Washington after he had won the Democratic primary for his reelection in 1987, just as the mayor was about to hold a press conference. Washington asked what percentage of Chicago's white vote he'd received. "And someone said, 'Well, you got 21 percent. And that's really good because last time'"— in his successful 1983 mayoral campaign—"'you only got 8,'" Axelrod recalled. "And he kind of smiled, sadly, and said, 'You know, I probably spent 70 percent of my time in those white neighborhoods, and I think I've been a good mayor for everybody, and I got 21 percent of the white vote and we think it's good.' And he just kind of shook his head and said, 'Ain't it a bitch to be a black man in the land of the free and the home of the brave?'

"That was Harold. He felt those things. He had fought in an all-black unit in World War II. He had come up in times—and that and the sort of indignities of what you had to do to come up through the machine really seared him." During his 1983 mayoral campaign, Washington was loudly booed outside a church in northwest Chicago by middle-class Poles, Italians, and Irish, who feared blacks would uproot them. "It was as vicious and ugly as anything you would have seen in the old South," Axelrod said.

Obama's ties to the South Side tradition that Washington represented were complicated. Like Washington, Obama attempted to forge a coalition between black South Siders and the broader community. But Obama, despite his adherence to black cultural mores, was, with his roots in Kansas and Hawaii, his Ivy League pedigree, and his ties to the University of Chicago, still an exotic out-of-towner. "They were a bit skeptical of him," says Salim Muwakkil, a journalist who has covered Obama since before his days in the Illinois State Senate. "Chicago is a very insular community, and he came from nowhere, seemingly."

Obama compounded people's suspicions by refusing to humble himself and go along with the political currents of the South Side. "A lot of the politicians, especially the black ones, were just leery of him," Kaye Wilson, the godmother to Obama's children and one of the president's earliest political supporters, told me recently.

But even as many in the black political community were skeptical of Obama, others encouraged him—sometimes when they voted against him. When Obama lost the 2000 Democratic-primary race against Bobby Rush, the African American incumbent congressman representing Illinois' First Congressional District, the then-still-obscure future president experienced the defeat as having to do more with his age than his exoticism. "I'd go meet people and I'd knock on doors and stuff, and some of the grandmothers who were the folks I'd been organizing and working with doing community stuff, they weren't parroting back some notion of 'You're too Harvard,' or 'You're too Hyde Park,' or what have you," Obama told me. "They'd say, 'You're a wonderful young man, you're going to do great things. You just have to be patient.' So I didn't feel the loss as a rejection by black people. I felt the loss as 'politics anywhere is tough.' Politics in Chicago is especially tough. And being able to break through in the African American community is difficult because of the enormous loyalty that people feel towards anybody who has been around awhile."

There was no one around to compete for loyalty when Obama ran for Senate in 2004, or for president in 2008. He was no longer competing against other African Americans; he was representing them. "He had that hybridity which told the 'do-gooders'—in Chicago they call the reformers the do-gooders—that he was acceptable," Muwakkil told me.

Obama ran for the Senate two decades after the death of Harold Washington. Axelrod checked in on the precinct where Washington had been so loudly booed by white Chicagoans. "Obama carried, against seven candidates for the Senate, almost the entire northwest side and that precinct," he said. "And I told him, 'Harold's smiling down on us tonight.'"

Obama believes that his statewide victory for the Illinois Senate seat held particular portent for the events of 2008. "Illinois is the most demographically representative state in the country," he told me. "If you took all the percentages of black, white, Latino; rural, urban; agricultural, manufacturing—[if] you took that cross section across the country and you shrank it, it would be Illinois."

Illinois effectively allowed Obama to play a scrimmage before the big national game in 2008. "When I ran for the Senate I had to go into southern Illinois, downstate Illinois, farming communities—some with very tough racial histories, some areas where there just were no African Americans of any number," Obama told me. "And when we won that race, not just an African American from Chicago, but an African American with an exotic history and [the] name Barack Hussein Obama, [it showed that I] could connect with and appeal to a much broader audience."

The mix of Obama's "hybridity" and the changing times allowed him to extend his appeal beyond the white ethnic corners of Chicago, past the downstate portions of Illinois, and out into the country at large. "Ben Nelson, one of the most conservative Democrats in the Senate, from Nebraska, would only bring in one national Democrat to campaign for him," Obama recalls. "And it was me. And so part of the reason I was willing to run [for president in 2008] was that I had had two years in which we were generating enormous crowds all across the country—and the majority of those crowds were not African American; and they were in pretty remote places, or unlikely places. They weren't just big cities or they weren't just liberal enclaves. So what that told me was, it was possible."

What those crowds saw was a black candidate unlike any other before him. To simply point to Obama's white mother, or to his African father, or even to his rearing in Hawaii, is to miss the point. For most African Americans, white people exist either as a direct or an indirect force for bad in their lives. Biraciality is no shield against this; often it just intensifies the problem. What proved key for Barack Obama was not that he was born to a black man and a white woman, but that his white family approved of the union, and approved of the child who came from it. They did this in 1961—a time when sex between black men and white women, in large swaths of the country, was not just illegal but fraught with mortal danger. But that danger is not part of Obama's story. The first white people he ever knew, the ones who raised him, were decent in a way that very few black people of that era experienced.

I asked Obama what he made of his grandparents' impressively civilized reception of his father. "It wasn't Harry Belafonte," Obama said laughingly of his father. "This was like an *African* African. And he was like a blue-black brother. Nilotic. And so, yeah, I will always give my grandparents credit for that. I'm not saying they were happy about it. I'm not saying that they were not, after the guy leaves, looking at each other like, 'What the heck?' But whatever misgivings they had, they never expressed to me, never spilled over into how they interacted with me.

"Now, part of it, as I say in my book, was we were in this unique environment in Hawaii where I think it was much easier. I don't know if it would have been as easy for them if they were living in Chicago at the time, because the lines just weren't as sharply drawn in Hawaii as they were on the mainland."

Obama's early positive interactions with his white family members gave him a fundamentally different outlook toward the wider world than most blacks of the 1960s had. Obama told me he rarely had "the working assumption of discrimination, the working assumption that white people would not treat me right or give me an opportunity or judge me [other than] on the basis of merit." He continued, "The kind of working assumption" that white people would discriminate against him or treat him poorly "is less embedded in my psyche than it is, say, with Michelle."

In this, the first lady is more representative of black America than her husband is. African Americans typically raise their children to protect themselves against a presumed hostility from white teachers, white police officers, white supervisors, and white coworkers. The need for that defense is, more often than not, reinforced either directly by actual encounters or indirectly by observing the vast differences between one's own experience and those across the color line. Marty Nesbitt, the president's longtime best friend, who, like Obama, had positive interactions with whites at a relatively early age, told me that when he and his wife went to buy their first car, she was insistent on buying from a black salesperson. "I'm like, 'We've got to find a salesman,'" Nesbitt said. "She's like, 'No, no, no. We're waiting for the brother.' And I'm like, 'He's with a customer.' They were filling out documents and she was like, 'We're going to stay around.' And a white guy came up to us. 'Can I help you?' 'Nope.'" Nesbitt was not out to condemn anyone with this story. He was asserting that "the willingness of African Americans [in Chicago] to help lift each other up is powerful."

But that willingness to help is also a defense, produced by decades of discrimination. Obama sees race through a different lens, Kaye Wilson told me. "It's just very different from ours," she explained. "He's got buddies that are white, and they're his buddies, and they love him. And I don't think they love him just because he's the president. They love him because they're his friends from Hawaii, some from college and all.

"So I think he's got that, whereas I think growing up in the racist United States, we enter this thing with, you know, 'I'm looking at you. I'm not trusting you to be one hundred with me.' And I think he grew up in a way that he had to trust [white people]—how can you live under the roof with people and think that they don't love you? He needs that frame of reference. He needs that lens. If he didn't have it, it would be . . . a Jesse Jackson, you know? Or Al Sharpton. Different lens."

That lens, born of literally relating to whites, allowed Obama to imagine that he could be the country's first black president. "If I walked into a room and it's a bunch of white farmers, trade unionists, middle age—I'm not walking in thinking, *Man, I've got to show them that I'm normal,*" Obama explained. "I walk in there, I think, with a set of assumptions: like, these people look just like my grandparents. And I see the same Jell-O mold that my grandmother served, and they've got the same, you know, little stuff on their mantelpieces. And so I am maybe disarming them by just assuming that we're okay."

What Obama was able to offer white America is something very few African Americans could—trust. The vast majority of us are, necessarily, too crippled by our defenses to ever consider such a proposition. But Obama, through a mixture of ancestral connections and distance from the poisons of Jim Crow, can credibly and sincerely trust the majority population of this country. That trust is reinforced, not contradicted, by his blackness. Obama isn't shuffling before white power (Herman Cain's "shucky ducky" act) or flattering white ego (O. J. Simpson's listing not being seen as black as a great accomplishment). That, too, is defensive, and deep down, I suspect, white people know it. He stands firm in his own cultural traditions and says to the country something virtually no black person can, but every president must: "I believe you."

IV. "You Still Gotta Go Back to the Hood"

Just after Columbus Day, I accompanied the president and his formidable entourage on a visit to North Carolina A&T State University, in Greensboro. Four days earlier, the *Washington Post* had published an old audio clip that featured Donald Trump lamenting a failed sexual conquest and exhorting the virtues of sexual assault. The next day, Trump claimed that this was "locker room" talk. As we flew to North Carolina, the president was in a state of bemused disbelief. He plopped down in a chair in the staff cabin of *Air Force One* and said, "I've been in a lot of locker rooms. I don't think I've ever heard that one before." He was casual and relaxed. A feeling of cautious inevitability emanated from his staff, and why not? Every day seemed to bring a new, more shocking revelation or piece of evidence showing Trump to be unfit for the presidency: He had lost nearly $1 billion in a single year. He had likely not paid taxes in eighteen years. He was running a "university," for which he was under formal legal investigation. He had trampled on his own campaign's messaging by engaging in a Twitter crusade against a former beauty-pageant contestant. He had been denounced by leadership in his own party, and the trickle of prominent Republicans—both in and out of office—who had publicly repudiated him threatened to become a geyser. At this moment, the idea that a campaign so saturated in open bigotry, misogyny, chaos, and possible corruption could win a national election was ludicrous. This was America.

The president was going to North Carolina to keynote a campaign rally for Clinton, but first he was scheduled for a conversation about My Brother's Keeper, his initiative on behalf of disadvantaged youth. Announcing My Brother's Keeper—or MBK, as it's come to be called—in 2014, the president had sought to avoid giving the program a partisan valence, noting that it was "not some big new government program." Instead, it would involve the government in concert with the nonprofit and business sectors to intervene in the lives of young men of color who were "at risk." MBK serves as a kind of network for those elements of federal, state, and local government that might already have a presence in the lives of these young men. It is a quintessentially Obama program—conservative in scope, with impacts that are measurable.

"It comes right out of his own life," Broderick Johnson, the cabinet secretary and an assistant to the president, who heads MBK, told me recently. "I have heard him say, 'I don't want us to have a bunch of forums on race.' He reminds people, 'Yeah, we can talk about this. But what are we going to *do*?'" On this afternoon in North Carolina, what Obama did was sit with a group of young men who'd turned their lives around in part because of MBK. They told stories of being in the street, of choosing quick money over school, of their homes being shot up, and—through the help of mentoring or job programs brokered by MBK—transitioning into college or a job. Obama listened solemnly and empathetically to each of them. "It doesn't take that much," he told them. "It just takes someone laying hands on you and saying, 'Hey, man, you count.'"

When he asked the young men whether they had a message he

should take back to policy makers in Washington, DC, one observed that despite their best individual efforts, they still had to go back to the very same deprived neighborhoods that had been the sources of trouble for them. "It's your environment," the young man said. "You can do what you want, but you still gotta go back to the hood."

He was correct. The ghettos of America are the direct result of decades of public-policy decisions: the redlining of real-estate zoning maps, the expanded authority given to prosecutors, the increased funding given to prisons. And all of this was done on the backs of people still reeling from the 250-year legacy of slavery. The results of this negative investment are clear—African Americans rank at the bottom of nearly every major socioeconomic measure in the country.

Obama's formula for closing this chasm between black and white America, like that of many progressive politicians today, proceeded from policy designed for all of America. Blacks disproportionately benefit from this effort, since they are disproportionately in need. The Affordable Care Act, which cut the uninsured rate in the black community by at least a third, was Obama's most prominent example. Its full benefit has yet to be felt by African Americans, because several states in the South have declined to expand Medicaid. But when the president and I were meeting, the ACA's advocates believed that pressure on state budgets would force expansion, and there was evidence to support this: Louisiana had expanded Medicaid earlier in 2016, and advocates were gearing up for wars to be waged in Georgia and Virginia.

Obama also emphasized the need for a strong Justice Department with a deep commitment to nondiscrimination. When Obama moved into the White House in 2009, the Justice Department's Civil Rights Division "was in shambles," former Attorney General Eric Holder told me recently. "I mean, I had been there for 12 years as a line guy. I started out in '76, so I served under Republicans and Democrats. And what the [George W.] Bush administration, what the Bush DOJ did, was unlike anything that had ever happened before in terms of politicized hiring." The career civil servants below the political appointees, Holder said, were not even invited to the meetings in which the key hiring and policy decisions were made.

After Obama's inauguration, Holder told me, "I remember going to tell all the folks at the Civil Rights Division, 'The Civil Rights Division is open for business again.' The president gave me additional funds to hire people."

The political press developed a narrative that because Obama felt he had to modulate his rhetoric on race, Holder was the administration's true, and thus blacker, conscience. Holder is certainly blunter, and this worried some of the White House staff. Early in Obama's first term, Holder gave a speech on race in which he said the United States had been a "nation of cowards" on the subject. But positioning the two men as opposites elides an important fact: Holder was appointed by the president, and went only as far as the president allowed. I asked Holder whether he had toned down his rhetoric after that controversial speech. "Nope," he said. Reflecting on his relationship with the president, Holder said, "We were also kind of different people, you know? He is the Zen guy. And I'm kind of the hot-blooded West Indian. And I thought we made a good team, but there's nothing that I ever did or said that I don't think he would have said, 'I support him 100 percent.'

"Now, the 'nation of cowards' speech, the president might have used a different phrase—maybe, probably. But he and I share a worldview, you know? And when I hear people say, 'Well, you are blacker than him' or something like that, I think, *What are you all talking about?*"

For much of his presidency, a standard portion of Obama's speeches about race riffed on black people's need to turn off the television, stop eating junk food, and stop blaming white people for their problems. Obama would deliver this lecture to any black audience, regardless of context. It was bizarre, for instance, to see the president warning young men who'd just graduated from Morehouse College, one of the most storied black colleges in the country, about making "excuses" and blaming whites.

This part of the Obama formula is the most troubling, and least thought-out. This judgment emerges from my own biography. I am the product of black parents who encouraged me to read, of black teachers who felt my work ethic did not match my potential, of black college professors who taught me intellectual rigor. And they did this in a world that every day insulted their humanity. It was not so much that the black layabouts and deadbeats Obama invoked in his speeches were unrecognizable. I had seen those people too. But I'd also seen the same among white people. If black men were overrepresented among drug dealers and absentee dads of the world, it was directly related to their being underrepresented among the Bernie Madoffs and Kenneth Lays of the world. Power was what mattered, and what characterized the differences between black and white America was not a difference in work ethic, but a system engineered to place one on top of the other.

The mark of that system is visible at every level of American society, regardless of the quality of one's choices. For instance, the unemployment rate among black college graduates (4.1 percent) is almost the same as the unemployment rate among white high-school graduates (4.6 percent). But that college degree is generally purchased at a higher price by blacks than by whites. According to research by the Brookings Institution, African Americans tend to carry more student debt four years after graduation ($53,000 versus $28,000) and suffer from a higher default rate on their loans (7.6 percent versus 2.4 percent) than white Americans. This is both the result and the perpetuator of a sprawling wealth gap between the races. White households, on average, hold seven times as much wealth as black households—a difference so large as to make comparing the "black middle class" and "white middle class" meaningless; they're simply not comparable. According to Patrick Sharkey, a sociologist at New York University who studies economic mobility, black families making $100,000 a year or more live in more-disadvantaged neighborhoods than white families making less than $30,000. This gap didn't just appear by magic; it's the result of the government's effort over many decades to create a pigmentocracy—one that will continue without explicit intervention.

Obama had been on the record as opposing reparations. But now, late in his presidency, he seemed more open to the idea—in theory, at least, if not in practice.

"Theoretically, you can make obviously a powerful argument that centuries of slavery, Jim Crow, discrimination are the primary cause for all those gaps," Obama said, referencing the gulf in education, wealth, and employment that separates black and white America. "That those were wrongs to the black community as a whole, and black families specifically, and that in order to close that gap, a society has a moral obligation to make a large, aggressive investment, even if it's not in the form of individual reparations checks but in the form of a Marshall Plan."

The political problems with turning the argument for reparations into reality are manifold, Obama said. "If you look at countries like South Africa, where you had a black majority, there have been efforts to tax and help that black majority, but it hasn't come in the form of a formal reparations program. You have countries like India that have tried to help untouchables, with essentially affirmative-action programs, but it hasn't fundamentally changed the structure of their societies. So the bottom line is that it's hard to find a model in which you can practically administer and sustain political support for those kinds of efforts."

Obama went on to say that it would be better, and more realistic, to get the country to rally behind a robust liberal agenda and build on the enormous progress that's been made toward getting white Americans to accept nondiscrimination as a basic operating premise. But the progress toward nondiscrimination did not appear overnight. It was achieved by people willing to make an unpopular argument and live on the frontier of public opinion. I asked him whether it wasn't—despite the practical obstacles—worth arguing that the state has a collective responsibility not only for its achievements but for its sins.

"I want my children—I want Malia and Sasha—to understand that they've got responsibilities beyond just what they themselves have done," Obama said. "That they have a responsibility to the larger community and the larger nation, that they should be sensitive to and extra thoughtful about the plight of people who have been oppressed in the past, are oppressed currently. So that's a wisdom that I want to transmit to my kids . . . But I would say that's a high level of enlightenment that you're looking to have from a majority of the society. And it may be something that future generations are more open to, but I am pretty confident that for the foreseeable future, using the argument of nondiscrimination, and 'Let's get it right for the kids who are here right now,' and giving them the best chance possible, is going to be a more persuasive argument."

Obama is unfailingly optimistic about the empathy and capabilities of the American people. His job necessitates this: "At some level what the people want to feel is that the person leading them sees the best in them," he told me. But I found it interesting that that optimism does not extend to the possibility of the public's accepting wisdoms—such as the moral logic of reparations—that the president, by his own account, has accepted for himself and is willing to teach his children. Obama says he always tells his staff that "better is good." The notion that a president would attempt to achieve change within the boundaries of the accepted consensus is appropriate. But Obama is almost constitutionally skeptical of those who seek to achieve change outside that consensus.

Early in 2016, Obama invited a group of African American leaders to meet with him at the White House. When some of the activists affiliated with Black Lives Matter refused to attend, Obama began calling them out in speeches. "You can't refuse to meet because that might compromise the purity of your position," he said. "The value of social movements and activism is to get you at the table, get you in the room, and then start trying to figure out how is this problem going to be solved. You then have a responsibility to prepare an agenda that is achievable—that can institutionalize the changes you seek—and to engage the other side."

Opal Tometi, a Nigerian American community activist who is one of the three founders of Black Lives Matter, explained to me that the group has a more diffuse structure than most civil-rights organizations. One reason for this is to avoid the cult of personality that has plagued black organizations in the past. So the founders asked its membership in Chicago, the president's hometown, whether they should meet with Obama. "They felt—and I think many of our members felt—there wouldn't be the depth of discussion that they wanted to have," Tometi told me. "And if there wasn't that space to have a real heart-to-heart, and if it was just surface level, that it would be more of a disservice to the movement."

Tometi noted that some other activists allied with Black Lives Matter had been planning to attend the meeting, so they felt their views would be represented. Nevertheless, Black Lives Matter sees itself as engaged in a protest against the treatment of black people by the American state, and so Tometi and much of the group's leadership, concerned about being used for a photo op by the very body they were protesting, opted not to go.

When I asked Obama about this perspective, he fluctuated between understanding where the activists were coming from and being hurt by such brush-offs. "I think that where I've gotten frustrated during the course of my presidency has never been because I was getting pushed too hard by activists to see the justness of a cause or the essence of an issue," he said. "I think where I got frustrated at times was the belief that the president can do anything if he just decides he wants to do it. And that sort of lack of awareness on the part of an activist about the constraints of our political system and the constraints on this office, I think, sometimes would leave me to mutter under my breath. Very rarely did I lose it publicly. Usually I'd just smile."

He laughed, then continued, "The reason I say that is because those are the times where sometimes you feel actually a little bit hurt. Because you feel like saying to these folks, '[Don't] you think if I could do it, I [would] have just done it? Do you think that the only problem is that I don't care enough about the plight of poor people, or gay people?'"

I asked Obama whether he thought that perhaps protesters' distrust of the powers that be could ultimately be healthy. "Yes," he said. "Which is why I don't get too hurt. I mean, I think there is a benefit to wanting to hold power's feet to the fire until you actually see the goods. I get that. And I think it is important. And frankly, sometimes it's useful for activists just to be out there to keep you mindful and not get complacent, even if ultimately you think some of their criticism is misguided."

Obama himself was an activist and a community organizer, albeit for only two years—but he is not, by temperament, a protester. He is a consensus-builder; consensus, he believes, ultimately drives what gets done. He understands the emotional power of protest, the need to vent before authority—but that kind of approach does not come naturally to him. Regarding reparations, he said, "Sometimes I wonder how much of these debates have to do with the desire, the legitimate desire, for that history to be recognized. Because there is a psychic power to the recognition that is not satisfied with a universal program; it's not satisfied by the Affordable Care Act, or an expansion of Pell Grants, or an expansion of the earned-income tax credit." These kinds of programs, effective and disproportionately beneficial to black people though they may be, don't "speak to the hurt, and the sense of injustice, and the self-doubt that arises out of the fact that [African Americans] are behind now, and it makes us sometimes feel as if there must be something wrong with us—unless you're able to see the history and say, 'It's amazing we got this far given what we went through.'

"So in part, I think the argument sometimes that I've had with folks who are much more interested in sort of race-specific programs is less an argument about what is practically achievable and sometimes maybe more an argument of 'We want society to see what's happened and internalize it and answer it in demonstrable ways.' And those impulses I very much understand—but my hope would be that as we're moving through the world right now, we're able to get that psychological or emotional peace by seeing very concretely our kids doing better and being more hopeful and having greater opportunities."

Obama saw—at least at that moment, before the election of Donald Trump—a straight path to that world. "Just play this out as a thought experiment," he said. "Imagine if you had genuine, high-quality early-childhood education for every child, and suddenly every black child in America—but also every poor white child or Latino [child], but just stick with every black child in America—is getting a really good education. And they're graduating from high school at the same rates that whites are, and they are going to college at the same rates that whites are, and they are able to afford college at the same rates because the government has universal programs that say that you're not going to be barred from school just because of how much money your parents have.

"So now they're all graduating. And let's also say that the Justice Department and the courts are making sure, as I've said in a speech before, that when Jamal sends his résumé in, he's getting treated the same as when Johnny sends his résumé in. Now, are we going to have suddenly the same number of CEOs, billionaires, etc., as the white community? In ten years? Probably not, maybe not even in twenty years.

"But I guarantee you that we would be thriving, we would be succeeding. We wouldn't have huge numbers of young African American men in jail. We'd have more family formation as college-graduated girls are meeting boys who are their peers, which then in turn means the next generation of kids are growing up that much better. And suddenly you've got a whole generation that's in a position to start using the incredible creativity that we see in music, and sports, and frankly even on the streets, channeled into starting all kinds of businesses. I feel pretty good about our odds in that situation."

The thought experiment doesn't hold up. The programs Obama favored would advance white America too—and without a specific commitment to equality, there is no guarantee that the programs would eschew discrimination. Obama's solution relies on a goodwill that his own personal history tells him exists in the larger country. My own history tells me something different. The large numbers of black men in jail, for instance, are not just the result of poor policy, but of not seeing those men as human.

When President Obama and I had this conversation, the target he was aiming to reach seemed to me to be many generations away, and now—as President-elect Trump prepares for office—seems even many more generations off. Obama's accomplishments were real: a $1 billion settlement on behalf of black farmers, a Justice Department that exposed Ferguson's municipal plunder, the increased availability of Pell Grants (and their availability to some prisoners), and the slashing of the crack/cocaine disparity in sentencing guidelines, to name just a few. Obama was also the first sitting president to visit a federal prison. There was a feeling that he'd erected a foundation upon which further progressive policy could be built. It's tempting to say that foundation is now endangered. The truth is, it was never safe.

V. "They Rode the Tiger"

Obama's greatest misstep was born directly out of his greatest insight. Only Obama, a black man who emerged from the best of white America, and thus could sincerely trust white America, could be so certain that he could achieve broad national appeal. And yet only a black man with that same biography could underestimate his opposition's resolve to destroy him. In some sense an Obama presidency could never have succeeded along the normal presidential lines; he needed a partner, or partners, in Congress who could put governance above party. But he struggled to win over even some of his own allies. Ben Nelson, the Democratic senator from Nebraska whom Obama helped elect, became an obstacle to health-care reform. Joe Lieberman, whom Obama saved from retribution at the hands of Senate Democrats after Lieberman campaigned for Obama's 2008 opponent, John McCain, similarly obstructed Obamacare. Among Republicans, senators who had seemed amenable to Obama's agenda—Chuck Grassley, Susan Collins, Richard Lugar, Olympia Snowe—rebuffed him repeatedly.

The obstruction grew out of narrow political incentives. "If Republicans didn't cooperate," Obama told me, "and there was not a portrait of bipartisan cooperation and a functional federal government, then the party in power would pay the price and they could win back the Senate and/or the House. That wasn't an inaccurate political calculation."

Obama is not sure of the degree to which individual racism played into this calculation. "I do remember watching Bill Clinton get impeached and Hillary Clinton being accused of killing Vince Foster," he said. "And if you ask them, I'm sure they would say, 'No, actually what you're experiencing is not because you're black, it's because you're a Democrat.'"

But personal animus is just one manifestation of racism; arguably the more profound animosity occurs at the level of interests. The most recent Congress boasted 138 members from the states that comprised the old Confederacy. Of the 101 Republicans in that group, ninety-six are white and one is black. Of the thirty-seven Democrats, eighteen are black and fifteen are white. There are no white congressional Democrats in the Deep South. Exit polls in Mississippi in 2008 found that 96 percent of voters who described themselves as Republicans were white. The Republican Party is not simply the party of whites, but the preferred party of whites who identify their interest as defending the historical privileges of whiteness. The researchers Josh Pasek, Jon A. Krosnick, and Trevor Tompson found that in 2012, 32 percent of Democrats held antiblack views, while 79 percent of Republicans did. These attitudes could even spill over to white Democratic politicians, because they are seen as representing the party of blacks. Studying the 2016 election, the political scientist Philip Klinkner found that the most predictive question for understanding whether a voter favored Hillary Clinton or Donald Trump was "Is Barack Obama a Muslim?"

In our conversations, Obama said he didn't doubt that there was a sincerely nonracist states'-rights contingent of the GOP. And yet he suspected that there might be more to it. "A rudimentary knowledge of American history tells you that the relationship between the federal government and the states was very much mixed up with attitudes toward slavery, attitudes toward Jim Crow, attitudes towards antipoverty programs and who benefited and who didn't," he said.

"And so I'm careful not to attribute any particular resistance or slight or opposition to race. But what I do believe is that if somebody didn't have a problem with their daddy being employed by the federal government, and didn't have a problem with the Tennessee Valley Authority electrifying certain communities, and didn't have a problem with the interstate highway system being built, and didn't have a problem with the GI Bill, and didn't have a problem with the [Federal Housing Administration] subsidizing the suburbanization of America, and that all helped you build wealth and create a middle class— and then suddenly as soon as African Americans or Latinos are interested in availing themselves of those same mechanisms as ladders into the middle class, you now have a violent opposition to them— then I think you at least have to ask yourself the question of how consistent you are, and what's different, and what's changed."

Racism greeted Obama in both his primary and general-election campaigns in 2008. Photos were circulated of him in Somali garb. Rush Limbaugh dubbed him "Barack the Magic Negro." Roger

Stone, who would go on to advise the Trump campaign, claimed that Michelle Obama could be heard on tape yelling "Whitey." Detractors circulated emails claiming that the future first lady had written a racist senior thesis while at Princeton. A fifth of all West Virginia Democratic-primary voters in 2008 openly admitted that race had influenced their vote. Hillary Clinton trounced him 67 to 26 percent.

After Obama won the presidency in defiance of these racial headwinds, traffic to the white-supremacist website Stormfront increased sixfold. Before the election, in August, just before the Democratic National Convention, the FBI uncovered an assassination plot hatched by white supremacists in Denver. Mainstream conservative publications floated the notion that Obama's memoir was too "stylish and penetrating" to have been written by the candidate, and found a plausible ghostwriter in the radical (and white) former Weatherman Bill Ayers. A Republican women's club in California dispensed "Obama Bucks" featuring slices of watermelon, ribs, and fried chicken. At the Values Voter Summit that year, conventioneers hawked "Obama Waffles," a waffle mix whose box featured a bug-eyed caricature of the candidate. Fake hip-hop lyrics were scrawled on the side ("Barry's Bling Bling Waffle Ring") and on the top, the same caricature was granted a turban and tagged with the instructions "Point box toward Mecca for tastier waffles." The display was denounced by the summit's sponsor, the Family Research Council. One would be forgiven for meeting this denunciation with guffaws: The council's president, Tony Perkins, had once addressed the white-supremacist Council of Conservative Citizens with a Confederate flag draped behind him. By 2015, Perkins had deemed the debate over Obama's birth certificate "legitimate" and was saying that it "makes sense" to conclude that Obama was actually a Muslim.

By then, birtherism—inflamed in large part by a real-estate mogul and reality-TV star named Donald Trump—had overtaken the Republican rank and file. In 2015, one poll found that 54 percent of GOP voters thought Obama was a Muslim. Only 29 percent believed he'd been born in America.

Still, in 2008, Obama had been elected. His supporters rejoiced. As Jay-Z commemorated the occasion:

My president is black, in fact he's half-white,
So even in a racist mind, he's half-right.

Not quite. A month after Obama entered the White House, a CNBC personality named Rick Santelli took to the trading floor of the Chicago Mercantile Exchange and denounced the president's efforts to help homeowners endangered by the housing crisis. "How many of you people want to pay for your neighbor's mortgage that has an extra bathroom and can't pay their bills?," Santelli asked the assembled traders. He asserted that Obama should "reward people that could carry the water" as opposed to those who "drink the water," and denounced those in danger of foreclosure as "losers." Race was implicit in Santelli's harangue—the housing crisis and predatory lending had devastated black communities and expanded the wealth gap—and it culminated with a call for a "Tea Party" to resist the Obama presidency. In fact, right-wing ideologues had been planning just such a resistance for decades. They would eagerly answer Santelli's call.

One of the intellectual forerunners of the Tea Party is said to be Ron Paul, the heterodox two-time Republican presidential candidate, who opposed the war in Iraq and championed civil liberties. On other matters, Paul was more traditional. Throughout the '90s, he published a series of racist newsletters that referred to New York City as "Welfaria," called Martin Luther King Jr. Day "Hate Whitey Day," and asserted that 95 percent of black males in Washington, DC, were either "semi-criminal or entirely criminal." Paul's apologists have claimed that he had no real connection to the newsletters, even though virtually all of them were published in his name ("The Ron Paul Survival Report," "Ron Paul Political Report," "Dr. Ron Paul's Freedom Report") and written in his voice. Either way, the views of the newsletters have found their expression in his ideological comrades. Throughout Obama's first term, Tea Party activists voiced their complaints in racist terms. Activists brandished signs warning that Obama would implement "white slavery," waved the Confederate flag, depicted Obama as a witch doctor, and issued calls for him to "go back to Kenya." Tea Party supporters wrote "satirical" letters in the name of "We Colored People" and stoked the flames of birtherism. One of the Tea Party's most prominent sympathizers, the radio host Laura Ingraham, wrote a racist tract depicting Michelle Obama gorging herself on ribs, while Glenn Beck said the president was a "racist" with a "deep-seated hatred for white people." The Tea Party's leading exponent, Andrew Breitbart, engineered the smearing of Shirley Sherrod, the U.S. Department of Agriculture's director of rural development for Georgia, publishing egregiously misleading videos that wrongly made her appear to be engaging in antiwhite racist invective, which led to her dismissal. (In a rare act of cowardice, the Obama administration cravenly submitted to this effort.)

In those rare moments when Obama made any sort of comment attacking racism, firestorms threatened to consume his governing agenda. When, in July 2009, the president objected to the arrest of the eminent Harvard professor Henry Louis Gates Jr. while he was trying to get into his own house, pointing out that the officer had "acted stupidly," a third of whites said the remark made them feel less favorably toward the president, and nearly two-thirds claimed that Obama had "acted stupidly" by commenting. A chastened Obama then determined to make sure his public statements on race were no longer mere riffs but designed to have an achievable effect. This was smart, but still the invective came. During Obama's 2009 address on health care before a joint session of Congress, Joe Wilson, a Republican congressman from South Carolina, incredibly, and in defiance of precedent and decorum, disrupted the proceedings by crying out "You lie!" A Missouri congressman equated Obama with a monkey. A California GOP official took up the theme and emailed her friends an image depicting Obama as a chimp, with the accompanying text explaining, "Now you know why [there's] no birth certificate!" Former vice-presidential candidate Sarah Palin assessed the president's foreign policy as a "shuck and jive shtick." Newt Gingrich dubbed him the "food-stamp president." The rhetorical attacks on Obama were matched by a very real attack on his political base—in 2011 and 2012, nineteen states enacted voting restrictions that made it harder for African Americans to vote.

Yet in 2012, as in 2008, Obama won anyway. Prior to the election, Obama, ever the optimist, had claimed that intransigent Republicans would decide to work with him to advance the country. No such collaboration was in the offing. Instead, legislation ground to a halt and familiar themes resurfaced. An Idaho GOP official posted a photo on Facebook depicting a trap waiting for Obama. The bait was a slice of watermelon. The caption read, "Breaking: The secret service just uncovered a plot to kidnap the president. More details as we get them . . ." In 2014, conservatives assembled in support of Cliven Bundy's armed protest against federal grazing fees. As reporters descended on the Bundy ranch in Nevada, Bundy offered his opinions on "the Negro." "They abort their young children, they put their young men in jail, because they never learned how to pick cotton," Bundy explained. "And I've often wondered, are they better off as slaves, picking cotton and having a family life and doing things, or are they better off under government subsidy? They didn't get no more freedom. They got less freedom."

That same year, in the wake of Michael Brown's death, the Justice Department opened an investigation into the police department in Ferguson, Missouri. It found a city that, through racial profiling, arbitrary fines, and wanton harassment, had exploited law enforcement for the purposes of municipal plunder. The plunder was sanctified by racist humor dispensed via internal emails among the police that later came to light. The president of the United States, who during his first year in office had reportedly received three times the number of death threats of any of his predecessors, was a repeat target.

Much ink has been spilled in an attempt to understand the Tea Party protests, and the 2016 presidential candidacy of Donald Trump, which ultimately emerged out of them. One theory popular among (primarily) white intellectuals of varying political persuasions held that this response was largely the discontented rumblings of a white working class threatened by the menace of globalization and crony capitalism. Dismissing these rumblings as racism was said to condescend to this proletariat, which had long suffered the slings and arrows of coastal elites, heartless technocrats, and reformist snobs. Racism was not something to be coolly and empirically assessed but a slander upon the working man. Deindustrialization, globalization, and broad income inequality are real. And they have landed with at least as great a force upon black and Latino people in our country as upon white people. And yet these groups were strangely unrepresented in this new populism.

Christopher S. Parker and Matt A. Barreto, political scientists at the University of Washington and UCLA, respectively, have found a relatively strong relationship between racism and Tea Party membership. "Whites are less likely to be drawn to the Tea Party for material reasons, suggesting that, relative to other groups, it's really more about social prestige," they say. The notion that the Tea Party represented the righteous, if unfocused, anger of an aggrieved class allowed everyone from leftists to neoliberals to white nationalists to avoid a horrifying and simple reality: A significant swath of this country did not like the fact that their president was black, and that swath was not composed of those most damaged by an unquestioned faith in the markets. Far better to imagine the grievance put upon the president as the ghost of shambling factories and defunct union halls, as opposed to what it really was—a movement inaugurated by ardent and frightened white capitalists, raging from the commodities-trading floor of one of the great financial centers of the world.

That movement came into full bloom in the summer of 2015, with the candidacy of Donald Trump, a man who'd risen to political prominence by peddling the racist myth that the president was not American. It was birtherism—not trade, not jobs, not isolationism— that launched Trump's foray into electoral politics. Having risen unexpectedly on this basis into the stratosphere of Republican politics, Trump spent the campaign freely and liberally trafficking in misogyny, Islamophobia, and xenophobia. And on November 8, 2016, he won election to the presidency. Historians will spend the next century analyzing how a country with such allegedly grand democratic traditions was, so swiftly and so easily, brought to the brink of fascism. But one needn't stretch too far to conclude that an eight-year campaign of consistent and open racism aimed at the leader of the free world helped clear the way.

"They rode the tiger. And now the tiger is eating them," David Axelrod, speaking of the Republican Party, told me. That was in October. His words proved too optimistic. The tiger would devour us all.

VI. "When You Left, You Took All of Me With You"

One Saturday morning last May, I joined the presidential motor-cade as it slipped out of the southern gate of the White House. A mostly white crowd had assembled. As the motorcade drove by, peo-ple cheered, held up their smartphones to record the procession, and waved American flags. To be within feet of the president seemed like the thrill of their lives. I was astounded. An old euphoria, which I could not immediately place, gathered up in me. And then I remem-bered, it was what I felt through much of 2008, as I watched Barack Obama's star shoot across the political sky. I had never seen so many white people cheer on a black man who was neither an athlete nor an entertainer. And it seemed that they loved him for this, and I thought in those days, which now feel so long ago, that they might then love me, too, and love my wife, and love my child, and love us all in the manner that the God they so fervently cited had commanded. I had been raised amid a people who wanted badly to believe in the possibil-ity of a Barack Obama, even as their very lives argued against that pos-sibility. So they would praise Martin Luther King Jr. in one breath and curse the white man, "the Great Deceiver," in the next. Then came Obama and the Obama family, and they were black and beautiful in all the ways we aspired to be, and all that love was showered upon them. But as Obama's motorcade approached its destination—Howard Uni-versity, where he would give the commencement address—the com-plexion of the crowd darkened, and I understood that the love was specific, that even if it allowed Barack Obama, even if it allowed the luckiest of us, to defy the boundaries, then the masses of us, in cities like this one, would still enjoy no such feat.

These were our fitful, spasmodic years.

We were launched into the Obama era with no notion of what to expect, if only because a black presidency had seemed such a dubi-ous proposition. There was no preparation, because it would have meant preparing for the impossible. There were few assessments of its potential import, because such assessments were regarded as speculative fiction. In retrospect it all makes sense, and one can see a jagged but real political lineage running through black Chicago. It originates in Oscar Stanton De Priest; continues through Congressman William Dawson, who, under Roosevelt, switched from the Republican to the Democratic Party; crescendos with the legendary Harold Washington; rises still with Jesse Jackson's 1988 victory in Michigan's Democratic caucuses; rises again with Carol Moseley Braun's triumph; and reaches its recent apex with the election of Barack Obama. If the lineage is apparent in hindsight, so are the limits of presidential power. For a century after emancipation, quasi-slavery haunted the South. And more than half a century after *Brown v. Board of Education,* schools throughout much of this country remain segregated.

There are no clean victories for black people, nor, perhaps, for any people. The presidency of Barack Obama is no different. One can now say that an African American individual can rise to the same level as a white individual, and yet also say that the number of black individuals who actually qualify for that status will be small. One thinks of Serena Williams, whose dominance and stunning achievements can't, in and of themselves, ensure equal access to tennis facilities for young black girls. The gate is open and yet so very far away.

I felt a mix of pride and amazement walking onto Howard's campus that day. Howard alumni, of which I am one, are an obnoxious fraternity, known for yelling the school chant across city blocks, sneering at other historically black colleges and universities, and condescending to black graduates of predominantly white institutions. I like to think I am more reserved, but I felt an immense satisfaction in being in the library where I had once found my history, and now found myself with the first black president of the United States. It seemed providential that he would give the commencement address here in his last year. The same pride I felt radiated out across the Yard, the large green patch in the main area of the campus where the ceremony would take place. When Obama walked out, the audience exploded, and when the time came for the color guard to present arms, a chant arose: "O-Ba-Ma! O-Ba-Ma! O-Ba-Ma!"

He gave a good speech that day, paying heed to Howard's rituals, calling out its famous alumni, shouting out the university's various dormitories, and urging young people to vote. (His usual riff on respectability politics was missing.) But I think he could have stood before that crowd, smiled, and said "Good luck," and they would have loved him anyway. He was their champion, and this was evident in the smallest of things. The national anthem was played first, but then came the black national anthem, "Lift Every Voice and Sing." As the lyrics rang out over the crowd, the students held up the black-power fist—a symbol of defiance before power. And yet here, in the face of a black man in his last year in power, it scanned not as a protest, but as a salute.

Six months later the awful price of a black presidency would be known to those students, even as the country seemed determined not to acknowledge it. In the days after Donald Trump's victory, there would be an insistence that something as "simple" as racism could not explain it. As if enslavement had nothing to do with global economics, or as if lynchings said nothing about the idea of women as property. As though the past 400 years could be reduced to the irrational resentment of full lips. No. Racism is never simple. And there was nothing simple about what was coming, or about Obama, the man who had unwittingly summoned this future into being.

It was said that the Americans who'd supported Trump were victims of liberal condescension. The word *racist* would be dismissed as a profane slur put upon the common man, as opposed to an accurate description of actual men. "We simply don't yet know how much racism or misogyny motivated Trump voters," David Brooks would write in the *New York Times*. "If you were stuck in a jobless town, watching your friends OD on opiates, scrambling every month to pay the electric bill, and then along came a guy who seemed able to fix your problems and hear your voice, maybe you would stomach some ugliness, too." This strikes me as perfectly logical. Indeed, it could apply just as well to Louis Farrakhan's appeal to the black poor and working class. But whereas the followers of an Islamophobic white nationalist enjoy the sympathy that must always greet the salt of the earth, the followers of an anti-Semitic black nationalist endure the scorn that must ever greet the children of the enslaved.

Much would be made of blue-collar voters in Wisconsin, Pennsylvania, and Michigan who'd pulled the lever for Obama in 2008 and 2012 and then for Trump in 2016. Surely these voters disproved racism as an explanatory force. It's still not clear how many individual voters actually flipped. But the underlying presumption—that

Hillary Clinton and Barack Obama could be swapped in for each other—exhibited a problem. Clinton was a candidate who'd won one competitive political race in her life, whose political instincts were questioned by her own advisers, who took more than half a million dollars in speaking fees from an investment bank because it was "what they offered," who proposed to bring back to the White House a former president dogged by allegations of rape and sexual harassment. Obama was a candidate who'd become only the third black senator in the modern era; who'd twice been elected president, each time flipping red and purple states; who'd run one of the most scandal-free administrations in recent memory. Imagine an African American facsimile of Hillary Clinton: She would never be the nominee of a major political party and likely would not be in national politics at all.

Pointing to citizens who voted for both Obama and Trump does not disprove racism; it evinces it. To secure the White House, Obama needed to be a Harvard-trained lawyer with a decade of political experience and an incredible gift for speaking to cross sections of the country; Donald Trump needed only money and white bluster.

In the week after the election, I was a mess. I had not seen my wife in two weeks. I was on deadline for this article. My son was struggling in school. The house was in disarray. I played Marvin Gaye endlessly—"When you left, you took all of me with you." Friends began to darkly recall the ghosts of post-Reconstruction. The election of Donald Trump confirmed everything I knew of my country and none of what I could accept. The idea that America would follow its first black president with Donald Trump accorded with its history. I was shocked at my own shock. I had wanted Obama to be right.

I still want Obama to be right. I still would like to fold myself into the dream. This will not be possible.

By some cosmic coincidence, a week after the election I received a portion of my father's FBI file. My father had grown up poor in Philadelphia. His father was struck dead on the street. His grandfather was crushed to death in a meatpacking plant. He'd served his country in Vietnam, gotten radicalized there, and joined the Black Panther Party, which brought him to the attention of J. Edgar Hoover. A memo written to the FBI director was "submitted aimed at discrediting WILLIAM PAUL COATES, Acting Captain of the BPP, Baltimore." The memo proposed that a fake letter be sent to the Panthers' cofounder Huey P. Newton. The fake letter accused my father of being an informant and concluded, "I want somethin done with this bootlikin facist pig nigger and I want it done now." The words *somethin done* need little interpretation. The Panthers were eventually consumed by an internecine war instigated by the FBI, one in which being labeled a police informant was a death sentence.

A few hours after I saw this file, I had my last conversation with the president. I asked him how his optimism was holding up, given Trump's victory. He confessed to being surprised at the outcome but said that it was tough to "draw a grand theory from it, because there were some very unusual circumstances." He pointed to both candidates' high negatives, the media coverage, and a "dispirited" electorate. But he said that his general optimism about the shape of American history remained unchanged. "To be optimistic about the long-term trends of the United States doesn't mean that everything is going to go in a smooth, direct, straight line," he said. "It goes forward sometimes, sometimes it goes back, sometimes it goes sideways, sometimes it zigs and zags."

I thought of Hoover's FBI, which harassed three generations of black activists, from Marcus Garvey's black nationalists to Martin Luther King Jr.'s integrationists to Huey Newton's Black Panthers, including my father. And I thought of the enormous power accrued to the presidency in the post-9/11 era—the power to obtain American citizens' phone records en masse, to access their emails, to detain them indefinitely. I asked the president whether it was all worth it. Whether this generation of black activists and their allies should be afraid.

"Keep in mind that the capacity of the NSA, or other surveillance tools, are specifically prohibited from being applied to U.S. citizens or U.S. persons without specific evidence of links to terrorist activity or, you know, other foreign-related activity," he said. "So, you know, I think this whole story line that somehow Big Brother has massively expanded and now that a new president is in place it's this loaded gun ready to be used on domestic dissent is just not accurate."

He counseled vigilance, "because the possibility of abuse by government officials always exists. The issue is not going to be that there are new tools available; the issue is making sure that the incoming administration, like my administration, takes the constraints on how we deal with U.S. citizens and persons seriously." This answer did not fill me with confidence. The next day, President-elect Trump offered Lieutenant General Michael Flynn the post of national-security adviser and picked Senator Jeff Sessions of Alabama as his nominee for attorney general. Last February, Flynn tweeted, "Fear of Muslims is RATIONAL," and linked to a YouTube video that declared followers of Islam want "80 percent of humanity enslaved or exterminated." Sessions had once been accused of calling a black lawyer "boy," claiming that a white lawyer who represented black clients was a disgrace to his race, and joking that he thought the Ku Klux Klan "was okay until I found out they smoked pot." I felt then that I knew what was coming—more Freddie Grays, more Rekia Boyds, more informants and undercover officers sent to infiltrate mosques.

And I also knew that the man who could not countenance such a thing in his America had been responsible for the only time in my life when I felt, as the first lady had once said, proud of my country, and I knew that it was his very lack of countenance, his incredible faith, his improbable trust in his countrymen, that had made that feeling possible. The feeling was that little black boy touching the president's hair. It was watching Obama on the campaign trail, always expecting the worst and amazed that the worst never happened. It was how I'd felt seeing Barack and Michelle during the inauguration, the car slow-dragging down Pennsylvania Avenue, the crowd cheering, and then the two of them rising up out of the limo, rising up from fear, smiling, waving, defying despair, defying history, defying gravity.

TOMMY PICO

■

Excerpt from *Nature Poem*

FROM *Tin House*

oh, but you don't look very Indian is a thing ppl feel comfortable
saying to me on dates.

What rhymes with, *fuck off and die?*

It's hard to look "like" something most people remember as a
ghost, but I understand the allure of wanting to know—

Knowledge, or its approximate artifice, is a kind of
equilibrium when you feel like a flea in whiskey.

I used to read a lot of perfect poems, now I read a lot of
Garbage

by A. R. Ammons

the old mysteries avail themselves of technique.

It's disheartening

to hear someone say *there's no magic left* bc I love that Youtube
of Amy Winehouse singing "Love is a Losing Game" at the
Mercury Awards and yesterday I overheard that Brooklyn

means "Broken Land"–there aren't many earthquakes in the city, but there's the fault line of my head that I'll always live on.

Pain is alienating, but blue breath breaking on a voice is the magic that makes ppl believe.

What, I learn to ask, *does an NDN person look like exactly?*

■

Hell

FROM *Vice*

IT WAS PEAK FOLIAGE, horned red leaves adrift on the duck pond, two-hand touch in the stadium's shadow, ripe-legged girls shivering in miniskirts under a harvest moon. It was the time of year for planning new debasements to perform on the pledges during Hell Week, the final test before their initiation. But we were short of ideas. Previous Gamma Phi upperclassmen had made their pledges do the elephant walk, in which they were marched through the house each holding the dick of the guy behind him, but we knew that that would no longer fly. It would be filmed on a phone and posted, drawing criticism. Previous upperclassmen had stripped the pledges to their underwear in the back of a van and dropped them off in what was thought to be gang territory in Springfield, but we considered that insensitive to the people who lived there. And the classic procedures— blindfolding the pledges and making them fellate cucumbers or eat bananas out of the toilet—had lost all power to surprise and deceive. The pledges had read online about any torment ever conceived by any pledgemaster. The exec board convened at its round plywood table, trying to think who might have some suggestions, when Glines, who was older than the rest of us, having taken time off after junior year to stretch rubber bands over the claws of lobsters and pay down his loans, mentioned a guy we'd never heard of: Michael Poumakis. When Glines was a pledge, Poumakis had been a house legend, spoken of in hushed tones by the seniors who remembered him. ROTC, hockey, rugby, Honors, Young Democrats, religious but still did something with girls in his room.

When Poumakis graduated, Glines said, he accepted a Navy commission. He was Lieutenant Poumakis now; Glines showed us the alumni database entry on his laptop. He lived in Crystal City, Virginia, a day's drive south.

"If he's an officer outside DC, guy's probably been through Navy Hell Week," Glines said. "That's SEALs Team Six shit. That's the state of the art. That, plus hazing in the Navy is probably harsher than anything we would ever come up with. They're preparing you for war."

I was with Glines. A Navy guy would know how to take an assortment of pledges and put them through something so strenuous that it would bind them into brothers. They wouldn't want to post a picture and get us all in trouble, because they'd be proud they got through it. They'd be proud to be one of us. That was Hell Week's whole point.

We composed the Facebook message as a group, with Glines's laptop on the table between us. We thanked the lieutenant for his service. Regretting that we couldn't provide travel money or accommodations, only Chef Bill's chili, no doubt the same as it had been back in the day, we invited him up for a weekend. "Please consider helping us plan Hell Week this year," we wrote. "We would be incredibly grateful to draw on the insights you have acquired in your military training as to how to make it an extreme experience for every pledge."

A response balloon with three dots appeared immediately in the blue window. "I would love to come."

We had seen full-body shots of him on Instagram, but he looked smaller in real life, stooped by eight hours at the wheel. Since the last picture, he'd grown a beard, and he petted the beard often, the way you would if your beard was new. He dressed like one of those hikers who strive always to be comfy: furry fleece hoodie, nubby fleece pants, canvas sneakers, moisture-repellant runner's socks, all shades of dun and brown. He petted his upper arms the same way he petted the beard. He was on the cusp of old, about thirty. He kept his hoodie up over his head and walked with his hands thrust in the front pocket, like people our age.

There was nothing about him that resembled the ads we'd seen for the Navy, buzz-cut sailors in starched whites, legs spread to shoulder width, hands clasped behind their backs on the deck of a carrier, links in the World's Strongest Chain. But his handshake had soft strength. All six of us in exec board showed him around the house, though our presence was unnecessary. We followed, while Glines led the way, walking backward as he talked.

Not much had changed in the house since Poumakis lived in it, so Glines didn't have that much to announce, and Poumakis didn't ask any questions. It was we who had questions for him. As we toured the Ping-Pong room, Glines finally asked, "So what's it like, being an officer in the military?"

Poumakis spoke in a high, quiet voice with his hood up. "The most important thing we do now," he said, "is try to change people's minds. Say, 'Hey, we know it's been hard in your country, we know you've been taught to view America as an enemy, but listen, we just want you on our side. We want you to help us create a world where people can vote, and there's basic human rights, and some kind of economic opportunity for everyone. You don't have to be like us, but please, join us.'"

Poumakis touched things: the sage and gold Gamma Phi letters painted on the dining room wall; the wooden owl mascot, carved by a chainsaw artist at the Three-County Fair; the air rifles racked on the back porch; the little bedrooms carved from larger bedrooms and crammed with loft beds. When we reached the threshold of the president's room, he touched the chin-up bar in the doorframe, said, "Yup, still here," and lifted off the ground, legs limp and straight.

Glines started to count Poumakis's chin-ups out loud, and then the rest of us had to join in, or Glines's love of Poumakis would be dramatically exposed. It was only fair; we were all a little gay for the soldier in our midst, and it would have been unbrotherly to let Glines stick out, like leaving an injured comrade behind. As soon as the group counting started—as soon as we all went, "Four, five" in chorus, like cadets—Poumakis dropped to the floor.

Glines gave Poumakis a beer from the fridge and guided him to the black couch on the back porch. He sat beside him and said, "So

level with us, dude. How real are the movies about Iraq and Afghani-
stan and everything? Is that what it's like?"

What Glines was trying to ask was, *Have you been in the shit?*

Poumakis wore no particular expression. There was a slot in his
beard that opened and shut.

"I thought *Zero Dark Thirty* was okay," he said. "They showed it
was a lot of people coordinating instead of one person doing everything. But they never showed anyone being funny, except for Chris
Pratt at the end. I liked Chris Pratt because he's funny. Still, when
they were working in the office in Pakistan, none of them were ever
funny. They were always serious. They were never like, 'Okay, it's
eleven o'clock, who wants donuts?'"

The sun had set over the decrepit unaffiliated green Victorian that
backed up against our yard. Rumor had it that it was all high-school
dropouts living off a grandma they kept in the attic. Their living-
room lights came on, and then music, a dance remix of a song about
being famous.

"But was it typical," Glines asked, "of how people go undercover
and find terrorists, and take them?"

What Glines meant was, *Have you gone undercover? Have you
killed?*

Poumakis picked at the label on his beer. "I wouldn't say typical,"
he said.

"I want you to know," said Glines, "that we're your brothers.
Whatever you say never leaves the porch."

"I can neither confirm nor deny," Poumakis said.

We sat there for a second and no one said anything. Poumakis
took a breath through his nose. He might have resumed talking for
no other reason but to fill the silence.

"The first mode of cover they teach in training," he said, "the one
that's most typical in the field, is called You Me Same Same. I don't
know where the name came from. I think it's probably African or
Caribbean, but some people think it's from this Vietnam movie from
the '80s. There's this Vietnamese girl, and she's really hot and she's
Viet Cong, and they've got her captured. And you're like, *Are they going to rape her?* And she points to her eyes, and she points at the eyes

of an American, you know, his white eyes, and goes, 'You, me, same, same.'"

We all looked at one another and pointed at one another's eyes. "You, me, same, same," we said, making come-hither faces.

Poumakis looked amused. We waited, rapt.

"If you're doing You Me Same Same," he said, "the first objective is to research the target's passions and interests. The second is to persuade the target that you're like her, only more confident, nicer. Which is all she has ever wanted in a lover or a friend. It's like dating."

Glines was grinning like a fool, like a shit-eater. He was grinning like a guy who's just asked his high-school sweetheart to marry him over the Jumbotron at Fenway and she's moaning, yes, yes, yes. I felt it too. I felt like my life had been a dream in which nothing mattered, and finally I was waking up into a world that was real, a world where people fought. It was really true that I was alive.

"So who would do that?" Glines asked Poumakis, his voice shaky with joy. "The CIA?"

"An agent who's doing You Me Same Same is usually conventional military granted temporary status as intelligence," Poumakis said. "CIA guys tend to take advantage of how everything kind of loosened up after 9/11 by farming out the fieldwork to us. The CIA is good at intelligence gathering, intelligence analysis, and planning paramilitary operations. But not when it comes to doing the actual ops. We're better at fieldwork than they are. It's there in the statistics. So what are we going to do? Tell them, like, 'Fuck off, I signed up for the Navy?'"

We were all nodding as if we related. We needed some way to express our exhilaration, and nodding was the available vehicle. But of the six of us, only Glines was so high on Poumakis that he could overcome his shyness of Poumakis, and ask him what we all wanted to ask.

"You've done that?" asked Glines. "Ops? You Me Same Same?"

Poumakis drew a vaporizer from a pocket of his sweatpants and puffed. The smoke was scentless, pleasant when it hit my cheek, like the breath of a girl.

"My first target was in Sudan. He loved the Canadian Brass. He was obsessed with these two albums, *Bach: The Art of Fugue* and *Live in Germany*. I bought them on old-school cassette from a University of Khartoum student at the Agriculture and Veterinary campus in Shambat. I sat in my apartment and listened to them for hours.

"I bought a new wallet, which was tan, not black like my real one. I bought a Paul Smith suit with subtle stripes and vintage Nike sneakers because my research indicated my target thought that those things were cool. I rented an apartment and got the kind of furniture he would've bought."

"So you knew you were going to get him to come to your apartment?" I asked.

He shook his head. "I knew that it might happen, but I didn't want it to. It's something they teach you to do, getting the furniture, so that you feel like a different person. And you need everything you can get that will make you feel like it will work, because you're not an actor, and here you are acting."

"It's all in the preparation and training," I said. I wanted to be the nuts-and-bolts guy, who didn't glamorize, so that Poumakis would pull me aside and say, "You seem like you've got a good head on your shoulders, have you ever thought about intelligence work?"

Poumakis didn't acknowledge what I'd said. "When I hung out with this guy, in my striped suit—we went to this cafe on Nile Street—I was worried I would spill my glass of tea down my suit because I was faking. I thought faking would be stressful. But then this weird thing happened. I found out I was more relaxed in cover than when I wasn't in cover. It was easier than being not in cover, kind of."

"That's because you're a natural," said Glines.

It brought me no end of relief that Poumakis also declined to acknowledge this comment. It meant that I was not the only one whom Poumakis found unanswerable.

"In cover, daily life wasn't that stressful at all," Poumakis continued. "Sometimes I liked pretending to enjoy horn quartets with a target more than I liked talking about, like, Arcade Fire, my actual favorite band, with a person I actually liked. It was just easier. The awkwardness of trying to be real with someone just went away. You didn't have to try to be real. I'm pretty sure I have mild PTSD, and I get this depression that comes for a little while and then goes. That didn't happen when I was in cover. It was like being drunk."

Glines gave himself a neck rub. "If it's like being drunk, sign me up," he said. "I'm going to Sudan."

No one laughed. Next door, someone threw a Frisbee into a tree, and water fell from the leaves, the sound of sudden rain.

Glines looked panicked now that his joke had bombed. To save him, I dove in, started talking. "It's great to have you here," I said to Poumakis. "But besides just getting to grill you about all the badass shit you've done, we were kind of hoping you could give us some advice. I mean, you've done Navy Hell Week, probably, right? Tell us the tricks you learned. How do you make things shitty for a bunch of pledges?"

Poumakis vaped again. "Navy Hell Week," he said, "is, you're swimming in the ocean on four hours of sleep catching hypothermia and there are drill instructors with megaphones telling you it's cool if you want to quit and go have coffee and donuts. They're shouting at you about how there's no dishonor in quitting, go set yourself free. They want 75 percent of you to quit, they expect you to bail. You're not trying to make these pledges quit. You're just trying to make things shitty for them, right? Because if 75 percent of your pledges quit, you don't have a fraternity."

We conceded that this was the case.

"Right. You want to make things shitty for a guy? Lock him up and leave him alone."

Glines seemed to see a chance to redeem himself here. He put on a serious face and nodded, as if he were about to take notes.

"Have you done that?" he asked. "In the field?"

"I've done interrogations," he said. "And the weird thing is, people can't stand it when you leave them by themselves. They bang on the walls until they elicit a response. Or they pretend to be sick until they elicit a response."

Glines was getting excited again. He had fully recovered from his failed joke. He rubbed his knees a little as he spoke. "You put them in a shithole?" he asked. "A box kind of thing?"

Poumakis shook his head. "With the guy in the Sudan, I put him in a room for a week. Not in a shithole. In a clean, plain room with food and water. Then I'd bring him out and You Me Same Same with him. He was always up for small talk, even to me. The next day, I offered him a sparkling water. We went for a walk, under guard. The day after that, I said, 'Come on up to our quote-unquote kitchen, we've got some cabbage, some yogurt, some eggs, some fruit. Let's see if we can slap together a real meal, because neither of us wants to be here but while we're stuck here, might as well, right?'

"The next thing you know, he's like, 'It's better than the food at camp.' And later, he's like, 'You think your rifles are shit? You should see the shit rifles we have.' Gradually, he gave me more and more of what I was after. He wanted to keep it going. He wanted company.

"He had to know what I was doing, but he went into denial about it. That's how much he hated being by himself. That's how badly he wanted some You Me Same Same. Can you imagine how he felt, when I put him back in his room and he thought about the information he'd given me in exchange for a little bit of bullshitting? It must have been torture for him. I tortured the guy, in a way, is I guess what I'm saying."

"He sounds like a pussy, though," said Glines. "It wouldn't have been torture for a guy with balls. It would have been dinner."

There was something about this last word, the way it hung in the air. Glines was just trying to be supportive of Poumakis. I knew him well enough to know that. But he had started to sound like an asshole. Glines, whose acquaintance with torture consisted of the lobsters of Vinalhaven snapping at his gloves, talking about what you would and wouldn't do if you had balls.

For the first time in the evening, Poumakis showed annoyance. He didn't look aggressive. It was more like he was shutting down. The lower half of his face disappeared into his hood. Instead of stroking his beard, or his fleeces, his hands lay still on his knees. His posture was erect.

"If you want to make Hell Week bad for a pledge," he said, "I'll tell you what you do. You bring him into this house, and you lock him in one of the bedrooms. Throw in some milk and bananas, throw in some water. Give him a bedroom that has a bathroom, with a toothbrush, a shower. Paint over the windows, take away his phone, don't let anybody come anywhere near him. For the first few days, he'll beg and plead with you. He'll say, 'Please, take me out of here.' Then he'll stop, and for the next few days, he'll cuss you out. He'll say, 'Fuck you, I don't care what you do to me anymore. I hate you. Don't come near me.'"

Poumakis drew the hood back from his face. He swiped at his cheeks as if there was a mosquito trying to bite him. His eyes were bright and brown and he raised his scant eyebrows, settling into his lecture. The music was different now, a song about going out and having a good time. It sort of fit the sagging house from which it issued. As the singer discussed a night in the club, the dance floor, the VIP, the labels on his clothing, a kid with a shaved head and full-sleeve tattoos had slouched out of the house and lit a cigarette. With the cigarette in his mouth, he got on a bike that was too small for him and rode it in a circle around the yard, one hand on the left handlebar, the other hanging at his side. His shin hairs were golden in a yellow light that shone from the garage.

"When the week is over, you let him out of the room. But don't let him out of the house. Let him take a walk down the hall. Let him look out the window. Let him walk up and down the stairs. Invite him to dinner."

Glines looked at the grass. He had his head down and was fiddling with the brim of his Sox cap. Without meaning to, I shook my head at Poumakis. I didn't want him to keep going, because I didn't want Glines to be further shamed. But Poumakis wasn't looking at me. He was looking out over the yard, tugging his beard into a triangle.

"Offer him the best food you have," he said. "Chef Bill's chili. Pour him a nice cold beer. Gather round the table, and say, 'Welcome, brother. Pull up a chair. We're the ones who did that to you, and we're in charge of everything. No need to be shy. Please, join us.'"

SONNY LIEW

■

The Most Terrible Time of My Life

FROM *The Art of Charlie Chan Hock Chye*

Part art book, part bildungsroman, part history of Singapore, Sonny Liew's The Art of Charlie Chan Hock Chye *documents the life and work of a fictional graphic artist from Singapore. The following excerpt is drawn from the second chapter of the book, and begins with a chance encounter between the story's eponymous protagonist and a young writer who will become his most instrumental collaborator.*

This page
VARIATIONS
1990

Character studies (self-portraits) for
The Most Terrible Time of My Life.

Opposite & following
**THE MOST TERRIBLE TIME
OF MY LIFE**
1991
Self-published

At the age of 53, Chan began
working on what was meant to be
a multi-volume autobiographical
comic. Only one volume was ever
completed, however, covering the
period 1955–1963.

DECEMBER 1955.

HEADING TO THE POST OFFICE WITH A PARCEL FOR OUR RELATIVES IN PENANG.

IT'S BEEN 15 MONTHS SINCE "*AH HUAT'S GIANT ROBOT*" WAS PUBLISHED IN *QIAN JIN*.

AFTER THE HOCK LEE BUS RIOTS, I WROTE A NEW "*AH HUAT*" STORY FOR THE MAGAZINE, EXPOSING THE *BAD BEHAVIOUR* OF THE POLICE AND THE COLONIALISTS.

BUT THEY TURNED IT DOWN THIS TIME, CITING SPACE CONSTRAINTS.

SINGLE-PANEL CARTOONS ARE BETTER FOR US...

YOURS HAS TOO MANY PAGES...

對不起

AND SO IT SEEMED THAT MY COMICS CAREER, NO SOONER HAD IT BEGUN, WAS FIZZLING OUT WITH BARELY A WHIMPER...

BUT ALL OF A SUDDEN...

HEY

HEY!

HEY!!

HEY!

COMICS!!

THIS IS MY BROTHER, ALEX.

HI.

COME ON UP!

HEY!

HEY! YOU MADE IT!

ALEX, GO GET US SOME ORANGE JUICE.

GET YOURSELF!

HE REALLY DID HAVE A LOT OF COMICS!

LET'S SEE... I WANTED TO SHOW YOU THESE...

YOU WEREN'T KIDDING!

I'M ALWAYS SERIOUS ABOUT MY COMICS!

THESE ONES FROM *E.C.* ARE GREAT...

TOP CLASS ART AND WRITING!

WOW.

PRETTY GOOD, RIGHT?

BERTRAND, IS THIS YOUR ARTIST FRIEND?

YES, MA.

HELLO, AUNTIE.

MA!!

ARE YOU SURE YOUR PARENTS DON'T MIND ME VISITING?

MY FAVOURITE IS THIS ARTIST CALLED *WALLY WOOD*...

ESPECIALLY HIS SCIENCE FICTION DRAWINGS...

NO LAH, DON'T WORRY ABOUT IT!

YOUR STYLE IS VERY DIFFERENT, OF COURSE...

BUT THAT'S NOT A BAD THING!

I'M A BIG FAN OF AN ARTIST CALLED *TEZUKA*...

HE'S FROM JAPAN.

I LIKE *EAGLE*!

I'LL SHOW YOU NEXT TIME!

SEE?

MM, VERY NICE!

EAGLE'S VERY GOOD TOO...

THEY'RE ABLE TO DO REALLY *REALISTIC* DRAWINGS BY BUILDING ACTUAL MODELS TO USE AS REFERENCES, AND GETTING PEOPLE TO POSE FOR PHOTOS AS WELL...

DAN DARE! HE'S A PILOT OF THE FUTURE!

BUT *AH HUAT*, MAN... *AH HUAT*!

FORWARD! 向上

WHAT? OH...

I THINK THAT COULD BE THE FIRST AND LAST ISSUE. THEY DON'T SEEM TOO KEEN TO PUBLISH ANY MORE...

YEAH, I GATHERED AS MUCH WHEN I WAS TRYING TO TRACK YOU DOWN.

FORWARD!

SO...

SO, I'VE GOT AN *UNCLE* WHO RUNS A PRINTING BUSINESS...

I THINK WE COULD GET HIM TO PUBLISH *AH HUAT* AS A PROPER COMIC.

Y'KNOW, I'VE GOT LOTS OF IDEAS FOR STORIES I WANT TO TELL...

BUT I CAN'T *DRAW* TO SAVE MY LIFE.

BUT WITH THE *TWO OF US* WORKING *TOGETHER*... WE MIGHT REALLY HAVE SOMETHING!

I CAN! I'M THE *BEST* AT DRAWING!

WHAT DO YOU THINK?

AH HUAT'S
GIANT ROBOT

陈福财

JANUARY 1956.

WONG PRINTING & Co.

DID YOU BRING YOUR DRAWINGS?

OF COURSE!

HI, UNCLE!

THIS IS THE FELLOW I TOLD YOU ABOUT.

HI, BERT.

AH, YES... THE ILLUSTRATOR.

THE *COMICS* ARTIST! HE'S VERY GOOD!

HELLO, MR. WONG.

BERT HERE THINKS THERE'S GOOD MONEY TO BE MADE IN COMICS.

YEAH! THE CREATORS OF *SUPERMAN*, THEY MAKE OVER $100,000 A YEAR!

I'VE ALSO HEARD THAT THIS *"ER TONG LE YUAN"** COMIC FROM HONG KONG SELLS **50,000** COPIES PER ISSUE.

ARE YOU BOYS PLANNING TO DO SOMETHING LIKE THIS?

NO, NO. WE'LL BE DOING OUR *OWN* STORIES, SOMETHING *NEW*.

NO NEED TO COPY ANYONE!

ARE YOU *SURE* ABOUT THAT?

*儿童乐园 ("CHILDREN'S PARADISE")

IF YOU COPY SOMETHING, YOU'LL JUST END UP WITH A POOR IMITATION.

CHARLIE ALREADY HAS A STORY WITH A GIANT ROBOT, AND WE'RE WORKING ON ONE NOW ABOUT THE WAR AND THE FIGHT AGAINST THE JAPS...

IT'S *FRESH* AND *NEW*, AND THAT'S WHAT PEOPLE WILL *WANT* TO READ!

ARE KIDS REALLY INTERESTED IN THESE KINDS OF THINGS?

SURE! ROBOTS ARE *VERY* POPULAR!

BESIDES, OUR WAR COMIC WILL FEATURE *ANIMAL* CHARACTERS... KIDS WILL LIKE THAT!

OK, OK. AS LONG AS IT *SELLS*, I DON'T MIND *WHAT YOU* BOYS DO.

HOW MANY PAGES IS THE ROBOT STORY?

ABOUT 20...

AH SENG, WRITE UP A VOUCHER.

I'LL GIVE YOU TWO DOLLARS A PAGE FOR NOW...

SO THAT'S 40 DOLLARS IN TOTAL.

WHAT ABOUT THE *OTHER* THING?

HMM?

OH, YES. OK...

SURE, NO PROBLEM FOR NOW. IT'S NOT BEING USED ANYWAY.

COME ON, CHARLIE!

WHAT OTHER THING?

HEH... MY UNCLE HAS A SPARE ROOM HERE...

WELCOME TO OUR *COMICS STUDIO*!

I CAN DO THE WRITING OVER HERE...

BOOKS AND REFERENCE MATERIALS CAN GO OVER *THERE*...

AND WE SHOULD GET YOU A PROPER *DRAFTING TABLE* AS WELL!

HOW ARE WE GOING TO PAY FOR ALL THIS?

EH?

THIS IS AMAZING...

BUT I'M NOT SURE HOW WE'LL BE ABLE TO *AFFORD* IT...

LET *ME* WORRY ABOUT THE MONEY SIDE OF THINGS FOR NOW. JUST FOCUS ON THE ART...

...YOU CAN PAY ME BACK WHEN WE HIT THE *BIG TIME*!

WONG P

LATER...

YOUR FIRST PAYCHECK, AND OUR VERY OWN STUDIO SPACE...

I THINK THAT CALLS FOR A *MOVIE* CELEBRATION!

AT THE ODEON?

NAH. LET'S GO TO THE REX. WE CAN HAVE SOME *POPIAH* AND *ROJAK* AFTERWARDS.

COMICS!

HEY! HEY!

HEY!

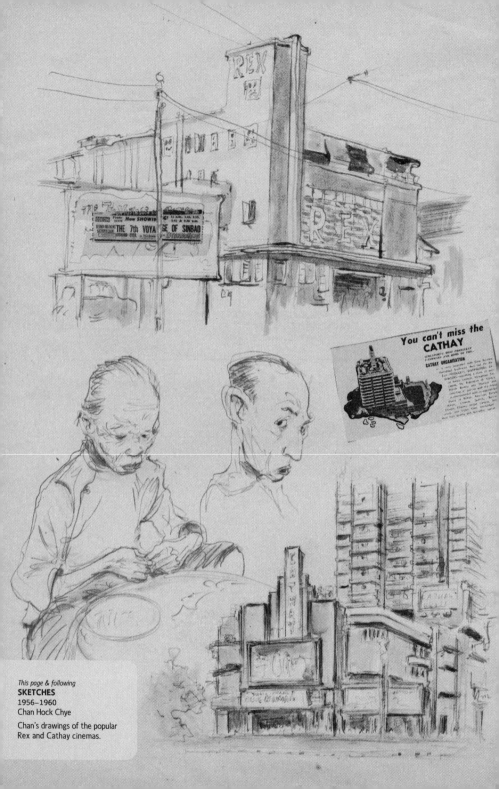

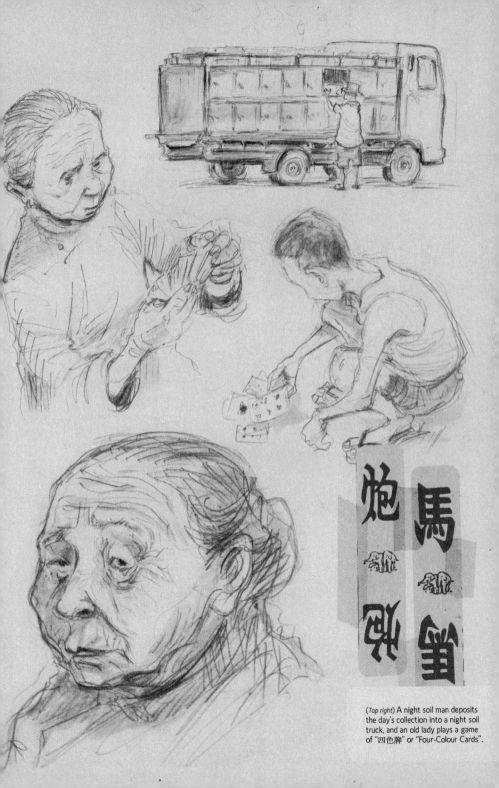

(*Top right*) A night soil man deposits the day's collection into a night soil truck, and an old lady plays a game of "四色牌" or "Four-Colour Cards".

Great World Amusement Park (*Tua Seh Kai*, or 大世界, *see bottom of page*), founded in 1929, was one of three popular amusement parks (along with New World and Happy World) offering affordable entertainment for the masses. Changing times and tastes led to their gradual decline, and Great World was closed for good in 1978.

c No 1374
GLOBE THEATRE
SINGAPORE
1st CLASS

JUNE 1956.

HEY.

ANY IDEA HOW SALES ARE GOING FOR *AH HUAT*?

OK, OK. NOT BAD! NOT *GREAT* YET...

BUT THINGS TEND TO PICK UP OVER TIME FOR *SERIALISED* COMICS...

WE JUST HAVE TO BUILD UP AN AUDIENCE AND GET THEM INVESTED IN THE CHARACTERS AND THE STORY.

DON'T WORRY, CHARLIE, WE'RE DOING ALRIGHT!

AND THIS TABLE...?

WHAT ABOUT IT?

I STILL DON'T KNOW WHY WE HAD TO GET SUCH A FANCY ONE...

IT'S ALL ABOUT THE ANGLES!

IF YOU'RE LOOKING AT YOUR DRAWING ON A FLAT SURFACE...

YOUR HEAD WILL BE AT A DIFFERENT ANGLE FROM THE DRAWING, SO IT CAN ALL TURN OUT A LITTLE *DISTORTED*...

A *TILTED* TABLE WILL HELP MAKE SURE THAT IT DOESN'T HAPPEN.

AND IT'S PROBABLY BETTER FOR YOUR *BACK* TOO!

NOT SURE ABOUT THAT!

HOW DO YOU KNOW SO MUCH ABOUT THESE THINGS?

YES, IT'S A REAL MYSTERY...

ALL THESE *SECRETS* THEY KEEP HIDDEN AWAY IN BOOKS AND SUCH...

DON'T YOU TEASE THE POOR BOY, BERT!

I BROUGHT YOU BOYS SOME ICED MILO.

LILY

MILO? BUT COMIC ARTISTS NEED *COFFEE!* KOPI-O! BLACK AS THE *DEVIL!*

THANK YOU!

THOSE WERE... THE HALCYON DAYS.

SITTING AT THE DRAWING TABLE, WITH BRUSH OR PENCIL IN HAND...

THINKING UP STORIES, PLOTS AND DREAMS...

OUTSIDE, YOU COULD HEAR THE SOUNDS OF THE CITY... MORE HUMAN VOICES THEN, FEWER CARS... AND THE COLOURS SOMEHOW MORE VIVID, IT FELT LIKE, EVEN IF THEY SEEM TO FADE WITH EACH YEAR IN PHOTOGRAPHS.

AND THEN...

AND THEN THERE WAS *LILY*.

UNCLE WONG'S YOUNGEST DAUGHTER, THE SAME AGE AS BERTRAND AND ME, SHE WAS A SPITTING IMAGE OF YU MING, THE MOVIE STAR.

HEY! CHARLIE!

I WAS JUST TELLING COUSIN HERE THAT WE COULD LOOK INTO MAKING SOME *AH HUAT* MERCHANDISE.

I THINK A ROBOT TOY WOULD BE QUITE SOMETHING!

MERCHANDISE...?

TIN TOYS, FIGURINES, BOOKMARKS, PLAYING CARDS, BADGES...

YEAH, MERCHANDISE! THAT'S THE TICKET!

BUT IT'S BACK TO THE GRINDSTONE FOR NOW...

ARE YOU BOYS STILL WORKING ON THAT WAR STORY?

THAT'S THE ONE... WE'VE COME UP WITH SOME *EXCELLENT* IDEAS!

CHARLIE, SHOW LILY THE CONCEPT DRAWINGS YOU DID.

WE'RE DRAWING THE LOCALS AS *CATS*...

THE JAPANESE AS *DOGS*...

...AND THE BRITISH AS *MONKEYS*!

IT'S FROM THE SONG THE CHINESE STUDENTS SING...

CHARLIE'S GOT A TRANSLATION!

THEY HAVE A *SONG* ABOUT CATS AND DOGS?

*"站起来!": HOKKIEN FOR "STAND ON YOUR OWN TWO FEET!"

我愛我的馬來亞

1=F

我爱我的马来亚
I love my Malaya

马来亚是我家乡
Malaya is my home

日本时期不自由
During the Japanese Occupation
We were not free

如今更苦愁
Now we are in greater misery

谁知狗去猴子来
Who knew when the dogs had gone
The monkeys would return

马来亚成苦海
And turn Malaya into a bitter sea

兄弟们呀姐妹们
Oh my brothers, my sisters

不能再等待
We can wait no more

同胞们呀快起来
Oh my compatriots
Let us all stand up

IVAN CHISTYAKOV

■

The Diary of a Gulag Prison Guard

FROM *Granta*

"Thanks to ideology," wrote the Soviet author and one-time prisoner Alek-sandr Solzhenitsyn in The Gulag Archipelago, *"the twentieth century was fated to experience evildoing on a scale calculated in the millions. This cannot be denied, nor passed over, nor suppressed." Next to nothing is known about the guard in a Siberian forced labor camp who kept a diary from 1935–36, excerpted here and published in 2016 with a translation by Arch Tait. A caption on a photo in his notebooks reads, "Chistyakov, Ivan Petrovich, repressed in 1937–38. Died at the front in Tula province in 1941." His is a homesick, frozen, and callous voice from the last century's mass grave.*

9 October 1935

A new stage in my life:

10 p.m. It's dark and damp in Svobodny. Mud and more mud. The luggage store is cramped and smoke-filled. A prop holds up the sagging ceiling, people sprawl on the floor. There is a jumble of torn quilted jackets with mismatched patches. It's difficult to find two people who look different, as they all have the same strange expression stamped on their faces, the same suspicious, furtive look. Unshaven faces, shaven heads. Knapsacks and trunks. Dejection, boredom. Siberia!

The town hardly lives up to its name. Fences and more fences, or empty land. Here a house, there a house, but with all the windows shuttered from the outside. Unwelcoming, spooky, depressing, cheerless. My first encounter: not a smart, upright soldier of the Red Army but some sort of scruffy partisan in a shabby greatcoat, no tabs on his collar, scuffed boots, cap plonked on his head, rifle over his shoulder. The local community hotel is a village house partitioned into cramped rooms. Overheated. Incessant snoring.

10 October 1935

Morning. I walk down Soviet Street. Unmetalled, no pavement. More fences, pigs, puddles, dung, geese. I could be in Gogol's *Mirgorod*, but this is Baikal–Amur Mainline Railway Central.

HQ is a two-storey brick building, with flowerbeds and a modern electric clock. Road signs: two reflective triangles and a 30-km speed limit. Same mud. Hostel. More mud.

First night in my life feeding bedbugs. Cold. No discipline here either. Incessant swearing.

"Panteleyev, don't give me that crap. Malingering, that's what it is. You know what we call that?"

We call it a crime.

Swearing to the rooftops, incessant, so dense you could lodge an ax in it.

VOKhR, the Armed Guards Unit. Bunks, colored blankets, illiterate slogans. Some men in summer-weight tunics, some in winter tunics, jackets quilted and not, leather or canvas or string belts. They lie on their beds, smoking. Two are grappling, rolling around locked together, one with his legs in the air, laughing, squealing. Another laments his lot with a wheezing accordion, bawling, "We are not afraid of work, we just ain't gonna do it." Men cleaning rifles, shaving, playing draughts, one even managing to read.

"Who's on duty here?" I ask. "Me," another partisan replies, getting up from poking embers in the stove. He's wearing padded winter trousers, a summer tunic, winter felt boots, and a convict's hat back to front on his head with a tuft of ginger hair sticking out. There's a canvas cartridge pouch on his belt. He starts trying to tidy himself up, shifting from foot to foot, uncertain how to behave. I find out later this sentinel has never been in the army and only had a few months' training on the job. What a hero! Few of them are any better.

What am I doing here? I ask myself. I feel ashamed of the little square lieutenant's insignia on my collar tab, and of being a commander, and living in 1935 across the road from the nationally celebrated Second Track of the Trans-Siberian Railway, shamed by a brilliant, soaring concrete bridge.

22 October 1935

I spent the night in a barracks hut. Cold. Killed a louse. Met the platoon commander. He seems pretty thick, etc. Walked back along the railway track.

My thoughts are all over the place, like pages torn out of a book, shuffled, stacked, crumpled, curling like paper on a fire. I'm disorientated. Lonely. Sad.

Twenty days ago I was in Moscow, alive, living my life, but now? There's no life here. There's no telling how high the clouds are, and it's impossible to take in the endlessness of the hills and the emptiness of the landscape. One hill, then another, then another, then another, on and on for thousands of kilometres. It's bewildering. Life starts to feel insignificant and futile. It gives me the creeps.

Moscow! Moscow! So far away, so out of reach!

Freezing temperatures. I hope they finish the earthworks on the bridge soon and I'm moved somewhere else. A comforting thought, providing I ignore the possibility it might be somewhere even worse.

23 October 1935

I slept all night in the warm. The joy of sleeping without needing a pile of bedclothes.

The day greets me with a stiff breeze as I walk along the track. *Zeks* grafting, inching toward freedom with every cubic meter of earth they shift and every meter of rail they lay, but what do I have to do to get demobbed? I didn't wash today: no water. Tomorrow? Probably still none. I can only dream of steaming in a bathhouse. Bathhouses make you happy. Bathhouses are heaven.

24 October 1935

Autumn is all around. There are haystacks, and the first ice on the River Arkhara appears. Autumn is brown. The haze above the distant hills merges with the horizon and you can't make out the sky, what are hilltops, what are rainclouds. A steady wind blows constantly and the oak leaves rustle in lifeless synchrony. The sun does shine, but it's pale and cold, a nickel-plated disk you can stare at. Was I really born to be a platoon commander at the Baikal–Amur Mainline forced labor camp? How smoothly it happened. They just called me in and sent me off. Party members have the Party Committee, the factory management, and the trade union to intercede, so Bazarov gets to stay in Moscow. For the rest of us, nobody puts in a word.

26 October 1935

A raging wind drives the thunderclouds low. Autumn! The russet incline of the hill is hacked into a cliff face day by day, exposing layers of geology. Trucks drive up, and moments later drive away, shuttling without respite between hill and railway station. The people, like ants, are patiently, persistently destroying the hill, transforming its hump into a square in front of the future station. The gash widens: fifteen hundred workers are a mere sprinkling in the maw of the hill, but their crowbars and shovels are having an impact. They count the cubic meters, fighting for the right to live outside, to be free. They rush through everything, whatever the weather. There is a hunger to work and work and work.

There are only statistics, statistics, statistics.

Days, cubic meters, kilometers.

If their strength did not give out, these people would work here night and day.

They work a ten-day week.

The USSR is impatient for the Second Track. The Soviet Far East is impatient for goods.

The Second Track will open up this region, speed its development. And so on.

29 October 1935

Rain and slush. The clay has been churned into sludge, which makes walking tough. Today is a footslog day. Twenty kilometers to Phalanx 13.

We've been invited to dinner by the section commander.

We walk into the village and enter a huge Ukrainian-style house that has been plastered from the inside with clay then whitewashed. Icons are draped with embroidered linen. The bedstead is a trestle bed with a lacy coverlet and the pillows are in gray chintz pillowslips. Everything is incongruous: the rags stuffed in windows where the glass is missing, the Russian stove, the icons, the bed. Dinner is different too. We have borscht with meat from a goat slaughtered yesterday, then noodles in milk with white gingerbread, homemade with butter. The Ukrainians are in their third year here and have a smallholding with a cow, three pigs, ten chickens. Sometimes they even have honey. Life could be worse for them.

The guards are permanently in a foul mood because their food is so bad.

'They're stashing food away for Revolution Day, so we get no fats.'

The camp administration have everything: meat, butter, everything.

In the evening we get an escape alert and everyone fans out. I walk along the track toward Ussuriysk. It's very still. The sun hovers over a hilltop, its last rays playing over the russet brown leaves of the trees, creating fantastic colors that contrast with equally fantastic shadows. It's exotic scenery for a European: a dwarf oak forest, the hills receding, one higher than the other far into the distance, their summits fanciful, humped animals. The haystacks look like the helmets of giants half rooted in the soil.

Construction of the Second Track is nearing completion. Only yesterday this was a graceless, jagged precipice with gnarled shrubs jutting out of it, but today? Today a women prisoners' brigade appeared and now for 150 meters there is an even, two-storey high embankment with regular lines and a smooth surface that is a sight for sore eyes.

Hills are sliced through, marshes drained, embankments embanked, bridges straddle streams coaxed into drainage conduits. It's the result of concrete, iron, human labor. Stubborn, persistent, focused labor.

And all around, the taiga, the dense forests of Siberia. As Pushkin never said, how much that word contains! How much that is untouched, unknown, unknowable! How many human tragedies, how many lives the taiga has swallowed up. I shudder when I think about the trek to Siberia, to exile, to prison. And now here is Petropavlovka, a village whose buildings bear the mark of a past of direst penury, but where a collective farm now thrives.

30 October 1935

To the bathhouse, the miraculous bathhouse! It's just a wooden shed, its inside walls pointed with cement, although you could stop up scores of cracks and still be left with as many again. There's a layer of slime on the floor, a cauldron plastered in place on top of the stove. The bathhouse is warm now, but how will it be in winter? The roof leaks—but still, I have a good scrub. It feels so good after twenty days!

I couldn't help getting nostalgic over the bathhouse in Moscow. It would be so nice to have a proper night's sleep too, but we are here to work. Nightfall brings disturbances, escapes, killings. For once, though, may the gentle autumn night extend its protective mantle over the captive. Two runaways this time. There are interrogations, pursuits, memoranda, reports to HQ. The Third Section takes an interest, and in place of rest night brings unrest and nightmares.

1 November 1935

Then there are prisoners who refuse to go out to work. They're just the same as all the others, no less human. They get just as upset at losing that roving red banner as anyone else. They cry just as bitterly. They have the same psychology as anyone serving a sentence, the same oppressive thoughts about backbreaking toil, bad conditions, hopes for the future. The same faith that some day they will be free, the same disappointed hopes, despair, and mental trauma. You need to work on their psychology, be subtle, be kind. For them kindness is like a second sun in the sky. The competitiveness here is cutthroat. A foul-up in recording their work credits can drive them to attempt escape, commit murder, and so on. No amount of "administrative measures" help, and nor does a pistol. A bullet can only end a life, which is no solution, and a dead prisoner can cause a lot of grief. A wounded *zek* is a wild beast.

4–5 November 1935

Five hours' sleep in the past forty-eight. It snowed during the night, icy cold. At five in the morning there's a noise, a knock. I hear the duty guard reporting to the deputy head of GHQ that it's not easing off. It's as cold in the room as outside in the snow.

We check out the huts. Oh, life! How can you do this to people? There are bare bunks, gaps everywhere in the walls, snow on the sleeping prisoners, no firewood. A mass of shivering people, intelligent, educated people. Dressed in rags filthy from the trackbed ballast. Fate toys with us all. To fate, none of us matter in the slightest.

They can't sleep at night, then they spend the day laboring, often in worn-out shoes or woven sandals, without mitts, eating their cold meals at the quarry. In the evening their barracks are cold again and people rave through the night. How can they not recall their warm homes? How can they not blame everyone and everything, and probably rightly so? The camp administration don't give a damn about the prisoners and as a result they refuse to go out to work. They think we are all bastards and they are right. What they are asking for is the absolute minimum, the very least we are obliged to give them. We have funds that are allocated for it, but our hoping for the best, our haphazardness, our reluctance, or the devil only knows what, means we deprive them of the very minimum they need to work.

10 November 1935

This life is nomadic, cold, transient, disordered. We are getting used to just hoping for the best. That wheezing accordion underscores the general emptiness. The cold click of a rifle bolt. Wind outside the window. Dreams and drifting snow. Accordion wailing, feet beating time.

12 November 1935

An influx of juvenile delinquents: the *zeks* call them "sparkies." We count them: five short. Count them again: still five short. We check them again: ten short, so another five have got away. We bring out extra security. Thirty sparkies are working; there is no way any of them can escape. We count again: twenty-nine. They cover themselves with sand or snow and, when everyone else has left, come out and leg it. Three more escaped during the night.

I talk to their top dog.

"Can you find them?"

"Sure!"

He did. They won't do it again. It turns out he sent them off himself and they got drunk but they're back now. Others will do the same tomorrow. I let a man out for a pee and he just disappeared. I saw a woman standing there. She pulled out a skirt she'd tucked into her trousers, put a shawl over her head, and before I knew it she'd vanished.

13 November 1935

I walked to Arkhara this morning. Twenty kilometers hardly counts here. We talked shop: someone got killed, someone else got killed. In 3 Platoon a bear ripped the scalp off a hunter and smashed up his rifle. They bayoneted it.

I bought frozen apples. They were a delight to eat. I spent the day hanging around at the station, which is regarded as normal. What can you do if there are no trains? Hang around.

16 November 1935

It's 26 degrees below zero and a gale-force wind is blowing. Cold. Cold outside, cold indoors. Our building seems to have more holes than wall. The building's superintendent comes in and cheers us up:

"Don't worry, lads, it's going to get twice as cold as this."

How wasteful human mismanagement is. Nobody thought to lay the sub-grade before the frost came and now the laborers are forced to dig a trench, thirty cm deep, into frozen clay as viscous as tin.

17 November 1935

Do you know what it feels like to be out in the taiga at night?

Let me tell you. There are oak trees, perhaps three hundred years old, their branches bare, like giants' arms, like tentacles, paws, beaks of prehistoric monsters, and they seem to reach out to seize and crush anyone they can catch.

You sit round a campfire and the flickering shadows make all these limbs look like they're moving, breathing, animated, alive. The quiet rustling of the remaining leaves and the branches tapping other branches make you think even more of the Cyclops or other monsters. You are overhearing a conversation you can't understand. There are questions being asked and answers given.

You hear melodies and rhythms. The flames of the fire pierce the darkness for five meters or so, and sparks fly like long glowworms in the air, swirling, colliding and overtaking each other. The face of your comrade opposite, vividly lit by the flames against the backdrop of the night, with shadows darting from his nose and the peak of his Red Army helmet, looks theatrically grotesque. You don't want to talk loudly. It would be out of place. You want to sit and doze and listen to the whispering of the trees.

23 November 1935

One more day crossed out of my life in the service of pointless military discipline. What if the Third Section read these lines, or the Political Department? They will interpret them their way.

24 November 1935

Have you seen the sun rise in these hills?

Something unexpected is the way the darkness disappears instantly. You look one way and it is dark, then you turn, close your eyes for a moment, and it is day. It's as if the light had been stalking you, waiting for you to open the door so that it could slip in, as iridescent as mother-of-pearl. The sun has not appeared yet but the sky is already ablaze, not only on the horizon but everywhere. It is aflame, changing like a theater set under the skilled hand of a lighting technician; as the action unfolds, it is painted every color. Rockets explode, firing rays of light from behind the hilltop. There is a stillness, a solemn silence, as if a sacrament is to be administered that cannot be celebrated without it. The silence intensifies and the sky reaches the peak of its brilliance, its apogee. The light grows no brighter but, in an instant, from behind the hill, the fireball of the sun emerges, warm, radiant, and greeted by an outburst of song from the dawn chorus.

Morning has broken. The day begins, and with it all the vileness. Here is one instance: there is a fight in the phalanx, a fight between women. They are beating one of the best shock workers to death and we are powerless to intervene. We are not allowed to use firearms inside the phalanx. We do not have the right even to carry a weapon. They are all 35-ers, but you feel sorry for the woman all the same. If we wade in there will be a riot; if they later recognize we were right, they will regret what they have done. You just get these riots. The devil knows but the Third Section doesn't. They'll come down on us and bang us up whether or not the use of firearms was justified. Meanwhile, the *zeks* get away with murder. Well, what the hell. Let the prisoners get on with beating each other up. Why should we get their blood on our hands?

27 November 1935
This is how we live: in a cramped room furnished with a trestle bed and straw mattress, a regulation-issue blanket, a table with only three out of four legs and a creaky stool with nails you have to hammer back in every day with a brick. A paraffin lamp with a broken glass chimney and lampshade made of newspaper. A shelf made from a plank covered with newspaper. Walls partly bare, partly papered with cement sacks. Sand trickles down from the ceiling and there are chinks in the window frames, door, and gaps in the walls. There's a wood-burning stove, which, while lit, keeps one side of you warm. The side facing toward the stove is like the South Pole, the side facing away from it is like the North Pole. The amount of wood we burn would make a normal room as warm as a bathhouse, but ours is colder than a changing room.

Will they find me incompetent, not up to the job, and kick me out? Why should I be sacrificed like so many others? You become stultified, primitive, you turn into a bully and so on. You don't feel you're developing, either as a commander or a human being. You just get on with it.

4 December 1935
Before I am even out of bed, another escape. I'll have to go looking for him tomorrow. We should just shoot three in each phalanx to put

them off the idea. Escapes disrupt everything. What a dog's life, sniffing around like a bloodhound, browbeating everyone all the time. Banged one *zek* up for twenty-four hours.

7 December 1935

I have to admit, I am growing into BAM. Imperceptibly the environment, the way of doing things, the life are sucking me in. Perhaps inevitably.

Tried studying Leninism but it only made me feel worse by rubbing in the kind of life we are living. What positive thing can I occupy myself with? Nothing.

8 December 1935

Above the hills there are whirlwinds and snowstorms. Everything is milky white. The silhouettes of trees make it look as if they are walking toward us as, now here, now there, the blizzard relents. But then there's another flurry, and tongues of dry, prickly snow inflict thousands, millions of venomous snakebites. Branches as thick as your arm, thicker even, snap off readily in the icy cold.

I sleep soundly and wake up refreshed. The air is clean and frosty and sometimes there is even a dusting of snow. My lecture program flaps on the wall. By lunchtime the temperature is down to minus 40 and the cold attacks every exposed part of my body. I stare longingly at a log of firewood, imagining the energy, the warmth within it. It's so cold in the room that a wet hand freezes to the door handle. Soap doesn't lather until the heat of my hand has melted it. Smoke from a steam engine doesn't disperse but hangs in the air like tufts of cotton wool. It mixes with steam to form snowflakes, an impenetrable haze obscuring a window like nets.

The lads have formed a jazz band with penny whistles and pipes, balalaikas and rattles. Music can also be warming, literally.

Meanwhile, *zeks* are on the run. Freedom. Freedom, even with hunger and cold, is still precious and irreplaceable. They may get away for only a day, but at least they get out of the camp. I wouldn't mind a day away from this job myself.

* * *

9 December 1935

Minus 42 degrees during the night and very, very quiet. The air chimes like crystal. The dry crack of a gunshot. It feels as if the air could break like glass and splinter. In places the ground has fissures as wide as my hand. It's so cold that even the rails can snap, with a sound unlike anything I've ever heard.

29 January 1936

My neck has frozen up and I can't bend or turn it. I have a headache and a runny nose. Went out to Territories 13 and 14. Squad Commander Sivukha goads his gray along at a gallop but my devil of a horse, snorting and twitching its ears and straining at the reins, doesn't let me take the lead.

My heart is so desolate, it alarms me.

I feel as if I'm not living in the real world but in some weird, unearthly world in which I can live and think but can't speak my thoughts. I can move, but everything is constrained. The sword of the Revtribunal hangs over everything I do. I feel constantly held back: you mustn't do this, you mustn't do that. Although I feel solidarity with society, I feel cut off from it by an insurmountable, if fragile, partition. I'm aware of my own strength, yet at the same time feel weak and powerless, a nonentity. I feel hopelessness and apathy, almost despair, that so much cannot be achieved. I stumble blindly along the paths of this world, unable to work out what is allowed and what is not. The thought that drills into my brain is, "How long will this go on for?" A lifetime? I have at least ten years of life ahead of me and I'm not being allowed to live them like a normal human being. Must I despair? We have to fight for every stupid little thing: a visit to the bathhouse, sugar, matches, clean linen, and more besides. As for heat, firewood, we almost risk our lives for that. We, the armed guards, are powerless.

5 February 1936

The sun warms us more kindly, and is even quite hot. During the day it gets as warm as 15–18 degrees. Not long now until summer and more escape attempts. The shortages of food, shoes, and underwear are so tiresome. We are promised everything, and in the

Center they clearly think we are living in a paradise. In reality, we are living in theories. We have theoretical semolina, butter, and new uniforms. Theoretically the Center is thinking about us. That's supposed to be encouraging. For some reason I simply do not believe it. Perhaps I'm the wrong sort of person. I would like to be provided, simply and without rhetoric, with the basic necessities. Today we had dumplings and homemade noodles, etc. Tomorrow, it will be homemade noodles and dumplings, and that has been going on for the past month.

11 February 1936
Making a little joke out of it, just barely hinting, the political adviser mentions mentoring. Incentivization. If a phalanx fulfills more of the Plan, the platoon commander gets paid more. I'm not swallowing that bait. How could I be a Stakhanovite when I have no wish to work at BAM for more than a year? If you stand out then you will never get away. In any well-ordered project you find some disorder, but we have more disorder than order. They put pressure on the guards and hint at incentivization, but make no attempt to address the real problem. There are all these miscellaneous "educators" in the Education and Culture Unit slobbing about, getting drunk and generally behaving scandalously, and the guards are expected to cover for the job they are not doing.

The phalanx leaders have it in for the guards. Our superiors are supposedly rehabilitating *zeks* and we're supposed to just put up with it. Why doesn't someone put those people in their place and stop them undermining our authority! If you dismissed me now without a month's notice I'd agree to it in a flash. In fact, I'd agree to donate a month's pay on top. What sort of work can you do in that kind of mood? All the same, I wonder what they do with educated people who would be capable of managing a phalanx, teaching them and so on.

12 February 1936
Today is a holiday in Moscow. I would be riding the tram home, planning my evening.

13 February 1936

The hills, the taiga, my thoughts, all exist in a kind of vacuum. Not only that, but a vacuum with constraints. There is another world abroad. I know it exists, but I can't get there.

23 February 1936

Red Army Day. I hand over 5 Platoon and prepare 4 for handover. Something is in the air. I'll be somewhere, somehow. I don't like moving, carting my belongings around, settling in. I'll even miss 4 Platoon a bit. They weren't such a bad lot.

25–26 February 1936

In Zavitaya. Spent a sleepless night in a truck. I feel doped all day. The boss calls me in and appoints me commander of a division. I've drawn the short straw, I'll have to serve in this army for decades now, like a serf. I sit with Savchuk and listen to the gramophone. It's emotionally unsettling.

I receive my letter of appointment. I have to start forming a divisional HQ. I have a meeting with the men from Moscow. Someone has a keen ear and long tongue. The company commander alludes to my demob yearnings. It feels strange, after the taiga, to be in an actual town. I'll have to get used to it. I'm not feeling quite right in the head. Must be the sleepless nights.

Also the jubilation, the wild, throbbing jubilation, has thrown me off balance. I receive a greetings telegram to mark Workers' and Peasants' Red Army Day. I'll enter . . . [sentence left incomplete]. The violin reduces me to a quivering wreck. There's nobody to exchange so much as a word with. There's no one to answer my questions.

I can't do this. I can't.

My pen is blunt.

Just breaking off in mid-sentence.

SHEILA HETI

■

A Correspondence with Elena Ferrante

FROM *Brick*

I interviewed Elena Ferrante by email over the summer of 2016. She read my questions (which were written in English) and wrote her responses in Italian. Her replies were translated by Ann Goldstein, the English translator of Ferrante's many books. I had been hesitant about conducting this interview when I was offered the opportunity, for I admire Ferrante's reticence. Yet, debating it over with myself, it seemed it would be a mistake not to ask this great writer questions, if I had the chance.

For those who are unaware, Ferrante is one of the most celebrated contemporary writers in the world, and rightly so. In 2011, she released the first of a series of four books (each around 350 pages in length) called The Neapolitan Quartet, *which follow two female friends from the time of their childhood in Naples in the 1950s to the present day. The books thrillingly unmask the consciousness and social situation of these women, tracing the complex bonds and political struggles of several generations of families in twentieth-century Naples. Reading these books, I felt a keen loss over the many great books that had not been written by women down through time; Ferrante made me long for even more first-rate writers to map (and to have mapped) the many underwritten aspects of the female experience. To me, the books have a distinctly female point of view: the point of view not of the natural victor but of one who has to fight for the right to observe.*

*Her three earlier and shorter novels (*Troubling Love, The Days of Abandonment, *and* The Lost Daughter, *published in Italian between*

1992 and 2006) are like tinctures of the quartet: exquisitely precise and intensely felt, they magnify moments in a life and are written in a style and language that calls to mind few others—perhaps Clarice Lispector, for being just as brutal, penetrating, and heartbreaking. Ferrante's books are profoundly contemporary while giving the same satisfaction as many nineteenth-century novels, as if Ferrante were not living in a landscape of busily competing media, but rather writing in a world where the quiet of readers can be taken for granted. She is formally risk-taking yet is a masterful storyteller. Her books rush you along in a swell of complicity, curiosity, feeling, and suspense. I cannot think of a single person I know who has not read Ferrante only to fall helplessly into her world. She has collapsed the gap between the sort of books that writers feel awe for and that the reading public can't get enough of—the rarest thing.

Speaking personally, as a writer who has engaged in the various publicity and marketing strategies that many of us allow, I was interested to talk to Ferrante about how she knew from the beginning that she wanted to avoid the performance of self; I wanted to ask about the relationship between her own "disappearance" and the many disappearances she writes about. To me, there is something special about Ferrante's disappearance as a body: unlike with, say, Salinger or Pynchon, disappearance is Ferrante's main literary theme, and so her choice seems artistically meaningful, not just personal. I wanted to ask about how she—as a great illustrator of the human condition—has navigated such experiences as motherhood, discipleship, and rebellion. Naturally, I was curious to know how she wrote her books, but I didn't ask too many craft questions because I know that for any writer, composition is ultimately a mystery.

Ferrante has managed, for decades, that difficult and enviable thing: the maintenance of total privacy as a human being, along with total openness as a creator through her art. I, and many of her devoted readers, hope there is even more of that art still to come. We are so grateful she took the time to do this interview, although as you will see, she doesn't consider this an interview at all.

—Sheila Heti

HETI: You've remarked that you forget the books you read. Do you think there's some connection between being a reader who forgets

(I am too) and being able to create and write? Maybe forgetting is a subconscious kind of remembering that allows writers to recombine what they've taken from literature in ways that are particular to them.

FERRANTE: Yes, that's probably the case. I do forget, I forget especially the books I've loved very much. I have an impression of them, I have a feeling for them, but to discuss them I would have to reread them. If I had a clear memory that allowed me to cite passages, point out crucial moments, any attempt at writing of my own would seem to me lost at the start. Imagination is said to be a function of memory. I prefer to think that it's a function of nostalgia. We compose stories knowing very well that we are the last to arrive. And yet every time it seems to us that we are returning to the moment when the first human being, with nothing but the truth of his experience and the urge to reinvent it at every step, began to tell a story.

HETI: Do you have any interest in writing short stories?

FERRANTE: I've written very few short stories. The form that suits me is the long story, not the novel: I surprised myself by the dimensions of *The Neapolitan Quartet*. The thickness of the volumes on the shelf makes me anxious, I have the feeling that I overdid it.

HETI: Is there something about "the book" as an idea or object that is particularly meaningful to you? And if books ceased to be printed, but were just read on tablets—not that I think this will happen— would you continue to write?

FERRANTE: I've never worshipped books. I've always had a sense of the provisional nature of forms—the world changes continuously and what seemed to us inconceivable soon becomes a habit. I admit, however, that I do worship writing. Everything will change, but I can't imagine the end of the possibility of writing, with whatever tool, on whatever surface.

HETI: Your three novels before *The Neapolitan Quartet*—were they written in fragments, which you later pieced into a narrative, or were they written from beginning to end? Some writers plan what's going to happen chapters before they get there; others can see only a few sentences ahead. What is the process like for you?

FERRANTE: I've always worked a lot on fragments. Sometimes there was almost no connection between them: they were good as self-sufficient pages, but there was no way to put them together. More often, though, a single fragment expanded and became a long story. The result almost always seemed to me artificial in tone because of an excess of invention, a maniacal attention to the sentence. I liked to tell stories—yes, I've always liked that—but I couldn't stick to what it seemed to me I had in mind in a satisfying way. Here I must explain myself: I always know what I want to tell but in a very confused way, so confused that I wouldn't be able to say it even to myself. In the past, to get out of that confusion, in the urgency to express myself and understand what was going through my own head, I would talk to a friend. But I soon discovered that the spoken story took away the desire to write, and so I learned to be silent. If I want the story to move from confusion to order, I have to write: for me, there is no other way. Naturally, once the story is under way, as it moves on from the beginning and seeks a conclusion, I may discover possible links to material already written, and I use it or rewrite it. But essentially, when I write, I myself am amazed at what emerges from the fog and becomes clear, establishes connections, finds junctions. Yet I should clarify here that not even this simple movement from confusion to story has ever seemed to me sufficient. The problem for me is naturalness of tone and preserving the truth. If, in telling a story, the writing loses truth, I throw it away.

HETI: You once said, "I tend to edit and then inevitably revert to the original draft, when I see what I've lost by editing." I agree: there is always some power in the way a person first catches the words on the page. Can you talk about balancing your instinct to keep the rawness with your instinct to clean up? If you often prefer the first draft to the edited draft, what does your editing process consist of?

FERRANTE: I detest vapid, sugary, sentimental tones and I try to get rid of them. I detest refinement when it cancels out naturalness, and so I look for precision without going too far. I could continue like that, with a fine list of intentions, but it's just talk. In fact, I move by instinct, a spontaneous movement that, if I put it in order, becomes merely a banal guidebook. So let's say that, pulled this way and that by countless readings, by varied layers of taste, by inclinations and idiosyncrasies, I generally aim at what seems to me perfection. Then, however, perfection suddenly seems an insane excess of refinement and I return to versions that seem effective precisely because they are imperfect.

HETI: Picasso said the new work of art always looks ugly at first, especially to its creator. Did you find your books ugly in the way Picasso meant?

FERRANTE: Yes, certainly yes, but not because I feel the book as new; rather because I feel it as mine, tarnished by contact with my experience.

HETI: Your books resist the pressure to be "correct" in a feminist sense. For me, I have noticed that often women will react negatively to portrayals of women that are "un-feminist." Why do you think such readers have a hard time with portrayals of women that conflict with their ideals? Do they feel the female author is somehow betraying them?

FERRANTE: "Correctness" has never been a concern of mine when I write. Nor have I ever felt, in telling a story, that I had to adapt the story or the character to the demands of a cultural alignment, to the urgent needs of political battles, even if I share them a hundred percent. Literature is not the sounding board of ideologies. I write always and only about what it seems to me I know thoroughly, and I would not bend the truth of a story to any higher necessity, not even to some ethical imperative or some prudent consistency with myself.

HETI: Jane Austen, Virginia Woolf, Elsa Morante, Clarice Lispector, Alice Munro. What are these writers, whom you cite among your favorite writers, able to do?

FERRANTE: *Pride and Prejudice* is perfect, but I find *Sense and Sensibility* and *Emma* more appealing. I like texts that are generous and thus imperfect. Elsa Morante's *House of Liars* and Clarice Lispector's *The Passion According to G. H.* also belong to this category, for different reasons.

HETI: Could you speak a bit about *Madame Bovary?* This book always upsets me. I can't take how unsympathetic Flaubert is to Bovary, how trite he feels her entrapment is, how foolish and narcissistic her fantasies. What do you think of the character of Bovary, and of Flaubert's relationship to his character?

FERRANTE: I think of Emma Bovary as the extraordinary incarnation, today more alive than ever, of how women can become the victims of debased liberating ideologies. Madame Bovary reads, and reads about what the full life of a romantic woman should be; that is to say, not a stupid, pious, provincial woman but a free woman worthy of a Byron. Flaubert shows in fact how his heroine's romanticizing is modeled more on male needs than on hers. Even structurally, the book shows the vise in which Emma is gripped. Not only does the author make her a victim of superficial lovers—although he concedes her the title, he denies her both the opening (devoted to Charles Bovary) and the end (devoted to the pharmacist Homais). Good books are not those that tell how things ought to go but those that tell how things do go.

HETI: Do you keep copies of the books you have written and published in the room where you write?

FERRANTE: No.

HETI: So much contemporary female writing is accused of narcissism. Have you escaped the charge of narcissism, or have you received it? I'd like to bind this question to your comments about women who "practice a conscious surveillance on themselves," who before were "watched over by parents, by brothers, by husbands, by the community." You have written that women who practice surveillance on themselves are the "heroines of our time," but it's precisely these women—real and fictional—who are accused of the sin of narcissism, as if a woman looking at herself (rather than being looked at by a man) was insulting to everyone. How do you understand this charge?

FERRANTE: I've never felt narcissism to be a sin. It seems, rather, a cognitive tool that, like all cognitive tools, can be used in a distorted way. No, I think it's necessary to be absolutely in love with ourselves. It's only by reflecting on myself with attention and care that I can reflect on the world. It's only by turning my gaze on myself that I can understand others, feel them as my kin. On the other hand, it's only by assiduously watching myself that I can take control and train myself to give the best of myself. The woman who practices surveillance on herself without letting herself be the object of surveillance is the great innovation of our times.

HETI: You've said, "Even if we're constantly tempted to lower our guard—out of love, or weariness, or sympathy, or kindness—we women shouldn't do it. We can lose from one moment to the next everything that we have achieved." This is very striking to me. What does it mean to you to lower your guard? Women are taught to give ourselves fully, with great trust, in love . . . but you think we shouldn't?

FERRANTE: It seems to me risky to forget that no one gave us the freedoms we have today—we took them. For that very reason they can at any moment be taken away again. So just that, we mustn't ever lower our guard. It's wonderful to give oneself fully to another, we women know how to do it. And we should continue. It's a serious mistake to retreat, giving up the marvelous feelings we're capable of. Yet it's indispensable to keep alive the sense of self. In Naples, certain girls who showed the marks of beatings would say, even with pleased half-smiles, He hits me because he loves me. No one can dare to hurt us because he loves us, not a lover, not a friend, not even children.

HETI: You've said, "I feel such a sense of unease and distrust these days that I can no longer write even half a word without fearing that, once published, it might be distorted or purposely taken out of context and used in a malicious way." I think this is something many writers feel. Have you found a solution for it?

FERRANTE: Yes. Be silent, recover my strength, start again.

HETI: Do you ever have the desire to publish under a new pseud-onym—to leave Ferrante behind and release a book into the world around which there are no assumptions? Or do you like building the oeuvre? Do you have a connection to the name?

FERRANTE: No, I don't enjoy playing with pseudonyms. That bit of "I" that I manage to put together as an author corresponds to the name of Elena Ferrante.

HETI: I think many male artists are flattered by the idea of having ar-tistic disciples, and many young men I know (writers, artists) enjoy being disciples of the older male artists they respect. This seems less the case among women who admire other women; women seem not to want imitators and seem not to want to imitate even the women they love. If this is true, how does a female literary tradition come into being? Or how do women become part of a non-gendered tradition, if tradition has anything to do with strong links between writers?

FERRANTE: I don't know. I've seen men in the most diverse fields fear young followers like the plague, terrified by the idea of being supplanted. And I've seen women of some power help other women without feeling threatened. It depends on the individuals. Of course, it's more likely that a certain number of disciples will crowd around a male writer because, in spite of everything, a male writer today ema-nates more power than a female writer. Perhaps the status of an es-tablished male writer is more solid than that of a female writer, and so it's possible that in his imitators he sees only the affirmation of his own reputation and not the threat of being overtaken so that he ap-pears instead to be the disciple of his imitator. But in my view what truly counts is not the crowd of followers who imitate you but the ca-pacity to distinguish who can be creatively grafted onto your experi-ence of writing and expand it, push it where you would be unable to take it. This is what establishes a tradition and this is what should be important to we women who write.

HETI: There's such a deep connection between your own anonymity and the many disappearances that haunt your work: Lila in *My Brilliant Friend*, the husband who abandons in *The Days of Abandonment*, the missing doll in *The Lost Daughter*, the dead mother in *Troubling Love*. In the case of all these disappearances, it is the disappearance that provokes the narrator's writing. Do you think your knowledge of your own "public absence" or "disappearance" likewise propels your writing-self? If so, what is the connection between your writing-self, which creates, and your disappearing author-self? Do you think you have to enact this disappearance to create the tension necessary to create, as we witness happening to the writers in your books?

FERRANTE: We have difficulty accepting that our lives acquire meaning more from losses than from gains, from absences rather than from presences. The same happens with creative activity. It's hard to accept that the author function is unstable. It emerges in its entirety in the making of the work and then it withdraws, vanishes; nothing assures us that it will return. In its place remains the label of the name on the cover, or we ourselves, emptied and yet engaged in frantically filling the void, in the spectacle of self-promotion organized by the culture industry. The only true filling of that void is the completion of the work. The author can offer himself to the public only in an aesthetic form, whether complete or incomplete.

HETI: Thinking of the amazing harmony between the stories you tell and how you choose to engage with the public brings to mind Andy Warhol, whose public performance and art had as perfect a harmony. Are there writers or artists you respect on this level of an aesthetic and symbolic consistency between their work and their self-presentation?

FERRANTE: Marina Abramovic seems to me to have represented this fact vividly in her work *The Artist Is Present*. The author's presence is possible only as it coincides precisely with her being the work.

HETI: Do you smoke cigarettes?

FERRANTE: Until a few years ago I smoked a lot, then I stopped abruptly. I tell you this because what is written while smoking seems better than that which fears for its health. But we have to learn to do well without necessarily doing harm to others and ourselves.

HETI: What is the role of a title for you? What sorts of titles do you like?

FERRANTE: I don't think that the title and the cover have much importance. I make use of them (sometimes polemically), but I think in essence only a good text makes a title lasting and a cover memorable.

HETI: You often use the words *authenticity* and *verisimilitude* as opposites. Can you clarify for me what you mean by these terms?

FERRANTE: One has to have great skill in order to write a story of which one can say, It seems true. I've tried to write such stories myself, and I read them with pleasure. And yet a text that skillfully gives an impression of truth is no longer convincing to me, as it used to be. Our world is based increasingly on effects of truth and less and less on truth. So I prefer books that it seems to me go back to an authentic experience. I don't at all despise skill—on the contrary. But more and more it interests me not as virtuosity in the reproduction of what is right before our eyes but as the capacity to adopt expressive means suitable for giving form to what is intimately ours and is difficult to say even to ourselves.

HETI: You've written, "A novel about today that is engaging and full of characters and events should be a novel about and against the suspension of disbelief." How does your work avoid the necessity of the suspension of disbelief, and do you find too many novels are written today that require the suspension of disbelief? If readers are trained to suspend their disbelief, are they less effective political actors on their own behalf?

FERRANTE: Those words of mine were a political metaphor. I was referring to what seems to me to have happened in recent decades: the transformation of citizens into a public involved in representations of the world that are skillfully constructed in order to suspend incredulity. The citizen risks acting like a fan, an enthusiastic consumer of media narratives that are plausible but deceptive, because those narratives are not the truth but have the appearance of truth. In other words, we have to return to not believing what they tell us. We have to relearn to distinguish between truth and verisimilitude.

HETI: Why do you do interviews? How do you decide which interviews to participate in? Are there rules you follow? Why not let the books exist without the interviews? Are you ever going to stop doing interviews altogether? Why not now?

FERRANTE: I no longer follow any rule. The main thing is that it doesn't seem to me that I'm giving interviews. You think that we're doing an interview? I don't. In an interview, the person being interviewed entrusts his body, his facial expressions, his eyes, his gestures, the way he speaks—an often-improvised speech, inconsistent, poorly connected—to the writing of the interviewer. Something that I can't accept. What we are doing resembles, rather, a pleasant correspondence. You think about it and write me your questions; I think about it and write my answers. It's writing, in other words, and I am fond of all occasions for writing. In the past it seemed to me that I was unable to come up with answers suitable for publication. Either they were too succinct, a yes or a no, or a short question became an occasion for reflection and I wrote pages and pages. Now I think I've learned something but not necessarily. So no, I don't give interviews, to anyone, but I find these exchanges in writing increasingly useful—for me, naturally. It's writing that should be placed beside that of the books, like a fiction not very different from literary fiction. I'm telling you about myself, but you too, a writer—I read one of your books in Italian, which I loved—with your questions are telling me about yourself. I talk about myself, as do you, as a producer of writing. I do it truthfully, addressing not only you and our possible readers but also myself, or at least that substantial part of myself that considers it completely senseless to waste so much time writing and needs reasons that justify the waste. In short, your questions help me to invent myself as an author, to give form, that is, to this unstable, elusive part that I myself know little or nothing about. Something that I imagine has happened to you too, as an author, when you have formulated the questions.

HETI: Do you think literature is possible without loneliness—either in the writer who writes it or in the reader who reads it?

FERRANTE: There are those who write or read in the midst of chaos; it depends on the need and on self-discipline.

HETI: In Magda Szabó's *The Door*, Emerence—the intelligent cleaning woman with a strong inner code of behavior, who keeps house for the intellectual woman-writer protagonist—reminds me a bit of your Lila, and Szabó's protagonist is reminiscent of your Elena. Yet Emerence is somehow the superior of the pair, as is Lila. Is there something in the figure of the intellectual woman writer that pales in comparison (from the perspective of the woman writing) to the (comparatively) unedu- cated woman who yet knows and understands the world? Why do so many female writers demean the "intellectual" female figures we cre- ate? Do we still not truly value female literary work, women who work with their minds? Is it a kind of self-loathing? Why do we often portray intellectual women as having lost more than they have gained?

FERRANTE: You pose a very interesting question; I have to think about it. Why do we invent cultivated, intelligent women and then lower their level or even their pleasure in life? Who knows. Maybe because we're still incapable of a convincing portrayal of female intel- ligence. We haven't completely set aside the literary model that rep- resented us at the side of a superior man who would take care of us and our children. Thus, though we have now acquired the sense of our inner richness and our intellectual autonomy, we portray them in a minor key, as if our capacity to produce ideas and culture were a presumptuous exaggeration, as if, even having something extra, we ourselves didn't really believe in it. From here, probably, comes the literary invention of secondary female figures who possess that something extra in themselves, remind us of it, assure us that it's there and should be appreciated. We are still in the middle of the crossing, and literature makes do however it can.

HETI: Do you ever regret not taking the path of not having children? I worry (for I think I will probably not have children) that maybe I won't be able to be a good enough writer if I don't have this experience. Obviously you can't have children for this reason. And Virginia Woolf and many other great writers were childless, yet I still have this fear; on the other hand, I want all my time to read and write. Do you think it's possible for a woman to experience her deepest humanity if she is not a mother? If not, isn't that a problem for someone interested in knowing humanity? Another version of this question might be: Do you think life naturally gives to everyone who writes enough experiences to write from—if writing is fed by having experienced life?

FERRANTE: I don't know how to answer. I know that literary creation requires such a concentration of the energies, of the affections we're capable of, that it certainly collides with motherhood: its urgent requirements, its pleasures, its obligations. Inserting oneself into the chain of reproduction diminishes, at times suffocates, the extremely violent impulse to enter into that other reproductive chain that is literary tradition. But then if the urge to write really is invincible, here it is, returning stronger than ever: it makes your existence as a mother more difficult than normal, burdens you with guilt, both unfounded and very well founded. What is better for a woman who wants to write—to have children or not to have them? I don't know. Living isn't only reading and writing. But reading and writing can have the force to claim our entire life. And I don't know if that's a good thing. But I don't know if it's a bad thing either. One has to deal personally with these issues.

HETI: What do you think is the greatest thing literature can do for people? For culture? For the writer herself?

FERRANTE: Take us where we have never been, where we are afraid of going.

HETI: You write in *Frantumaglia* that you were the sort of child who "apologized for everything." But as an adult, you realize that goodness "derives not from the absence of guilt but from the capacity to feel true loathing for our daily, recurring, private guilt." Yet how can a woman ever truly know what she should be guilty for when women live in a world of codes that have been created by men, when we live in "male cities" (as you have termed it), and when the route to understanding who one is necessarily involves exploring one's instinct to "disobey"? How can you tell the difference between what you should feel guilty for and what you are made to feel guilty for but shouldn't?

FERRANTE: Our future depends on this connection. There is no true liberation without a strong sense of self. The systematic practice of disobedience is in fact an integral part of male values, and so doesn't really free us; rather, at times, it crushes us, makes us even more acutely the victims of men's needs, especially in the realm of sex. We need an ethics of our own to oppose that which the male world has imposed on and claimed from us. We need a hierarchy of our own of merits and faults, and we need to reckon with truth. But that's possible only if we consider ourselves to be exposed to good and evil like any human being. When literature represents us as the positive pole of life or as having been exposed to evil only as victims—an evil that in the end will turn out to be a good, if looked at with spectacles different from those imposed by males—it is not doing its duty. The duty of literature is to dig to the bottom. We are a subject both unpredictable and unknown even to ourselves. We have an urgent need for representation and for an ethics of our own. We have the right and the duty to explore ourselves thoroughly, to slip away, to cross the borders that make us suffer. I insist on self-surveillance, which means choice, assumption of responsibility, and the necessity of losing restraint in order to know ourselves, not lose ourselves.

HETI: You have said that if you weren't a writer you'd be a dressmaker, like your mother was. When I read that, I thought about your books as a kind of dressmaking; perhaps the craft of dressmaking that you witnessed your mother practice is sublimated into the act of writing, as some writers sublimate their desire to dance, compose music, act . . . You refuse to shroud the female body in obscuring drapery, which, as you write, dressmakers do, in order to protect the sons who wish not to see their mothers' shape. And you refuse to show the female body to its best advantages, as the inappropriately feminizing dress the protagonist dons in *Troubling Love* does. Rather, you cut a dress to the exact specifications of the woman you write about. My mother was a pathologist. I think the act of looking at slides, of doing autopsies on the human body, is part of how I understand writing—is my inheritance from my mother's life's work.

FERRANTE: I believe that everything that comes to us from our mothers has a power that we have to learn to draw on. But that power of suggestion at first frightens us or makes us ashamed. Our mothers seem, instead of a constant inspiration, a stumbling block to our growth, an annoyance. We spend much, perhaps too much, time in order to truly feel that we are their daughters, that is to say, an outlet of their story as women, not as mothers.

HETI: I only ever saw my mother reading self-help books, and now as an adult I find them particularly inspiring and fascinating, in a literary sense. You once wrote, "Over the years . . . I've become less ashamed of how much I like the stories in the women's magazines . . . It seems to me that this cellar of writing, a fund of pleasure that for years I repressed in the name of Literature, should also be put to work."

FERRANTE: I think that it's not the great writers of the twentieth century but their followers who committed the extremely serious error of thinking of the pleasure of reading as a sign of triviality. Boredom is not a mark of distinction. In fact, there has never been a great or very great book that doesn't give primary importance to the enjoyment of readers, even if it's a handful of highly competent readers.

HETI: For a while, I had a theory that you must have published as an author under a different name before publishing these books—not only because I figured you must have first-hand experience of the literary circus that you write about so well in the body of Elena, but because your books seem like those of someone in the middle of her career, not at the beginning. Perhaps you just have higher standards, or more restraint, than many of the people who publish today. Do you think today people often publish books too young?

FERRANTE: Not at all. Good books are written at all ages, and if one feels that one has produced a good thing, it does one as well to publish at twenty as at eighty. The problem is precisely the feeling of one's own value. I've written a lot, but sometimes I've had a hard time considering what I've written to be worth publishing. As for the knowledge of the literary circus that you attribute to me, what to say? A circus is a show. So it's enough to sit in a corner as a spectator, in silence, and observe with unillusioned eyes.

HETI: Did you ever fear what you would lose by not participating in the media, festivals, etc.? How did you set about so confidently not pleasing your publisher? And do you think it's possible for a writer who has sent herself around in the world as a writer to stop? Or does the fact of ever having been seen mean that something is forever lost and any retreat is useless? Finally, have you ever signed a book?

FERRANTE: Yes, I made the mistake of signing a hundred copies, some years ago. It was naive. It seemed to me that since I was doing it at home, in private, it wouldn't cost me much. Today I think that I could have spared myself even that. I remain of the opinion that a book has to absolutely make it on its own; it shouldn't even use advertising. Of course, my position is extreme. And among other things, the market has by now absorbed it and made the most of it, while the media have readily changed it to gossip and a puzzle to be solved. But for me the small cultural polemic underlying the choices I made twenty-five years ago remains important. I will never consider it finished, and I trust that no one who feels that writing is fundamental will completely set it aside. Good books are stunning charges of vital energy. They have no need of fathers, mothers, godfathers, and godmothers. They are a happy event within the tradition and the community that guards the tradition. They express a force capable of expanding autonomously in space and time.

MARK POLANZAK

■

Giant

FROM *The Southern Review*

THE SURPRISINGLY FEW eyewitness reports stated that the giant walked, more or less, up Main Street from the west, stepping on the pavement and sometimes in patches of trees in parks and backyards, just before dawn. He stopped in the square, choosing to sit in the brick courtyard of the city hall, and leaned back against the big stone church, blocking off traffic on Elm and Putnam. Authorities discovered that he had successfully avoided stomping on parked cars and most of the city's infrastructure, but that many swing sets, water fountains, jungle gyms, basketball hoops, grills, and gardens had been "smooshed." No one knew if any birds or squirrels, likely sleeping in the parks and backyards, had been flattened.

The giant was still sitting in the square in the morning. A crisp and blue Monday morning in September. We found police cruisers and fire trucks parked with lights flashing in a two-block radius around the giant. Residents of the buildings within the zone were evacuated. Businesses were cleared and shuttered. There wasn't a TV or radio station broadcasting anything but news of the giant. Live footage from a helicopter aired endlessly. The giant was taller than the city hall, the stone church, and the apartment buildings, even while sitting. Few of us saw him erect. He wore baggy tattered brown pants drawn by a red rope, an ill-fitting faded green shirt, and no shoes. He was human. He had human feet. Human hands. A brown satchel was strapped around his torso. He occasionally reached into the satchel to remove handfuls of giant berries and something else that crunched and echoed throughout town. He had long, stringy blond hair that fell on either side of his face, down to his shoulders—except in back, where a few strands had been pulled and tied up with a giant red band. No one had heard him speak. No one, as far as we knew, had attempted to communicate.

Since the giant seemed to have purposefully avoided crushing our homes and cars and had made no indication that he wanted to hurt us, we did not panic. Even the flashing lights and sirens did not inspire anxiety. The newscasts were not fear-driven. The reporters were curious. It wasn't an emergency to anyone. It was awe-striking. Eventually, the sirens were silenced. The flashers were shut off. You could hear laughter in the streets. When he reached for more food, there were gasps of joy. Children were held on shoulders to have a look.

The mayor, around three o'clock that first day, was raised up on a cherry picker and handed a megaphone. He said to the giant, "Hello." The whole town was silent, awaiting a response. When, after a minute had passed and the giant had reached for another handful of food, the mayor repeated himself, adding his name, title, the name of our city, and a welcome message. To our great delight, the giant finally acknowledged the mayor, turning to him and emanating a ground-shaking, three-syllable reply. But we could not understand. He was not an English speaker.

Professors from the language department of the university listened to the recording, determining that it was not something they had ever heard before. Linguistic anthropologists then went to work on the recording. They were not sure either. Verbal communication was placed on hold.

None of us went to work that first day. No child went to school. Many of us chuckled after remarking that the giant had put things in perspective. Our work seemed small. Our schools seemed small. The giant was all we cared about, and no one disputed it. How could we get our paperwork done with the giant down the street? How could any teacher concentrate on her lesson? There was no way our kids would do math problems with a real, live giant outside.

The influx of reporters and visitors slammed our streets and hotels and bars and restaurants that first night. You could talk with the person seated next to you. There wasn't a chance they'd be discussing anything else. You could talk with anyone on the street. What do you do in a situation like this? He doesn't want to hurt us. He can't talk with us. He just looks tired, don't you think? He keeps sighing and eating. Have you seen that he fell asleep? He sleeps with his head resting on the post office? Did you hear him snore? It sounded like low rolling thunder. Yes, it was soothing. And how he scoops gallons of water from the river with his hand?

Although the mayor had spoken with him, no one had attempted to touch him until the third day. After town meetings to devise the best plan to approach the giant, it was decided that the mayor and thirty policemen would carry flags with every conceivable peaceful symbol drawn on them. A peace sign. A pure-white flag. Two hands shaking. The word *LOVE*. The word *WELCOME*. Pictures of people waving and smiling. Big flags. Big signs. They would walk cautiously up to the giant. We decided to make an offering. A barrel of orange juice. A loaf of bread the size of a school bus. We would place these before him and back away, waiting for him to notice that we were being kind. Then the mayor and policemen would walk closer and closer, extending hands and shaking each others' hands to demonstrate what we meant.

Everything went as planned. But the giant never reached down to touch anyone. When the mayor got close enough, he touched the giant's heel. The giant did not notice. This was frustrating. He ate the bread in a single chomp. He tossed the barrel of OJ into his mouth, crunched, and swallowed. He went back to sighing, wiping his brow, and resting.

The giant is not interested in us. He is not curious about us in the slightest. He eats, drinks, rests, sighs, and sleeps. He has made no attempt to look any of us, save for the mayor that first day, in the eye. He has not thanked us for the food. He has not apologized for trampling our parks and gardens and recreation areas. He has not offered any help of any kind.

Not long ago, we began to wonder why we were so curious. What, apart from his obvious size, made him any more interesting than any of us? Why were we constantly talking about him, for days and weeks on end? Why were we fascinated every time he reached for his satchel or scratched his forearm? We all still talked to each other, but the conversation turned. We had waited long enough. We wanted to know if anything was going to happen, or if we were just going to have to live with a giant in our square. A dumb oaf that caused people to move out of their homes, that caused the government to move the offices of city hall and the post office to other buildings. If he were of normal size, he would be completely uninteresting. He would be mentally deficient, mangy. We would pity him. He contributed nothing. He took. He stole. He trespassed. He destroyed. He frustrated and incensed. He was boring.

When we travel, when we mention where we live and people ask, *Isn't that the town with the giant?* we sigh, *Yes.* When we return home, we ask if it is still there. And our neighbors give the sarcastic answer, *Oh, he wouldn't go anywhere, don't you worry.* When we walk to the bus stop, we glance up at him with as much amazement as we do down to our watches. We know what we'd see. We would see a giant, sitting there, eating and drinking. We'd see a tired monster, not interesting enough to even hurt us. We'd see him wipe his brow. Then we'd check the time.

■

Tattoo

FROM *Epiphany*

IT TOOK A WHILE for him to tell me he was God. It was maybe the second or third talk we had. Talks were special times when San would take only one of us girls into his room at the back of the house, where we'd station ourselves in the two pumpernickel leather chairs by the windows. Above one chair was a portrait of his father, above the other his mother. He told us he had painted them himself.

I had been in the single-storied clapboard house for a few weeks before I was summoned for a talk. My stomach burned when he called me, like how the whale must have felt when Jonah lit a candle inside its belly.

I entered with mugs of chamomile tea, spoons circling around the lip of the cups as I walked across the floor. The tea's steam rose between us. San had told us, when he went over the rules of the talk, that when the steam stopped, the words could start. It wouldn't matter who spoke first, just as long as they were words worthy of the talk. Most of us let San start. Even Shelly-Rebecca, the girl who wasn't afraid to roll her golden-dollar eyes when he turned away, displaying his wide, linen shoulders. She could be seen, only by us girls, muttering under her breath as she swept up the kitchen.

I was sitting in the chair across from San, making sure my cottoned knees touched. My feet were wide apart in heavy, black boots tied in bows with serrated ribbons. He commented positively on them, and I looked down into myself and squeaked out a thanks. My zipper scratched my chin where it would break out every month. San said the breakout was how he knew when I was bleeding.

He lifted my face with his secure hands. That's when I first noticed a tattoo peeking out of his shirtsleeve on the top of his wrist, where a watch's face would be. "Is that a peacock?" I asked, since I always did fancy birds. And unlike the other girls, blue was my favorite color. But then I saw this tattooed bird's red wattle, which I didn't think peacocks had—but I had never been to a zoo, so I wasn't sure what it was.

"It's not, Nora-Lynn. It's a cassowary. It's like a peacock but different. They both don't fly," he said, his voice slow and definite, paved with pebbles like the road into town. His teeth were small, but cleanly bright. He took care of them and taught us to as well. His gift to each of us when we first joined the house was a soft-bristled toothbrush in princess colors with stars and hearts on the handles.

"That is a shame, isn't it? When a bird can't get off the ground?" I tensed up and looked down at my feet after I spoke. My right bow was bigger than my left. San could put me in the closet for this, for asking a question. Lara-Michelle was put in the pantry for two days for asking San why the pumpkins he grew weren't as big as the pumpkins they saw down at the German's farm on the way to the market. We were supposed to spit on her whenever we opened the door for canned goods. In a slice of light, Lara-Michelle winced when our saliva hit her sallow face. It might have been harsh, but we all learned something from it. Shelly-Rebecca thought it was cruel, but I told her to keep an eye on Lara-Michelle after the punishment. Watch what she does. After she was allowed to leave the closet, I gave her a hug. As I released the embrace, I grabbed her face, gently but automatically. She was softened, I could tell. As Shelly-Rebecca lurched to hug her, Lara-Michelle breezed passed us both to sit next to San. She bowed her head in forgiveness, and I could feel San pass some warm thought to her. I would have liked to say I was jealous—that would be expected. I wasn't. I felt I conveyed the same message to Lara-Michelle that San had. That of protection and pride, like I imagined a caretaker might feel.

San said questions were just fine, as long as they weren't trap questions. "If you ask me something trying to catch me without an answer just to prove a point, I know you must have some evil in you."

It was his belief, and consequently the belief of all of us girls, that evil became confused in the dark. It was so dark itself that when it was confronted with nothing but the same, it fell into itself like a black hole. Bad things don't exist in the dark, San used to like to say. That's why punishments were in the closet.

"It is a shame isn't it? When you realize something's limitations. But people can't fly and we somehow managed to figure out how to make a machine that does. So our limitations don't have to be a burden. They can be an inspiration," San drawled his thoughts while patting my head. My honey hair frizzed, since the curly hair shampoo and conditioner I used to use was too expensive for us girls' budget. We took ivory-white bars of soap and smoothed them over our wet scalps. We could wash ourselves in our bathroom with warm water and a rough cloth whenever we felt necessary, but we got a proper bath with soap once a week in San's tub. His bathroom would steam as he drew the water as hot as skin could take it. He'd watch us as we dipped our toes in to test it. We wore white cotton dressing gowns in the tub, as San had read they did years ago, when people still believed in the sanctity of the human form. He'd make sure we were safe and comfortable as the cloth shielded our nakedness. As I would recline deeper in the bath, the water made the gown transparent, almost forming just another layer of skin. San would light a candle and give us privacy as he sat on the other side of the closed door, ready with a towel.

That day of the talk my hair was clean, so I didn't flinch when he stroked it. I was relieved; I had asked a thoughtful question, one he could teach me a lesson with. "Is that why you have that tattoo? To remind you of your limitations?" I thought this was a proper follow-up and he would stroke my hair again. He pulled back into the comfort of his chair, swigged some chamomile and brushed his adroit fingers over the bird with its plumed cape of feathers.

"Nora-Lynn, I'm going to tell you something. I haven't told the other girls yet." There was a tightness in my body, an automatic response to his stimuli. The other girls had more talks. Shelly-Rebecca was on her eighth, so close to the dozen you needed for the transformation. Yet I was being treated as special.

"I knew it would happen, but I didn't know when. It's begun," he beamed, his cheeks expanding like a bullfrog sated with flies.

"What is it?" I was no longer timid; I lurched forward, feeling sweat forming on my lower back where the patch of hair grew that my brothers had always made fun of back when I was at home. I unzipped my jacket and unsheathed my arms. I could smell the pie I had helped bake that morning on my aproned paisley dress. When San extended his fist toward me, I sank back in fear, but he was just showing me the cassowary up-close. It was true, sometimes I just got things wrong.

"I was told to get this tattoo, not in a dream really—I wasn't asleep. I was just working. Filling in potholes down in Tatonville last summer. And I heard the voice. I was supposed to defile my body for the sake of the Lord, and in turn I would find out why. But I never knew when. Now it's all becoming clear." He told me, in the lambent light of the sun, that it would burn. The mark flamed red in the brutal heat and needed to be soothed with petroleum jelly several times a day. He heard a voice saying the pain was worth it. And that as it healed, it would only burn again when he was close to someone with the potential to go beyond her limitations. And how it burned when he met Ann-Eleanor truantly smoking at High Cliff Park, Shelly-Rebecca at the bus station coming off a Greyhound from Jackson City, Lara-Michelle by the tracks down on High Street, and me when I was begging for change by the Family Dollar, two weeks shy of my fifteenth birthday. I was already out of the money I had pilfered from the hall closet of the house I grew up in. I had fingered each pocket for bills and change before I left early one morning. Seventeen dollars had lasted me a few sunrises, but it was gone soon enough. I had been living off chicken bones for a few days and hoping to get enough money to buy myself a burger. And that's when I had met San.

As we sat under the portraits of his parents, he continued his story. The tattoo he got, the cassowary, was created on the back of his hand. The tattoo artist, an Asian woman—which was rare around these parts, he noted—had to shave some stray hairs off his fist. Now the tattoo was on his wrist. It had moved. It was the proof that San was divine. He told me, and I believed him.

* * *

The first summer we were all with San, when it got too hot in the house, our perspiration sticking to everything our bodies touched, San would take us in the flatbed to the pond on Lynchfield Road. If we went early enough, it would just be the five of us. Sometimes there were newborns with their mothers in skirted bathing suits or old couples holding hands under shading umbrellas. San would sit on the blanket draped over the sand, letting the breeze cool him while us girls dove into the crisp water. Ann-Eleanor was a crack swimmer. She'd breaststroke to the other side and back, Lara-Michelle at the ready with plump splashes upon her return. I liked to go underwater, grabbing a handful of sand and scrubbing my skin with it. I always felt so clean after a dip in the pond. I thought that was why San would usually pick me for talks on those days.

By then, all the girls had noticed the tattoo. San wanted to be modest and wear a shirt to the beach, but it was too hot. We all understood when he unfastened the white buttons of his shirt, slipping his arms out of his sleeves, and then lifted off his tank top. He had the body of a worker, strong and dense with muscle. We tried not to look at his chest, and our pharmacy sunglasses camouflaged our gazes. But we all saw the cassowary making its way up his arm. By then it sat right over the crook in his elbow. We were fascinated by its migration and spent hot nights in our pitch-black room guessing its destination.

"It's going to go down his other arm. And then disappear! And something big will happen, like a war. And San will protect us." Lara-Michelle craved the destruction of the world, and, I thought, the rest of us girls, so she could be alone with San.

I thought it might stop when it got to his heart, and I nodded off thinking of it beating, the bird moving on the skin above it. If it got to his heart, maybe it would finally fly.

Shelly-Rebecca was confused by the tattoo. She couldn't wrap her mind around the impossible. It scared her that San might be that powerful, might be chosen. She felt she didn't deserve to be so close to a deity. All throughout that summer, she threatened to leave. Not to San. But to us.

One day, in the kitchen, evaluating the intake from the garden, Shelly-Rebecca told me she wondered if the tattoo was even real.

"You can leave whenever you want. You're not a prisoner. Don't go talking garbage about your family." I chopped the overgrown stem off of a rutted carrot. It looked like green feathers, like the kind on a boa. I tickled her arm with it, making my way up to her shoulder.

"Shoulda stayed with my mother. At least she would pass out sometimes. I don't know what he wants. It's hard to trust a man with a fake tattoo."

I could have run to San and told on Shelly-Rebecca right then. He was painting in his room, something he hadn't shown us. He never said not to disturb him while he was creating, but I felt it would be wrong. I didn't want to end up in the closet. The best I could spit out was, "Nonsense, Shelly-Rebecca."

She grabbed the carrot out of my hand like a child in an outburst. I reached out and took her cool, damp grip in mine. She withdrew. "It's just Rebecca. And you're just Lynn. You don't have to go by the name he gave us. You don't have to do anything someone tells you to do."

"I'm Nora-Lynn now. I will miss you if you go. I'll pray for you." I let go of her hands and left the kitchen. I needed to change into my dress. San had requested a talk, my tenth, and I had to prepare. Knee high socks. Bowed boots. Paisley dress.

Shelly-Rebecca was gone a week later, back at her mother's. A roof over her head, but no home like she had with us. After hitchhiking and panhandling for bus fare, she arrived back in her hometown. Her mother had moved her boyfriend into their house in Shelly-Rebecca's absence, and now neither of them was all too happy to have a third mouth to feed. Shelly-Rebecca's mother was so angered by that mouth she often slapped it, and her boyfriend, like a parrot, would repeat her actions. Shelly-Rebecca wrote us on fringed notebook paper to see if it would be okay if she returned. It had been my chore to walk down to the mailbox. I didn't show the letter to the other girls. And I never could bring myself to reply in secret. It pained me to take the letter and toss it into the fire so it wouldn't upset San. So it wouldn't upset the other girls. It was hard enough for them when she left, I didn't know what would happen if she was allowed back in.

Summer was a time for San to make money. He continued to work for the roads department whenever he could. With double shifts and overnights installing signs and highway dividers, he could save up enough not to have to work in the winter. He believed we shouldn't be slaves to currency, that it dulls the senses and that when you make money, you only want more. "Isn't it better to try to find ways to live outside of the greed that everyone falls prey to? It's all bloodthirsty lust." Whatever cash we took in, he handled—we never even saw it and we never needed it.

We lived modestly, growing most of our food and keeping chickens for eggs and meat. San's dad had built a coop years before he died, and his mother, the mythical Ida-Renee, whose recipes, scripted on yellowed index cards, we followed, let it fall into disrepair before her own passing. When San came back into town and moved into the house he had inherited, he borrowed tools from the neighbors, a mile walk in either direction. The chicken coop was fixed up and painted a periwinkle blue. He turned over the soil and planted the garden. Anything we couldn't eat in-season we froze or canned for those dinners huddled by the fire, wrapped in our jackets that absorbed the scent of cinnamon from Ida-Renee's apple strudel that I loved to bake all autumn.

We would make our clothes, leaving most of the sewing to Ann-Eleanor, who once wanted to run away to New York and live on Seventh Avenue, where she said there was a big, red statue of a button and a needle. "It's called the Garment District and all they do there is make clothes. The most beautiful things you ever saw!"

On our birthdays, we were allowed to pick out one present, which San would purchase for us. The girls would make each other something, fabricating a hair clip out of metal scraps in the garage or collaging melted wax from the colorful candles we burned to save money on the electric bill.

My sixteenth birthday came, and I thought San would let it pass by, since he had not called me for a talk in a while. He hadn't had any of us come to his room. We didn't know why, but sometimes we did hear him whimper late at night. Lara-Michelle thought he was keeping a puppy to surprise us with, especially since she heard a sound like whipping or swatting, like you'd have to do to house-train a dog. But no pet ever came. I thought he was just working on his painting, and if that's the way he worked, we should let him be.

None of us had gotten to that twelfth meeting, where we would be approved for the ascension to the next level. I had asked San what that would entail, what rapture I would feel. He looked through to my insides, made them feel like they were going to come right out of the darkness of my body. What would they do in the light of day? San's throaty croak unsettled me. "You will find out when you're able to understand." I chastised myself for not being ready.

For my gift, I asked to go to Millman's Book Shop on the east side of town. I didn't want anything to read, really, but I knew they had elegant stationery sets, some with glamorous women who looked like movie stars, and some embellished with sparkles and the Eiffel Tower. They even sold old-fashioned pen-and-ink sets, complete with squat, brown jugs of slick ink and midnight-black plumes.

San dropped me off and gave me thirty minutes to look around while he went to the post office. I was free to roam and picked out a set of notecards, blue-speckled with bursts of white. They reminded me of a hovering summer sky. It made me crave tomatoes eaten like apples.

Holding on to my gift, I wandered through the store, coiling around each aisle, stopping when something hit my eye. I approached the animal section, denoted by a mural of a jungle. The animals looked friendly, so as not to scare children. A thick, black-and-white spine adorned with birds picked up the gleam of the overhead lights. I pulled out the book, because it seemed like one of those teeming with glossy color photos that were so sharp you could remember them years later like you were actually in them. I was thinking of San and how I hadn't seen his tattoo in a while. It was too cold for any flesh to be exposed, and I was afraid to ask him about it. Lara-Michelle claimed she'd spied him changing his shirt when he thought no one was looking, and it was all the way up on his shoulder next to a grouping of red marks. In the book, I looked up the cassowary.

I learned they were native to Australia, and that they were usually heavy—only the ostrich was heavier. On the middle toe of each of their feet grew a claw about four inches long. I tried to visualize that length. Looking at my hand, I thought maybe it was from the tip of my thumb to my wrist. The size of the cigarettes I pulled from my father's slack mouth so he wouldn't start another fire. The markers I used in third grade that smelled of cherries and grapes.

On a cassowary's head grows a crest made of keratin, like our fingernails. Their eyes are yellow, and they're big enough for a person to hop on one's back and ride it like a carousel animal. They are so strong they can kill humans, and they have.

The bell from the shop's front door trilled and I sensed it was San. He walked in without his coat, in a sweater I had knitted under the tutelage of Ann-Eleanor. Next to him was a girl, younger than me, but almost as tall as San. With his coat caped around her shoulders, she tried to settle the chattering of her teeth. Her cheeks had no meat on them. Her eyes were hungry, and I suddenly felt so blessed, as I had been like her only a little over a year before. San came over to me, and she followed, tripping over her mammoth feet.

San introduced her. "Nora-Lynn, this is Veronica. I thought maybe we could bring her home, get her a meal."

"No, nuh-uh. I didn't say I'd go to your house. We can get something to eat but I can't go anywhere else." Veronica seemed cornered, even out in the open. Her eyes could not settle on any one place, like she was always looking for something to come at her.

I wanted to stroke her hair, and I wanted to tell her how lucky she was to have found us. But I didn't want to come on too strong. "Have you ever had quiche? I know it sounds fancy, but it's really just eggs in a pie crust. I made a big one this morning with cheese and peppers and sweet potatoes. Come home with us and warm up and have a big piece. All of us girls will. And we won't give any to San!" I laughed and San's eyes lazed softly at me and Veronica. I guessed his cassowary tattoo had been burning when he saw Veronica. I could feel it too. She was a new sister to expand the family. Another person I could love and who could love me back. Maybe not even a sister. I felt miles above and years ahead. An aunt?

"What do you think Nora-Lynn? Does she look like a Veronica to you?"

I looked at her and bore the warmth of the summer I felt when I looked at my birthday notecards. "No, I think she seems like a Skye," I said with pride, like a mother when she first sees her newborn.

Before she ate, Skye-Veronica needed to be cleaned. Ann-Eleanor lit the stove and tore fresh leaves of salad while San ran a bath. I brought our new girl into the bedroom and opened the wardrobe. Inside, there were laundered white gowns folded in a pile. She made sure the door was closed and found no lock. She undressed in front of me, accepting the soft, white dress and slipping it over her head as if a snake were trying to get back into its skin.

In the bathroom, San shut off the faucet. Skye-Veronica stood close to me. It felt like she was using me as a shield. I saw white in my periphery. I took San aside and said to him, as I got him near the door, "She's scared. Let me help her." He smiled at me and kissed the top of my head, matting down the bush of curls I had yet to ask Lara-Michelle to cut or style in the way I had seen Ida-Renee's in the photos I had found in a keepsake trunk—slicked-up bun with two pieces of hair framing her face and curling under at her shoulders. As Skye-Veronica stepped into the bath, San pulled me out of the room for a moment, into the chamber of his bedroom. He pulled something out from under the bed. It was a canvas.

"I'm going to hang this. And when you're done helping Skye-Veronica, you can see it."

After I had made sure she washed her face and behind her ears, and after I had wrapped her in a large yellow towel and put a comb through her string hair, the other girls picked her up at San's door and led her into the fire-warmed kitchen.

When we were alone, San turned me to the wall with the chairs and his parents' pictures. Not right next to them but over to the right, nearer to his bed, was the painting San had just hung. It was a likeness of me so exact I thought it might be a photograph. I went closer and felt the bumps of the paint strokes and the roughness of the canvas beneath. It was really me, I thought, and San had made it.

Soon after, San called me for my last talk. I brought in the tea and sat below the painting of his mother. I had tried to wear my hair in a bun that day, like her, but it was too difficult to tame. From my seat, I saw my painting, but I didn't want to stare. I knew it was there. The girls knew it was there. San leaned back in the tatty leather under the stern likeness of his father. I spoke first, giddy with anticipation of my soon-to-be transformation. "Oh, San, thank you for thinking I'm ready. I know I am and you won't be disappointed."

He got up and went over to the closet, "Your dress is getting threadbare. And I think it only proper you wear something new." San pulled out a white-laced dress, cinched at the waist and flared out like a paper fan below it. A tag dangled from a seam. I gave him a questioning look and he nodded, so I got up to feel the dress. It was soft like a cloud and just about the prettiest thing I had ever seen. And it was mine.

"I want you to put this on. I'm taking you down to the pond. You will bathe in the waters there and I will bless you." He patted my head as I breathed in the new smell of the white fabric. "I've seen how you've taken Skye-Veronica under your wing. You've shown her such kindness. More like a mother to her than a sister. And that's all part of your potential. You have so much love."

I felt the love, so hot, like a poison, make my limbs go numb. My fingers burned and I was afraid I would scorch the innocent dress. He left me to change, and I felt honored to have San's room all to myself. The dress fit me well—it was a little short, but I was sure with Ann-Eleanor's help I could take the hem down. I came out into the kitchen and all the girls fawned over me. I hugged each one before I joined San in the truck and headed over to Lynchfield Road, riding down bumpy streets. The potholes still hadn't been filled from the winter's icy reign.

It wasn't warm enough to go in the pond, I thought, but San said that it was all part of the process. I just had to feel it was warm and it would be warm. We lingered around the edge of the water until I felt ready to go in. The sun was out, reflecting itself off my full skirt. My bare feet dipped in the water and the cold hurt like talons. But San was there next to me. He held my hand those first steps I took in. When I got used to the temperature, it was as if I could feel the pond heating up. I was thinking it, and then it was so.

San stopped me from going in further. "Nora-Lynn, as you are moving forward, ascending into a deeper understanding of the world and your place in it, I want you to recognize you will be a new person. This acts not as a baptism, but as a new birth." He added I would be taking his name. That made me feel that I was truly his family. "And as a baby is born of its mother, with nothing but its purity, so will you be reborn."

San assisted in unzipping the white dress. He folded it and placed it carefully on the sand. I shivered at the breeze on my belly and only wanted to face him, so he didn't see the patch of hair on my back, as if a slight imperfection could dissolve love. I beckoned the sun to warm me and knew it would come, as I already felt the acute blister of acceptance.

He looked at me to continue. "You need to be unencumbered by anything the world puts on you." I understood and took off my bra and my underwear. I walked deeper into the water, until it covered my chest, so I didn't feel undressed. The cold battled me, and I was like a baby, no defenses against it. But I knew I just had to dive in and make the water warm around me. I smiled at San to let him know I was all right. He watched me, hands on his hips, his swath of sable hair vibrating in the wind. He kept his eyes on me, and I kept mine on his until I went under the surface.

It was dark. Everything was obscured. I grabbed sand and scrubbed my arms. The temperature of the water was insignificant. I thought of how I could touch a flame, extinguishing a candle between two fingers. I thought of my sisters. I thought of my love for San and how he had saved me. I would do anything for them, and that was all the warmth I needed.

Coming up through the water, grabbing onto a deep breath of air, I saw San. He had taken off his shirt and shoes and was bent over to one side pulling off his pants. He wore cotton boxer shorts that we had darned so much they looked like an injured soldier returning from battle, unable to fight any more. I stood where I was, my feet barely touching the ground, with the water covering my breasts. My frizzy hair was tamed by the murky pond. His cassowary was now close to his heart, where I hoped it would end up.

He removed his shorts and stood on the edge of the water. I had never seen a man naked before. My brothers, sure, but they were all boys. And my old neighbor Kyle, who I always forgot about. He would notice when I was home alone, which was often, and stand naked in his living room, whose full windows faced my childhood bedroom. He'd swivel his hips and look at me like I was a fried-chicken dinner.

San entered the pond. I swear the level of the water went higher, like he'd displaced it with his presence. I waited where I was. When he got to me, his arms surrounded my body, and he dwarfed me with his considerable presence. His smile was so clean and easy. Down under the water he brought me, and then we rocketed back up to the atmosphere. He let go of me. In his excitement, he flapped around like a fish victoriously getting free from a hook. I wanted to celebrate as much as San could, but I still felt like I was just a girl. I felt no transformation yet. I shyly looked down into my chest and wanted to pretzel my arms to cover my nipples, in case the water wouldn't.

I saw a smear on my skin, deep, dark, almost-black blue, with dots of red. I thought it might be a pond creature, some sort of leech or lamprey that had attached itself to me. But it wasn't alive. It was just paint or ink. My eyes met San's chest, stubbly in places like maybe he had shaved it. His cassowary was fading, like it was melting away into the water. The tattoo's ink sloughed off into the pond, mixing with the algae and the tadpoles and the bugs that carpeted the place. I hugged him, my arms barely fitting around the whole of his broad shoulders. I wrapped my legs around his waist and held on. I didn't want him to see what I had just seen.

MIRIAM TOEWS

■

Peace Shall Destroy Many

FROM *Granta*

IN 1962, a young scholar from Saskatchewan by the name of Rudy
Wiebe caused outrage and scandal in Mennonite communities
throughout North America when he published his first novel, *Peace
Shall Destroy Many*. The title, taken from a verse in the Book of Daniel, encapsulated the contention of the novel—that pacifism and non-
conflict, core tenets of the Mennonite faith, may in fact be sources
of violence and conflict, all the more damaging because unacknowl-
edged or denied.

Although the book was published two years before I was born, I
can remember my parents discussing it at the kitchen table, conspir-
atorially, as if the topic was in itself dangerous. My mother would
later tell me that she had driven herself to the city, Winnipeg, the day
it was made available in stores—it would never have been sold in my
little conservative Mennonite town—to find out what all the fuss was
about. By the time I was buying books myself, I had learned to think
of this novelist named Rudy Wiebe as controversial and heroic, as an
intellectual whose work was *groundbreaking* and *revolutionary*. These
were exciting words to me.

All the fuss was about the challenging questions posed by the novel's central character, Thom Wiens, an earnest young farmer living
in a small isolated community in Saskatchewan (much like the community Rudy Wiebe grew up in). It is 1944, wartime, and the local
men have either gone to conscientious objector work camps around
Canada, or stayed behind to tend the crops and raise livestock. Wiens

begins to wonder whether the Mennonite opposition to war may be self-serving. How can Mennonites stand aside while others are dying to protect the freedoms they enjoy? How can Mennonites justify selling their produce to the Canadian army, at a profit no less, and continue to preach peace and love for one's enemies?

Rudy Wiebe hadn't intended to stir things up with his novel. He was no Mennonite provocateur or self-appointed rabble-rouser. He wanted to write honestly and philosophically about the conflicts that arise from non-conflict. He also wanted to raise questions of sexuality and racism, and to test the established perception of Mennonites as a people "*in* the world but not *of* the world."

At the time, Wiebe was a devout Christian and respected member of the Mennonite establishment. After the book was published he was fired from his job as the editor of a Mennonite newspaper and denounced, by some, as a liar, an upstart, and a traitor. Even worse, an atheist. Others, like my parents, were supportive, secretly though, as was and is the custom among dissenting Mennonites. When my mother said, "Rudy Wiebe has aired our dirty laundry and it's about time," she whispered. It was important to keep the peace in all matters, including the matter of *Peace Shall Destroy Many*.

"I guess it was a kind of bombshell," Wiebe told an interviewer in 1972, "because it was the first realistic novel ever written about Mennonites in western Canada. A lot of people had no clue how to read it. They got angry. I was talking from the inside and exposing things that shouldn't be exposed."

Shouldn't be exposed. These are telling words. The conviction that certain realities *shouldn't be exposed* is what lurks behind the time-honored Mennonite practice of avoiding conflict and refusing engagement. Everyday life in these remote towns and colonies is punctuated by conflicts, big and small—just like anywhere else—but Mennonites have a number of distinctive methods for dealing with them. You can, for example, whisper about them with your spouse late at night in bed and hope he or she doesn't betray you to the elders. Pray for resolution. Ask for guidance from your church pastor, who may also be the source of the conflict. Turn the other cheek, according to the words of Jesus. And, if it's bad enough, freeze out the individual creating the problem until they cease to exist in your thoughts, or even better, have that person shunned. (Shunning happens by order of the elders. It involves a complete denial of the individual's existence. It is a method of conflict avoidance that maintains the righteousness of the community while preventing any resolution or possibility of justice. It is murder without killing and it creates deep-seated wells of rage that find no release.)

War is hell, it's true. *Shouldn't be exposed* is another hell. *Shouldn't be exposed* stifles and silences and violates. *Shouldn't be exposed* refuses and ignores and shames. *Shouldn't be exposed* shields bullies and tyrants. I have seen it in my own life.

When my sister was ten years old, she was grabbed off the street, driven around for a while by a group of teenage boys unknown to her or any of our family, doused in some brown, toxic liquid and dropped back off in front of our home. The white furry hat that she'd just received as a Christmas present was ruined and had to be thrown into the garbage. That's all I know about that. I don't know what else happened in the car. Police weren't called, nobody was called, it had happened and then there was silence and over time it seemed as though it might not have happened after all.

My grandmother, my father's mother, was a secret alcoholic. Our community was dry, drinking was a sin, but she shoplifted bottles of vanilla extract from the local grocer and drank them one by one alone in the darkness of her small apartment. My parents would let themselves in with a key that they kept, pick her up, clean her up, and put her to bed. My mother had mentioned to me that she suspected that my grandmother had been assaulted by a group of local men when she was a young woman, but it was never spoken of, never investigated. Every few weeks, the owner of the grocery store where my grandmother stole vanilla would call my father and tell him the sum total of the missing bottles—he never confronted my grandmother directly—and my father would write him a check and that was that, until the next time, when the same process would be repeated.

My other grandmother, my mother's mother, was stood up at the altar twice by my grandfather until finally, on the third try, they were married. She had thirteen children, buried six of them as babies and spent a great deal of time praying. She would never even have suggested to my grandfather that his sexual desire was becoming an inconvenience. In fact, it was killing her, each pregnancy posing another threat to her life. At the onset of menopause and with the blessed end of pregnancies clearly in sight, she dropped dead of high blood pressure.

My father had a nervous breakdown at the age of seventeen and was diagnosed with bipolar disorder, then called manic depression. His family never spoke of it except to berate him for being weak and effeminate and not devout enough a Christian, even though he attended church relentlessly, taught Sunday school, prayed his heart out for relief, and never missed a sermon.

When I was twelve, the car dealership next door wanted to expand their parking lot and they put pressure on my father to sell our house. My father didn't want to sell the house he had built himself for his new bride and the offspring that followed, and my mother encouraged him to fight, but he didn't once argue or put up any kind of resistance. Business was next to godliness in our town and if my father refused to sell his house and beautiful yard filled with chokecherry trees and Saskatoon trees and petunias and tiger lilies and homemade birdhouses painted with cheerful colors then he truly was a sinner. He sold the house for cheap and mourned his loss quietly. I remember my mother slinging her arm around my father's broad shoulders and whispering, "Defend yourself, man," and my father smiling mysteriously, with no words attached.

My mother's cousin received a Rhodes Scholarship to study at the University of Oxford and just a few months into the first term he died there, mysteriously, under suspicious circumstances, or according to God's will, in which case what was there to do about it? His parents chose not to hear any details of an investigation or an autopsy. What if their son had died from a drug overdose, or sexual misadventure, or suicide? If they don't know, then they don't feel obligated to condemn him as a sinner, and they can imagine their bright, young, beloved son in heaven.

My son's girlfriend told me a story about an Italian friend of hers. This Italian friend had an aunt who was absolutely furious with her brother for something they've all since forgotten. In order for her brother to know the extent of her rage she dragged a dead and blood-

ied deer carcass (I'm not sure where she got it from) onto his driveway for him to discover in the morning. That dead deer carcass said,
"Don't Fuck With Me!" Her brother got the message. He apologized.
She made him prove he meant it. He convinced her of his contri-
tion. They laughed. They clinked shot glasses of grappa and drank to
peace. *Basta!* Well, I don't know exactly how it all went down but I've
been so envious of this Italian brother and sister duo ever since my
son's girlfriend told me the story.

During my twenty-year marriage, which ultimately ended in di-
vorce and a tsunami of agony and madness and guilt for thinking
that I had destroyed my innocent family out of pure selfishness and
conceit, and with the thought that I should probably destroy myself
before I could cause more damage, I would sometimes air my complaints to my husband after he'd been drinking and when he was
just about to fall asleep. I knew that he wouldn't remember what I
had said but at least I would have gotten it off my chest. It was a perfect arrangement. I could speak up but it wouldn't turn into a huge
blowout. I would talk about mundane things, mostly, how it bugged
me that we always had to have supper at 6 p.m. sharp, for instance,
or that he didn't seem enthusiastic about my decision to join the Da-
kar Desert Rally, but I'd often get into bigger issues too; fundamental
questions about our happiness and our compatibility. He would nod
and smile, his eyes closed, and tell me we'd work it all out, he had to
sleep, sorry. In the morning he'd have no memory of the conversation. In true Mennonite fashion, I had managed to take the edge off
my disappointment and dissatisfaction (by saying a kind of prayer,
pretending that someone was listening), without exposing myself,
without provoking a big, ugly fight, and without changing a thing.

Between 2005 and 2009, in a very isolated Mennonite colony in Bo-
livia, 130 women and girls between the ages of three and sixty were
raped by what many in the community believed to be ghosts, or Sa-
tan, as punishment for their sins. These girls and women were waking up in the morning sore, in pain, and often bleeding. These mys-
terious attacks went on for years. If the women complained they
weren't believed and their stories were chalked up to "wild female
imagination."

Finally, it was revealed that the women had been telling the truth. Two men from the community were caught in the middle of the night as they were climbing into a neighbor's bedroom window. The men were forced into a confession. They and seven other locals would spray an animal anaesthetic created by a local veterinarian through the screen windows of a house, knocking unconscious all occupants. They would climb in, rape the victims, and get out.

These Mennonite colonies are self-policed, except in cases of murder. The bishop and the elders came up with a solution to the problem of how to punish the offenders. They locked all nine men into sheds and basements, and the idea was that they would stay there for decades. Also, they would instruct these men to ask for forgiveness from the women. If the women refused to forgive these men then God would not forgive the women. If the women did not accept the men's apology they would have to leave the colony for the outside world, of which they knew nothing.

Eventually, this outside world was made aware of the Mennonite "ghost rapes" and the perpetrators were arrested by the Bolivian police and put on trial by the Bolivian criminal court. According to sources within the community, the rapes have continued and no offers of counseling have been accepted by the elders on behalf of the women and girls. One explanation they made for refusing help was that, because the victims were sedated during the attacks, they couldn't possibly be suffering from psychological trauma.

Abe Warkentin, founder of *Die Mennonitische Poste*, the most widely read Mennonite newspaper across North and South America and whose headquarters are located in my home town, has called the Mennonites "a broken people." He has said that in our communities there continues to resound a "deafening silence" when it comes to these crimes and issues, and he describes the scandal as "little more than an enlargement of social problems, in which more energy is put into hiding them than confronting and solving them."

My father, after politely inquiring as to when the next freight train was scheduled to pass through the tiny village he had walked to, killed himself by kneeling in front of it. Blank pieces of paper were found scattered next to his body. My sister killed herself twelve years later in an identical fashion. Earlier she had left a note that listed the many people she had loved and had added a plea for forgiveness and the hope that God would accept her into His kingdom. When I was a teenager my sister put her hands on my shoulders, as though knighting me, and told me that I was a "survivor." What does that mean? What does that require?

In 2008, I met Rudy Wiebe for the first time. A book tour had been arranged for the two of us in Germany. We would travel together from one small Mennonite village to the next, reading from our work and answering questions from audiences. A tall long-haired Lithuanian Mennonite living in Bonn drove us around from colony to colony and acted as our cultural attaché. He and Rudy Wiebe sat in the front seat of the car and told each other hilarious stories in Plautdietsch, the unwritten language of the Mennonites, and I sat in the back seat amazed that I was on a book tour with the guy who everybody had whispered about—the myth himself!

Rudy Wiebe was the same age my father would have been. They had a similar body type: tall, slightly stooped. He was formal and polite, like my father, with a way of looking up at things suddenly from a bowed head, so that in that instant, when he looked up or at you, his eyes were wide and his forehead was creased. He was a sort of folk hero in these communities, no longer condemned as a renegade traitor but sweetly embraced by these conservative Mennonites as a famous writer they could call their own, a prodigal son who spoke their language and who was no longer as harsh a critic of their culture as he'd been in his youth.

Rudy and I spent a week together on the road and had come to our last event in a tiny Mennonite town whose name I can't remember. Once again, the audience was overjoyed to hear Rudy speak and mostly puzzled or just indifferent when it was my turn. I don't speak Plautdietsch so a translator had to help me out when there were questions from the audience. I was reading from my novel, *A Complicated Kindness,* which is about a sixteen-year-old girl whose Mennonite family is torn apart by fundamentalism. My reading didn't leave a great taste in the mouths of these German Mennonites. Afterwards, an angry-looking woman stood up and asked to be given the microphone. Her question was directed at me. It went on for a long time, in Plautdietsch, and when she was finished the translator faltered, a bit reluctant to tell me what the woman had said. Rudy Wiebe had understood it all and was busy making notes on a pad of paper. The translator told me that the woman had said my book was filthy and that my characters' mockery of Menno Simons, the man who started the Mennonites in Holland five hundred years ago, was sacrilegious and sinful. She said that if she had a sixteen-year-old daughter she would not allow her to read my book. As the translator translated I smiled and nodded politely. When he was finished I thanked the woman for her comments. I was at a loss as to what to say next. Rudy Wiebe motioned for me to hand over the microphone. He walked to the edge of the stage and spoke directly to this woman in her language. After a minute or two, the woman stormed out of the room, dragging her mortified husband along with her. Rudy continued to talk for a while and then handed the microphone to the translator who translated everything back into English for me and the few other English speakers in the room.

Rudy had defended me. He had told this woman, "No. You're wrong." He said that the reaction to my book had reminded him of the Mennonite reaction to his first novel, *Peace Shall Destroy Many.* He told the people in the room that however they might feel about the swearing in the book, it was at least an honest book, and that the conversations it had generated were important ones and that it, in its way, was advocating for necessary change within our culture; it was holding us accountable as Mennonites to our humanity, our humanness; it was asking us to be self-critical, to accept reality, and to love better. He may have said other things that weren't translated, I don't know.

What I'll remember is that on that day Rudy Wiebe stood up in front of a Mennonite "congregation" and fought for me. My father would have approved. He may not have been able to do it himself but I know he would have appreciated the scene, this long-ago subversive hero defending his very own daughter.

Rudy and I took a train to Frankfurt the next day, where we were catching different flights home to Canada. The train was packed and, with the exception of one seat, there was standing room only. Rudy gestured for me to take the seat, but I hesitated. He looked tired and I knew the week had been hard on him. Again he reminded me of my father before he died, smiling valiantly, sadness in his eyes. I shook my head and gestured for him to take the seat. I was happy to stand, no problem. The train was moving fast and things, life, on the outside became a blur. I watched him as he gazed through the window out at the German countryside, pensive. Soon he was asleep and the train ticket he held in his hand slipped from his fingers and fell to the floor.

DAVID KAISER AND LEE WASSERMAN

∎

The Rockefeller Family Fund Takes on ExxonMobil

FROM *The New York Review of Books*

In March 2016, the Rockefeller Family Fund announced its plan to divest from the fossil fuel industry. The following is the second part of a two-part article, in which the president and the director of the organization explain their reasons for that decision. They focus their argument on ExxonMobil, one of the corporate descendents of Standard Oil and a source of the Rockefeller family's wealth. ExxonMobil, the authors assert, has long understood the reality of climate science, but has worked to sow disinformation regarding that science and to impede actions that would mitigate the consequences of climate change.

In the first part of this article, we described recent reporting that ExxonMobil's leaders knew humans were altering the world's climate by burning fossil fuels even while the company was helping to fund and propel the movement denying the reality of climate change. Ever since the *Los Angeles Times* and *InsideClimate News* started publishing articles showing this in late 2015, ExxonMobil has repeatedly accused its critics of "cherry-picking" the evidence, taking its statements out of context, and "giving an incorrect impression about our corporation's approach to climate change." Meanwhile, New York Attorney General Eric Schneiderman is one of several officials who have been investigating whether the company's failures to disclose the business risks of climate change to its shareholders constituted consumer or securities fraud.

Since ExxonMobil claims that it has been misrepresented, we encourage it to make public all the documents Schneiderman has demanded, so that independent researchers can consider all the facts. In the meantime we suggest that anyone who remains unconvinced by the record we have collected and published of the company's internal statements confirming the reality of climate change consider its actions, especially its expenditures. Regardless of its campaign to confuse policymakers and the public, Exxon has always kept a clear eye on scientific reality when making business decisions.

In 1980, for example, Exxon paid $400 million for the rights to the Natuna natural gas field in the South China Sea. But company scientists soon realized that the field contained unusually high concentrations of carbon dioxide, and concluded in 1984 that extracting its gas would make it "the world's largest point source emitter of CO_2 [, which] raises concern for the possible incremental impact of Natuna on the CO_2 greenhouse problem." The company left Natuna undeveloped. Exxon's John Woodward, who wrote an internal report on the field in 1981, told *InsideClimate News*, "They were being farsighted. They weren't sure when CO_2 controls would be required and how it would affect the economics of the project."

This, of course, was a responsible decision. But it indicates the distance between Exxon's decades of public deception about climate change and its internal findings. So do investments that Exxon and its Canadian subsidiary Imperial Oil made in the Arctic. As Ken Croasdale, a senior ice researcher at Imperial, told an engineering conference in 1991, concentrations of greenhouse gases in the atmosphere were increasing "due to the burning of fossil fuels. Nobody disputes this fact." Accordingly,

> any major development with a life span of say 30–40 years will need to assess the impacts of potential global warming. This is particularly true of Arctic and offshore projects in Canada, where warming will clearly affect sea ice, icebergs, permafrost and sea levels.

Croasdale based these projections on the same climate models that Exxon's leaders spent the next fifteen years publicly disparaging. But following his warnings that rising seas would threaten buildings on the coast, bigger waves would threaten offshore drilling platforms, and thawing permafrost would threaten pipelines, Exxon began reinforcing its Arctic infrastructure.

Similarly, as Steve Coll wrote in *Private Empire: ExxonMobil and American Power* (2012), the company's

> investments in skeptics of the scientific consensus coincided with what at least a few of ExxonMobil's own managers regarded as a hypocritical drive inside the corporation to explore whether climate change might offer new opportunities for oil exploration and profit.

The company tried to use the work of one of its most celebrated earth scientists, Peter Vail, to predict how alterations to the planet's surface made by the changing climate could help it discover new deposits of oil and gas. "'So don't believe for a minute that ExxonMobil doesn't think climate change is real,' said a former manager . . . 'They were using climate change as a source of insight into exploration.'"

Soon after Rex Tillerson replaced Lee Raymond as CEO at the start of 2006, he created a secret task force to reconsider the company's approach to climate change—"so that it would be more sustainable and less exposed," according to one participant. Tillerson may have been afraid that the company's aggressive denial campaign had made it vulnerable to lawsuits.

Under his leadership, as Coll has shown, the company gradually began to change its public position on climate. In 2006 its British subsidiary promised the UK's Royal Society it would stop funding organizations that were misinforming the public about climate science. In 2007 Tillerson stated, "We know the climate is changing, the average temperature of the earth is rising, and greenhouse gas emissions are increasing." (That was more than Raymond had ever admitted, but Tillerson still wouldn't acknowledge that fossil fuel combustion caused global warming.) In January 2009—twelve days before President Obama's inauguration would situate the company in much less welcoming political territory—Tillerson announced that ExxonMobil had become concerned enough about climate change to support a carbon tax.

The climate measure then under active discussion in Washington, however, was a cap-and-trade bill. There was almost no political support for a carbon tax at the time, and Tillerson's announcement may have been meant to divert support from the reform that seemed most plausible. Indeed, since then, although ExxonMobil continues to claim that it supports a carbon tax, it has given much more money to members of Congress who oppose such a tax than to those who endorse one. As of last year it was still funding organizations that deny global warming or fight policies proposed to address it. And at its annual shareholder meetings it still fiercely resists almost all meaningful resolutions on climate change.

The Securities and Exchange Commission requires companies to disclose known business risks to their investors, and Exxon's leaders have been acutely conscious of the changing climate's danger to the oil business for almost forty years. The company didn't start telling its shareholders about that danger until 2007, however, and in our opinion has never disclosed its full scope. To take just one very important example, the valuation of any oil company depends largely on its "booked reserves," meaning the quantities of buried oil and gas to which it owns the rights. Ultimately, however, ExxonMobil may not be able to sell most of its booked reserves, because the world's governments, in trying to prevent catastrophic climate change, may have to adopt policies that make exploiting them economically unfeasible.

In 2013 the Intergovernmental Panel on Climate Change (IPCC) formally endorsed the idea of a global "carbon budget," estimating that, to keep warming to the two degrees Celsius then considered the largest increase possible without incurring catastrophe, humanity could only burn about 269 billion more tons of fossil fuels. (We are currently burning about ten billion tons a year.) As of 2009, however, the world had 763 billion tons of proven and economically recoverable fossil fuel reserves.

If ExxonMobil can sell only a fraction of its booked reserves—if those reserves are "stranded"—then its share price will probably decline substantially. The company has long been familiar with the concept of a carbon budget, but claims to believe it is "highly unlikely" that the world will be able to comply with the IPCC's recommendation for such a budget. In 2014 it stated, "We are confident that none of our hydrocarbon reserves are now or will become 'stranded.'" Because it is a matter of the highest urgency that humanity find a way to adopt the IPCC's global carbon budget, however, it seems to us that ExxonMobil has been much too sanguine about its business prospects. As a *Baltimore Sun* editorial about the company's long history of climate deceptions put it, "Surely there ought to be consequences if a for-profit company knowingly tells shareholders patent falsehoods (and then those investors make decisions about their life savings without realizing they've been lied to)."

It is up to government officials, not public interest advocates, to determine whether ExxonMobil's conduct has violated any state or federal laws within the relevant statutes of limitations. Recognizing this, the Rockefeller Family Fund (RFF) informed state attorneys general of our concern that ExxonMobil seemed to have failed to disclose to investors the business risks of climate change. We were particularly encouraged by Schneiderman's interest in this matter, because New York's Martin Act is arguably the most powerful tool in the nation for investigating possible schemes to defraud. If ExxonMobil fully complies with Schneiderman's subpoena, he will be able to make a thorough review of the company's disclosures to shareholders on climate change and the history of its internal knowledge. He will then be able to decide whether or not to hold ExxonMobil legally responsible based on all the facts.

No state AG's office can easily compete with ExxonMobil's legal resources, however, not even New York's. Schneiderman has been intrepid so far, but would benefit greatly from cooperation from the AGs of Massachusetts, California, and other states, as well as from the federal government. ExxonMobil has already launched aggressive legal actions against the Virgin Islands, Massachusetts, and New York in response to their investigations, and this may deter others from joining Schneiderman's efforts. Still, we hope that other AGs will recognize how dangerous it is when a corporation can use its wealth to discourage enforcement of possible violations of laws governing securities and consumer protection. If they believe the laws of their states may have been violated, they should initiate investigations of their own.

The RFF has also consulted with other advocates about ways to use what we know about ExxonMobil to educate the public about climate change. The company's suggestion that our communications with governmental officials and like-minded public interest advocates constitutes "conspiracy," however, is absurd, ignoring the long record American civic associations have of addressing deep societal problems by use of the First Amendment.

ExxonMobil's success in forestalling any sort of adequate response to climate change for a quarter-century makes it imperative that Congress address this swiftly descending crisis now with all possible force and urgency. If the companies that bear so much responsibility for blocking climate action have broken any laws in the process, we hope they will be held accountable. We also hope, secondarily, to make it difficult for elected officials to accept ExxonMobil's money and do its bidding.

Texas Congressman Lamar Smith has taken more money in campaign contributions from oil and gas companies, including Exxon-Mobil, than from any other industry during his congressional career. It is not hard to see why companies intent on blocking new climate policies are eager to support him. Last year, for example, the National Oceanic and Atmospheric Administration published an article in *Science* refuting the already discredited canard that climate data show no warming over the past two decades. In response Smith issued a subpoena to the agency, demanding all its internal emails about climate research. An article in *US News and World Report* observed that Smith's "brand of oversight may signal a new era for science, one where research itself is subject to political polarization." According to Eddie Bernice Johnson, the ranking minority member of the House Science Committee, Smith has repeatedly called former tobacco industry scientists, consultants, and public relations firms to testify at his committee's hearings, and has relied on their guidance in previous investigations. *Wired* last year called him "Congress' Chief Climate Denier."

Recently, Smith has accused several AGs and environmental organizations, including the Rockefeller Family Fund, of "undermin[ing] the First Amendment of the Constitution." He has told us at the RFF that "Congress has a duty to protect scientists and researchers from the criminalization of scientific inquiry" and "a responsibility to investigate whether [the state inquiries into ExxonMobil] are having a chilling effect on the free flow of scientific inquiry and debate regarding climate change." As the dean of the Yale Law School wrote in the *Washington Post,* "It is hard to exaggerate the brazen audacity of this argument." Johnson wrote to Smith that "in a Congress in which the Committee on Science, Space, and Technology's oversight powers have been repeatedly abused, this latest action stands apart . . . Never in the history of this formerly esteemed Committee has oversight been carried out with such open disregard for truth, fairness, and the rule of law." The *San Antonio Express-News,* Smith's hometown paper, which had previously endorsed his bids for reelection, declined to do so this year because of his "abuse of his position as chairman" and his "bullying on the issue of climate change."

Congressional committees have very limited jurisdiction over state law enforcement officers engaged in the good-faith execution of their duties, and never before has Congress subpoenaed a state attorney general. The AGs investigating ExxonMobil are trying to determine whether the company has defrauded shareholders according to the laws of their states. Fraud, of course, is not protected by the First Amendment, and since the AGs are responsible for prosecuting fraud, they must be free to investigate it.

As for the nonprofit organizations the Science Committee has subpoenaed, including our own, it is obviously not within our power to violate anyone's First Amendment rights. The Supreme Court has called it "a commonplace that the constitutional guarantee of free speech is a guarantee only against abridgment by government, federal or state." That aside, we have no wish to silence anyone, or to interfere with free scientific inquiry. For the best ideas to prevail, however, people must be allowed to point out instances of inaccurate or dishonest speech. And indeed, by calling attention to the deep, largely orchestrated dishonesty that has characterized the climate denial movement ever since its inception, we are supporting genuine scientific inquiry.

We have tried to reach a reasonable accommodation with the Science Committee. But we do wish to criticize ExxonMobil on moral grounds for its long effort to confuse and deceive the public about climate change. Moreover, we believe that the willingness of some members of Congress to echo and defend ExxonMobil's obfuscation of established climate science is an inexcusable breach of the public trust. It is our First Amendment right to express these views.

In fact, the Science Committee is doing to the people and organizations it subpoenaed exactly what it accuses us of doing. It is trying to chill the First Amendment rights of those who would petition government, speak freely, and freely associate to advocate for responsible climate policies. The legal fees we have incurred because of its demands are bearable for the RFF, but they would be crippling for many smaller organizations. We also face civil or criminal liability if we are held in contempt of Congress because we will not accede to these demands.

More seriously, the committee's actions now force all organizations that would collaborate with others when taking on powerful special interests to consider that they might be ordered to reveal their strategies to any hostile member of Congress with subpoena power. This is a clear injury to the First Amendment right of association. As the Ninth Circuit wrote in *Perry v. Schwarzenegger* (2010):

> Implicit in the right to associate with others to advance one's shared political beliefs is the right to exchange ideas and formulate strategy and messages, and to do so in private. Compelling disclosure of internal campaign communications can chill the exercise of these rights.

Many commentators have noted that the committee is doing the same things to us that it falsely accuses us of doing. By accusing us of harming the First Amendment rights of others when it is attacking ours, it is trying to turn what would otherwise be self-evidently outrageous conduct into a dispute. This is not so different from ExxonMobil's politicized variant of the "Tobacco Strategy"—people will be tempted simply to take the side with which they sympathize ideologically. Meanwhile, the committee is creating a distraction from the real issues, which are what Exxon knew, and when; what it did with its knowledge; and what options humanity has left to prevent the worst consequences of climate change.

Thousands of scientists from around the world contribute to the Intergovernmental Panel on Climate Change's reports, reviewing and synthesizing the published literature on climate science every few years. The summaries for policymakers that encapsulate those reports must then be considered and approved, line by line, by representatives of over 120 different countries. Because of the remarkable number of scientists participating in the IPCC's work, it is generally considered the world's greatest institutional authority on climate science. But because it requires the approval of so many nations, including oil producers like Saudi Arabia and Kuwait, and because it is subject to political manipulation, as happened when ExxonMobil convinced the Bush administration to have its chairman replaced in 2001, the IPCC's conclusions are generally considered quite conservative.

Still, the predictions of the IPCC's latest report, published last year, are dire. In this century, disastrous weather events such as storms, droughts, floods, fires, and heat waves will become more common and more severe. Changes to regional weather will have especially serious consequences in places that are already poor, as areas that are semiarid now, for example, become too dry to farm at all. Low-lying islands and coastal cities around the world will be threatened by rising sea levels. In many parts of the world, both the quantity and the quality of fresh water will decline.

For a time, some places will see agricultural productivity increase as the planet warms and rainfall distribution shifts; but others will face shortages of food and the possibility of famine. Globally, total agricultural output is expected to be lower at the end of the century than it is now. The challenge of feeding the world's people will be exacerbated by declining fisheries as the oceans warm and turn more acidic. Many plant and animal species will become extinct as climatic changes outpace their ability to adapt, others will migrate to new regions, and all of this will have cascading effects on most ecosystems. (For example, the combination of much larger wildfires than we are used to seeing and invasive beetle species may endanger the world's boreal forests—and if they disappear, they will release vast additional quantities of carbon dioxide into the atmosphere.) Old diseases will spread and new ones emerge.

These different effects of climate change will interact with each other in complex ways, some of which may not be predictable now. It seems clear, however, that the poorest parts of the world will become poorer still, and economies everywhere will be threatened. (A 1980 American Petroleum Institute meeting in which Exxon participated concluded that at a "3% per annum growth rate of CO_2, a 2.5° C rise [in average global temperature] brings world economic growth to a halt in about 2025.") Conflict over dwindling resources will increase around the world; so, dramatically, will human migration and political instability.

As a group of retired American generals and admirals who studied the national security implications of climate change concluded in 2007:

> Economic and environmental conditions in already fragile areas will further erode as food production declines, diseases increase, clean water becomes increasingly scarce, and large populations move in search of resources. Weakened and failing governments, with an already thin margin for survival, foster the conditions for internal conflicts, extremism, and movement toward increased authoritarianism and radical ideologies.

It is true that scientists still disagree about precisely how severe the effects of climate change will be, and when. But, the generals and admirals wrote, "As military leaders, we know we cannot wait for certainty. Failing to act because a warning isn't precise enough is unacceptable."

The world's governments should have acted decades ago. When the Exxon scientist James Black wrote in 1978 that "the need for hard decisions regarding changes in energy strategies might become critical" in "five to ten years," he was right. That was humanity's best chance to start making the transition to a clean energy economy before so much CO_2 was released into the atmosphere that a great deal of warming became unavoidable. In our opinion, the reason the world has failed to act for so long is in no small part because the climate denial campaign that Exxon helped devise and lead was so successful.

Just as the tobacco industry gained decades of huge profits by obfuscating the dangers of smoking, the oil industry secured decades of profits—in Exxon's case, some of the largest profits of any corporation in history—by helping to create a fake controversy over climate science that deceived and victimized many policymakers, as well as much of the public. The bogus science it paid for through front groups, which was then repeated and validated by industry-funded, right-wing think tanks and a too-easily cowed press, worked just as well for ExxonMobil as it had for R. J. Reynolds. A 2004 study by Naomi Oreskes in *Science* examined 928 peer-reviewed papers on climate science and found that not a single one disputed global warming's existence or its human cause. But according to a recent Yale University study, only 11 percent of Americans understand that there is a scientific consensus on these points.

The climate deniers succeeded in politicizing a formerly nonpartisan issue and a threat to all humanity. In consequence, for decades now, meaningful congressional action to address climate change has been impossible. Without the agreement and leadership of the United States, the world's largest cumulative emitter of CO_2, it has been impossible to achieve a meaningful global accord on climate change. The recently completed Paris agreement on climate, for which the Obama administration fought, will be effective—but only if the world's nations live up to the commitments they made in it. Although, as a result in part of the actions of ExxonMobil, we have already missed our best chance to prevent a reordering of the world's ecological balance due to climate change, we can still avoid its worst effects. There is an enormous difference between the new, local disasters that the changing climate is already causing around the world and the global catastrophe that will become unavoidable within a few decades unless humanity takes decisive action soon.

WILLIAM PANNAPACKER

■

Selected Tweets from @WernerTwertzog

FROM *Twitter.com*

A Twitter feed emulating the voice of German film director Werner Her-zog, whose bleak if deadpan narration of his own documentaries in-cludes Teutonic pronouncements such as this zinger from Grizzly Man: "I believe the common denominator of the universe is not harmony, but chaos, hostility, and murder."

Jan 1, 2016: This day is meaningless, like all measures on the hu-man scale, to those of us who have gazed into the abyss of time. #HappyNewYear

Jan 3, 2016: #Coffee should not include whipped cream or sweet syr-ups. It should be a black, bitter foretaste of what we must face before the day is over.

Jan 11, 2016: It is Monday, my coffee is cold, the streets are filled with dirty slush, and, like my soul, #DavidBowie is dead.

Jan 13, 2016: I am told that the cheese I enjoy kills the cancer caused by the cured meats I enjoy, so I am, as the Americans say, "Even Steven."

Jan 17, 2016: "It gets better." No. It does not. It gets worse. And your body falls apart until you beg for death. #FakeGrownUpFacts

Jan 17, 2016: "Everything happens for a reason." Yes, and that reason is our stupidity. #FakeGrownUpFacts

Jan 18, 2016: One is not born German. One becomes German through ecstatic visions, years of self-recrimination, vigorous hiking, and beer.

Jan 18, 2016: *Charlotte's Web* is about the life of the artist: if you write for pigs and simpletons, you die alone in an abandoned fairground.

Jan 23, 2016: I do not own a "selfie stick" because the "self" does not exist.

Jan 24, 2016: We celebrate the Puritans, who came to these shores, in great adversity, because they were not powerful enough to oppress anyone at home.

Jan 27, 2016: Blessed are the nihilists, for one way or the other, they do not care.

Jan 29, 2016: I do not want to watch a "movie." I want an experience that will destroy everything I once believed about human nature. For $9.00.

Jan 30, 2016: No, "Beastie Boys," you should fight for something of greater substance, such as "the right of the People peaceably to assemble."

Jan 31, 2016: Men do not climb mountains because "they are there." They do so because life is meaningless.

Feb 20, 2016: Those who choose the road less travelled typically are murdered by paramilitary gangs.

Feb 20, 2016: I must agree, Elvis Presley, we cannot go on together with suspicious minds, but the alternative is a comprehensive surveillance state.

Feb 22, 2016: The "Truth" shall not make you free, because it is socially constructed, contingent, and contextual. Whoever claims to possess it is lying.

Mar 3, 2016: As we all know, school exists because children are an inherently criminal demographic that needs to be institutionalized. #Algebra

Mar 6, 2016: Man is born free, but everywhere he is checking work-related email.

Mar 6, 2016: Americans: You do not need standing desks. You need desks that teeter on the edges of open graves for the moment you stop working.

Mar 6, 2016: #Twitter needs something stronger than "block." Something involving hostages.

Mar 7, 2016: The universe will expand into a cold, thin haze of elementary particles. Nothing you did will matter. #mondaymotivation

Mar 8, 2016: And so I asked, "Why is there only one set of footprints?" And He answered, "Because that is when I hurled you 300 cubits for ingratitude."

Mar 16, 2016: Planetariums are important for introducing the next generation to Pink Floyd.

Mar 19, 2016: Alone, naked, afraid, in a Ford Econoline van, near the George Washington Bridge, #ChrisChristie ponders, briefly, how it all came to this.

Mar 19, 2016: It is too late in the winter to die, and too early in the spring to be happy.

Mar 24, 2016: Farewell, #GarryShandling. You often made me think about what it might be like to laugh.

Mar 28, 2016: I do not wear a sports jersey because I am not a proletarian seeking vicarious honor from people who despise me.

Apr 2, 2016: And then they came for the nihilists, and I said nothing, because, you know, nothing really matters. Everyone dies at some point.

Apr 9, 2016: It is important to ask subordinates to "speak freely" to identify the traitors.

Apr 11, 2016: Two roads diverged in a yellow wood. And I took them. It did not matter. Both lead to death.

Apr 21, 2016: Farewell, #Prince: shaman, libertine, androgyne—you bestrode Reagan's '80s like a colossal satyr in Edwardian drag.

Apr 29, 2016: Rereading Cormac McCarthy's *The Road* for pointers about surviving the next decade.

May 7, 2016: No, Steven Spielberg, we do not need "a bigger boat." We need, instead, a more comprehensive eschatology.

May 15, 2016: At times like this, I ask, "What would Thoreau do?" He answers: "Build cabin on rich friend's land. Take home laundry. Write dull book."

May 27, 2016: Coca Cola tasted better when it came in easily shattered glass bottles. And there was a Cold War that could kill all of us in 30 minutes.

May 27, 2016: As a child, I never won a "spelling bee" because I understood that correct spelling is historically contextual and rooted in imperialism.

Jun 3, 2016: The red jelly inside some donuts reminds us that civilization is built upon murder. #NationalDonutDay

Jun 25, 2016: When a tree falls in the forest, it does, of course, make a sound, because, you need to realize, it is not all about you.

Jun 21, 2016: No, "Frank" Sinatra, it was not possible to have done it "your way," since the self is a construct and free will is an illusion.

Jun 29, 2016: Jerry Seinfeld meets death. Asks, "What's up with the scythe? Is the scythe really necessary? Are we wheat?" He dies. The rest is silence.

Aug 1, 2016: My knees hurt. And David Bowie is dead.

Aug 4, 2016: "To irritate your conservative Christian parents" is not a good reason to convert to Islam. Just major in Art History.

Aug 4, 2016: It's important to tell the young they can be "anything they can dream," so that, one day, they'll blame themselves instead of the system.

Aug 5, 2016: Abraham Lincoln wrestled with depression, but that did not stop him from becoming the top steampunk cosplayer in Illinois.

Aug 28, 2016: Camping is important for remembering that nature is disgusting and wants to kill us.

Sep 5, 2016: Roses are red, violets are blue. They reflect different wavelengths of light. Neither have objective value.

Oct 3, 2016: College is important for making you a slave to the choices of your 18-year-old self.

Oct 13, 2016: It is important for fitted sheets to be too small to stay on the mattress to make us despair of ever finding true rest in this life.

Oct 28, 2016: Teach a man to fish, and you have condemned him to labor in a declining industry.

Nov 8, 2016: Dear Americans, remembering Fort Sumter, Crash of '29, Pearl Harbor, deaths of JFK and MLK, and 9/11. Yet you persisted. I am sorry. Werner.

Nov 12, 2016: Leonard Cohen: Take me with you.

Nov 12, 2016: I'd like to buy the world a Coke so that billions of humans will simultaneously know the emptiness of sugary drinks and Western ideology.

Nov 15, 2016: Jerry Seinfeld meets Hitler: "So, what's with the tiny mustache?" He is shot.

Nov 23, 2016: When interviewing the white working class, it is important to get lots of b-roll: junkyards, vacant stores, lonely churches, RAM Trucks.

Nov 25, 2016: Florence Henderson is dead. The Brady Bunch are orphans. As are we all.

Nov 29, 2016: Dear America: Your average liberal-arts college librarian now has more tattoos than the Hell's Angels chain-murderers at Altamont. What's up?

Dec 10, 2016: Love is patient. Love is kind. Love is the leading cause of murder.

Dec 20, 2016: It is important, if you teach English at a university, to dress as though you were an ironworker from the 1870s.

Dec 22, 2016: Coffee should not be a confection of syrups and cream. As a foghorn in the morning of Icelandic fjords sounds, so should your coffee taste.

Dec 31, 2016: Calendars and clocks are meaningless. But one thing is true: We are closer than ever to death. #HAPPYNEWYEAR

LIN-MANUEL MIRANDA

■

You'll Be Back

FROM *Hamilton Songbook*

On the following page you will find sheet music from the Broadway musical Hamilton. *We have chosen this number sung by King George III because, unlike the play's hip-hop hits, this one could be more easily performed by the takers of piano lessons. Also, given that this book represents the election year of 2016—not necessarily American representative democracy's finest hour—an ode from the king who was the butt of the joke in the Declaration of Independence seemed funnier while at the same time sad.*

YOU'LL BE BACK

Words and Music by LIN-MANUEL MIRANDA
Arranged by Alex Lacamoire and Lin-Manuel Miranda

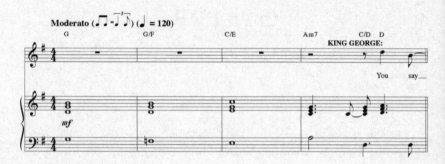

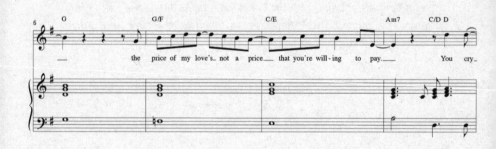

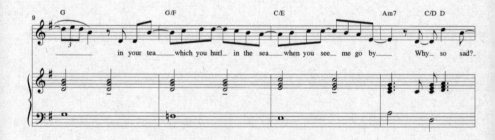

■

Excerpt from *Utah, Petitioner v. Edward Joseph Strieff, Jr.*

FROM *The Supreme Court of the United States*

We have abridged Justice Sonia Sotomayor's dissent and edited out her legal citations to make it legible for the general reader. And it is a compelling, if disturbing, read. Her unabridged opinion can be found at supremecourt.gov. Also, to those citizens who insist on crossing streets: stick to crosswalks.

ON WRIT OF CERTIORARI TO THE SUPREME COURT OF UTAH
[June 20, 2016]

JUSTICE SOTOMAYOR, with whom JUSTICE GINSBURG joins as to Parts I, II, and III, dissenting.

The Court today holds that the discovery of a warrant for an unpaid parking ticket will forgive a police officer's violation of your Fourth Amendment rights. Do not be soothed by the opinion's technical language: This case allows the police to stop you on the street, demand your identification, and check it for outstanding traffic warrants— even if you are doing nothing wrong. If the officer discovers a warrant for a fine you forgot to pay, courts will now excuse his illegal stop and will admit into evidence anything he happens to find by searching you after arresting you on the warrant. Because the Fourth Amendment should prohibit, not permit, such misconduct, I dissent.

I.

Minutes after Edward Strieff walked out of a South Salt Lake City home, an officer stopped him, questioned him, and took his identification to run it through a police database. The officer did not suspect that Strieff had done anything wrong. Strieff just happened to be the first person to leave a house that the officer thought might contain "drug activity."

As the State of Utah concedes, this stop was illegal. The Fourth Amendment protects people from "unreasonable searches and seizures." An officer breaches that protection when he detains a pedestrian to check his license without any evidence that the person is engaged in a crime. The officer deepens the breach when he prolongs the detention just to fish further for evidence of wrongdoing. In his search for lawbreaking, the officer in this case himself broke the law.

The officer learned that Strieff had a "small traffic warrant." Pursuant to that warrant, he arrested Strieff and, conducting a search incident to the arrest, discovered methamphetamine in Strieff's pockets.

Utah charged Strieff with illegal drug possession. Before trial, Strieff argued that admitting the drugs into evidence would condone the officer's misbehavior. The methamphetamine, he reasoned, was the product of the officer's illegal stop. Admitting it would tell officers that unlawfully discovering even a "small traffic warrant" would give them license to search for evidence of unrelated offenses. The Utah Supreme Court unanimously agreed with Strieff. A majority of this Court now reverses . . .

IV.

Writing only for myself, and drawing on my professional experiences, I would add that unlawful "stops" have severe consequences much greater than the inconvenience suggested by the name. This Court has given officers an array of instruments to probe and examine you. When we condone officers' use of these devices without adequate cause, we give them reason to target pedestrians in an arbitrary manner. We also risk treating members of our communities as second-class citizens.

Although many Americans have been stopped for speeding or jay-walking, few may realize how degrading a stop can be when the officer is looking for more. This Court has allowed an officer to stop you for whatever reason he wants—so long as he can point to a pretextual justification after the fact. That justification must provide specific reasons why the officer suspected you were breaking the law, at twenty-one, but it may factor in your ethnicity, where you live, what you were wearing, and how you behaved. The officer does not even need to know which law you might have broken so long as he can later point to any possible infraction—even one that is minor, unrelated, or ambiguous.

The indignity of the stop is not limited to an officer telling you that you look like a criminal. The officer may next ask for your "consent" to inspect your bag or purse without telling you that you can decline. Regardless of your answer, he may order you to stand "helpless, perhaps facing a wall with [your] hands raised." If the officer thinks you might be dangerous, he may then "frisk" you for weapons. This involves more than just a pat down. As onlookers pass by, the officer may "'feel with sensitive fingers every portion of [your] body. A thorough search [may] be made of [your] arms and armpits, waistline and back, the groin and area about the testicles, and entire surface of the legs down to the feet.'"

The officer's control over you does not end with the stop. If the officer chooses, he may handcuff you and take you to jail for doing nothing more than speeding, jaywalking, or "driving [your] pickup truck . . . with [your] 3-year-old son and 5-year-old daughter . . . without [your] seatbelt fastened." At the jail, he can fingerprint you, swab DNA from the inside of your mouth, and force you to "shower with a delousing agent" while you "lift [your] tongue, hold out [your] arms, turn around, and lift [your] genitals." Even if you are innocent, you will now join the 65 million Americans with an arrest record and experience the "civil death" of discrimination by employers, landlords, and whoever else conducts a background check. And, of course, if you fail to pay bail or appear for court, a judge will issue a warrant to render you "arrestable on sight" in the future.

This case involves a suspicionless stop, one in which the officer initiated this chain of events without justification. As the Justice Department notes, *supra*, at 8, many innocent people are subjected to the humiliations of these unconstitutional searches. The white defendant in this case shows that anyone's dignity can be violated in this manner. But it is no secret that people of color are disproportionate victims of this type of scrutiny. For generations, black and brown parents have given their children "the talk"— instructing them never to run down the street; always keep your hands where they can be seen; do not even think of talking back to a stranger—all out of fear of how an officer with a gun will react to them.

By legitimizing the conduct that produces this double consciousness, this case tells everyone, white and black, guilty and innocent, that an officer can verify your legal status at any time. It says that your body is subject to invasion while courts excuse the violation of your rights. It implies that you are not a citizen of a democracy but the subject of a carceral state, just waiting to be cataloged.

We must not pretend that the countless people who are routinely targeted by police are "isolated." They are the canaries in the coal mine whose deaths, civil and literal, warn us that no one can breathe in this atmosphere. They are the ones who recognize that unlawful police stops corrode all our civil liberties and threaten all our lives. Until their voices matter too, our justice system will continue to be anything but.

I dissent.

■

"Woman Fries and Eats Pet Goldfish After Fight With Husband"

—headline, Associated Press

FROM *The Southern Review*

I made sure the pan was plenty hot—
   the pain over quick—
all seven sizzling in butter and salt,
   heads and tails flipped,
just once, to the other side.
   That day we bought them
at Sunny Pointe Mall—the tied
   plastic bags bouncing
in our hands—we floated along,
   certain about the feeding
and caring, that soon we'd add
   a swim-through pagoda,
a little bridge. He stared at the tank
   first thing each morning,
waiting for coffee, always
   complaining: "It's too weak!"
I felt that way about his kisses,
   excuses, his whines
over the fish needing more space.

He called me mean
when I netted the black-spotted one
    in a corner, for only
a minute, so that the others
    could reach their fair share
of food. He knew how much
    I wanted a special anniversary,
but he gave me a sweat shirt,
    our trip to Reno out
because he couldn't trust
    the guy next door
with a key, let alone with the fish.
    I'm not sorry I gulped
them down without chewing—
    no scales left clinging
to my teeth, no bones
    sticking in my throat.
But I wish he hadn't walked in
    to see one pair left,
those stony eyes, ragged faces,
    burnt fins matching.

CASEY JARMAN

■

An Oral History of Gabriel DePiero

FROM *Death: An Oral History*

There weren't really any strangers in my hometown of twelve thousand people, but Tony and Gabe, rosy-cheeked identical twins from a big Italian family, were especially hard to miss. They were affable and outgoing, their family was well-liked, and as one of the community's only sets of twins (there were four, Gabe remembers, but he and his brother were the only identical twins), they were an inherent curiosity. They were special, even from a distance, whether they liked it or not.

Then, at age thirteen, Tony took his father's gun and shot himself. He died instantly.

For the larger community of Florence, Oregon—a scenic coastal tourist trap with crumbling fishing and timber industries—it was a shock. But shock and disbelief gave way to finger-pointing and speculation. Painful rumors flew almost as fast as word of Tony's death. In one version of events, he had left an angry suicide note. He and his middle-school girlfriend had been in a huge fight, according to another. The most malicious rumors were that Tony's twin brother, Gabe, had pulled the trigger. Those rumors always made their way back to the family. It was as if the likeliest culprits—a teenager's failure to grasp the nature of his own mortality; a momentary madness that could never be taken back—were too simple for the community to accept.

Beyond the rumor and blame, Tony's absence in the community was tangible. No one felt it more profoundly than his twin brother. "Every time people looked at me, they thought of Tony," Gabe told me in the living room of his mobile home, his dog, Nix, at his feet. "Every time I look in the mirror, still, I see him."

—Casey Jarman

I'm Surprised That We Survived Childhood

On the surface, my family life was very Brady Bunch. That's what my dad strove for. He wanted everything to be perfect. It was very traditional small town: Dad worked, Mom worked, all of us four kids were into sports, and we played outside and whatnot. Mom worked at the school, so in the summers she stayed at home with us. When she wasn't around, my oldest brother usually babysat us—and tormented us—and we did all the normal shit you go through growing up in a small town. We built forts, we made booby traps, we lit the pitch on the trees on fire, and then, you know, pissed the fire out when our parents drove up—because every time you light anything on fire, your parents show up. I guess in some ways I'm surprised that we survived childhood.

My mom was brought up Presbyterian, and my dad was brought up Catholic, but we weren't raised religious as kids. The only religious thing that ever happened to us as children is when we went to go visit my grandparents on my dad's side. We went to church on Sundays if we were with them, and man, Catholic services suck. There was all this kneeling, standing, sitting, kneeling. Going to church is a workout! Especially when you're a little kid, and you're antsy, and you wanna go do something else.

My mom and her whole family are very open in talking about death. We still, even now, we talk about it. Her father—my grandfather—just recently passed away, and we've talked a lot about that. He was ninety-two years old. Toward the end he was forgetting things, and he called me everything but my own name. He would call me different grandkids' names each time I visited him, but at least he knew that I was his grandkid.

My grandparents on my dad's side had some property near Eugene, with a big garden and orchard, and so we ate vegetables and fruit and played. We had a great time. My grandfather, Jeno, was a woodworker. He taught me how to write in cursive. He died a couple of years prior to Tony. He passed away from cancer, and that affected me because we were close. But when I lost Tony, I lost me, too. I know that I was not the same person afterward that I was before. Because that connection—well, it was weird.

"If You Blink, It's Gonna Snap!"

Tony and I were the clinical definition of mirrored twins. As a young child I was predominantly left-handed: I wrote left-handed, threw a baseball with my left hand—that kind of stuff. But when I hit school, I got made fun of for writing left-handed because it looked funny. You know, kids are mean. Tony was right-handed. He was into hunting and sports. I was kind of athletic, but the hunting and fishing I could have done without, you know? I didn't want to get up at five in the morning to go kill a bird or a deer, that didn't appeal to me. But it was very big in my family, and since I didn't really hunt, I helped do the cleanup. I remember holding a deer by its legs while my dad gutted it, and he handed me the heart, and there was blood running down my arms. I was a part of the whole process except actually taking the life of the animals. Tony would hunt, but I'd carry a gun for someone. Give me a tag, great. That's kinda how it happened when I was younger. I went through hunting safety classes, I knew how to handle a gun, and I'm still not fearful of guns. Clearly, I know what guns can do.

Tony and I weren't in any sort of "twin bubble." There were always four of us. We had Dominic, who was the oldest by two years, and then Mario, two years younger than him. There are two years between me and Mario, but there were only two minutes between me and Tony. We were the youngest. But whenever we did things as brothers, like when we would play any kind of sports or games, it was always me and Dominic against Mario and Tony. That's how we always matched it up.

We were close. I mean, I was never alone. We shared a bedroom our whole lives. For a long time we shared a queen-sized bed. He had one side, and I had the other. That's just how we were. We got bunk beds when we started getting a little bit older. We were independent, but still had a lot of the same qualities. We never did do the whole "let's wear matching clothes" thing. We never did any of that kind of shit. Tony was into music; he played the drums at school. I played trombone and bass clarinet.

School wasn't easy for Tony. He struggled with it. It was easy for me, in regards to the academic side of things. Tony was really social.

He liked to please people and make sure they were happy. I don't give a shit about other people. I'm an asshole. I mean, the mouth I have right now is the mouth I had when I was a child, so my growing up wasn't as peachy keen as my brothers' was. I stood up for myself where my brothers backed down easily. When Tony got in trouble, I would do things to provoke my dad to take the punishment away from Tony. That was a big thing for me.

My dad's very intelligent. He's got a photographic memory, and he's super smart. But when I was a kid, he didn't know how to be a dad, except "I bring in the money, I put a roof over your head, I bring the food home." Providing was how he showed you that he loved you. I never felt a lot of love, other than that.

Socially, school wasn't the greatest for me because I was overweight. I was made fun of for that. And I was always called *gay, fag,* and stuff like that growing up. That started in elementary school. This kid Taylor was a big perpetrator of it. He called me "Gay Gabe." I got that a lot. You've got to love having a name that rhymes with *gay.* I mean, I knew from a young age that I was gay, but living in Florence, and in my family, it was a sign of weakness—and I'm not weak. I'm a strong person. But I was fat, too, and I got a lot of shit for it. I had friends, but I was picked on a lot.

By the time we were teenagers I was two inches taller than Tony. He was more active, so he shed weight and wasn't nearly as rotund as me. I was round. But I always stood up for myself. If someone said something, I said something right back to them. I didn't take it. I wasn't meek. I wasn't shy by any stretch of imagination. When Taylor or whoever would say things, I'd come back with, "Really? I'm that important that you took the time out of your life to insult me?" I was creative, you know?

I was never physically hit or anything because of my size. I was always taller and bigger than the other kids, and I never backed down from an altercation, so no one would try to pick on me in a physical way. As a small child, my dad told me this—and I'll never forget it— he was like, "If you get in a fight at school and I find out you threw the first punch, your ass is grass. If you are defending yourself, and you kick the shit out of them, I will fight tooth and nail to make sure nothing happens to you." I mean, Dominic and Mario picked on us as kids. I remember my parents going off to some function, and my brother setting mouse traps and holding them in front of our faces: "If you blink, it's gonna snap!" Now I can beat anybody in a staring contest. [Laughs.] You know how bad it hurt to have the trap snap your face? It stings.

Like most families, ours looked nice on the surface, but when you scratched just a little bit, it bled like a motherfucker. But when I turned twelve, it was like, *life*. That's when my parents divorced, and it just felt like everything went downhill from there. Tony and I moved out with my mom to a little apartment behind the middle school. My two older brothers stayed with my dad at our childhood home. We moved out in July, prior to sixth grade. So Tony and I went from taking the bus to school to walking across the street.

Tony and I would spend every other weekend at my dad's house. Dominic and Mario mostly chose to live with him because he had less rules and stipulations. They were older, so that was easier for them. Tony and I had just turned thirteen. I remember when they first moved out, one of the first things that Mario told us was, "We eat ice cream after dinner every night." I was like, "Good for you." I mean, my mom struggled, and we worked really hard. That was one thing that my mom did really well—and my dad, as well—is to teach me that you have to earn what you have. Nothing's ever given to you.

It Startled Me Awake, But I Didn't Move

Tony died on spring break during our seventh-grade year. The last time I talked in this kind of detail about it, it was about two years after that. I remember, it was at a football game. My friend McKenzie and a couple of other people started asking questions, so I went into detail and told the whole story. But it has been a while . . . [takes deep breath].

It was just a normal Saturday night. We were staying at my dad's house. Everything was fine. We went to see a movie—*Naked Gun 33⅓*. Then in the morning, Dad came in and told Tony, "You need to get up. I'm taking Dominic to school." Dominic was going on a field trip with the golf team, and he'd be gone during spring break. Dad was going to come home, and we were going to go to work with him for the day. He was a plumber—he was going to go work on a project or whatever he had going on. So that was the plan.

Tony woke up and I stayed in bed. It was just us in the house. At some point that morning, he came in and said, "Hey, dude, get up," and I was like, "I wanna sleep. I'm still tired, leave me alone." Tony said, "All right," and he walked out.

The next thing I remember is hearing a very loud noise. My dad being a business owner for a plumbing business, he had very large invoice books—I mean like fifty-pound, huge books—and what it sounded like is it came from the dining room–kitchen area. I thought maybe it was one of those falling and slapping against the linoleum floor. So I didn't get out of bed. I just laid there because it startled me awake, but I didn't move.

I went back to sleep. Dad came home and asked, "Is Tony here?" I was like, "Nope." He went down the hallway, looked in Dominic's room, looked in Mario's room, said his name, and then looked in his room and he screamed . . .

The scream is the part that still bothers me. I still have nightmares now about the scream that my dad let out. He said, "Oh my god, Tony, no!" Then he came running down the hallway. At that point I was out of bed, and I remember stomping on a Nintendo system, then on a remote control, and then tripping over the corner of Tony's bed to get out of the door. I come swinging out of the room, into the dining room, and he's on the phone with 911, and I'm like, "What's going on?" My dad says, "My son shot himself, please send an ambulance," and that was pretty much the end of the conversation. He looks me directly in the eyes and says, "If you can see the white of my carpet, you're too close to my room. Don't go near my room." I'm like, "What the fuck's going on?" He's still not telling me what's happening, and he starts just calling people.

I think to myself, *Tony shot himself. What a douche.* You know, he was very accident-prone. He crashed a three-wheeler into a tree and cut open his hand once. I'm thinking he shot himself in the foot— what an idiot. It hadn't occurred to me that he could be dead. Dad called everyone. He called my mom and said, "Call someone to give you a ride. There's been an accident with Tony. You need to get out here now." He called my grandparents and my aunts, and they started calling all the family in Eugene. We had a couple of different uncles, and an aunt who lived in Springfield, and so people started getting these calls.

I went outside and pet the dog on the porch. We had a tree stump across the yard, and I went and sat on that with the dog. I could hear the ambulance, so I walked out to the driveway. Of course, they drove past our driveway, so I ran out to the street and ran after them a little bit to get them to turn around and come to our house. That's when it started to dawn on me that there was something really wrong, because they weren't rushing. I was like, "Hello, the accident's over here." But they weren't in a rush.

Then Mr. L [a local teacher] got there right after the ambulance did. He was the first one to respond. He was at church when he heard a dispatch radio go off, and then that's when all the other police started showing up.

When the police and everyone started showing up, that's when I went back in the house and sat on the couch in the living room. I had to put the dog out because he kept getting pissed off and barking with all these strangers in the house. I was sitting on the couch, and I remember my mom got there. Chuck, a family friend who got there right after Mr. L, said, "That's the mom." The cops separated, and Chuck grabbed my mom and just lifted her onto our deck. I had stepped out at that point to give my mom a hug, and she just collapsed in my arms. I had to ask the police officer to help me because I was falling over. She didn't know what was going on, so she ran into the house, and that's when Dad came out and said Tony had shot himself, and he was gone. I stayed outside at that point. I don't know if my mom went into the house and saw him or not. I know that at one point my dad went into the kitchen and got a glass of water. I was sitting on a recliner outside of the kitchen doorway, and he was like, "He hasn't been baptized. Can I baptize him?" That was before anyone showed; the ambulance, the paramedics had just gotten there. They couldn't pronounce him dead until the coroner showed up, which was like two hours later.

The vice-principal brought Dominic back from school after he was dropped off there for his golfing trip. Then he and I went to get my brother Mario from his friend's house, where he had stayed the night. I remember that my necklace had broken somehow, and I was picking up beads from the ground when a family friend came through the door. My dad was standing there, and the woman was like, "You killed him, motherfucker!" and she pushed him and, like, assaulted my dad. My dad immediately said, "Get this bitch off my property!"

When the police came, they asked me a lot of questions. "Was he unhappy? Was he this or that?" He had a girlfriend at the time, and they asked about her. I was like, "No, there's no indication of anything bad." I mean, come on, it was a seventh-grade romance. What did they do—they passed notes, they held hands. There was nothing going on that I can think of in his life at that point that was so bad that he needed to end it. He had a lot of friends that he was close with, that he socialized with. He wasn't alienated or anything like that. He wasn't ostracized for anything. He wasn't bullied at all. I mean, I can see me pulling the trigger before anyone else. I truly believe in my heart that it wasn't suicide, and I will defend that until I die.

At that point, after I answered those questions, I kind of shut down. I remember saying, "He didn't fucking kill himself. It wasn't suicide." Then I kind of snapped, and Chuck stepped over and told them, "You have to leave him alone." They didn't ask me another question after that.

My uncle Terry showed up, and he could see I needed to get out of there. He had just got back from a trip to Germany. He took me up the coast just to get away from the house and everyone, and all he did was talk about his trip to Germany. I don't even remember what he said about it because all I did was stare out the window of his truck. I remember staring at the trees. We parked in a parking lot next to the ocean, and I just stared out the window and listened to sound. Then he drove us to Saint Mary's Church, where he got out and said a prayer. I just sat in the back of the church.

When we got back, they took Tony out of the bedroom in a red body bag. They set him behind the ambulance, and our dog went and laid next to the body bag. I had to walk over and take him away because, when they grabbed the body bag to put him in the ambulance, he sort of attacked the paramedic. I had to walk over and grab the dog to walk him away. At that point, I knew I had to leave. That was when I grabbed my mom and was like, "We have to go. I have to go. You have to take me home now." That's when I finally left.

There Was No Feeling, There Was Nothing

Tony died on my classmate Matt's birthday. So I went to the birthday party that same day. My mom and her friend Lynette thought that it might take my mind off things. Which was really kind of odd because, when I got there, it put all of them in a very weird place. My friend Spencer—I'll never forget this—he walked into the living room where I was sitting on the couch, and he was like, "I don't know what to say." And I was like, "Neither do I." I said, "How are you doing?" He was like, "I'm okay. How are you?" I said, "It's been a rough day." And that was how the conversation started. Then we all just started talking about normal stuff. Things started feeling normal again. We went to the video store to get a video game to play, and I remember running into a girl from school. I told her, "Tony died this morning." She said, "Nuh uh." I said, "No, he shot himself and died this morning." And she said, "No, he didn't."

We grew up around guns. We had hunters' safety, the whole works. We knew how guns worked: pistols, rifles, shotguns, anything in between. What had happened was that Tony had already cleaned two pistols. He had cleaned two, and he had taken a revolver, and he had all of the shells in his pocket but one. So what they believe he was doing was playing Russian roulette, and he lost. They don't believe it was a suicide thing—that he killed himself that way intentionally—but "I'm the invincible teenager." He was stupid in doing shit, and I could see him being like, "I can win!" And he lost. It was a hollow-point bullet. It went through his right eye and completely removed all of this . . . [motions toward back of his skull].

He didn't know what happened. No, he did not know what happened. It was instant. There was no feeling, there was no nothing. That's the only peace of mind that I get from it, that he didn't know what happened. The click. If he even heard the click of the hammer, he was gone. He was sitting at my dad's bed with his knees under the bed, so when my dad found him, he was partway under the bed. There were two full-door mirrors behind him, with a small section of wall between them that was painted white. I remember after the whole thing, I went in the room, and they had cut the carpet out of my dad's bedroom and torn up everything under it, the base, wood floor, everything. They had completely repainted the wall and cleaned stuff out, so that there was no . . . everything was gone by the time I had seen it. I never saw it or anything. The only time I saw Tony prior to them burying him was we did get to view him in his casket. They reconstructed all of this . . . [motions at back of his head], and he had an eye patch on when I saw him.

The Voice

I'm not a religious person, and I wasn't then. I'm somewhat spiritual, but I'm not religious. One thing I do remember and I won't forget, though, is while everyone was at the house—the paramedics and police and neighbors—I went and laid down on my bed, and I remember hearing Tony's voice very clearly telling me, "I'm sorry," and "Everything's going to be okay." There was no one around because I immediately got up like, "Who fucking said that?" I looked out my bedroom door, and no one was around. It was Tony's voice, very clearly. It was Tony's voice telling me it would be okay.

Kid Gloves

Everyone treated me differently after that. Kid gloves. It was like, "I'm a human being. Treat me normal." That was the one thing that drove me crazy. I was so tired. I wasn't a child. I wasn't an adult by any means; I was a teenager. But it was like, "Quit treating me like a baby." I think all teenagers feel like that, but when you throw in the death of your twin brother, it's worse. Family, friends, everyone— everyone took a step back. I felt like I had the plague.

Everyone was kind of looking over their shoulders or side-eyeing me. Like, "Poor him." They wouldn't say anything to me. It was like,

"Say something or do something!" I felt very alienated. And everyone, kids, teachers—the teachers were the worst in regards to the baby gloves because it wasn't just me. It was everyone around me, too. When I walked into the room, it was like, "Okay, the plague just got here, so how is everyone else going to respond now that Gabe's in the room?" I wasn't just worried about me. It was the stress of everybody around me. Like, "What's going to happen today?" I had breakdowns at school. I had a couple of them. It was awful. And I had to go to the office and leave because there were a couple of really bad breakdowns that I just couldn't get myself under control. It would come out of nowhere. I would all of a sudden get overwhelmed and couldn't handle it.

It was like standing in a room full of people screaming my head off, and no one responded. That's exactly how I felt. It was like, I was screaming bloody murder for anyone and everyone, but I didn't exist. At the same time it was like everyone was on me, but no one listened. It was all about what was best for *them* in the situation, not what was best for me. It was about what made them comfortable, not what made *me* comfortable.

I'd never felt alone before. I'd always had Tony around. At the end of the day, he was in the same room with me sleeping, too, you know? I never felt alone. After he died, that was the first time. You have all these people around you, trying to support you. Friends' families made our lunches for a month after Tony died. I remember going to school every day, and this girl handing me a lunch because her mom made me a lunch, too.

I felt like such a burden. Like, "Oh god, here comes Gabe." Then, the bullying didn't stop when Tony died. I mean, it didn't get any worse, but didn't get any better. I was still Fat Gabe, Gay Gabe, whatever. That was just part of it. But that was almost better than the fact that most people didn't look at me when I spoke. I just wanted them to acknowledge that I existed.

I mean, if I had had one person who sat there and just looked at me when I spoke, it would have made a world of difference. I didn't have that. I felt so alone. I mean, pluck me and put me in the middle of nowhere, and I think I would have found a friend there before I found one in Florence.

My family had to look at me every day, and it reminded them of Tony. I know how that feels because I look in the mirror and I have to see myself. I mean, I'm thirty-four years old. I'll be thirty-five at the end of this month, and there isn't a day that goes by that Tony doesn't pop into my mind. People say that cliché, but it's true. Every time I look in the mirror, still, I see him. I wonder, *Would we look the same now, or would we look different?* There are all these questions.

It was overwhelming, so I tried to kill myself. I thought, *If I'm this alone, why even be here?* It was so overwhelming, and it drove me nuts. One night I was home alone at my mom's house, and I swallowed a bottle of Tylenol and chugged a bottle of rum out of the liquor cabinet. I woke up in a big pile of puke. That was a few months after Tony died. The pills seemed like the easy way out. But it wasn't so easy. I felt like shit for like three days afterward.

We Didn't Know What to Say

I've met a lot of other twins throughout the years. When I was in college, there were like five sets of identical twins living in the dorms. It's difficult, especially when they don't know me from my childhood, and they don't know that I'm a twin. They're like, "Oh, you were a twin." And I say, "Yeah, I'm still a twin. He's just not alive." I'm absolutely a twin. That's who I am. He's my other half.

I met another twin recently, a guy, and he asked, "What is that like? I couldn't imagine that." I said, "Don't." There are certain pains and certain horrible experiences in life that you don't have to go through, and you should never have to imagine. Because you can't. It's not just the loss of that person; it's the aftermath. It was almost like I died with Tony. Then my death happened every day after that for a long time. It's everything after. It's how people treat you.

Looking back now that I'm older I just want to ask everyone, "Why did you do that? Why did you stop talking to me? What was wrong with me that you couldn't talk to me after Tony died?"

We didn't know what to say.

Neither the fuck did I! I was thirteen. You were the adult in the situation! Like, what the fuck!? I mean, I had a lot of rage. I had a lot of anger. Awful rage and anger.

Looking back at it now, I get it. It's a hard situation. But still—why was I punished after he died? What did I do wrong to be treated that way? It still bothers me to this day. Even when I've spoken to people about it, all they can say is, "I didn't know what to say." It's a bullshit excuse. Spencer, at the age of twelve or thirteen, said the same thing, but then the conversation started after that. So, really? You were the adult, and you couldn't do anything? Zip? I mean "fuck you" is better than being ignored. What did I do that you couldn't say, "How do you feel?" or "How are you doing?" Like, why couldn't you ask me that? You asked everyone else that. When Tony died I magically gained the ability to never be asked, "What's up?"

Sometimes I wish my family and friends would have said, "I can't talk to you anymore because Tony died." I would have had closure there. "You're dead to us, too, because Tony died." Yeah, that would've hurt, but I would have had closure. I would have known why. Being ignored, I was left wondering if I was only ever included because Tony was there, too. You know, did people just want to hang out with him? Those were my thoughts as a teenager. Maybe it was because I'm the youngest by two minutes—I'm just the little brother—I felt expendable.

I can talk to anyone now. I don't care. I freak a lot of people out, that's fine. How many people want to put themselves into situations that make them uncomfortable? Or make them feel something fearful or feel something that they don't like? Not many. Not many, if any at all. Journalists, maybe. And gay people! Gay people will talk to you.

There Was No Pain

I lost a lot of family and friends when I came out. It's okay. I care about you the way you care about me. Probably in my late twenties, I realized that there were certain things in life that were out of my control—things that I absolutely couldn't do anything about. Why should I stress over those things? If something happens and I can't get over it in three seconds, there's a problem. I need to address that problem and fix it because I don't like feeling that way. I don't want stress in my life. I don't need stress in my life. My home is my sanctuary. I want to be comfortable and relaxed. So things don't bother me. I don't let things bother me anymore.

That took me a lot of years to figure that out. I've been through a lot of therapy. I've had my lows. I was a cutter. I was a drinker. It affected me really bad when I first started college. It was really hard seeing all these sets of twins. That was when my second suicide attempt happened, in college. I was at a very low point. I don't remember doing it. I don't remember how it happened. But when I came to, I had cut my arm twenty-six times with a serrated blade.

I just turned the whole back of my arm into hamburger. I remember looking down, and my whole shirt being covered in blood, and I'm like, "Oh my god, I stabbed myself." I go rushing into the bathroom to find out where the hole is at, what did I do. Remember, I had the knife in my hand. I was wearing a white T-shirt, and it was just hanging heavy with blood. That's when I realized my arm was covered in blood, and I grabbed a washcloth and I wiped it. It was just like, *holy shit*. I had taken the Gerber—it was one of those serrated knives, a Gerber tool—and just sat there.

I had cut myself and burned myself and did those things after Tony had died. I have different scars on me from different incidents, on my hands and legs, wounds that I inflicted on myself. But I hadn't done it in years. I was drinking heavily, and I was living out on my own. My roommates were gone, and I was watching a movie about Matthew Shepard.* At the end of it his mother went out to where they tied him up to that fence. When she walked up to that, it put me into a crying rage. It made me think of Tony, and it made me think about how I hadn't come out yet. All these different things and all these different feelings, and I just started . . . that's what triggered my crying. That movie. I watched that movie and I remember sitting on my couch. But it put me way in deeper than that. I blacked out. I think when I get put into that situation of total panic and fear and pain and

---

* A gay University of Wyoming student who was brutally tortured and murdered in 1998. His death led to significant hate crime legislation.

everything, my mind shuts down. My brain doesn't want to do it any-more. It has dealt with so much for so long that it hits capacity and it just stops. I don't remember grabbing the knife. I don't remember opening it. I don't remember any of that. To this day I don't remem-ber doing anything. Except I remember I had just sliced the shit out of my arm and it never hurt. That was the weird thing. There was no pain. It was bad, like the scars. There's still certain lines that you can see, different cuts that are still there. A lot of them went away. Some of them I covered up with a tattoo. It was like I went after these veins right here: [points to the inside back of his left forearm].

That one was the worst. I was going to therapy at the time, and I told my therapist that I had cut myself, and he said, "What do you mean?" I pulled up my sleeve and showed him, and he's like, "You know that we can put you away for that." I said, "What do you mean?" He said, "You're inflicting pain on yourself. You have to see your doc-tor about antidepressants right now." I showed my doctor what I did, and that's when the whole world kind of came crashing in on me be-cause, basically, I lost my ability to make my own decisions. It was, *Now that you've inflicted pain upon yourself, we could hospitalize you for three days and put you under surveillance and blah blah blah blah.* You would lose the ability to make the decisions for medications and any-thing; those decisions would be made by your parents, even as an adult.

I fought taking antidepressants. I was like, "I don't need drugs." I had friends who took different antidepressants, and you could see the change in them. I didn't want that. But my doctor made a really good point. He was like, "You're worried about changing, but what are you in control of right now? This medication is to give you the tools to get things back under control. Then once things are easier, you can start getting off of them. But you're not in control now, so what's the dif-ference?" That made sense. That's when I first started taking antide-pressants. I took them for a few years, and then I weaned myself off of them. I haven't taken them since.

The antidepressants made things easier to deal with. After Tony died, I worried about everything. If I wasn't around my mother, I was calling her every hour—"How are you doing? What's going on?" I worried. After Tony died, every nightmare I had, every dream I had,

I lost someone close to me. Someone I cared about died. I was so scared that someone else I cared about was going to die. I was always super stressed about that, and I was taking a lot of antacids and stuff. I worried about anything and everything.

Oh, it was awful. If a friend said, "Hey I'm going to call you in a little bit," I'd be like "How long is a little bit?" If they said half an hour, and then they didn't call within that half-hour mark, I was devastated. I'd think they hated me, or I'd be freaked out. I'd think, *Oh my god, their house blew up*. I mean, everything. *Oh my god, they slipped in the shower and strangled themselves with the curtain*. Everything horrible you can think of, that's what I always thought had happened.

I didn't have my childhood ripped away. I had my teenage years ripped away. I got to have a childhood. But as a teenager, you're trying to figure out who you are, and that was all torn away.

My Turn to Be Selfish

I was scared. Everything was built on "I'm not gay." I didn't come out because I was scared that I would lose the family that I had. Because that was a sign of weakness, being gay. They'd all made their comments. I heard all the comments my dad made. It's never been a positive thing in my family. It's not talked about, even now. I was in a relationship for an extended amount of time, and he never met my parents. My mom's comment was always, "I have concerns about the lifestyle." AIDS, and all that, STDs. But I could have sex with women, too, and the same things could happen. I'm not stupid. I use a condom, hello.

I didn't come out until I was twenty-four, but I figured it out in middle school. I remember first changing my status on MySpace from "straight" to "unsure." And the controversy that caused at my job, you wouldn't believe it.

This is me. If you don't like it, kick rocks. Don't let the door hit ya' where the good lord split ya'. I'm not going to stress my life over how you feel. That's been very important to me. When I die, that's one thing I want to be said at my funeral: Gabe cares about every one of you the way you cared about him. Because I know 60 percent of the people in that room didn't give two shits for me, but are there because of the other people that are there. That's how my family is. They're there for show. And that's fine. I know who cares about me, and the rest can kiss my ass. I don't want to worry about everyone else. I want to worry about me. You know what? It's my turn to be selfish. I've earned that right.

In my mid-twenties I was back in Florence, and I was like, "I haven't been to a football game since high school! Let's go to a football game." It's like six years after high school. There were four people there. Three of them I had graduated with [in a class of about 110 people]. I told a girl I'd been friends with that I was gay. She said, "No, you're not." And I'm like, "Yeah, I am." She wouldn't believe me.

I'm your typical guy who grew up in a small town, except I like to be with other men.

Sometimes it's just, "Why was I dealt this hand?" Be a twin, lose your twin. Be gay in a small town. Struggle with your weight. It's like, what the fuck did I do to deserve this? What did I do in a previous life that put me on this path?

At the same time, it has made me a more compassionate person. When someone tells me they lost a loved one, I tell them I'm so sorry for their loss, but I don't stop the conversation there. I know how that kid felt. I wanted someone just to listen, to sit there and stare at me while I talked. No one did any of that kind of stuff. That's what I got out of all this pain—it was compassion. It taught me compassion. Everything else about me is just me. The compassion I have is a direct result of all that horrible shit I went through. I don't want anyone to ever, ever feel like that.

I tell my friends, "If you need anyone, you call me, day or night." I truly mean that. Because you never know when you need someone. I've needed people at 3 a.m.

My Whole Life, It Was Tony's Life

I don't think anyone else has been through what I've been through. I know people go through horrific things every day. Is mine any worse or better than theirs? Yes and no. Everyone handles things differently. I mean, I tried to end it twice. It wasn't my time. I feel like I was put here to go through all these horrible, awful things because I can handle it. I've had to. After Tony died, I had to move on. I had to deal, you know? No one was there to support me. I had to pull up my bootstraps on my own.

People will tell you, "Oh, we were there. We were supportive." I'm like, just because you were in the room doesn't mean you were there. What did you say to me when you were in the room? *Well, nothing.* I'm very vocal when I walk in a room. I say hello; I want people to know I'm there. I don't want anyone to feel that way I felt for a lot of years. It wasn't just that moment after Tony died. It almost felt like my whole life, it was Tony's life. How I felt after all that happened was that everyone wanted Tony, and I was just the tagalong because we shared the embryo at birth. I was expendable, disposable.

There's no guidebook for something like this. The one thing when going through death and mourning is just ask questions. Ask a question. Doesn't matter what that question is—I mean, "What's your favorite color?" Engaging that person in anything no matter what it is or how minute it is could mean the world. I truly believe that. That would have meant the world to me, if someone would have just asked me anything, made me feel like they cared about the answer I gave. If someone would have said, "What's your favorite color?" and I told them "Yellow," and they listened to me, that would have meant so much.

I Like the View from Here

When his anniversary comes around, in March, it's rough. My birthday's really hard, too.

It's weird. I went years without going up and seeing his grave. And other times, I just want to go up there and hang out. It's a peaceful place. I like going up there. It's beautiful. It's up at the top of the cemetery, next to that big tree. I signed his casket—"I will always love you. Love, Gabe." I wrote that in black Sharpie on his casket.

It's weird: I'm thirty-four years old, and I have a cemetery plot.

I don't own my own home, but I do know where I'm going to be buried. I have a plot right next to Tony's. When he died, my parents chose to buy the plot right next to his. They bought it for me. It's weird knowing I have a cemetery plot. I wouldn't say it's comforting, but—and I know this sounds really morbid—I'm the one who chose where Tony got buried. I sat there, as a kid, and then I laid on the ground. I would lay on the ground in different places and be like, "I like the view from here." I told them that the spot near the tree was where I wanted Tony to be buried. And that's where they put him.

I wanted him to be buried right under the tree, actually, but because of the roots and all that, they don't allow it. Rules. The whole idea of being planted and becoming a tree still interests me. I love that. I think that is the coolest idea. Like, when my dog dies, I will plant her under a tree. My wild fern grows somewhere. I think that is the coolest way to remember someone, to have that. Because the tree can live on forever, you know? It gets its life from you. How cool is that? My energy's all gone because I'm dead, but what's left of me is in this tree.

But I know where I'm going to end up. Saying that out loud, it sounds weird. I've never thought about it much until just the other day, when I was talking to someone and I'm like, "I know where I'm going to be buried when I die." I'm thirty-four years old and I know where I'm going to be buried when I die.

That World Is Gone

I remember flipping through channels one day with my mom and landing on *The Jenny Jones Show*. It was an episode about "twinless twins," and my mom was like, "We have to watch this!" I was like, *really?* After Tony died my mom went through this kind of crazy death thing. Twinless twins are networks of people who have lost their twins. I've never contacted one. I've looked into it, but I've never reached out to a twinless twin.

Why would I reach out to another pained soul? I can't answer for what happened then. Back then, I felt worthless. I was the leftover, the remnant. Why would I want to bring another person into that feeling? Or why would I want to surround myself with people who felt that same way? That'd just make me feel even worse. Nothing like a little more death in the room. Ugh, no thanks.

I don't want to reach out to a community where all they're going to do is bitch and moan or talk about the loss of their twin. I lost my twin. I don't want to dwell on it. Your story is your story and my story is my story. I'm not trying to one-up you or any of that stuff with my loss, but then again . . . good luck beating my story.

There's always death. I mean, everyone in the world is going to experience death, close to them, somehow. An animal, a parent, a family member. But there's a certain pain when you lose that other half of you. It's indescribable. I can't put it into words.

I don't want to say it's a special kind of alone because, when you say it's special, it makes it a good thing. It makes it sound positive. It's the worst. There are certain things you don't wish on your worst enemy, and the loss of a twin, that feeling of abandonment and loneliness—I don't wish that on anyone in the world.

At the same time, I'm proud that I've survived all of the things I've gone through. Those experiences have made me a stronger person. They've made me much more of a compassionate person because I know how fragile life is. I know how hurtful words are cause I grew up with bullying my whole life.

My childhood ended when Tony died, and I don't even think about what happened prior to his death because that world is gone. I can't ever get it back, so why dwell on it? I believe your life is a specific path that you're meant to take. I was put on this world to take the path I've taken. I take it full charge. Sometimes I have someone next to me help out. Most times I don't. That's okay. Let's go. I don't know why my path was lined with such awful, horrible things along the way, but I've survived it. And I'm still surviving it, you know?

Here's the New Planet You Live On

After Tony died, I was living in that awful negativity. Because one moment everything was—I don't want to say *normal*, I hate using that word—but everything was the way it was supposed to be, and in this one little fraction of a second, my whole world was gone.

Now here's the new planet that you live on. Here's everything new that you're supposed to get used to. Here's the semicolon.

Finally, in my thirties, I was like, "Why am I living in such a horrible, negative world? I want to be happy." I can't say that I've been happy very much in my life. When I met my ex, I remember that feeling, that feeling of happiness. I was like, "Wow. I feel loved." He made me feel cared about. I thought, *This is what being a human feels like. This is what it feels like to be treated with respect and to be cared about.* He showed me what that was like. It was very eye-opening. That's when I was like, *I need to stop doing all this shit. I need to stop letting all these little things bother me. I want to feel like this more often.*

That relationship ended, but I wanted to keep that feeling. I needed to stop worrying, and I needed to stop taking things so personal. Everything that happened, I took so personally. So I just stopped. I mean, it's hard. There are all these what-ifs. My whole world is what-if. But I've finally stopped living the what-if, and that's when I stopped feeling alone. I can't live in a what-if world. I need to live in this world that I have right now.

I'm content right now where I'm at. Ever since I got Nix, it's been a lot better. You know, coming home and being excited for her to be excited that I'm home, and vice-versa. Not coming home to an empty house helps a lot. She has helped me so much, just in the last nine months that I've had her.

It's a day-by-day process. When you lose someone close to you, it doesn't go away. You deal with it on a regular basis. It gets easier to deal with, and some days are just a cakewalk and some days I don't want to get out of bed. I still have those days. But I've got to feed the dog.

I celebrate my birthday. Every year, I'm glad I made it through. I've been on my own since I was thirteen. I truly feel that way. I may not have supported myself financially and stuff, but I've been alone since I was thirteen. Not until I hit my thirties did I feel like I wasn't alone.

It gives me solace that I've lived a life of honesty and I've been myself. I know that one day I'll meet all the people that I care about and have lost. Before my grandfather died a few weeks back, I told him, "Please tell everyone I love them. I'm jealous that you get to see them. I know I'll get to see them one day. Just tell them all hi for me. Give them my love." People are gone, but they're not gone forever. That's what gets me through. There will come a day that I will get to see these people again.

I've always wondered, too: *Is Tony going to be the thirteen-year-old version of him, or am I going to see him as an adult?* Is he going to age along with me? How is that going to work?

CHEN CHEN

■

I am reminded via email to submit my preferences for the schedule

FROM *Poets.org*

But really
I would prefer
to sit, drink water,
reread some Russians
a while longer
—a luxury
perhaps, but why
should I, anyone,
call it that, why
should reading
what I want,
in a well-hydrated fashion,
always be what I'm
planning to finally
do, like hiking
or biking, & now
that I think of it, reading
should make me, anyone,
breathe harder, then
easier, reach for cold,
cold water, & I
prefer my reading

that way, I prefer
Ivan Turgenev,
who makes me work for
not quite pleasure
no, some truer
sweatier thing,
Turgenev,
who is just now,
in my small room
in West Texas,
getting to the good part,
the very Russian part,
the last few pages
of "The Singers"
when the story
should be over,
Yakov the Turk
has sung with fervor,
meaning true
Russian spirit,
meaning he's won
a kind of 19th century
Idol in the village
tavern, The End, but
Turgenev goes
on, the narrator walks
out, down a hill,
into a dark
enveloping mist,
& he hears
from misty far away
some little boy
calling out for
Antropka!
calling hoarsely,
darkly,
Antropka-a-a!

& it's that voice that stops
then opens my breath
that voice
& all Monday-Wednesday-Fridays
all Tuesday-Thursdays
are gone
I have arrived
in the village of
no day   none
& I am sitting
with the villagers
who are each at once
young   old
who have the coldest
water to give me
& songs
I think I have sung   before
they sing
their underground
tree-root syllables
they give me silences
from their long
long   hair

GEORGE SAUNDERS

■

Who Are All These
Trump Supporters?

FROM *The New Yorker*

He Appears

Trump is wearing the red baseball cap, or not. From this distance,
he is strangely handsome, well proportioned, puts you in mind of
a sea captain: Alan Hale from *Gilligan's Island,* say, had Hale been
slimmer, richer, more self-confident. We are afforded a side view of a
head of silver-yellow hair and a hawklike orange-red face, the cheeks
of which, if stared at steadily enough, will seem, through some opti-
cal illusion, to glow orange-redder at moments when the crowd is especially pleased. If you've ever, watching *The Apprentice,* entertained
fantasies of how you might fare in the boardroom (the Donald, recognizing your excellent qualities with his professional businessman's
acumen, does not fire you but, on the contrary, pulls you aside to assign you some important non-TV, real-world mission), you may, for
a brief, embarrassing instant, as he scans the crowd, expect him to
recognize you.

He is blessing us here in San Jose, California, with his celebrity,
promising never to disappoint us, letting us in on the latest bit of in-
side-baseball campaign strategy: "Lyin' Ted" is no longer to be Lyin'
Ted; henceforth he will be just "Ted." Hillary, however, shall be "Lyin'
Crooked." And, by the way, Hillary has to go to jail. The statute of limitations is five years, and if he gets elected in November, well . . . The
crowd sends forth a coarse blood roar. "She's guilty as hell," he snarls.

He growls, rants, shouts, digresses, careens from shtick nugget to shtick nugget, rhapsodizes over past landslides, name-drops Ivanka, Melania, Mike Tyson, Newt Gingrich, Bobby Knight, Bill O'Reilly. His right shoulder thrusts out as he makes the pinched-finger mudra with downswinging arm. His trademark double-eye squint evokes that group of beanie-hatted street-tough Munchkin kids; you expect him to kick gruffly at an imaginary stone. In person, his autocratic streak is presentationally complicated by a Ralph Kramdenesque vulnerability. He's a man who has just dropped a can opener into his wife's freshly baked pie. He's not about to start grovelling about it, and yet he's sorry—but, come on, it was an *accident*. He's sorry, he's sorry, okay, but do you expect him to *say it*? He's a good guy. Anyway, he didn't do it.

Once, Jack Benny, whose character was known for frugality and selfishness, got a huge laugh by glancing down at the baseball he was supposed to be first-pitching, pocketing it, and walking off the field. Trump, similarly, knows how well we know him from TV. He is who he is. So sue me, okay? I probably shouldn't say this, but oops—just did. (Hillary's attack ads? "*So* false. Ah, some of them aren't that false, actually.") It's oddly riveting, watching someone take such pleasure in going so much farther out on thin ice than anyone else as famous would dare to go. His crowds are ever hopeful for the next thrilling rude swerve. "There could be no politics which gave warmth to one's body until the country had recovered its imagination, its pioneer lust for the unexpected and incalculable," Norman Mailer wrote in 1960.

The speeches themselves are nearly all empty assertion. Assertion and bragging. Assertion, bragging, and defensiveness. He is always boasting about the size of this crowd or that crowd, refuting some slight from someone who has treated him "very unfairly," underscoring his sincerity via adjectival pile-on (he's "going to appoint beautiful, incredible, unbelievable Supreme Court Justices"). He lies, bullies, menaces, dishes it out but can't seem to take it, exhibits such a muddy understanding of certain American principles (the press is free, torture illegal, criticism and libel two different things) that he might be a seventeenth-century Austrian prince time-transported here to mess with us. Sometimes it seems that he truly does not give a shit, and you imagine his minders cringing backstage. Other times you imagine them bored, checking their phones, convinced that nothing will ever touch him. Increasingly, his wild veering seems to occur against his will, as if he were not the great, sly strategist we have taken him for but, rather, someone compelled by an inner music that sometimes produces good dancing and sometimes causes him to bring a bookshelf crashing down on an old Mexican lady. *Get more*, that inner music seems to be telling him. *Get, finally, enough. Refute a lifetime of critics. Create a pile of unprecedented testimonials, attendance receipts, polling numbers, and pundit gasps that will, once and for all, prove—what?*

Apply Occam's razor: if someone brags this much, bending every ray of light back to himself, what's the simplest explanation?

"We're on the cover of every newspaper, every magazine," he says in San Jose in early June. "*Time* magazine many times. I just learned they're doing yet another cover on Trump—I love that. You know, *Time* magazine's a good magazine. You grow up reading *Time* magazine—who ever thought you'd be on the cover of *Time* magazine? Especially so much?"

It's considered an indication of authenticity that he doesn't generally speak from a teleprompter but just wings it. (In fact, he brings to the podium a few pages of handwritten bullet points, to which he periodically refers as he, mostly, wings it.) He wings it because winging it serves his purpose. He is not trying to persuade, detail, or prove: he is trying to thrill, agitate, be liked, be loved, here and now. He is trying to make energy. (At one point in his San Jose speech, he endearingly fumbles with a sheaf of "statistics," reads a few, fondly but slightingly mentions the loyal, hapless statistician who compiled them, then seems unable to go on, afraid he might be boring us.)

And make energy he does. It flows out of him, as if channeled in thousands of micro wires, enters the minds of his followers: their cheers go ragged and hoarse, chanting erupts, a look of religious zeal may flash across the face of some non-chanter, who is finally getting, in response to a question long nursed in private, exactly the answer he's been craving. One such person stays in my memory from a rally in Fountain Hills, Arizona, in March: a solidly built man in his mid-forties, wearing, in the crazy heat, a long-sleeved black shirt, who, as Trump spoke, worked himself into a state of riveted, silent concentration-fury, the rally equivalent of someone at church gazing fixedly down at the pew before him, nodding, Yes, yes, yes.

A Tiny Pissed Voice Rings Out

"Wow, what a crowd this is," he begins at Fountain Hills. "What a great honor! . . . You have some sheriff—there's no games with your sheriff, that's for sure . . . We have a movement going on, folks . . . I will never let you down! Remember. And I want to tell you, you know, it's so much about illegal immigration and so much has been mentioned about it and talked about it, and these politicians are all talk, no action. They're never going to do anything—they only picked it up because when I went, and when I announced, that I'm running for President, I said, 'You know, this country has a big, big problem with illegal immigration,' and all of a sudden we started talking about it . . . And there was crime and you had so many killings and so much crime, drugs were pouring through the border." ("STOP IT!" someone pleads from the crowd.) "People are now seeing it. And you know what? We're going to build a wall and we are going to stop it!"

Mayhem. The Wall is their favorite. (Earlier in the afternoon, Jan Brewer, the former governor of Arizona and legislative mother of that state's Draconian immigration policies, nearly undoes all the good right-wing work of her career by affirming that, yes, Trump is "going to build *the Fence.*" Like new Americans who have just been told that Hulk Hogan was the first president, the crowd rises up in happy outrage to correct her.)

"THANK YOU, TRUMP!" bellows a kid in front of me, who, later in the speech, will briefly turn his back on Trump to take a Trump-including selfie, his smile taut, braces-revealing, grimacelike yet celebratory, evoking that circa-1950 photograph of a man in a high-velocity wind tunnel.

"I only wish these cameras—because there's nothing as dishonest as the media, that I can tell you." ("THEY SUCK!") "I only wish these cameramen would spin around and show the kind of people that we have, the numbers of people that we have here. I just wish they'd for once do it, because you know what?" ("PAN THE CAMERAS!") "We have a silent majority that's no longer so silent. It's now the loud, noisy majority, and we're going to be heard . . . They're chipping away at the Second Amendment, they're chipping away at Christianity . . . We're not going to have it anymore. It comes Christmas time, we're going to see signs up that say 'Merry Merry Merry Christmas!' Okay? Remember it, remember it. We have become so politically correct that we're totally impotent as a country—"

Somewhere in the crowd, a woman is shouting "Fuck you, Trump!" in a voice so thin it seems to be emanating from some distant neighborhood, where a girl is calling home her brother, Fuckhugh Trump.

The shouter is Esperanza Matamoros, tiny, seventeen years old. The crowd now halts her forward progress, so she judiciously spins and, still shouting, heads toward the exit. As she passes a tall, white-haired, professorial-looking old man, he gives her a little shove. He towers over her, the top of her head falling below his armpit. She could be his daughter, his granddaughter, his favorite student. Another man steps in front of her to deliver an impromptu manners lesson; apparently, she bumped him on her way up. "*Excuse me,*" he says heatedly. "Around here, we say *excuse me.*"

An ungentleness gets into the air when Trump speaks, prompting the abandonment of certain social norms (e.g., an old man should show forbearance and physical respect for a young woman, even— especially—an angry young woman, and might even think to wonder what is making her so angry), norms that, to fired-up Trump supporters, must feel antiquated in this brave new moment of ideological foment. They have thought and thought, in projective terms, about theoretical protesters, and now here are some real ones.

This ungentleness ripples out through the crowd and into the area beyond the fence where the protesters have set up shop. One of them, Sandra Borchers, tells me that out there all was calm (she was "actually having dialogues" with Trump supporters, "back-and-forth conversations, at about this talking level") until Trump started speaking. Then things got "violent and aggressive." Someone threw a rock at her head. A female Trump supporter "in a pink-peachy-color T-shirt" attacked a protester, kicking and punching him. Rebecca LaStrap, an African American woman, twenty years old, wearing a "FUCK

TRUMP" T-shirt, was grabbed by the breast, thrown to the ground, slapped in the face. (She was also told to "go back on the boat," a perplexing instruction, given that she was born and raised in Mesa.) Later that day, in Tucson, two young Hispanic women, quietly watching the rally there, are thrown out of the venue, and one (as a member of Trump's security staff bellows, "Out! Out! Out!") is roughly shoved through a revolving door by a Trump supporter who looks to be in his seventies and who then performs a strange little quasi-karate move, as if he expects her to fly back in and counterattack. A pro-immigration protester named George Clifton, who is wearing a sign that says "VETERAN: U.S.M.C. AND C.I.A.," tells me that two Trump supporters came up to him separately after the Fountain Hills rally and whispered "almost verbatim the same thing, not quite, but in a nutshell": that they'd like to shoot him in the back of the head.

I'm Here for an Argument

In Tucson, Trump supporters flow out of the Convention Center like a red-white-and-blue river, along hostile riverbanks made of protesters, who have situated themselves so as to be maximally irritating. When a confrontation occurs, people rush toward it, to film it and stoke it, in the hope that someone on the other side will fly off the handle and do something extreme, and thereby incontrovertibly discredit his side of the argument. This river-and-shore arrangement advantages the Trump supporters: they can walk coolly past, playing the offended party, refusing to engage.

Most do, but some don't.

"Trump is racist, so are YOU!" the protesters chant, maximizing the provocation. A South Asian–looking youth of uncertain political affiliation does a crazy Borat dance in front of the line as a friend films him. An aging blond bombshell strolls by in a low-cut blouse, giving the protesters a leisurely finger, blowing them kisses, patting one of her large breasts. A matronly Hispanic protester says that the woman has a right to do what she likes with her breasts since, after all, "she paid for them." A grandmotherly white woman tucks a strand of graying hair behind her ear, walks resolutely over, and delicately lifts a Mexican flag from where it lies shawl-like across the shoulders of a young, distractedly dancing Hispanic girl, as if the flag had fallen across the girl's shoulders from some imaginary shelf and the grandmother were considerately removing it before it got too heavy. The girl, offended, pulls away. But wait: the woman shows her anti-Trump sign: they're on the same side. The girl remains unconvinced; she'll keep the flag to herself, thanks. "So *sorry*," the white woman says and rejoins a friend, to commiserate over the girl's response, which strikes her, maybe, as a form of racial profiling.

Two tall Trump supporters tower over a small liberal in a green T-shirt.

"Stupid! Uneducated!" Trumpie A shouts. "Do you know anything that goes *on* in the world?"

"Articulate a little more," the guy in the green shirt says.

"I don't want to live in a fascist country!" Trumpie B says.

"You don't know what fascism *is*," Green Shirt says.

"Oh, I'm getting there, man!" Trumpie B says. "Obama's teaching me!"

"Go back to California," Trumpie A shouts at Green Shirt. "Bitch!"

The four of us stand in a tight little circle, Trumpie A shouting insults at Green Shirt while filming Green Shirt's reaction, me filming Trumpie A filming Green Shirt. The bulk and intensity of the Trumpies, plus the fact that Green Shirt seems to be serving as designated spokesperson for a group of protesters now gathering around, appears to be making Green Shirt nervous.

"Obama's teaching you what fascism is?" he sputters. "Obama's a fascist? The left is the fascists? This is so rich! So, like, the people who are being oppressed are the oppressors?"

"Do you know what's going on in the world, man?" Trumpie A says. "You're not fucking *educated*."

This stings.

"I am very educated," Green Shirt says.

"You have no *idea* what's going on," Trumpie B says.

"I am very educated," Green Shirt says.

"You've got no idea, bro," Trumpie A says sadly.

"Ask me a question, ask me a question," Green Shirt says.

The Tall Trumpies, bored, wander away.

Green Shirt turns to one of his friends. "Am I educated?"

"You're fucking educated," the friend says.

Green Shirt shouts at the Tall Trumpies (who, fortunately for him, are now safely out of earshot), "And I'll stomp the fucking *shit* out of you!"

Spotting a round-faced, brown-skinned youth in a "Make America Great Again" T-shirt, who's been quietly listening nearby, Green Shirt snarls, "And *you* can get your fat fucking Chinese face out of here."

The kid seems more quizzical than hurt.

I ask Green Shirt for clarification: did he just tell that guy to get his Chinese face out of here?

"No, I was calling his *shirt* Chinese," he clarifies. "I told him to get his Chinese *shirt* out of here. The Trump campaign gets those shirts from China."

I'm relieved. My liberal comrade did not commit a racial slur.

"I did call him fat, though," he admits, then dashes back over to the kid, hisses, "Why don't you make your *waistline* great again?," and slips away into the crowd.

"This is America!" a Trump supporter rages desperately into the line of protesters, after one of them forces his phone camera down. "I'm American! I'm Mexican American! Are you a marine?" he demands of an elderly protester in a floppy fatigue hat. "I'm a veteran. I'm a *veteran*. You're idiots. You're *idiots*. I'm a Navy corpsman! I saved marines' *asses*. Mexican, white, and black. We're red, white, and blue!" The guy in the floppy hat answers, in heavily accented English, that, yes, he was a marine. This conflict rapidly devolves into a bitter veteran-off: two old guys, who've presumably seen some things in their time, barking hatefully at each other. I know (or *feel* I know) that, on another day, these two guys might have grabbed a beer together, jump-started each other's cars, whatever—but they're not doing that today.

"What are you *doing* here?" a girl shouts at the Trump-supporting Mexican American former corpsman. "You should be ashamed!"

"What am I doing?" he shouts back. "I'm supporting a man who's going to clean up Mexico, build a wall, fix the economy!"

"*Puto!*" a protester snaps, as the corpsman storms off, to go home and, I'm guessing, feel like crap the rest of the day.

If you are, as I am, a sentimental middle-aged person who cherishes certain Coplandian notions about the essential goodness of the nation, seeing this kind of thing in person—adults shouting wrathfully at one another with no intention of persuasion, invested only in escalating spite—will inject a palpable sadness into your thinning, under-exercised legs, and you may find yourself collapsing, post-rally, against a tree in a public park, feeling hopeless. Craving something positive (no more fighting, no more invective, please, please), forcing yourself to your feet, you may cross a busy avenue and find, in a minimall themed like Old Mexico, a wedding about to begin. Up will walk the bridesmaids, each leading, surprisingly, a dog on a leash, and each dog is wearing a tutu, and one, a puppy too small to be trusted in a procession, is being carried, in its tutu, in the arms of its bridesmaid.

And this will somehow come as an unbelievable relief.

Let's Call the Whole Thing Off

Where is all this anger coming from? It's viral, and Trump is Typhoid Mary. Intellectually and emotionally weakened by years of steadily degraded public discourse, we are now two separate ideological countries, LeftLand and RightLand, speaking different languages, the lines between us down. Not only do our two subcountries reason differently; they draw upon non-intersecting data sets and access entirely different mythological systems. You and I approach a castle. One of us has watched only *Monty Python and the Holy Grail*, the other only *Game of Thrones*. What is the meaning, to the collective "we," of yon castle? We have no common basis from which to discuss it. You, the other knight, strike me as bafflingly ignorant, a little unmoored. In the old days, a liberal and a conservative (a "dove" and a "hawk," say) got their data from one of three nightly news programs, a local paper, and a handful of national magazines, and were thus starting with the same basic facts (even if those facts were questionable, limited, or erroneous). Now each of us constructs a custom informational universe, wittingly (we choose to go to the sources that uphold our existing beliefs and thus flatter us) or unwittingly (our app algorithms do the driving for us). The data we get this way, pre-imprinted with spin and mythos, are intensely one-dimensional. (As a proud knight of LeftLand, I was interested to find that, in Right-Land, Vince Foster has still been murdered, Dick Morris is a reliable source, kids are brainwashed "way to the left" by going to college, and Obama may yet be Muslim. I expect that my interviewees found some of my core beliefs equally jaw-dropping.)

A Trump supporter in Fountain Hills asks me, "If you're a liberal, do you believe in the government controlling everything? Because that's what Barry wants to do, and what he's pretty much accomplished." She then makes the (to me, irrational and irritating) claim that more people are on welfare under Obama than ever were under Bush.

"Almost 50 million people," her husband says. "Up 30 percent."

I make a certain sound I make when I disagree with something but have no facts at my disposal.

Back at the hotel, I Google it.

Damn it, they're right. Rightish.

What I find over the next hour or so, from a collection of web sites, left, right, and fact-based:

Yes, true: there are approximately 7 million more Americans in poverty now than when Obama was elected. On the other hand, the economy under Obama has gained about seven times as many jobs as it did under Bush; even given the financial meltdown, the unemployment rate has dropped to just below the historical average. But, yes: the poverty *rate* is up by 1.6 percentage points since 2008. Then again the *number* of Americans in poverty fell by nearly 1.2 million between 2012 and 2013. However, true: the proportion of people who depend on welfare for the majority of their income *has* increased (although it was also increasing under Bush). And under Obama unemployment has dropped, GDP growth has been "robust," and there have been close to seventy straight months of job growth. But, okay: there has indeed been a "skyrocketing" in the number of Americans needing some form of means-tested federal aid, although Obama's initiatives kept some 6 million people out of poverty in 2009, including more than 2 million children.

So the couple's assertion was true but not *complexly* true. It was a nice hammer with which to pop the enemy; i.e., me. Its intent:

discredit Obama and the liberal mind-set. What was my intent as I Googled? Get a hammer of my own, discredit Bush and the conservative mind-set.

Meanwhile, there sat reality: huge, ambiguous, too complicated to be usefully assessed by our prevailing mutual ambition—to fight and win, via delivery of the partisan zinger.

LeftLand and RightLand are housemates who are no longer on speaking terms. And then the house is set on fire. By Donald Trump. Good people from both subnations gape at one another through the smoke.

Who Are They? (Part I)

It's clear enough to those of us who don't like Trump why we don't like him. What isn't clear is why it isn't clear to those who like him. The Trump supporter is your brother who has just brought home a wildly inappropriate fiancée. Well, inappropriate to *you*. Trump support, nationwide, stands at around 40 percent. If you had ten siblings and four of them brought home wildly inappropriate fiancées, you might feel inclined to ask yourself what was going on in your family to make your judgment and that of your siblings so divergent.

It seems futile to try to generalize about a group as large and disparate as "Trump supporters"—like generalizing, say, "people who own riding lawnmowers," who, of course, tend to be, but are not exclusively limited to, people with large or largish lawns, but can also include people with small yards, who, for whatever reason, can't manage a push mower, and/or people (both large- and small-yarded) who may have received a riding mower from a father-in-law or an uncle and don't want to rock the boat. But sometimes, standing at a rally among several thousand madly cheering Trump supporters, I'd think, All these people have *something* in common. What is it?

I didn't meet many people who were unreservedly for Trump. There is, in the quiver containing his ideas, something for nearly everyone to dislike. But there is also something for nearly everyone to *like*. What allows a person not crazy about Trump to vote for him is a certain prioritization: a person might, for example, like Trump's ideas about trade, or his immigration policies, or the fact that Trump is, as one supporter told me, "a successful businessman," who has "actually done something," unlike Obama, who has "never done anything his entire life."

The Trump supporters I spoke with were friendly, generous with their time, flattered to be asked their opinion, willing to give it, even when they knew I was a liberal writer likely to throw them under the bus. They loved their country, seemed genuinely panicked at its perceived demise, felt urgently that we were, right now, in the process of losing something precious. They were, generally, in favor of *order* and had a propensity toward the broadly normative, a certain squareness. They leaned toward skepticism (they'd believe it when they saw it, "it" being anything feelings-based, gauzy, liberal, or European; i.e., "socialist"). Some (far from all) had been touched by financial hardship—a layoff was common in many stories—and (paradoxically, given their feelings about socialism) felt that, while in that vulnerable state, they'd been let down by their government. They were anti-regulation, pro small business, pro Second Amendment, suspicious of people on welfare, sensitive (in a "Don't tread on me" way) about any infringement whatsoever on their freedom. Alert to charges of racism, they would pre-counter these by pointing out that they had friends of all colors. They were adamantly for law enforcement and veterans' rights, in a manner that presupposed that the rest of us were adamantly against these things. It seemed self-evident to them that a businessman could and should lead the country. "You run your family like a business, don't you?" I was asked more than once, although, of course, I don't, and none of us do.

The Trump supporter comes out of the conservative tradition but is not a traditional conservative. He is less patient: something is bothering him and he wants it stopped *now*, by any means necessary. He seems less influenced by Goldwater and Reagan than by Fox News and reality TV, his understanding of history recent and selective; he is less religiously grounded and more willing, in his acceptance of Trump's racist and misogynist excesses, to (let's say) forgo the niceties.

As for Trump's uncivil speech—the insults, the petty meanness, the crudeness, the talk about hand size, the assurance, on national

TV, that his would-be presidential dick is up to the job, his mastery of the jaw-droppingly untrue personal smear (Obama is Kenyan, Ted Cruz's dad was in cahoots with Lee Harvey Oswald, U.S. Muslims knew what was "going on" pre-Orlando), which he often dishonorably eases into the world by attaching some form of the phrase "many people have said this" (*The world is flat; many people have said this. People are saying that birds can play the cello: we need to look into that*)—his supporters seem constitutionally reluctant to object, as if the act of objecting would mark them as fatally delicate. Objecting to this sort of thing is for the coddled, the liberal, the élite. "Yeah, he can really improve, in the way he says things," one woman in Fountain Hills tells me. "But who gives a shit? Because if he's going to get the job done? I'm just saying. You can't let your feelings get hurt. It's kind of like, get over it, you know what I mean? What's the big picture here? The big picture is we've got to get America back on track."

The ability to shrug off the mean crack, the sexist joke, the gratuitous jab at the weak is, in some quarters, seen as a form of strength, of "being flexible," of "not taking shit serious." A woman who wilts at a sexist joke won't last long in certain workplaces. A guy who prioritizes the sensitive side of his nature will, trust me, not thrive in the slaughterhouse. This willingness to gloss over crudeness becomes, then, an encoded sign of competence, strength, and reliability.

Above all, Trump supporters are "not politically correct," which, as far as I can tell, means that they have a particular aversion to that psychological moment when, having thought something, you decide that it is not a good thought, and might pointlessly hurt someone's feelings, and therefore decline to say it.

Who Are They? (Part II)

I observed, in Trump supporters' storytelling, a tendency to conflate things that, to a non-Trump supporter, might seem unrelated. For example, in 2014, Mary Ann Mendoza's son, Brandon, an openly gay policeman in Mesa, who volunteered at the local Boys and Girls Club, was killed in a car accident caused by an intoxicated, undocumented Mexican man who had spent at least twenty years drifting in and out of the United States and had been charged with a number of crimes, including assaulting a police officer, and was convicted of criminal conspiracy, but was free at the time of the crash, having been shown leniency by a Colorado court. At the rally in Fountain Hills, Ms. Mendoza gave a moving speech about her son, which she concluded this way: "This was the kind of man my son was . . . *Was.* Not is. *Was.* Because of the lack of concern that this Administration has for American citizens . . . Brandon's. Life. Matters." The crowd roared. Something key lay in that juxtaposition and that roar. What was the connection between her son's death and the Black Lives Matter movement? Couldn't a person be against the killing of innocent black men *and* against illegal immigration (or drunk driving, or the lax enforcement of existing laws, etc.)?

A man comes to Arizona from Vermont and finds that "the illegals" are getting all the kitchen jobs for which he's qualified. "So once Trump started talking about the Wall," he says, "I was like, all right, now I think I've got to start paying attention to this." How does he know those workers were undocumented? He doesn't; there's no way, situationally, that he could. Stephanie, an executive administrator for a finance group in Minnesota, gets laid off, and the only benefit she qualifies for is "a measly little unemployment check." Standing next to her at the government office are "these people, that are from other countries, non-speaking—I'm not biased, I have no reason to be—but . . . I'm seeing them getting cash, getting their bills paid, and, as a taxpaying citizen, I don't get anything. And so the border thing really resonated with me." Does she know for a fact that these were illegal immigrants? "That's a good question, and I don't know the answer," she says. "I'm not a hundred percent on it."

Bill Davis, a funny, genial sales rep in the packaging industry, has nothing against legal immigration but feels that illegal immigration is "killing" the area in Southern California where he lives. How, specifically, is it doing this? He mentions a neighbor of his who speaks no English, has two hundred chickens running around his yard, goats everywhere, doesn't "play by the rules"—and hence Bill's property values are going down. Is his neighbor undocumented? It doesn't matter, he says. He's "not assimilated." Growing up, Davis says, he had a lot of first-generation Hispanic friends. These people took pride in assimilating. "Those days are over," he explains. "So Trump is onto something about that. We don't want you guys throwing your fast-food wrappers out your windows when you're driving down the freeway. Take some pride in what you do. And learn to work in this country by the rules and regulations that we've developed over two hundred and fifty years. I'm not opposed to immigration, by any means. Come here, but when you leave Mexico—when you leave Germany, when you leave Russia, wherever—you've left that culture for a reason. It's America now. So you can have your parties and your stuff at your house, but don't expect us to cater to your culture."

"Thousands of Cubans coming in," Kathryn Kobor, a Trump supporter and animal-rights activist in her seventies, tells me in Phoenix, as she sits in protest of the Hillary Clinton rally across the street, beneath an umbrella provided by a Clinton supporter. "Three hundred sixty thousand Guatemalan kids and mothers standing at the border, they have to be taken in. We're going to be taking in thousands of Syrians, whom we cannot vet." I tell her that the thought of deporting and dividing families breaks my heart. "Of course it does—you're a human, you care about people. That's not the question. The question is, Do you want to live like India? Sewage running in the streets? . . . The infrastructure is crumbling . . . I'm not speaking for tomorrow. I'm not speaking for a year, two years from now. I'll be gone. I'm speaking for my descendents. I have a granddaughter. I have a son. I want them to live a decent, clean life . . . Trump just wants the laws enforced . . . He's not a mean-spirited person."

A former marine in line for a Trump rally in Rothschild, Wisconsin, tells me that, returning to the United States from a deployment overseas, he found himself wondering, "Where did my country go?" To clarify, he tells me that he was in Qatar on the day that Obama was first elected. "I was actually sitting in the chow hall when they announced the results and he gave his speech," he says. "I saw such a division at that time. Every black member of the military was cheering. Everybody else was sitting there mute. Like stunned."

What unites these stories is what I came to think of as usurpation anxiety syndrome—the feeling that one is, or is about to be, scooped, overrun, or taken advantage of by some Other with questionable intentions. In some cases, this has a racial basis, and usurpation anxiety grades into racial nostalgia, which can grade into outright racism, albeit cloaked in disclaimer.

In the broadest sense, the Trump supporter might be best understood as a guy who wakes up one day in a lively, crowded house full of people, from a dream in which he was the only one living there, and then mistakes the dream for the past: a better time, manageable and orderly, during which privilege and respect came to him naturally, and he had the whole place to himself.

How Do You Solve a Problem Like Noemi?

Talking to a Trump supporter about Trump's deportation policy, I'd sometimes bring up Noemi Romero, a sweet, soft-spoken young woman I met in Phoenix. Noemi was brought to the United States when she was three, by undocumented parents. A few years ago, she had the idea of applying for legal status through the Deferred Action for Childhood Arrivals (DACA) program. But the application costs $465, money her family didn't have. Hearing that a local Vietnamese grocery was hiring, she borrowed her mother's Social Security card and got the job. A few months later, the store was raided. Noemi was arrested, charged with aggravated identity theft and forgery, and taken to jail and held there, within the general prison population, for two months. She was given spoiled milk, and food that, she said, had tiny worms in it. Her lawyer arranged a plea bargain; the charges were reduced to criminal impersonation. This was a good deal, he told her, the best she could hope for. She accepted, not realizing that, as a convicted felon, she would be permanently ineligible for DACA. Puente, a local grassroots organization, intervened and saved her from deportation, but she is essentially doomed to a kind of frozen life: can't work and can't go to college, although she has lived virtually her whole life in the United States and has no reason to go back to Mexico and nowhere to live if she's sent there.

I'd ask the Trump supporter, "What do we do about Noemi?" I always found the next moment in our exchange hopeful.

Is she a good person? the Trump supporter might ask. I couldn't feel more sorry for her, he might say. That kid is no better or worse than I am and deserves the best God can give her. Or he might say that deportation would have to be done on a case-by-case basis. Or propose some sort of registry—Noemi, having registered, would go back to Mexico and, if all checked out, come right back in. There had to be some kind of rule of law, didn't there? Tellingly, the Trump supporter might confess that she didn't think Trump really intended to do this mass-deportation thing anyway—it was all just campaign talk. The most extreme supporter might say that, yes, Noemi had to go—he didn't like it, but ultimately the fault lay with her parents.

Sometimes I'd mention a Central American family I met in Texas, while reporting another story. In that case, the father and son were documented but the mother and daughters weren't. Would you, I'd ask, split that family up? Send those girls to a country in which they'd never spent a single day? Well, my Trump-supporting friend might answer, it was complicated, wasn't it? Were they good people? Yes, I'd say. The father, in spare moments between his three jobs, built a four-bedroom house out of cinder blocks he acquired two or three at a time from Home Depot, working sometimes late into the night. The Trump supporter might, at this point, fall silent, and so might I.

In the face of specificity, my interviewees began trying, really trying, to think of what would be fairest and most humane for this real person we had imaginatively conjured up. It wasn't that we suddenly agreed, but the tone changed. We popped briefly out of zinger mode and began to have some faith in one another, a shared confidence that if we talked long enough, respectfully enough, a solution could be found that might satisfy our respective best notions of who we were.

Well, let's not get too dreamy about it. We'd stay in that mode for a minute or two, then be off again to some new topic, rewrapped in our respective Left and Right national flags. Once, after what felt like a transcendent and wide-ranging conversation with a Trump supporter named Danny (a former railroad worker, now on disability), I said a fond goodbye and went to interview some Hillary supporters across the street. A few minutes later, I looked over to find Danny shouting at us that Hillary was going to prison, not the White House. I waved to him, but he didn't seem to see me, hidden there in the crowd of his adversaries.

The Elephant in the Room

The average Trump supporter is not the rally pugilist, the white supremacist, the bitter conspiracy theorist, though these exist and are drawn to Trump (see: *the Internet*)—and, at times, the first flowerings of these tendencies were present among some of the rank-and-file supporters I met. A certain barely suppressed rage, for example, is evident in the guy in Phoenix who wears his gun to a protest against Hillary ("I'm out here with two friends, Smith and Wesson"). One of his fellow-protesters tells me that Hillary has had oral sex with many female world leaders ("She's munched with a lot of our enemies, man").

After a rally in Eau Claire, a handful of Trump protesters stand silently in the Wisconsin cold as the Trump supporters file out— a spontaneous little lab experiment investigating the Trumpies' response to silent rebuke. "I guess you guys don't read too much," someone shouts at the protesters. "Or watch the news. *Fox News!* Watch that once in a while!" Other Trump supporters yell over incredulously, "Fifteen bucks an hour?" And "Go to socialist Europe! Save your checks and move to a socialist country!"

But the line I won't forget comes from a guy leaving the rally, alone, who shout-mutters, if such a thing is possible, "Hey, I'm not paying for your shit, I'm not paying for your college, so you go to Hell, go to work, go to Hell, suck a dick."

Not far away, a group of enterprising Girl Scouts is out late, selling cookies under a winter-leafless tree. "Cookies for sale, last time this season," they seem to sing. "Girl Scout cookies, last weekend to get them."

So, yes, there are bigots in the Trump movement, and wackos, and dummies, and sometimes I had to remind myself that the important constituency is the persuadable middle segment of his supporters, who are not finding in Trump a suitable vessel for their hate but are misunderstanding him or overestimating him, and moving in his direction out of a misplaced form of hope.

Who Are They? (Part III)

Sometimes it seemed that they were, like me, just slightly spoiled Americans, imbued with unreasonable boomer expectations for autonomy, glory, and ascension, and that their grievances were more theoretical than actual, more media-induced than experience-related.

Before the rally in San Jose on June 2, I talk to a group of construction workers, each of whom is in some state of layoff: current, recent, chronic. One, who's hoping to get a job working construction on the Wall, rails against millennials, the unions, a minimum-wage hike for fast-food workers, and "these people" who get fired, then turn around and sue. I ask for examples. He says he isn't going to give me any names. I say forget the names, just tell me a particular story. A guy got fired from his workplace just last week, he says. "Is he suing?" I ask. "Well, probably," he says.

I ask one of his friends, a thoughtful Chinese American guy, how his life has been made worse over the past eight years. He comes up with this: he pays more for his insurance because of Obamacare. Anything else? Not really. How has he personally been affected by illegal immigration? He hasn't, he tells me, but he's been fortunate enough to have the resources to keep his family away from the danger.

At one point, in line at the Fountain Hills rally, frustrated by a litany of anti-Obama grievances being delivered by the woman in front of me, I say that I think life is good, pretty good, you know?

"You think this is *good*?" she says.

"I do, yeah," I say. "We're out here on a nice day, having a beautiful talk—"

She groans, meaning, You know that's not what I mean.

But I don't, really, so I ask her what, in terms of her day-to-day life, she thinks is wrong with America.

"I don't like people shoving Obamacare down my throat, okay?" she says. "And then getting penalized if I don't have insurance."

Is she covered through Obamacare?

No. She has insurance through her work, thank God, but "every day my rights are being taken away from me, you know?" she says. "I mean—this is America. In the U.S., we have a lot of freedoms and things like that, but we're not going to have all that if we have all these people coming in, that are taking our—"

"We have our own people to take care of, I'm sorry," interjects a seventeen-year-old girl who is standing nearby, holding up a sign that says "MARRY ME DON."

Who Are They? (Part IV)

American presidential campaigns are not about ideas; they are about the selection of a hero to embody the prevailing national ethos. "Only a hero," Mailer wrote, "can capture the secret imagination of a people, and so be good for the vitality of his nation; a hero embodies the fantasy and so allows each private mind the liberty to consider its fantasy and find a way to grow. Each mind can become more conscious of its desire and waste less strength in hiding from itself." What fantasy is Trump giving his supporters the liberty to consider? What secret have they been hiding from themselves?

Trump seems to awaken something in them that they feel they have, until now, needed to suppress. What is that thing? It is not just (as I'm getting a bit tired of hearing) that they've been *left behind economically*. (Many haven't, and au contraire.) They've been left behind in other ways, too, or feel that they have. To them, this is attributable to a country that has moved away from them, has been *taken away* from them—by Obama, the Clintons, the "lamestream" media, the "élites," the business-as-usual politicians. They are stricken by a sense that things are not as they should be and that, finally, someone sees it their way. They have a case of Grievance Mind, and Trump is their head kvetcher.

In college, I was a budding Republican, an Ayn Rand acolyte. I voted for Reagan. I'd been a bad student in high school and now, in engineering school, felt (and was) academically outgunned, way behind the curve. In that state, I constructed a worldview in which I was not behind the curve but ahead of it. I conjured up a set of hazy villains, who were, I can see now, externalized manifestations, imaginary versions of those who were leaving me behind; i.e., my better-prepared, more sophisticated fellow-students. They were, yes, smarter and sharper than I was (as indicated by the tests on which they were always creaming me), but I was . . . what was I? Uh, tougher, more resilient, more able to get down and dirty as needed. I distinctly remember the feeling of casting about for some worldview in which my shortfall somehow constituted a hidden noble advantage.

While reporting this story, I drove from New York to California. During all those days on the highway, with lots of time on my hands for theorizing, generalizing, and speaking my generalized theories into my iPhone while swerving off into the spacious landscape, I thought about this idea of grievance, of feeling left behind. All along the fertile interstate-highway corridor, our corporations, those new and powerful nation-states, had set up shop parasitically, so as to skim off the drive-past money, and what those outposts had to offer was a blur of sugar, bright color, and crassness that seemed causally related to more serious addictions. Standing in line at the pharmacy in an Amarillo Walmart superstore, I imagined some kid who had moved only, or mostly, through such bland, bright spaces, spaces constructed to suit the purposes of distant profit, and it occurred to me how easy it would be, in that life, to feel powerless, to feel that the local was lame, the abstract extraneous, to feel that the only valid words were those of materialism ("get" and "rise")—words that are perfectly embodied by the candidate of the moment.

Something is wrong, the common person feels, correctly: she works too hard and gets too little; a dulling disconnect exists between her actual day-to-day interests and (1) the way her leaders act and speak, and (2) the way our mass media mistell or fail entirely to tell her story. What does she want? Someone to notice her over here, having her troubles.

But, Then Again, Come On

A bully shows up, is hateful, says things so crude we liberals are taken aback. We respond moderately. We keep waiting for his supporters,

helped along by how compassionately and measuredly we are responding, to be persuaded. For the bully, this is perfect. Every fresh outrage
pulls the camera back to him, and meanwhile those of us moderately
decrying his immoderation are a little boring and tepid, and he keeps
getting out ahead of us. He has Trumpmunity: his notions are so low
and have been so many times decried, and yet they keep arriving, in
new and escalating varieties, and the liberal imagination wilts.

I have been mentally gathering all those nice, friendly Trump
supporters I met and asking them, Still? Even after the Curiel fiasco
and the post-Orlando self-congrat fest, and Trump's insinuation that
President Obama was in cahoots with the terrorists? Guys, still, really? The tragedy of the Trump movement is that one set of struggling people has been pitted against other groups of struggling people by someone who has known little struggle, at least in the material
sense, and hence seems to have little empathy for anyone struggling,
and even to consider struggling a symptom of weakness. "I will never
let you down," he has told his supporters, again and again, but he
will, and in fact already has, by indulging the fearful, xenophobic,
Other-averse parts of their psychology and reinforcing the notion
that their sense of being left behind has no source in themselves.

All That Bad Energy Comes Home to Roost

Ah, how fondly I now recall those idyllic rally days in Fountain Hills,
Tucson, Rothschild, and Eau Claire, back in March and early April,
when the punching was being done by Trump supporters.

After the San Jose rally in early June, protesters bullied and spat on
straggling Trump supporters. Sucker punchers lurched up, punched
hard, darted away, hands raised in victory. A strange little protester,
mask around his neck, mumbled, as he scuttled past a female reporter conducting an interview, "Fuck you in the pussy." Some sick
genie, it seemed, had been let out of the bottle. I had to pull an older
white woman out of a moblet of slapping young women of color, after she'd been driven down to one knee and had her glasses knocked
off. When I told the young African American woman who'd given
the first slap that this was exactly the kind of thing the Trump move-

ment loved to see and would be happy to use, she seemed to suddenly come back to herself and nearly burst into tears. The slapped woman was around sixty, tall, lean, sun-reddened, scrappy, a rancher, maybe, and we stood there a few minutes, recovering ourselves. Seeing something unsteady behind her eyes, I suggested that she be sure to take a few deep breaths before driving home. She said she would, but a few minutes later I saw her again, at the edge of the crowd, watching the protesters in fascination, as if what had just happened to her made it impossible for her to leave.

The order to disperse was given, first from a helicopter circling above, then barked out repeatedly on the ground, through megaphones. Police, in riot gear, stepped forward, shoulder to shoulder, chanting, "MOVE MOVE MOVE!," and the kids played at revolution, chanting back, "HANDS UP! DON'T SHOOT!" and "FUCK TRUMP!" and "FUCK THE SYSTEM!" and "FUCK THE POLICE!," occasionally dashing ahead of the advancing line to gain a few minutes to call home on their cells to reassure their worried parents. The police line formed a human wiper blade that, over the next couple of hours, drove the protesters around and around the downtown area. It was like some large-form board game: the longer the blue wiper blade pushed forward, the more protesters fell off the game board and went home, until, finally, only a handful remained, regrouping in the dark under the freeway.

Up on grassless viaduct slopes, whippet-thin young men of color gathered stones, carried them down furtively in clenched fists. When asked not to throw them, they averted their eyes guiltily, the way a busted third grader might. Some dropped their rocks; others just slipped away into the crowd. I saw two friends hurl their rocks at once, high, weak, arcing throws that burst up through street-light-yellow, low-hanging branches. I told an African American kid wearing an elaborate Darth Vaderish multi-mask arrangement that this made him look like he was up to no good and aggravated the ambient white-privileged notion of the protesters as thugs out to make trouble. He sweetly agreed, but then (dashing off) said that, still, the protesters "have to do what we have to do."

They were so young, mostly peaceful, but angered by the hateful rhetoric addressed at their communities, and their disdain for

Trump morphed too easily into disrespect for the police, a group of whom, when all was over, huddled in a bank doorway, bathed in sweat, a couple of them taking a knee, football style, and when their helmets came off it was clear that they'd been scared, too, and I imagined them later that night, in darkened living rooms, reviewing the night, assessing how they'd done.

Early in the evening, a protester about my age asked me, "Where's your sheet?" Seeing my confusion, he regrouped. "If you're a Trump supporter, I mean." Later, I saw him again, shouting to the police that they were all "pigs." Still smarting over his Klan crack, I asked how he could hold a sign claiming that hate doesn't work while calling a group of people he didn't know "pigs." "They *are* pigs," he said. "Every one of them." His wife was murdered a few years ago, he added, and they did nothing about it.

So there you go. Welcome to America.

The night was sad. The center failed to hold. Did I blame the rioting kids? I did. Did I blame Trump? I did. This, Mr. Trump, I thought, is why we practice civility. This is why, before we say exactly what is on our minds, we run it past ourselves, to see if it makes sense, is true, is fair, has a flavor of kindness, and won't hurt someone or make someone's difficult life more difficult. Because there are, among us, in every political camp, limited, angry, violent, and/or damaged people, waiting for any excuse to throw off the tethers of restraint and get after it. After which it falls to the rest of us, right and left, to clean up the mess.

The Somewhat Better Angels of Our Nature

Well, it wasn't all doom and gloom. Who could fail to be cheered by the sight of a self-described "street preacher" named Dean, whose massive laminated sign read "MUHAMMAD IS A LIAR, FALSE PROPHET, CHILD RAPING PERVERT! (SEE HISTORY FOR DETAILS)" and, on the flip side, "HOMO SEX IS SIN—ROMANS I," being verbally taken down by an inspiring consortium consisting of a gay white agnostic for Trump, a straight Christian girl for

Trump, and a lesbian Latina agnostic for Bernie? Who could resist the raw wonder in the voice of a rangy young Trump supporter who reminded me of a gentler version of Sid Phillips, the bad neighbor boy in *Toy Story*, as he said, rather dreamily, "I love that everything in Trump's house is gold. That's like real-life Batman. That's some real Bruce Wayne shit." A group of anti-Trump college students in Eau Claire concocted the perfect Zen protest: singing and dancing en masse to Queen's "Bohemian Rhapsody." If there's anything common across the left-right divide, it's the desire not to come off as tight-assed or anti-rock and roll, and what could the passing Trump supporters do but dance and sing along, a few holdouts scowling at the unfairness of the method?

Outside a Clinton rally in Phoenix, a Native American–looking man in an Aztec-patterned shirt joined the line of Trump supporters, with his megaphone, through which he slowly said, one word at a time, "Make. America. White. Again." Once the Trump supporters caught on to the joke, they moved away, but he was a good sport and scooted down to join them.

"Make. America. White. Again," he said, in the calmest voice.

"We don't want you," one of the Trumpies said. "We don't want your racism!"

And civility is still alive and well, if you know where to look for it. Outside a Lutheran church meeting hall in Mesa that is being used as a polling place on primary day, for example, where an eighty-eight-year-old woman sits, beautifully dressed for the occasion. "Oh, my goodness," she says. "I've never seen anything like this."

Hundreds of voters are waiting in a line that runs around the parking lot and down the street. She came earlier, she says, and thought she might just forget it. "But then," she says, "I thought, I'm getting up there in years—not going to have that many more chances to vote. I don't want to skip it. Because I always vote."

The voters move slowly, under crossed palm fronds, up for Palm Sunday, past a grapefruit tree in a gravelled breezeway: its three trunks have been whitewashed, and it looks like a three-legged creature in white pants, standing on its head.

For the next five hours, America passes by, wearing work badges, fanny packs, surgical scrubs, sparkly dance-short-leotards, suspenders, wool caps, head scarves, dreadlocks; pushing walkers, baby strollers, a fat-wheeled trail bike, a shopping cart (containing a bamboo cane and a Burger King crown); carrying walkie-talkies, books, a man-purse shaped like a gigantic tennis shoe, squirming babies, portable fold-up seats that never get used.

Someone says that in twenty-nine years she's never seen this level of excitement. Someone says that it takes all kinds. Someone says that this is what makes the United States great: so much difference, and everyone gets a chance. Someone says that there are so many extremes at play in this election, people are coming out just to resist the extreme they're most against.

A man says, "I'm a good guy, I hope," and his wife nods.

A hipster dad picks up a bit of cookie his kid has dropped on the sidewalk and eats it.

A college-age kid in a *Captain America* shirt demonstrates that there is a certain portion of one's elbow flesh that will never hurt, no matter how hard one pinches it.

At seven, the polls are supposed to close, but the line is the longest it's been all day.

No one seems angry. There isn't much political talk, and what there is is restrained, chatty. They are here to vote, and that is a privilege and a private matter.

How fragile this mind-set is, I think. It could be lost in a single generation.

By 8:18 p.m., per the Internet, with only 1 percent of precincts reporting, it's over: Trump wins, Clinton wins.

Even though their votes now seem technically meaningless, there is no mass exodus. The people just keep coming. They've raced over from work, weary kids trudging along beside them. They are fantastically old people; people in terrible health, in wheelchairs or hobbling along on walkers, or joining me on my bench to stretch out a stiff leg or adjust a bad back. What makes them do it? Keep standing in line, after dark, at the end of a long day, to vote in an election that is already over?

A young woman says, cheerfully, to her toddler, "Don't hit yourself. You only have one face, one head. That carries your brain.

Which is very important."

"After all these many years, in the back of my head," a man says thoughtfully, "I still hear this voice: 'Wait until your father gets home.' And that's my mom's voice."

At 9:50 p.m., the last person in line disappears inside.

I am joined by a trans woman about my age. People get afraid, she tells me, and nobody wants to feel afraid. But if you get angry, you feel empowered. Trump is playing on people's fears, to get them angry, which in turn makes *us*, on the other side, feel fearful. It's a domino effect. And, she says, it will continue even if Trump is out of the equation.

Another trans woman, apparently a stranger to the first, comes out of the church, holding a journal.

"All I have to write in here," she says, "is: I voted from Hell."

The last fifty or so voters are still visible inside: patient, calm, plodding forward a few steps at a time.

Mailer described what he called democracy's "terrifying premise" this way: "Let the passions and cupidities and dreams and kinks and ideals and greed and hopes and foul corruptions of all men and women have their day and the world will still be better off, for there is more good than bad in the sum of us and our workings."

Well, we'll see.

From the beginning, America has been of two minds about the Other. One mind says, Be suspicious of it, dominate it, deport it, exploit it, enslave it, kill it as needed. The other mind denies that there can be any such thing as the Other, in the face of the claim that all are created equal.

The first mind has always held violence nearby, to use as needed, and that violence has infused everything we do—our entertainments, our sex, our schools, our ads, our jokes, our view of the earth itself, somehow even our food. It sends our young people abroad in heavy armor, fills public spaces with gunshots, drives people quietly insane in their homes.

And here it comes again, that brittle frontier spirit, that lone lean guy in our heads, with a gun and a fear of encroachment. But he's picked up a few tricks along the way, has learned to come at us in a form we know and have forgotten to be suspicious of, from TV: famous, likably cranky, a fan of winning by any means necessary, exploiting our recent dullness and our aversion to calling stupidity stupidity, lest we seem too precious.

"DONALD J TRUMP A GUARDIAN ANGEL FROM HEAVEN," reads a poster I retrieved from the floor of the Rothschild rally. "HIS SPIRIT AND HARD WORK AS PRESIDENT WILL MAKE THE PEOPLE AND AMERICA GREAT AGAIN!!!"

Although, to me, Trump seems the very opposite of a guardian angel, I thank him for this: I've never before imagined America as fragile, as an experiment that could, within my very lifetime, fail.

But I imagine it that way now.

CONTRIBUTORS' NOTES

Chen Chen is the author of *When I Grow Up I Want to Be a List of Further Possibilities,* winner of the A. Poulin, Jr. Poetry Prize (BOA Editions, 2017). His work has appeared or is forthcoming in *Poetry,* the *New York Times Magazine, The Best American Poetry,* and *Bettering American Poetry.* He is a PhD student at Texas Tech University.

Ivan Chistyakov was a Muscovite who was expelled from the Communist Party during the purges of the late 1920s and early 1930s. He commanded an armed guard unit on a section of BAM, the Baikal–Amur Railway, which was built by forced labor. He was killed in 1941.

Ta-Nehisi Coates is a national correspondent for the *Atlantic,* where he writes about culture, politics, and social issues. He is the author of *The Beautiful Struggle* and *Between the World and Me.*

Teju Cole is a writer and photographer. He is the author of four acclaimed books, each in a different genre: the novella *Every Day Is for the Thief,* the novel *Open City,* the essay collection *Known and Strange Things,* and the genre-crossing *Blind Spot,* a work of photographs and text. Raised in Nigeria and living in Brooklyn, Cole uses words and images to explore cosmopolitanism, migration, and transnational identity. His work has been translated into sixteen languages, and his honors include the PEN/Hemingway Award, the New York City Book Award for Fiction, the Internationaler Literaturpreis, and the Windham Campbell Prize.

Meagan Day is a freelance writer who focuses on politics, social movements, labor, law, and history. Her book *Maximum Sunlight*, excerpted here, is available from E. M. Wolfman Books.

Viet Dinh was born in Vietnam and grew up in Colorado. He received his degrees from Johns Hopkins University and the University of Houston and currently teaches at the University of Delaware. A recipient of a National Endowment for the Arts Fiction Fellowship, he is the author of *After Disasters* (Little A Books, 2016), a finalist for the PEN/Faulkner Award, and his short stories have appeared in *The O. Henry Prize Stories, Zoetrope: All-Story, Ploughshares, Fence, Threepenny Review, Five Points,* and other journals. He rarely gets seasick.

Louise Erdrich is the author of fifteen novels as well as volumes of poetry, children's books, short stories, and a memoir of early motherhood. Her novel *The Round House* won the National Book Award for Fiction. *The Plague of Doves* won the Anisfield-Wolf Book Award and was a finalist for the Pulitzer Prize, and her debut novel, *Love Medicine,* was the winner of the National Book Critics Circle Award. Erdrich has received the Library of Congress Prize in American Fiction, the PEN/ Saul Bellow Award for Achievement in American Fiction, and the Dayton Literary Peace Prize. She lives in Minnesota with her daughters and is the owner of Birchbark Books, a small independent bookstore.

Masha Gessen is the author of several books on Russia, including *The Man Without a Face: The Unlikely Rise of Vladimir Putin* and *The Future Is History: How Totalitarianism Reclaimed Russia,* forthcoming from Riverhead in October 2017.

Smith Henderson is the author of the debut novel *Fourth of July Creek*. His short fiction has won a Pushcart Prize and appeared in *The Best American Short Stories 2016* anthology.

Sheila Heti is the author of seven books, including the novel *How Should a Person Be?* She is the former interviews editor of the *Believer* magazine. She lives in Toronto.

Casey Jarman has served as the music editor at the Pulitzer Prize–winning weekly *Willamette Week* in Portland, Oregon, and managing editor of the *Believer* in San Francisco. He cofounded Party Damage Records in 2013. He has written for the *Believer, Nylon, Portland Monthly, Willamette Week, Next American City,* and *Reed Magazine,* as well as various online publications. His book, *Death: An Oral History,* is a collection of interviews with Americans about death and dying, and includes pieces with legendary cartoonist Art Spiegelman and songwriter David Bazan, among others. He lives in Portland, Oregon, with his wife and two cats.

Kima Jones has been published at *GQ, Guernica,* and NPR among others and in the anthologies *Long Hidden: Speculative Fiction from the Margins of History* and the *New York Times* bestseller, *The Fire this Time,* edited by Jesmyn Ward. She is an MFA candidate in fiction and Rodney Jack Scholar in the MFA Program for Writers at Warren Wilson College. Jones lives in Los Angeles, where she operates Jack Jones Literary Arts, a book publicity company.

David Kaiser is president of the Rockefeller Family Fund, a family-led public charity that works to promote a sustainable and just society.

Sonny Liew's *The Art of Charlie Chan Hock Chye* was a *New York Times* and Amazon bestseller, and the first graphic novel to win the Singapore Literature Prize. Other works include *The Shadow Hero* (with Gene Luen Yang), *Doctor Fate* (with Paul Levitz), and *Malinky Robot,* as well as titles for Marvel Comics, DC Comics, DC Vertigo, First Second Books, Boom Studios, Disney Press, and Image Comics. He has been nominated for multiple Eisner Awards for his writing and art and for spearheading *Liquid City,* a multivolume comics anthology featuring creators from Southeast Asia.

Lin-Manuel Miranda is an award-winning composer, lyricist, and performer, as well as a 2015 MacArthur Foundation Award recipient. His current musical, *Hamilton*—with book, music, and lyrics by Mr. Miranda, in addition to originating the title role—opened on Broadway in 2015. *Hamilton* was awarded the 2016 Pulitzer Prize in Drama and earned a record-breaking sixteen Tony nominations, winning eleven Tony Awards including two personally for Mr. Miranda for Book and Score of a Musical.

Benjamin Nugent's fiction has appeared in *Best American Short Stories* and *The Unprofessionals: New American Writing from the Paris Review*. His first story collection, *Fraternity*, is forthcoming from Farrar, Straus and Giroux.

William Pannapacker has a PhD in American Civilization from Harvard University; he lives in the woods and teaches courses on American literature, opinion journalism, and comedy writing. Since 2013, Pannapacker has been inspired by the great New German Cinema director, Werner Herzog, to channel his voice in a semi-eponymous short-form genre called the "Twertzog": To tweet (verb) or a tweet (noun) in a Bavarian accent that is erudite, existential, and that changes your life, forever. September 5 is the globally celebrated #Twertzog Day on Twitter.

Simon Parkin is a British journalist and a contributing writer to *The New Yorker* online. During the past decade he has also contributed to the *New York Times*, the *Guardian*, *Harper's Magazine*, the BBC, and many others. His first book, *Death by Video Game*, was published in 2016.

Tommy "Teebs" Pico is a poet originally from the Viejas Indian reservation of the Kumeyaay Nation. He currently lives in Brooklyn, where he co-curates the reading series Poets with Attitude (PWA) with Morgan Parker, and cohosts the podcast *Food 4 Thot*.

Mark Polanzak's first book is the hybrid fiction/memoir *POP!* (Still-house). He is a founding editor for *draft: the journal of process,* and a producer at *The Fail Safe* podcast. He teaches at the Berklee College of Music and lives in Salem, Massachusetts.

Melissa Ragsly is a fiction writer whose work has appeared in *Joyland, Epiphany, Green Mountains Review,* and *Cosmonauts Avenue.* She is an assistant editor at *A Public Space* and lives in the Hudson Valley. Her website is melissaragsly.com.

Christine Rhein is the author of *Wild Flight,* a winner of the Walt McDonald First Book Prize in Poetry (Texas Tech University Press). Her poems have appeared widely in literary journals and have been selected for *Poetry Daily, The Writer's Almanac, Best New Poets,* and other anthologies. A former automotive engineer, she lives in Brighton, Michigan.

Elizabeth Lindsey Rogers is the author of the poetry collection *Chord Box* (University of Arkansas Press, 2013), which was a finalist for the Lambda Literary Award. Her poems and essays appear in the *Missouri Review, Boston Review, Prairie Schooner,* and elsewhere. She is the Murphy Visiting Fellow at Hendrix College and a contributing editor at the *Kenyon Review.*

George Saunders is the author of nine books, including *Tenth of December,* which was a finalist for the National Book Award, and won the inaugural Folio Prize (for the best work of fiction in English) and the Story Prize (best short story collection). He has received MacArthur and Guggenheim Fellowships, the PEN/Malamud Prize for excellence in the short story, and was recently elected to the American Academy of Arts and Sciences. In 2013, he was named one of the world's 100 most influential people by *Time* magazine. He teaches in the creative writing program at Syracuse University.

Sonia Sotomayor is a United States Supreme Court justice. She holds degrees from Princeton University and Yale Law School. Prior to being appointed to the Supreme Court by President Barack Obama, she served as a judge on the United States Court of Appeals for the Second Circuit.

Andrew Sullivan pioneered political blogging at the *Daily Dish* from 2000–2015, with over a million monthly readers. From 1991–1996, Sullivan was the editor of the *New Republic*, winning three National Magazine awards in his tenure. He is a *New York Magazine* contributing editor covering politics and culture.

Arch Tait was awarded the PEN Literature in Translation prize in 2010 for his translation of Anna Politkovskaya's *Putin's Russia*. To date he has translated another twenty-seven books from Russian, most recently the memoirs of Akhmed Zakayev.

Miriam Toews's most recent novel is *All My Puny Sorrows*. She lives in Toronto, Canada.

Lee Wasserman has served as director of the Rockefeller Family Fund since 1999. Lee's work has led to creation and implementation of initiatives to address climate change; advance women's economic interests; and expand citizens' ability to influence their democratic institutions.

Anna Wiener is a writer based in San Francisco. She has written for the *Atlantic*, the *New Republic*, and *The New Yorker* online.

Madison DeVry is currently a senior at Summit Shasta High School in Daly City. When she's not at BANR she is reading, writing, procrastinating, or binge-watching Netflix. She drinks caffeine all the way until 8 p.m. but she is still able to fall asleep. Hard to believe, she knows.

 Emilia Villela Fernández is a senior at Lick-Wilmerding High School in San Francisco. She loves sleeping, reading, and spending time in Yosemite with her extended family. She has been known to fantasize about getting locked in a library, and considers it a danger to even set foot in a bookstore before she has finished all the other things she has to do that day. Last night she had a dream about swimming in pool of warm sand. She hopes this is not a bad omen.

Asha Fletcher-Irwin has been compared to a loaf of sourdough bread, Henry the Eighth, and the caterpillar from *A Bug's Life*. She graduated from Oakland School for the Arts and now attends Hollins University. She's extremely happy to have been a part of BANR and hopes you enjoy this book.

Marcus Gee-Lim is a freshman at Occidental College. Last June he graduated from Lowell High School in San Francisco. His hobbies include listening to music, long walks on the beach, and keeping it loopy. He struggles to find adequate desktop backgrounds.

Emma Hardison is a senior at Oakland School for the Arts and this was her second year on the BANR committee. She enjoys long walks on the beach and romantic candle-lit dinners. She doesn't want to toot her own horn or anything, but she is pretty funny.

Sidney Hirschman is from San Carlos, California, and they are a senior at Lick-Wilmerding High School. Sidney spent the spring semester of 2017 at The Oxbow School in Napa, California, where they learned how to cut hair, grow food, and fall in love. You can contact Sidney by manually rewinding a VHS tape of *The Land Before Time* under a gibbous moon (waxing and waning are both fine).

Althea Kriney is a junior at Lowell High School in San Francisco. She turned this bio in a week late and this is all she could come up with. That's all you need to know about her.

Sian Laing is a senior at Mission High School in San Francisco. She has been known to cartwheel at inopportune times. Once, she was a flower girl at a wedding and she cartwheeled down the aisle. Long story short, she made a mess and the guests were covered in flowers.

Lola Snowflake Leuterio (the middle name is her sister's fault) is a junior at Tamalpais High School. She loves Steinbeck books, *Lord of the Rings* movies, Chance the Rapper, satisfying math problems, Jesse, and Whole Foods Tasters. Being on the BANR committee this year was the best and she's excited to continue doing it!

Zoe Olson is a senior at Mission High School and this is her second year on the BANR committee. She likes cookies, cats, and arts and crafts. You can't see, because the image is zoomed in, but she's waving at you from the little picture on the left. Hi!

Isaac Schott-Rosenfield is a freshman at Columbia University. He reads, writes, etc. For reasons that are not entirely clear to him, there is a life-size cardboard cut-out of Tom Hanks in the BANR meeting room. It has been there for much of the year, staring impassively at

the committee as it goes about its work. The cut-out is facing away from Isaac as he writes this, and yet, he has the sense that it is watching him.

Annette Vergara-Tucker is a junior at Lick-Wilmerding High School. This is the second BANR book she has been involved in, and it's been very interesting for her to get to see the contrast between the 2015/2016 and 2016/2017 literature being published. It goes without saying, but it was a big year for politics. She hopes that the readers of this year's anthology learn as much as she has from these fascinating pieces.

Very special thanks to Dave Eggers, Nicole Angeloro, Mark Robinson, and Kenard Pak. Thanks also to Rachel Kushner, Adam Johnson, Daniel Handler, Rebecca Marcyes, Mikayla McVey, Angela Hui, Kristin Gore, Fred Armisen, Bill Heinzen, Andi Winnette, Ruby Perez, Sunra Thompson, Claire Boyle, Kristina Kearns, Chris Monks, Mimi Lok, Gerald Richards, Kait Steele, Lauren Broder, Maggie Andrews, Daniel Cesca, Yusuke Wada, Lindy Caldwell, Cecilia Juan, Jonathan Hsieh, Okailey Okai, Alyssa Aninag, Dana Belott, Elaina Bruna, Bianca Catalan, Lizzie Jean Coyle, Ricardo Cruz Chong, Lauren Hall, Allyson Halpern, Caroline Kangas, Kona Lai, Kiley McLaughlin, Molly Parent, Christina Villaseñor Perry, Amy Popovich, Meghan Ryan, Susan de Saint Salvy, Ashley Smith, Anton Timms, Jillian Wasick, Byron Weiss, Ryan Young, Diana Adamson, Juliana

Sloane, Zebunissa Bradley, Kate Bueler, Rita Bullwinkel, Nirvana Felix, Marisela Garcia, Cristian King, Courtney Lee, Jessica Li, Monica Mendez, Oliver Pascua, Veronica Ponce-Navarrete, Francisco Prado, Piper Sutherland, Timothy Tu Huynh, Nick Watson, and Alma Lucia Zaragoza-Petty.

THE NONREQUIRED 2016
ELECTION APPENDIX

KENYA BARRIS, "Lemons," *Black-ish*, ABC, January 11, 2016. Anthony Anderson as Andre:

"Do I understand what anybody in their right mind could have seen in Trump? No! But maybe that's why we lost. Over fifty million people felt something. And I'm not saying that they were right. But I don't think it's possible that all, half, or even most of them were nuts. Or racists. Or hated women . . . It's time to stop calling each other names. And we start trying to have those conversations. If we don't, we'll end up being in a country that's even more divided for a long time."

VINCENT BEVINS, Facebook post, June 24, 2016. Reporter pinpoints the reasonable concerns underlying the rise of Trump and Britons' vote to leave the European Union:

"Both Brexit and Trumpism are the very, very, wrong answers to legitimate questions that urban elites have refused to ask for thirty years. Questions such as: Who are the losers of globalization, and how can we spread the benefits to them and ease the transition? Is it fair that the rich can capture almost all the gains of open borders and trade, or should the process be more equitable? Can we really sustainably create a media structure that only hires kids from top universities (and, moreover, those prick graduates that can basically afford to work for free for the first 5–10 years) who are totally ignorant of regular people, if not outright disdainful of them? Do we actually have democracy, or do banks just decide? Immigration is good for the vast majority, but for the very small minority who see pressure on their wages, should we help them, or do they just get ignored?"

KEN BURNS, "2016 Stanford Commencement Address," delivered June 12, 2016:

> "For 216 years, our elections, though bitterly contested, have featured the philosophies and character of candidates who were clearly qualified. That is not the case this year. One is glaringly *not* qualified. So before you do anything with your well-earned degree, you must do everything you can to defeat the retrograde forces that have invaded our democratic process, divided our house, to fight against, no matter your political persuasion, the dictatorial tendencies of the candidate with zero experience in the much maligned but subtle art of governance; who is *against* lots of things, but doesn't seem to be *for* anything, offering only bombastic and contradictory promises, and terrifying Orwellian statements; a person who easily lies, creating an environment where the truth doesn't seem to matter; who has never demonstrated any interest in anyone or anything but himself and his own enrichment . . ."

DAVE CHAPPELLE, monologue, *Saturday Night Live*, NBC, November 12, 2016. Imagining President-elect Trump's conversation with President Obama at the White House:

> "Hello, Donald. How ya feeling?"

> "Oh, God. Got to tell you, this job looks like it's going to be a lot harder than I thought."

> "Really? It's not that hard, I mean at least you get to be white while you're doing it."

TAYLOR DOBBS and ANGELA EVANCIE, "How the Iowa Caucus Works, In 2 Minutes (Starring Legos)," Vermont Public Radio, January 27, 2016. Delightful animation explaining the mechanics of the Iowa Caucus using toys. Answers the age-old question of how precinct captains convince a plastic Yoda to join their candidate's preference group.

ROD DREHER, "Tribune of Poor White People," *American Conservative*, July 22, 2016. Question and answer with J. D. Vance, author of *Hillbilly Elegy*. Vance:

> "No one seems to understand why conventional blunders do nothing to Trump. But in a lot of ways, what elites see as blunders people back home see as someone who—finally—conducts themselves in a relatable way. He shoots from the hip; he's not constantly afraid of offending someone; he'll get angry about politics; he'll call someone a liar or a fraud. This is how a lot of people in the white working class actu-

ally talk about politics, and even many elites recognize how refreshing and entertaining it can be! So it's not really a blunder as much as it is a rich, privileged Wharton grad connecting to people back home through style and tone. Viewed like this, all the talk about 'political correctness' isn't about any specific substantive point, as much as it is a way of expanding the scope of acceptable behavior. People don't want to believe they have to speak like Obama or Clinton to participate meaningfully in politics, because most of us don't speak like Obama or Clinton."

DAVE EGGERS, "None of the Old Rules Apply," *Guardian*, November 18, 2016. *BANR*'s founding editor drives across the country in the aftermath of the election:

"I left the memorial and turned on to a two-lane road, part of the Lincoln Highway that runs through the state—part of the first coast-to-coast highway in the United States. Just beyond a sign advertising home-grown sweetcorn, there was a residential home, the first house anyone might encounter when leaving the United 93 Memorial, and on this home, there is a vast Confederate flag draped over the front porch.

It's important to note that this was the Lincoln Highway. And that the Civil War ended 160 years ago. And that Pennsylvania was not a state in the Confederacy. So to see this, an enormous Confederate flag in a Union state, a mile from a symbol of national tragedy and shared sacrifice, was an indicator that there was something very unusual in the mood of the country. Ancient hatreds had resurfaced. Strange alliances had been formed. None of the old rules applied."

ALEC MACGILLIS, "Revenge of the Forgotten Class," *ProPublica*, November 10, 2016. The Rust Belt angle:

"Tiffany Chesser, said she was voting for [Trump] because her boyfriend worked at a General Electric light-bulb plant nearby that was seeing more of its production lines being moved to Mexico. She saw voting for Trump as a straightforward transaction to save his job. 'If he loses that job we're screwed—I'll lose my house,' she said. 'There used to be a full parking lot there—now you go by, there are just three trucks in the lot.'"

LIZ MERIWETHER, "Which *Game of Thrones* Characters Would be Republicans, According to Delegates at the RNC," Vulture.com, July 22, 2016:

"Mike refused to assign a party to the psychotic King Joffrey, because 'I don't think you want to say that any political party is necessarily going to take a crossbow and shoot a naked woman to a bedpost 17 times. That would just be rude. We're trying to be respectful in our political discourse.'"

MATTHEW SCHMITZ, "Donald Trump, Man of Faith," *First Things*, August 2016. Theological journal traces the Republican nominee's religious beliefs back to Norman Vincent Peale, pastor and author of the best-selling self-help book, *The Power of Positive Thinking*. Trump attended Peale's church and often cites him as a major influence in his life:

> "At a campaign event in Iowa, Trump shocked the audience by saying that he had never asked God for forgiveness. All his other disturbing statements—his attacks on every vulnerable group—are made intelligible by this one. The self-sufficient faith Trump absorbed from Peale has no place for human weakness. Human frailty, dependency, and sinfulness cannot be acknowledged; they must be overcome."

WRITING STAFF OF *PARKS AND RECREATION*, "A Letter to America from Leslie Knope, Regarding Donald Trump," Vox.com, November 10, 2016. A beloved fictional public servant offers hope and apologies to American girls:

> "When I was in fourth grade, my teacher Mrs. Kolphner taught us a social studies lesson. The 17 students in our class were introduced to two fictional candidates: a smart if slightly bookish-looking cartoon tortoise named Greenie, and a cool-looking jaguar named Speedy . . . Before we voted, Greg Laresque asked if he could nominate a third candidate, and Mrs. Kolphner said 'Sure! The essence of democracy is that everyone—' and Greg cut her off and said, 'I nominate a T. rex named Dr. Farts who wears sunglasses and plays the saxophone, and his plan is to fart as much as possible and eat all the teachers,' and everyone laughed, and before Mrs. Kolphner could blink, Dr. Farts the T. rex had been elected president of Pawnee Elementary School in a 1984 Reagan-esque landslide, with my one vote for Greenie the Tortoise playing the role of 'Minnesota.'
>
> After class, I was inconsolable. Once the other kids left, Mrs. Kolphner came over and put her arm around me. She told me I had done a great job advocating for Greenie the Tortoise . . .
>
> 'Greenie was the better candidate,' I said. 'Greenie should have won.'
>
> She nodded.
>
> 'I suppose that was the point of the lesson,' I said.
>
> 'Oh, no,' she said. 'The point of the lesson is: People are unpredictable, and democracy is insane.'"

NOTABLE
NONREQUIRED READING
OF 2016

MICHAEL ANDREASEN
   Bodies in Space, *Tin House*

CHLOE CALDWELL
   Hungry Ghost, *I'll Tell You in Person*

MICHAEL CHABON
   My Son, the Prince of Fashion, *GQ*

JAI CHAKRABARTI
   A Small Sacrifice for an Enormous Happiness, *A Public Space*

KATHLEEN COLLINS
   Whatever Happened to Interracial Love?, *Whatever Happened to
Interracial Love?*

CHAUNA CRAIG
   Hidden in Plain Sight, *Ploughshares*

DEXTER FILKINS
   The End of Ice, *The New Yorker*

AMITY GAIGE
   Hollow Object, *Ploughshares*

JOSH HARKINSON and KYLE TAYLOR
   Confessions of a Gun Range Worker, *Mother Jones*

ANNA JOURNEY
Little Face, *AGNI*

JACOB S. KNABB
A Portrait of a Coal Town on the Brink of Death, *Vice*
SAMUEL CLARE KNIGHTS
The Manual Alphabet, *Fence*

ALYSA LANDRY
Presidents and Native Americans series, *Indian Country Today*

AMY MARGOLIS
Don't Look Up, *Iowa Review*
DAVID TOMAS MARTINEZ
Triptych on Ambition, *Tin House*
ELIZABETH McCRACKEN
A Walk-Through Human Heart, *Zoetrope*

ASHLEY NELSON LEVY
Auntie, *Zyzzyva*

MOLLY OSHATZ
College Without Truth, *First Things*

NATHAN POOLE
Open Season, *Ecotone*

KATHRYN SCHULZ
Citizen Khan, *The New Yorker*
DANYEL SMITH
When Whitney Hit the High Note, *ESPN*

DEB OLIN UNFERTH
The First Full Thought of Her Life, *Wait till You See Me Dance*

ABOUT 826 NATIONAL

Proceeds from this book benefit youth literacy

A percentage of the cover price of this book goes to 826 National, and its network of seven youth tutoring, writing, and publishing centers in seven cities around the country.

Since the birth of the 826 Network in 2002, the organization's goal has been to help students ages 6–18 explore their creativity and improve their writing skills, while helping teachers get their classes excited about writing. 826's mission is based on the understanding that great leaps in learning can happen with individualized attention, and that strong writing skills are fundamental to future success.

Established in 2008, the 826 National office provides strategic leadership, administration, and resources to ensure the success of seven—soon to be eight—writing and tutoring centers in San Francisco, New York City, Los Angeles, Ann Arbor/Detroit, Boston, Chicago, Washington, DC, and, beginning in 2018, New Orleans. Each 826 chapter offers five core programs: after-school tutoring, field trips, workshops, the Young Authors' Book Project, and in-school programs—all offered completely free of charge for students, teachers, and schools. Each program offers innovative and dynamic project-based learning opportunities that build on students' classroom experience and strengthen their ability to express ideas effectively, creatively, confidently, and in their own voice.

The demand for the 826 Network's services is tremendous. In 2015–16, 826 chapters worked with nearly 5,000 active volunteers and over 32,000 students nationally, hosted 676 field trips, completed 240 in-school projects, offered 568 evening and weekend workshops, held over 1,500 after-school tutoring sessions, and produced 898 student publications. At many of the chapters, field trips are fully booked almost a year in advance, teacher requests for in-school tutor support continue to rise, and the majority of evening and weekend workshops have waitlists.

826 Network volunteers are local community residents, professional writers, teachers, artists, college students, parents, bankers, lawyers, and retirees from a wide range of professions. These passionate individuals can be found at all of the writing centers and neighboring schools each day, running morning field trips, sitting side-by-side with students after school, and helping entire classrooms learn the art of writing.

Read on to learn more about each 826 chapter.

826 VALENCIA

Named for its street address in San Francisco, 826 Valencia was founded in 2002 by educator Nínive Calegari and author Dave Eggers. 826 Valencia comprises two writing centers—the flagship location in the Mission District and a new center in the Tenderloin neighborhood—and three satellite classrooms at nearby public schools. 826 Valencia offers tutoring and workshops at both centers, supports teachers in their classrooms through in-school projects, and hosts field trips from local public schools in which students collectively write stories, create choose-your-own-adventure books, or write and record their own podcasts. This year 826 Valencia will produce 47 major student-written publications, and cultivate wonder, confidence, and an affinity for writing for 7,000 under-resourced students all over San Francisco.

826NYC

826NYC's writing center opened its doors in September 2004. It provides more than 3,000 students a year with the opportunity to build their writing skills and confidence in their creative voice, through a combination of after-school, in-school, and field trip programs. 826NYC operates year-round programs out of the world famous Brooklyn Superhero Supply Co., the South Williamsburg Branch of the Brooklyn Public Library, and its East Harlem Writers Room located at M.S. 7/ Global Tech Prep. In addition, 826NYC runs short-term programs with Title 1 schools throughout the city. 826NYC publishes more than 25 publications each year, supported by a corps of more than 300 volunteers annually.

826LA

826LA benefits greatly from the wealth of cultural and artistic resources in the Los Angeles area. The organization regularly presents free workshops at the Armand Hammer Museum in which esteemed artists, writers, and performers teach their craft. 826LA has collaborated with the J. Paul Getty Museum, the Los Angeles  County Museum of Arts, and, most recently, the Broad Museum. Since opening in March 2005, 826LA has provided thousands of hours of free individualized writing support, held summer camps for English language learners, and given students sports-writing training in the Lakers' press room.

826CHI

826CHI is headquartered in the Wicker Park neighborhood of Chicago and serves thousands of students from over 120 different schools throughout the city. Originally opened in 2005, 826CHI moved to a new base of operations in 2014 and opened their new storefront, the Secret Agent Supply Co., full of products that unlock creativity  and trigger new adventures for agents of all ages. Over 400 active volunteers support 826CHI's programs, which strive to strengthen each student's power to express ideas effectively, creatively, confidently, and in their individual voice.

826MICHIGAN

 826michigan opened its doors on June 1, 2005, on South State Street in Ann Arbor. In October of 2007 the operation moved downtown, to a new and improved location on Liberty Street. Today, 826michigan operates Liberty Street Robot Supply & Repair in Ann Arbor, the Detroit Robot Factory in the city's Eastern Market neighborhood, and dozens of writing and tutoring programs in venues across Ann Arbor, Detroit, and Ypsilanti. 826michigan students—all 4,000 of them—write poems and essays, stories and plays in field trips, in-classroom residencies, drop-in writing programs in public library branches, and much more. The organization has a staff of 11 and a diverse, vibrant volunteer corps of 500+ adults across southeastern Michigan.

826 BOSTON

826 Boston opened its doors to the Greater Boston Bigfoot Research Institute in 2007. Working with traditionally underserved students ages 6–18 out of its headquarters in the Roxbury neighborhood of Egleston Square, as well as through a network of full-time Writers' Rooms located within Boston public schools,

826 Boston has served 19,000 students. Its community of more than 2,500 volunteers—including college students, professional writers, artists, and teachers—helped 826 Boston secure a "Best Places to Volunteer" distinction from the *Boston Globe*. Recent collections of 826 Boston student writing include *I Rate Today A –1,000*, inspired by Jeff Kinney's *Diary of a Wimpy Kid* series, and *Attendance Would Be 100%: Student Proposals for High School Redesign Boston*.

826DC

826DC opened its doors to the city's Columbia Heights neighborhood in October 2010. 826DC provides after-school tutoring, field trips, workshops, in-school publishing programs, help for English language learners, and assistance with the publication of student work. It also offers the District its only magic shop—Tivoli's Astounding Magic Supply Company, Illusionarium & De-Lux Haberdashery—right in the heart of the city. In 2016, 826DC students crafted personal narratives and college admission essays at the White House in collaboration with First Lady Michelle Obama's Reach Higher initiative.

ABOUT SCHOLARMATCH

Founded in 2010 by author Dave Eggers, ScholarMatch began as a simple crowdfunding platform to help under-resourced students pay for college. In just a few short years, ScholarMatch grew into a thriving hub for all things college access. Today, we support the college journeys of more than 1,500 students each year. We serve students at our San Francisco drop-in center, at local schools and organizations, and online through a virtual college coaching initiative. We also pioneer innovative resources like the ScholarMatcher—the first free college search tool built specifically with the needs of low-income students in mind.

Our mission is to make college possible for underserved youth by matching students with donors, resources, and colleges. More than 70 percent of ScholarMatch students are the first in their families to go to college, and on average come from families making $28,000 or less annually. With the support of donors, volunteers, schools, and community organizations, we ensure that college is possible for underserved students in the San Francisco Bay Area and beyond. To support a student's college journey or learn more, visit scholarmatch.org.

THE BEST AMERICAN SERIES®

FIRST, BEST, AND BEST-SELLING

The Best American Comics

The Best American Essays

The Best American Mystery Stories

The Best American Nonrequired Reading

The Best American Science and Nature Writing

The Best American Science Fiction and Fantasy

The Best American Short Stories

The Best American Sports Writing

The Best American Travel Writing

Available in print and e-book wherever books are sold.

Visit our website: *www.hmhco.com/bestamerican*